cousins to ⟶ **COHEN** ⟵ **Friedlands cousins to**

FATHER COHE[N]
MOTHER COH[EN]

Five
brothers
remained
in Russia

| Joe married to Lily | Sam married to Mima | Jack married to Edith Friedland | Sol married to Fanny | Ben married to Dora | Leah see Harry Katz | Eshka see Saul Katz |

[w]ife
[...]itch

Shirley
married
2 children

Marty
married to
Julie

girl   Harvey

Marvin
married
2 children

Elaine

[S]am [m]arried [to] [M]argo

Jonathan married to Sheila

Sara married to Mike

Ed   girl

[M]ark

girl   boy   Marybell

[...]ry

Katz-Cohen

Katz-Cohen

A NOVEL BY *Samuel Astrachan*

Macmillan Publishing Co., Inc.

NEW YORK

Macmillan Publishing Co., Inc.
866 Third Avenue, New York, N.Y. 10022
Collier Macmillan Canada, Ltd.

Library of Congress Cataloging in Publication Data

Astrachan, Samuel.
    Katz-Cohen.

    I. Title.
PZ4.A842Kat [PS3551.S7]   813'.5'4   77-20128
ISBN 0-02-503950-4

FIRST PRINTING 1978

Printed in the United States of America

The Doctor

PRINCIPAL CHARACTERS

THE KATZES:

Saul Katz, the doctor, married to his cousin Eshka, father of *Lazarus* (Larry) and *Max*.

Harry Katz, Saul's oldest brother, a house painter, married to Leah, father of *Anna* and *Eli*.

Irving Katz, Saul's older brother, a prominent physician, married to *Mary*.

Dan Katz, the doctor's youngest brother, lives in France.

The Katz sisters are *Esther*, married to a politically active writer in Palestine, *Sonia* in Russia, and *Nuissa* and *Judith* in Warsaw with their parents. *Ruth* is the daughter of Judith.

Lazarus, a younger brother of the doctor, was killed in Russia.

THE COHENS:

Mother Cohen, mother to thirteen children, among whom are the five Cohen brothers and two sisters in New York.

Joe Cohen, stiff-necked, the most successful of the Cohen brothers. Like them all he is a furrier. Married to *Lily*, his son is *Marty*.

Sam Cohen lives in Rockaway with his wife *Mima*. He is a pinochle player, his hands are palsied.

Jack (Jacob) Cohen lives in the Bronx, childless, with his wife *Edith*. He is in business with his younger brother Ben.

Sol Cohen, a small man, partially deaf, married to *Fanny*.

Ben Cohen, youngest of the brothers, married to his former bookkeeper *Dora*, father of *Marvin* and *Elaine*.

Leah Katz, Cohen sister married to Harry Katz.

Eshka Katz, Cohen sister married to the doctor, Saul Katz.

The oldest of the Cohen brothers was *Itcha*, who was twice married. Itcha's only child by his first marriage is *Louis*. By his second marriage, his children were: *David*, who limps; *Sam*, who is gentle; *Jonathan*, who will rise, and *Sara*. Orphans, they were taken to America by their uncles, and Sam and Jonathan work with and are partners to Ben and Jack in their fur business.

OTHERS:

Emma, rich cousin to both the Katzes and Cohens, married to *Bill*, has a daughter. Her father was a Nissnievitch, who came to America, changed his name to Nelson, became a millionaire, and committed suicide in 1930.

Herman Friedland, leader of the Friedland clan, cousin to both the Katzes and Cohens, brother of Jack Cohen's wife Edith.

CHAPTER *One*

T HAT TIME WAS out of darkness as if the family, the Katzes and Cohens, had, when it came to New York City, left behind in Russia and Poland not only pogroms, civil war, and hunger, but disease and death.

Joe, Jack, and Sam had been the first of the five Cohen brothers and two sisters to come to America. They came separately before the First World War. The other brothers came with their mother and sisters in 1921 and went into the fur businesses the first arrivals had begun. The three Katz brothers to come to America, Harry, Irving, and Saul, came with that group.

It was a time of weekly family meetings and of quarterly meetings of a family association that included more than 100, the Nissnievitches, Starobinetzes, Feldbaums, and Friedlands, so intermarried that all relationships were in a tangle, that no one at those meetings, or so it seemed, was not a cousin to everyone there. It was a tribal time, and at the tribe's center were: the widowed mother of the Cohens, five sons and two daughters in America, five sons in Russia, her eldest son dead, three children dead in infancy, miscarriages. she now eighty-five years old; Eshka Katz, the younger of the Cohen sisters, married to Dr. Saul Katz; and Dr. Saul Katz.

He was a slender man, five foot three. He had wanted to be an engineer, but there had been room in the imperial engineering school for only one Jew from his region and there had been five with perfect grades. They had drawn lots, and he had drawn a place in medical school, two of the five drawing blanks. He had been drafted as medical captain in the czar's army, then drafted as colonel in the Red Army. But in America he had had to complete again his fourth year of medical studies and his internship. An uncle, a Nissnievitch, who had come to America before the turn of the century and had become a millionaire (his name changed to Nelson), paid for his schooling and advanced him the money to set himself up in an office in the East Bronx. He was thirty-four years old, and he wrote to his parents in Warsaw that he was going to marry his third cousin, Eshka Cohen. His mother replied: "It's enough that your brother Harry who has no profession has married a Cohen." The girl, after all, ten years his junior, spoke Russian badly and was still learning English at a P.S. night school. Her sister, his sister-in-law Leah, said when he broke the engagement, "You will not do that to my sister and go on living under my roof." So he shared rooms with a pinochle-playing doctor, and they spoke Russian, and for a time he avoided all the Cohens as if he had chosen doctors and Russian to Yiddish and Cohens. But one day he put on his best suit and tie and went back to Eshka, asked her out for a walk, wanted to tell her something from the heart, but finally turned to her to speak in English of her duties as a doctor's wife.

He began paying off his debt to Nelson and, after Nelson's suicide in 1930, paid to Nelson's daughter. He paid regularly, even after his meager savings disappeared in the Crash, even when it was all he could do to pay the rent, to make car payments, to send money to his parents and sisters in Warsaw, he practicing medicine all day long, and often in the night, for fifty cents here, a dollar there, the "Bronxers" not even able to pay with chickens and eggs. There was a first child, a girl who died in infancy, and there were two sons: Lazarus, and me, Max.

He was a proud man, an intellectual, and sarcastic. He had a rare talent for diagnosis. Perhaps for that, bad news always homed to him.

In that time, Katzes and Cohens lived in the Bronx, though three of the Cohen brothers, newly prospering, had moved to the same

building on Weeks Avenue in the West Bronx. And on the Grand
Concourse close by lived the three orphaned sons and one daughter
of Itcha Cohen, the eldest of the Cohen brothers. Joe Cohen lived in
Westchester; his son was attending Harvard College. One of the
Katz brothers, Irving, a dermatologist, had married a slender
American-born Jewish girl and lived in Manhattan. But the family
center was in the East Bronx, where the Cohen sisters Leah and
Eshka, married to the Katz brothers Harry and Saul, lived a block
apart, and where, in an apartment separated from her daughter
Eshka's by Dr. Katz's medical office, lived Mother Cohen. The
Cohen sons came every Sunday to the East Bronx to visit their
mother.

They came in Chevrolets and Pontiacs. Joe had a Buick. The sons
of Itcha had a Packard. Other family came, cousins from Brooklyn,
New Jersey. Their cars too would be parked just outside the ground-
floor apartments and office, and around the corner, and across the
street.

They came with wives and children—men and women wore hats
—and passed immediately through the doctor's waiting room, down
a short dark corridor to Mother Cohen's small apartment. Almost in
a line they approached the small, shawl-covered, wizened old lady
and bent to kiss her. In Yiddish they told her their chagrins, hopes,
accomplishments. Sometimes they whispered into her ear and she
nodded, having already heard that story or one like it, and touched
a hand or a cheek reassuringly. "Have children," she would say to a
wife. "Give him a college education," she would say to a father.
"Honor your father," to a son. Her older daughter Leah served silently, cookies, fruit, offering a small whisky glass of homemade
raspberry wine. Mother Cohen's bed was in the room; sometimes
she received while in bed. On the bed table was a framed photograph of Joe's Harvard son.

The visitors brought honey cakes, bottles of sweet wine, boxes of
chocolate. Everything was opened and served, and when there was
too much, one of the children would carry what was left over to
Eshka's apartment, where the big dining-room table was spread,
every Sunday by three o'clock, with Eshka's homemade cakes and
cookies, with platters of bananas and oranges, plates of nuts, dried
figs and raisins. There was a continual flow from one apartment to

the other, and midway, in the doctor's waiting room, the most private place in the two apartments, there would be groups tem-
porarily settled in the sofa and chairs, a Cohen brother whispering
business with a Feldbaum.

At one end of Eshka's dining-room table, cakes and platters
pushed toward the center, sat, in big straight upholstered chairs, the
pinochle players: Dr. Saul Katz and Joe, Sam, and Jack Cohen. They
removed their jackets, they opened their vests. They played four
handed, the dealer out of the game. They played for nickels, dimes,
and quarters, spades was double. There were kibitzers in folding
chairs who craned forward or sideways to see the players' tightly
held cards. Children, standing behind, watched too—the silver in
the "kitty" mounting, dollar bills passing, the son's hidden excitement, for he knew he must not say a word or even give a sign, as his
father turned over one by one his three bought cards. Sam Cohen's
palsied hands trembled. Jack played slowly and evenly and never
won or lost much. The real match was always between Joe and Saul.
Joe a big man and a born winner; Saul's pleasure less to win than to
put Joe down, double, in spades. He would snap his card down as if
to bluff it into a winner. They played for hours, this was Sunday.
With new arrivals, the game might slow, but would always pick up,
and if Saul were called to the phone and had to leave for an emergency, someone would slip into his place and keep it warm for
him.

The trigger finger of Jack's right hand was sewn to the middle
finger. "How did that happen?" the boys asked, though not within
Jack's hearing, he a big taciturn man, the strongest of the Cohens.

"Sh . . ." Jonathan, the youngest of Itcha Cohen's sons, who
worked with Jack, said, "that was the czar's punishment."

And the boys imagined Jack a great marksman shooting cossacks
down. And imagined the scene of punishment, the czar watching, Jack
not even wincing as an old lady bent over his hand and pierced his
flesh over and under with a needle.

To the boys the uncles were all giants, but Jack was bigger even
than Joe, and for that, as for his sewn-together fingers, and for his
deep quiet gentleness, as for his silent anger, he was special. Of all
his brothers-in-law, the doctor respected Jack most. He, Saul would
say, is a strong man.

"Can we come with you?" the boys asked Dr. Saul. Two sat in the front of the two-door Chevy with the doctor and three were in the rear. Down Hunts Point, the cobblestoned avenue divided by trolley rails and hanging cables; past two Loews movie theaters on Southern Boulevard. Into a neighborhood of Irishers, or an Italian neighborhood of two-family houses, and wrestling in the car, and the doctor coming back, his black bag, but something in his walk, in him, announcing him even more: The Doctor.

Eshka, kneeling on a chair, leaning over the table at the other end from the pinochle players, turned over cards and read a niece's fortune. Eshka was no taller than the doctor, but was big, big-busted, and her face big and her lips thick, and for her coloring and spirit she was called gypsy or *schwartze*.

"Darling," she said, "I see a young man. He has dark hair and dark eyes. He will come calling carrying flowers."

The other aunts, hatted still, feathers in their hats, said, "Only let him not be a *Galitziana!*"

"Only let him not be a *schnorrer* like the last one!"

Eshka said, and that was the kind of surprising detail that lent force to her fortunes, "Sh, he's wearing a uniform. He's a soldier."

Underneath this glass-covered table—the cookies and cakes, fruits, boxes of chocolate (the smell now of orange peel, the smoke, though for respect of Eshka no one here smoked cigars as next door no one smoked at all) between the glass and the fine lace cloth, for the whole length and width of the table, were the faces, the hundreds of photographs Eshka placed without any order. Cousins here in America, babies, but mainly the cousins, uncles, and aunts, the parents, in Russia and Poland. A brown-tinted photograph of a well-dressed man carrying a cane in one hand, holding the hand of a little boy in the other, walking on a boardwalk. "He is in Danzig." Dr. Katz's father and mother sitting on a bench in a Warsaw park; little children in Warsaw. You sat at the table and you saw past fragrant orange peel, through reflections of the pinochle players, the handsome face of a cousin almost forgotten or never met.

At sundown the boys came in from the street, their hands dirty from slapping, punching, and catching the pink Spalding. They had played curb ball into the gutter, boxball on the sidewalk, stoop ball, punchball. On Manida Street, between the iron fence of a last large private property and the high walls of a convent, they had used a broomstick to play stickball. There had been a pitcher who wound up to throw his fast ball, his spitball, who could make the ball curve. More than one batter met the pitched ball like Mel Ott, with one foot off the ground. Cousin Eli, fourteen years old, could hit the ball a mile. Cousin Marty, six foot three, home from Harvard, would umpire. Neighborhood boys—their names Guilfoyle, Cook, Prieto— joined the game. They were quieter than usual, they strove, like all of us, to do well.

Then there would be more cars, for almost no one left before late and cousins were still arriving. A new Chrysler and the boys said, "Morris is here." A Cadillac with Jersey plates—the mild Feldbaum who owned a liquor store in Harlem.

The pinochle game was ending; Eshka was in the small narrow kitchen, water steaming; the aunts served tea in the fine flowered china. If necessary, they used the daily service; they could go higher too, the upper kitchen shelves packed with newspaper-covered dishes. The fine china had a cream and sugar set, there was another in polished soft silver. Some guests preferred to take their tea in glasses. Eshka, when she finally had her tea, poured it very hot from her glass into her saucer and drank it from there, blowing on it, a lump of sugar in her mouth. On the long-marble-topped buffet, under the gilt-framed mirror as long as the buffet—inclined into the room, in which you could see the reflection of nearly all the room, yourself, the tabletop, the glass-enclosed bookcase—was a polished and unused brass samovar. The boys, standing about the table be-hind parents and uncles, slipped their hands into the clutter on the table and then snuck off into Lazarus and Max's bedroom with chocolates, cookies, slices of cake.

There, perhaps they came upon an uncle napping. He, waking, straightening his clothes, finding this as good an occasion as an-other, passed each of the nephews a dollar bill, good-looking, curly-haired Ben Cohen peeling the bills off a roll. Joe, who gave two dollars to each, needed no such effect. They lay then across the twin beds and played a dice-throwing baseball or football game, spoke low, for in the dining room the uncles, aunts, cousins were listening to Drew Pearson or to Walter Winchell, who, in that nasal, excited voice, with the sense of urgency emphasized by the Morse code telegraph sounds he used between items, gave gossip and exposed our enemies.

"The way he speaks," Joe said, "you'd think the world was coming to an end."

The boys listened to "Gangbusters."

In the dining room they were reading out loud letters from abroad. Letters still mainly of gossip, though even then each letter writer took himself very seriously, was a spokesman, that sense communicated even through the way the cousin or brother read the letter aloud, he that spokesman's voice.

"What can happen?" asked Bill, the American-born son-in-law of Nelson. "All they want is bigger checks."

His wife Emma, handsome and heavy, smiled thinly. And the other rich and moderately rich smiled too, for they were the ones taxed the most. And they were proud of that, but sometimes felt a little put on.

Saul Katz's eyes blazed angrily. He said, "We must get them out." For besides what he had gleaned from letters and rumors he had heard from patients, from German emigrants, he had read the reports in the *New York Times* and the *Jewish Daily Forward.*

Jack, who had been, in spite of his sewn-together fingers, drafted for eight years into the czar's army, who had deserted, who had traveled across Siberia to Japan, who had been hunted and hungry, nodded his head.

"Some of us have already taken care of our own," said Herman Friedland, who with his brothers, some years before, had brought a sister and her family out of Poland.

Ben said, "There are so many of them. If I sell my business to raise money, who'll give them jobs when they get here?"

"The Germans are gentlemen," Saul's brother Irving said. He had been a prisoner of war of the Germans. One year older than Saul, he was tall; he wrote learned articles in German, as well as in English, on arsenic and mercury pharmacology.

"Irving," Joe said, "how many times have you tried to convince your parents to come to America?" Irving would not deign to answer. Joe said, "Over there, there are proud people, and among them are some who are stubborn."

Sam Cohen said as stutteringly as he played cards, "It—would—be—better—to—have—them—here."

"Who says it wouldn't be better?" Joe snapped impatiently.

Bill, tall, leaned down to whisper a joke to a cousin.

Mother Cohen entered to say good-night to her children and family. In the boys' room, she pressed nickels into Lazarus and Max's hands that they, when they would go to bed, would say the *Shma Yisrael* that she had taught them months before, in a summer cottage, each bedtime adding a word, nodding, repeating, correcting, leaning over them then, looking deeply at them, another world in her eyes, framing their heads with her hands and touching then her lips to their foreheads. They did recite the prayer—after they had counted all their money—their light out, most of the guests gone, whispering sounds coming still from the dining room, the sound outside of a last trolley.

CHAPTER *Two*

1

SAUL AND ESHKA SLEPT in twin beds, a night-table with a lamp and telephone between them. The built-in closet in the short hallway between the dining room and their room was hers; he had a metal wardrobe opposite his bed with his suits hung on one side, his starched shirts and his linens on shelves on the other. He preferred the metal to wood even though it did not go at all with the other furnishings; it closed almost hermetically, it was easy to keep clean. At night, in the kitchen and bathroom, there were, no matter what products Eshka used, no matter when the exterminator had last been there, cockroaches; once a year, the apartment was invaded by termites; every month or so, one of the kitchen mousetraps snapped shut on a mouse, and Eshka picked the trap up and dropped it in a paper bag and dropped that down the kitchen dumbwaiter. Saul told a story of his life in the trenches, of waking and beginning to pull on a boot, and feeling a moving thing in it, and pouring out a mouse. He tried to make the story funny, to give it something of Chaplin's *Charley, The Soldier*, but he was a very clean man; he washed his hands tens of times a day.

He went to bed every night with a journal of the AMA or of the New York State Medical Association, which he read with a red pencil at hand. He kept a pocket diary in Russian in which he

recorded money affairs, his wife's migraines, his children's sick-
nesses, in which he once or twice allowed himself to write of himself: shortness of breath. He was forty-eight years old. He rarely
slept a night through. The telephone would ring, he would grope for
it, uncradle it, switch on the light, and answer, "Doctor here."

He listened then to the sick person's wife or mother, to the worried, anxious, panicky, to the timid, to fools, with an iron patience.
Never to permit his interrupted sleep to determine his response. To
interrupt only in order to get the facts: temperature, location of
pain. "I'll be there in twenty minutes."

At night he did not bother to put on a tie.

The cool night, the Chevy that started right up, deserted streets,
streetlights on. Somewhere, someone waiting for him. For him these
were the hours of greatest and most secret struggle. The sick died
before dawn, the fever broke at dawn. He brought his arms: miracle
sulfa drugs, adrenaline. He had in the pocket of his neatly pressed jacket
pens and a prescription pad, a penlike flashlight, a scalpel. Science
was on his side, he battled with darkness. The patient's temperature
was 105, his breathing was shallow; his wife called for a priest. He
had administered drugs, he had controlled the room's temperature.
He stayed on knowing the crisis would be soon, that no respiratory
accident would be final, that if the man began to fail he could rush
in a last element. The room was hot; the priest, murmuring last rites,
was sweating. He took the man's pulse, he arranged his pillow so
that his head was raised. He waited an hour, and then the patient's
breathing was suddenly regular. "Thank you, father," the wife said.
And to him, she said, "Doctor, how much do I owe you?" Which
rendered him, as often as it happened, quietly furious. You owe me
what you think you owe him. Only not me—Science, Progress, Hygiene. Only I too must make a living. "Three dollars," he replied.

There were nights that he lost, and yet would have to put his bag
in order and go off with a doctor's dignity, someone asking, "Doctor,
how much do we owe you?"

"Three dollars."

There were nights Eshka would call him to tell him there was a
second emergency.

There was a rhythm to these nights, to waking, dressing, starting
and warming the car, checking his black bag, driving, the dark roll-

ing thoughts while driving, of Eshka restless or sleeping whom, dressing, he had only glimpsed but now saw, his boys sleeping in their twin beds, the money thoughts. The thoughts of the sick waiting, of disease, the visualizing of disease, of diseased blood, diseased cells, the model of a heart on his office desk, the compartments that opened, the matter that could grow flabby or sticky. The tiny face of his infant daughter, the terrible cough, the terrible trembling, and then the sudden descent, the instant of silence, she slipping out of his hands. His parents, doors closing on them. Climbing stairs he felt the dark of the sleeping apartments, felt himself drawing close to the lit apartment where he was waited for. There was the washing of hands. The taking of pulse, blood pressure, the stethoscope sounding. There was boiling water. There was the waiting. Sometimes the wife offered him something to drink. "Tea please. One sugar."

The drive home was slow, the darkest moment in his day, he and his arms having failed, or the most relaxed. He would have liked to drive to the river, to park there and smoke a cigarette. It was dawn, and on Hunts Point, Karp, a Bereziner townsman, was opening his vegetable store. He did not look up, checking crates of lettuce, oranges, that had been delivered during the night. The long row of unseparated low apartment houses on one side of Hunts Point, with stoops. On the other side of the wide avenue, the stores on the ground floor of brown apartment buildings: bakeries, delicatessens, laundries, pharmacy, candy. Grocery and butcher shops, the fish store. The barbershops. At the corner of Hunts Point and Lafayette, outside a delicatessen, diagonally across from the boys' bedroom, was a taxi stand, a driver already there saluting him as he stepped out of his car. A first trolley was roaring, swaying up the easy rise of Hunts Point; a man with a lunch bag was waiting for it to take him to the subway to Manhattan.

Driving too most mornings on house calls through all the Bronx, for he was not only a neighborhood GP, but house physician of the family association, of the Bereziner Mutual Aid Society, of a Jewish workmen's group, knowing the Bronx even as well as a taxi driver would. He was differently alert now, quick regardless of sleep, driving more quickly, cursing other drivers: *"Swolitch!"* or "Son of a bitch!" His thoughts clearer now, simpler, the order of his morning calls, of his day, the papers and phone calls necessary for a hospitalization, a new drug he thought he might use and control to relieve someone's high blood pressure.

Horowitz, a Bereziner who was the first of his generation to have a heart attack, said, "When I called you in the middle of the night, I paid you only what I pay you now, on a house call in the morning, three dollars."

"I can't in good faith charge extra for someone's having a heart attack in the middle of the night."

"Saul," Horowitz said warmly, "what have you against us? The pact? I assure you, Stalin made the pact only to gain time. One of these days, he'll strike."

"I am waiting."

Horowitz had left Berezin a young man before the Revolution, had made money in America, bought apartment buildings, and had joined the Communist party. Epstein, who had a small laundry service, whose stout handsome wife sang professionally at bar mitzvahs and weddings, said, "Poland has always been a dagger in Russia's back."

In the waiting room, Mr. Matter graciously insisted on being taken last. He came, with a urine sample in a small jar, twice a year. Saul weighed and measured him, looked into his eyes, ears, nose, and mouth, had him drop his suspenders and open his shirt to sound him with a stethoscope. He took his blood pressure. He was an older landsman, a bachelor; he had a candy store–magic store somewhere in the Bronx. Saul examined him even though he knew—and his knowing disturbed him, as if he had no right to know without accumulated, verified observations—that nothing was wrong with him. Something in Matter's simplicity, in his smiling blue eyes. He came really more to visit than for the examination, but the doctor was the doctor and was a Bereziner Katz, and perhaps he thought things would have a more formal and respectful base if he came, small jar in hand, as a patient. After the examination, after Saul conscientiously recorded his findings on one of the index cards he kept for all his patients, Matter said, "Here is your honorarium, doctor."

"Mr. Matter, please!"

Smiling, buttoning his vest, he put two crisp dollar bills on the doctor's desk. The doctor took the bills, folded them into one of Matter's pockets, and said, "How can I take a fee from a guest? Matter, will you take potluck with us?"

"Doctor, such potluck I should have all the days of my life."

Wall-eyed Lipshutz was at the dining-room table one evening when Matter came in with the doctor. A big man with a big head, his hair long, full, silver, he was speaking in his elaborate Yiddish of exotic places. He traveled about America giving speeches, raising funds for Jewish causes, he had been three times to Palestine. Nothing that happened to him was uninteresting. He knew well many important Jewish figures. In his leisure time, he translated Shakespeare into Hebrew.

"Eshka, my dove, I've seen Jews in such Godforsaken places you'd think they'd become savages. But they're held together by something. I've seen Jews in Casablanca and Livorno. In Waco, Texas, and in Kansas City, Missouri. What is it that holds us together?" he asked and paused for effect.

"Blood?

"The Bible?

"Our sufferings?

"Is it not at least a little our womankind? You are the pride of our nation, our mothers and sisters." He waxed on even as Eshka laughed and left the room to stir a pot on the kitchen stove, waxed on from dining room to kitchen.

To the boys, he said, "You will be pioneers. How is your Hebrew?" But he was wall-eyed, and the boys were young and never knew to whom he was speaking. He was disappointed they were learning only to read and pronounce Hebrew. "Fountain-pen Jews!" he said, referring to the usual bar mitzvah gift.

Lipshutz had studied Hebrew in the same *chedar* as the doctor. The doctor had gone on to a Russian *gymnasium*, Lipshutz had continued Hebrew studies. Matter, of a poor Bereziner family, had received little education. With Lipshutz and the doctor in the room, he took up little place after his entry. Out of a paper bag, such light in his blue eyes, he drew three pink Spaldings. He juggled the balls once in one hand and then so easily let them fly, one after the other, to little Max, who caught only the first, everyone laughing. For Lazarus, he had five different colored pencils and a small pencil sharpener. For Eshka, he had a fortune-reading book and a deck of cards to go with it that he opened in one hand into a fan and then dropped, like moving stairs, into the other.

The boys set the table.

"The best chicken soup in all the Bronx," Lipshutz said, reserving the option of later enlarging his compliment: "A chicken soup that is a chicken soup."

Eshka, eating, serving, spoke of family, landsmen, children. She had seen this one and that, she had spoken on the phone with this other. She was a link to everyone, she knew what was happening sometimes even without having been told. There were things she would not tell, secrets, troubles. Sometimes even the doctor found himself listening to her like sounding her. Her Yiddish, her first language, was sprinkled with English expressions and Russian, with smiles and frowns, and her conversation too was an element of the meal, flavoring it. In Russia, Saul had seen hard times. He would say to his children, "Eat it all up. Not a scrap of waste. People are starving." But Eshka poured the food on as if, starving people or not, what one had to encourage in life was an appetite.

"What do you hear from your parents?" Lipshutz asked when the meal was over.

Saul answered, a finger tapping nervously, "Have you seen the envelopes? They're cut open, and the letter is read and censored, and they stamp the letter with their eagle holding a swastika. It's my sister Nuissa who writes." He heard from his sons' room the sound of the Lone Ranger music, riding music. He saw Nuissa at a table writing the letter. "She writes that Cousin Hunger is moving in next door."

After a moment, Matter said, embarrassed, "Doctor, I too, when I was a boy, learned Morse. All this time you have been tapping S-O-S." Saul laid his hand flat on the table.

Lipshutz too had news of Warsaw. The head of the Jewish Council there was occasionally permitted to communicate with representatives of American Jewry and had reported that he had received official assurances that the Germans would not create a ghetto; he asked for money, food packages, matzoh for Passover. News filtered too from escapees in Istanbul; they spoke of wanton murder, typhus, mass resettlement.

"The English won't open Palestine for fear of offending the Arabs. America too has closed its doors. Nine hundred Jews sailed up and down the coast of America kept from landing by Coast Guard cutters-like-dogs, and who here even raised his voice that refuge be given to those homeless men, women and children? In Palestine, the English soldiers greet such boatloads of Jews who have arrived even in sight of the Promised Land with shots! In Poland, without help from the Germans, Colonel-General Beck said, 'We have one million Jews too many.' Without help from the Germans, Hungary and Rumania persecute the Jews. In France, there are half a million Jewish refugees without papers. The French round them up and put them in camps. What will happen to them if, God forbid, France falls? In Europe are eight million Jews!"

2

Several times a year, the doctor went to the towering New York University Medical Center to attend lectures. Sometimes he met his brother Irving there. Good work was being done in those skyscrapers overlooking the East River, disease was being fought not merely on a doctor-to-patient basis, but by the discovery of scientific truths, of weapons of miraculous scope. Here, in quiet laboratories, light was being brought to bear on darkness, and one by one, areas of darkness were being illumined once and for all. Sitting there in a lecture hall, taking notes, he was regularly renewed. And he felt between him and Irving, seated side by side, a great warmth, an ideal equality of brothers, men of science engaged in a common struggle.

The other equality, the social one, he would never even want to lay claim to. Irving was a year older than him, he was tall, handsome, he inspired confidence, he was a specialist, a professor, he earned twice what Saul did. Irving wrote learned articles; in all his career, Saul had published two or three paragraphs—observations like footnotes of banal diseases that he had felt a duty to add to the storehouse of medical knowledge.

They met before one such lecture, Irving dressed in Brooks Brothers gray flannel, a black felt hat, looking, except for his small black bag, a diplomat. Today, he was pale, tired. He had returned from Washington, D.C., the night before. He said, "Still there are no visas. They make promises, but then there are delays. I sat in waiting rooms whole mornings and afternoons. No matter, I saw our senator and he, at least, is on our side. You can imagine how many hundreds there are in our position."

In the middle of the lecture, the doctor said aloud, "Ach!" Doctors turned to look at him. Irving looked at him quizzically and then nodded as if he understood, and then returned his attention to the lecturer, indicating that his brother should too. But the doctor could not. Taking form in his mind all these months was the inside of an apartment building, a stairwell, a cold apartment in which lived his mother and father, his sisters, their children. Now and then he would glimpse father, mother, or sister seated alone, motionless, staring.

"I'll go to Washington," he said to his brother at the end of the lecture.

"You'll go?"

He did not take offense. "I'll see the people you saw. That way they'll know there are two American citizens concerned."

After a moment, Irving said, "Don't discuss it with the Cohens."

"My wife is a Cohen."

"I'm speaking of your nephews, *Itcha's* sons, the playboys who come to me . . ." He interrupted himself as if he had already revealed too much. "They are people who get what they want by *greasing palms.* In any event, the Cohens are only cousins. They've nothing to do with our parents and sisters!"

The Cohens were, in fact, cousins twice and three times removed from the Katzes, though some were cousins on both the maternal and paternal sides. Some Cohens had worked for the doctor's grandfather, who had been a lumber broker; Itcha Cohen had learned that business in which he had later become wealthy working for the doctor's grandfather and had, after a brief first marriage, married a Nissnievitch, which—there was such Katz-Nissnievitch intermarriage—was almost like marrying a Katz. The Cohens and Katzes had celebrated weddings, sat *shiva* for the dead together. But the Katzes had spoken Russian and the Cohens Yiddish; the Katzes traced themselves to *hassids* honored in the Pale, and the Cohens had slipped into Berezin two generations before, and no one, not even they, knew from where, and they had only their name to show they might have a calling.

He had cancelled his appointments, Drs. Shellin and Konstam would take his calls. His Chevy was in Leo's garage, and Leo would check it out and do what had to be done—he liked the dank dark, the smells of that place, to receive his car all gassed, oiled and greased, polished, tuned and alert. Leo called him "Doc"; he hardly minded. It was, he thought now, his train speeding south, a good enough neighborhood with, not far from his apartment, a public school and a big playground. With the East River beyond the Consolidated Edison gasworks—where the trolley line ended—and the narrow Bronx River seven blocks down the Lafayette Street hill. It was a family neighborhood, Italians living closer to the rivers, three generations together in small houses, their crowded vegetable gardens. It was a workers' and small businessmen's neighborhood, and mothers sat knitting on folding chairs outside their apartment buildings or wheeled their babies to playground benches, or to the East River. Eshka, always a great walker, had regularly wheeled Lazarus across the bridge to Manhattan. Shopping too could be a pleasure, though the doctor rarely did that—the fish that the fishman netted live out of a tank or that lay all silvery on ice on sloped tile counters, the sawdust floor; barrels of sour pickles; the smell of fresh bread; three-cent sodas, or the Coke that Edelman, the druggist, served in Coca-Cola top-bowled glasses in a small corner of his store, a small round wire-legged table and wire-legged, wirebacked chairs; the storekeepers gossiping outside their stores, the barber ushering him in to a barber chair.

Eshka had packed his suitcase for him—packed twice as well as she would for herself, knowing how particular and neat he was—into which he had put at the last minute a stethoscope, a syringe kit, some emergency drugs. She and the boys had stood with him at the trolley stop across the street from their ground-floor apartment, and as the trolley had swayed on its tracks up the cobblestoned avenue,

he had kissed his boys and Eshka on the cheek and then had
boarded. Moving down the aisle, the trolley swaying off, he had
seen the boys waving still and, though he thought any demonstra-
tiveness that was not formal in bad taste, he waved once; Eshka had
just watched him. He was able to imagine her then as she would be
a moment later, shaking off her heaviness, stretching her arms
around her boys' shoulders, glancing right and left for traffic, and
then sweeping her boys home across the street.

Now it was twilight and it occurred to him that back there, in the
East Bronx, Mother Cohen, alone in her bed-sitting room would
surely have begun the daily evening prayers, a white prayer shawl
over her head and shoulders, the worn book that she did not need in
her hands, the pages of which she turned sometimes one after the
other, finding again her place against her voice with wetted finger.
On Faile Street nearby were two synagogues in each of which there
were, surely, a *minyan* of ten and few more, toward the river was an
old age home and there there was every evening a crowd and a great
singing and wailing.

Soon Eshka would put the boys to bed. She would kneel on her
chair at one end of the table with her Jewish paper spread open
before her, her eyeglasses on, and read the *roman*, the serialized
novel the paper was running, which she spoke of with her brothers,
sister, and sisters-in-law, with her neighbors and friends. They spoke
about characters in the *roman* as if they were real, or as if the *roman*
were Literature. Mrs. Kreindel, a neighbor, might come in with a
potful of newly made sauerkraut, and they would taste it and speak
of beautiful Rosie, of whether Sidney would marry the Gentile.

He saw her kneeling, her head framed in her hands, her elbows on
the glass-topped table. She was a thick-lipped, heavy-breasted
woman; sometimes when she read to herself she would form the
words on her lips. He thought that it had not been given to him to
love. Was it his fault? Was it his nature? That she was who she was?
He had lived with Harry, his brother, who so loved his wife, Leah,
her sister; he had seen Leah's look of adoration for Harry, their
bright children. He too had wanted wife and family—What was a
man without a family? What was a man without a son?—and he had
chosen Eshka that she was there, and a cousin, and young, and that
he had sensed that in a very deep way she *needed* him. He could

have asked a half-dozen educated women, sisters of doctor friends, thin and ironic like him, to be his wife; when he broke the engagement he went occasionally to a concert or play with such women. Why then had he returned to her? Did she love him still? After the death of their daughter, a distance had grown between them. Well, now there were the sons, though when they awoke Sunday mornings they did not come, bare feet pattering, then racing with that joyous expectation, to his bed but to hers.

The doctor was—the deep steady rhythm of the train, the time and distance before him—caught up in a deep introspection he did not need. He felt cut off, going where, a hotel room in a city he did not know. He opened a medical journal.

The night was impenetrable.

When he shaved, yes, one or both of the boys might stand in the bathroom doorway and watch. He might, in Rockaway—where, in a rooming house owned by his brother-in-law Sam Cohen, his wife, boys, and mother-in-law spent some summers, he staying with them for the weekend—put on his Panama, take up a walking stick a patient had given him, and say, "Come boys, we'll go for a walk." Of course, he would have to give them at the boardwalk penny arcade pennies and nickels and wait for them, his hands clasped behind his back, and then buy them ice cream. There would be the hot sun, the ocean breeze, bathers, the wide expanse of clean sand, the three of them walking together on the endless boardwalk, the railing at which here and there solitary people stood looking out to the sea.

He had left Berezin in a wagon to go to a neighboring town to begin the long train trip to Riga. With Irving. The first time, all the family had accompanied them to the railroad station, the sisters, all five brothers there, his mother and father. No, that was when Irving went alone for the first time.

He had been commissioned a captain and sent off to the front direct from his school in Riga. A long lumbering troop train, fifty freight cars filled with soldiers in their greatcoats and forage caps, each with his pack and long rifle, and slatted cars for the horses, and some junior-officer–packed passenger wagons, stopping twenty times in a day, for ten minutes, an hour, several hours; the railroad stations-become-encampments close to the front, the hundreds of small fires, the smoke and mist, and the sound, finally, distantly, of cannons. And he, badly shaven, was long gone pale, the sweat and stench of packed officers, the horse stench covering the whole train, bedbugs already, fleas. Then more days to make his way through confusion, misdirection to his assigned post, always pale, stiff, only a doctor and not entitled to a salute, but sometimes mistakenly saluted and, so small, wondering if some soldier's obsequiousness was not mockery, that he was so small, a little Jew, a scared little Jew.

"I had a horse and orderly. An orderly, Max, is a soldier assigned to an officer to take care of his personal needs. I'd never ridden a horse before."

In the photograph album, there was a photograph of him in uniform seated uncomfortably on a horse. There was one of him and his brothers lying in a field, the grass high and dry, Harry, Irving, himself, Lazarus, and Dan.

"Where are they?" Lazarus asked.

There was a blown-up photograph under the glass of the table, of his parents on a park bench. Probably a Sunday, his mother wearing a hat with a feather, a buttoned-up caracul coat, his father in derby hat, a heavy overcoat, his trimmed little beard. His mother, the fineness of her features, more than seventy years old. His father almost eighty. The faint gray-eyed smiles of them both, the picture taken for their sons and grandsons in America. Why hadn't they come to America when it was still possible? Why had they preferred to stay there, in Warsaw, where they had not even been born, where they did not even speak the language?

He had, even from his childhood, been an "American." Others of his age had been Socialists, Communists, Zionists. It was a period of such darkness that everyone had a dream. Jews were not citizens. They could live only within the Pale of Settlement and could be expelled at any time from their village within the Pale of Settlement. There was a *numerus clausus* in the professions, in the universities, even in the high schools; Jews could not own land, they could not engage in certain trades and businesses. Forty percent of the Jewish population lived on Jewish charity. The government accused the Jews of parasitism. Jews were accused of being behind every political assassination, behind all revolutionary movements. Jews, it was said, committed ritual murder. The government policed

the Jews, recruited spies among them, and withdrew its police only
to give free rein to the bands of hoodlums it had organized, the
Black Hundreds, who rode into villages and pillaged, burned, raped,
and murdered.

In the doctor's father's childhood, Jewish children would be
drafted into the army for thirty years. Twelve, thirteen years old,
they would be beaten until they would renounce their faith, they
would be ducked under water until they would accept baptism.
They would die or become Christian. When a Jewish child was so
kidnapped or sold—for the rich could buy protection for their
children—the family would gather and sit *shiva*, the rite for the
dead.

The doctor's father was a proud enlightened Jew who had read
Voltaire, Rousseau.

The doctor had admired German industry, science, philosophy,
and music. He loved France for Victor Hugo, Emile Zola, and the
Rights of Man, for Napoleon battling all of Europe's kings, for his
making Jews full-fledged citizens, for his exporting the Revolution.
But America, that was new, vital, and the future. That was Natty
Bumpo, Jack London, and *A Connecticut Yankee in King Arthur's
Court*. That was real separation of church and state; that was one
man, one vote. That was government divided into executive, legisla-
tive, and judicial, two to be elected, the three to be, under the
greatest constitution in the world, real checks on each other, tyranny
abolished.

Zionism had not interested him. Why establish a nation in Palestine? An ideal worth its salt is larger than any religious group or
any people. How can one be for separation of church and state in
Russia and yet want to create a Jewish nation? He thought Jews
wanting to be farmers was romantic, an anachronism.

His sister Esther had married a Zionist cousin and lived in Palestine, his sister Sonia had returned from Warsaw to Russia in 1925,
his younger brother Lazarus had also been a Bolshevik.

In 1919, during the civil war, he had seen the Reds as incompe- ⋆
tent and merciless as the Whites. He had seen their leather-jacketed
adolescent commissars. He had heard the salvos of their firing
squads. "The peasants," his brother Lazarus had said, "suffer twice
what the Jews do. The workers in factories are slaves. What is a

numerus clausus to the life a peasant leads! How can we be such egoists!"

3

He had forgotten what it was to sit in waiting rooms.

Patients waited for him every day, and it was always first come, first served. Sometimes a patient might have to wait an hour; sometimes, if he had an urgent call, he would leave his patients waiting an hour or two. He never thought twice about it, priorities were simple enough in medicine, and when they were not, time was too short. He thought, waiting now, the room full of people and no one entering the senator's office, that the senator had been, even as might happen to him, suddenly called away.

He was, in any event, the first to be called. He stood before the senator, his topcoat over his arm, his hat in hand. The senator looked up from papers and said as if surprised, "Doctor Katz?"

"Yes, senator. Perhaps you thought I was my brother."

The senator laughed. "Sit down, doctor. Sit down."

He asked him about his practice, his neighborhood. He knew the East Bronx well, he said. Hard-working people lived there, Italians, Irishmen, Jews. He spoke of the doctor's brother, a fine man, a credit to his people, a distinguished physician.

"What, sir, can I do for you?"

The doctor reminded him that he had promised to intercede with the Immigration Service in behalf of his parents, who were in Warsaw. Of course, the senator said. Yes, he had sent a letter to Visas. He would ask his secretary if there had been a reply. He buzzed her. There had not. He said, "We'll see about that!" and asked his secretary to call Miss Gleason at Visas.

This is the way things should be done, the doctor thought.

But the line, the senator said, was busy. He held onto the phone, smiled at the doctor, and began tapping a pencil restlessly as if he were being kept from other pressing business.

"Still busy," he said. "I've an idea, doctor. Why don't I give you a letter of introduction to Miss Gleason?"

The doctor went first to his congressman's office. He had a letter of introduction to him from his state senator, but he was told to come back the following day.

Immigration was an enormous room with, on one side of a counter, perhaps thirty desks, each with typewriter, racks of seals, files of papers, and clerk. Beyond the furthest of those desks were offices whose thin partitions did not reach to the idle-fanned ceiling. On the visiting side of the counter was a narrow area with rows of benches where were waiting about 150 people. They were new or recent immigrants. They were Greek, Italian, but mostly Jews. They spoke German, Polish, Yiddish. They sat on the benches, a bench place was a place on line, but they were often standing up, asking questions, finding their way to the ladies' or men's room. The men wore European suits and American ties, or American suits and European shoes. Some wore loud ties proudly. There were parents with young children, infants crying. There was a group of Italian or Greek women all in black, grandmothers, mothers, widows, young girls, black kerchiefs tight about their heads. There were men eating sandwiches and drinking sodas, although from time to time one of the clerks would announce, "No eating, no smoking. Silence, please."

The doctor presented his letter of introduction to a clerk. The clerk would not take the letter and said, "You'll have to fill out a form." He saw a man on a bench smiling sardonically at him; he too had an envelope in hand.

He sat down when there was room at the end of the farthest bench. The form asked for name, address, place of birth, age, nationality, race, nature of business. People about him asked his advice on how to fill out their forms. What address should they list? What was their nationality?—they had fled. Some treated these forms as if their fate depended on how well they filled them out.

He pressed up the bench like everyone else and crossed from one bench to another at the rate of one place every ten minutes. Men and women clerks came to the counter and called, "Next!" They would open a door in the counter and lead the immigrant to a desk, where, seated behind a typewriter, they would look at one form and fill out another, would ask questions. Some clerks typed with two fingers and never looked up from the machine at their clients. There was a continual movement of clerks to central filing cabinets, there was a desk where people were sent to have their fingerprints taken; at a certain time a woman came briskly out of an office, went to a group of waiting people, and witnessed, one after the other, twenty oaths sworn on the Bible. At four o'clock, a clerk announced that no one else would be seen and that those waiting could return the following morning.

In his congressman's office, a little man turned to him and said, "Does a Jew say hello to a Jew?" The doctor was embarrassed, but the man jumped right in. His wife and children were in Cracow. He said there was no way out. Maybe the Germans would let one train-load of "Americans" out.

"Who do you know, doctor?"

"Who do I know?"

"Who is your fixer?"

"I have no fixer."

"You know no one in Washington?"

"No one."

The man was not even aware of the pride with which the doctor answered. He could not care less. And so genuine was his loss of interest, so serious and single-minded did he seem to be, that when, a short time later, he took a pencil and paper from his pocket and wrote a name and number on it and said, like giving charity, "Give him a call," the doctor, in spite of himself, took the paper.

Miss Gleason did not look up from her papers. Behind her was an American flag on a short flagpole. On the wall was a framed parchment membership in the Daughters of the American Revolution.

She said, "Your senator only clutters my desk with these letters. He doesn't want to understand the rules. Our policy is dictated by law. There is a quota. When the quota is full, the door closes. You Greeks come here to earn and save money for your old age, but there are many Americans who are unemployed."

"Excuse me," the doctor interrupted. "I am not a Greek. My name is Katz, Doctor Saul Katz, and I am an American citizen."

"Of course you are an American citizen," she said, putting one paper on top of another. "Why wouldn't you be?"

He went to the offices of Jewish refugee organizations. There too were lines, crowds. He looked about him at the faces of these people. He could now distinguish immigrants like himself from more recent arrivals by something in the face. He had his parents abroad, a brother, sisters; he had not seen them in almost twenty years. They had wives and young children, they were ready to wring their hands, to crawl.

A sharply dressed man approached him. He whispered, "I'm leasing a ship to bring two thousand Jews from Poland. You look like a man of intelligence. How many times do you think I can succeed such an operation? I lease the ship for twenty thousand dollars. I fly the flag of Costa Rica."

"Where will you load?"

"Where will I load? I'll load in Istanbul."

"But how will the Jews get to Istanbul?"

"How? By train, of course!"

"Why will the Germans let them go?"

The man laughed at his simplicity and made a gesture of buttering his palm.

"You'll buy them out," the doctor said nodding.

He gave his price. "One thousand dollars per person, half for children."

"When do you want payment?"

"For you, I'll take half the total now and half when I land them in New York."

"In New York? How will you land them in New York?"

"In the night, on the Seagate beach!"

Another man said he owned an amphibious airplane, that his pilot had flown with Lindbergh. The pilot would land the seaplane on the Vistula, there would be just enough time to load sixty people, but listen, no baggage.

They had a flair, these Noahs. They whispered their plans, they laughed at the timid, at greenhorns, they comforted the miserable. They looked at their snapshots and said, "Yes, she's a beautiful little girl. Yes, yes, we must save her." They had, of course, contacts in Istanbul, in Bucharest, they had contacts even among the Germans. They demanded full confidence—no less, anyhow, than 50 percent.

To stand before a door and beg for entry. Why was this hopeless role familiar to him? Only, he was on the inside with his wife and sons, and brothers, and the Cohens, Starobinetzes, Nissnievitches, with the whole Bereziner Mutual Aid Society. It was only an oversight, an accident, that his parents were in Warsaw. *There* were children and mothers who did not know which way to turn, fathers who would not desert their wives and children. They were beating their fists against the door. Let them in! Only no one had reason to let them in. What for? Why should Miss Gleason care? All over the world bureaucrats were being swamped from nine to four with refugees who only caused disorder.

Make them wait in the hallway! Make them wait in the street!

He too was petitioning, and what had he to offer?

If *they* want to make you people stateless, if *they* want to punish you for something you may or may not have done, what has that to do with us? We have our laws, rules, and hours!

He saw himself in a hotel room studying maps, and he began to tremble.

He went from fixer to fixer. They promised him what he knew they could not deliver. One, a young man, promised nothing, but opened up a possibility. An honest man, the doctor thought, 50 percent honest anyhow. The young man could obtain Cuban passports. The doctor's parents, sisters could, for dollars, become citizens of Cuba.

The three Katz brothers met on a Sunday morning in Harry's apartment in the East Bronx; it was on the second floor of a private home, and its front room was a sunlit parlor filled with big potted plants, little tables, Harry's big soft armchair. He was the oldest of the five Katz brothers and four sisters and was the only brother not to have attended a university. He had served seven years in the czar's army and had been a sergeant. He told how Saul, newly arrived at the front, had eaten with him, how shocked Saul had been to see him draw a spoon from his boot and without even wiping it begin to eat. From his other boot, he told, smiling so richly, he had drawn a knife, and he had cut bread and offered Saul the first slice and Saul had begun a lecture on hygiene. He was laughing now, scrunching up his body to imitate his brother nervously lecturing, bombs bursting.

Even as Irving had an air about him of being an officer—his manner, his carriage—Harry had the air of being an NCO, calm,

capable, patient. Able to take commands and to roar them out, able
to roll up his sleeves and get in there and do. When Harry relaxed,
he wore his suspenders but no shirt, he wore his shoes but no socks.
And he smoked a cheap corncob pipe. He was a house painter, he
worked hard, he had money worries; he followed baseball closely,
listened to weekend games, and took his children several times a
season to see the Yankees. He had a sergeant's big mustache, and
though he was not as tall as Irving he was a big man.

Leah, his wife, appeared only to greet and serve.

They drank tea. Lazarus and Max came in with the *Sunday News*,
the *Journal American*, and the *Jewish Daily Forward*. They were
surprised to see their father. The doctor could tell they did this
every Sunday. "We'll read the funnies later," Harry said, dismissing
the boys.

What a sunny room this was! And the many plants in the windows and on the floor. The doctor could see the funnies spread open
on the table, "Prince Valiant," and Harry, his eyeglasses on, reading
to Lazarus and Max as he had read until a few years ago to his own
son and daughter. The smell of Harry's pipe, the three brothers
sipping their tea. Now, with no argument, they would, he knew,
tighten their belts. Irving would not trade in his car this year or the
next, he himself would have to borrow on his life insurance, what
would Harry borrow on? No one would weigh one thing against
another, but one could, yes, regret a new car, a new sofa, a nest egg
for a son.

He said, "In Washington, wherever you go, you meet desperate
people. No one even listens to them. They beg you only to look at
their snapshots. There's not one of them who doesn't believe in one
last train making it out of there, in one last ship. They believe in a
last clipper ship, they speak of it as if it were being gotten ready
now."

After a moment, Irving said, "Who can guarantee the authenticity
of the passports?"

"He says," the doctor answered, "the ambassador himself touches
a percentage."

"*He* says! *Who* says? You're speaking of a confidence man!"

"I'm speaking of a fixer."

"I've made contact with the Catholic archbishop's office. Caritas has an office in Warsaw." But they already knew he had done that and knew what that contact was worth. Perhaps Irving was this way showing that they were making a choice, he would continue to petition senators, he would deal through Caritas, they chose to deal with fixers. He said, but the way he said it the doctor knew he would pay his share or more, "This is no way of doing things, people are getting fat on other people's misery."

They would have to raise $9,750. The passport price was $1,500 per adult. Right up the line—fixer, undersecretary, oversecretary, whoever—they had decided children's passports would be half.

He was in charge. Irving would have no direct contact with fixers. Perhaps Irving still refused to believe what was happening. He had been in a hospital behind the lines, his sector had been overrun, he had continued treating the wounded and dying even until the Germans arrived. German soldiers had not interrupted, German doctors had given him medicines. In a German prison camp for one year, he had worked as a German physician's assistant. After the war, the German had sent him with a letter of recommendation to a friend at a Dutch university, where he had learned his specialty. He had seen nothing of the Russian Revolution and civil war. If he now detested the Nazis, it was that he scorned the rabble. He was guest speaker that spring at the annual dinner meeting of the Russian Medical Association. He bought a new tuxedo and gave his old one to Saul to have cut down that he could attend. He spoke of the doctor's wartime role, that in war as in peace the doctor was not only a healer but, by his example, a teacher of ethics; his moral code was the highest, he served his nation, he served all the wounded; he was a patriot, he acted unwaveringly, unstintingly, with courage, compassion, and decency. To these tuxedoed White Russian émigrés and some few Russian Jews who had seen not a little of life. He received a standing ovation; Saul, with a mist before his eyes, applauding for his parents too, in the tailored-down Brooks Brothers tuxedo he wore only that once; that Irving caught in them, had never let go in himself, the highest ideals of their youth, that he steadfastly addressed the coming times.

Denmark and Norway fell. Jews in Poland had to wear a Star of David. Jews in Austria were being deported to Poland. The government general of Poland would be one great prison for Jews. In Lodz, the first prison-ghetto was established. The Germans began their offensive against France. The English would send fifty divisions, fleets of airplanes. The Germans would be smashed against the Maginot Line. Everyone spoke, those May days, of the end of Hitler. And then suddenly Holland and Belgium surrendered, the British evacuated Dunkerque, and France was in rout and then fell.

The doctor's brother-in-law Joe wanted to bet that now the English would make a separate peace. "This Churchill," he said, "is only a headline hunter."

Irving had $4,000 cash, Saul raised 3,000, Harry raised 2,000. It was only a beginning. In Washington, the fixer was now asking 10 percent more.

Harry parked his Chevy behind the doctor's. He wore a suit but no tie; in the back of his car were cans of paint, piles of paint-stained canvas, overalls. His car always smelled of paint. He would not sit down in the crowded waiting room, and when the doctor opened his office door to let one patient out and another in, Harry stepped forward, cutting off the incoming patient, the doctor disturbed by the interruption but standing his ground in the doorway. Harry said, "How will the passports be gotten to them?"

"We'll find a way."

"Let's say the passports are gotten to them. Who will help them out? Our father is eighty years old."

"We'll find a way."

"Who do you think you're speaking to?" Harry said angrily and only then noticed the doctor's pallor.

4

Emma lived on Park Avenue. In the Crash her father lost a great deal of money and committed suicide. Still he left her rich, and the apartment buildings she owned were all in her name; her husband Bill had an office as a real estate agent.

There were large Persian rugs on the parquet floors of her apartment. In the large living room the large windows were bordered by

velvet draperies and veiled by silk gauze. On the walls were dim
mirrors, dark, gilt-framed oil paintings of mills and streams. There
were deep sofas and armchairs. There was a fireplace with a high
mantel that Bill would lean his elbow on, there was a highly polished dark grand piano on which Bill, at the end of a gay evening,
might play songs.

Emma was alone when the doctor called on her. She wore a dark
dress, pearls. She was handsome still. Her father had had mistresses,
she had been his princess; her husband, it was said, played around.
They had one daughter.

"That's a lot of money," she said. "And it's strange you come to me
when you think so little of me. You're surprised? You think we're not
worth your respect. You think we're only rich."

He asked, "What do you want me to do?"

"What? No irony now?" She said as if wanting to be stopped,
"Why didn't you bring Eshka with you? She's the only one of you I
love."

He would tell no one of Emma. Bill employed Harry regularly on
apartment building painting jobs, Harry would only tell Bill off.

He went to Thirtieth Street off Seventh Avenue to see his brothers-
in-law Ben and Jack Cohen, there in the tall-buildinged, teeming fur
market, jobbers and dealers dealing and gossipping at the street
corners; delivery boys pushing and pulling coatrack wagons full of
fur coats or bunches of skins, mink skins hanging 100 to a bunch; a
big manufacturer with silver hair, a cigar, a fast talker at his side
trying to sell him something, passing through the crowd like royalty,
dealing out a smile, a wave.

The language of the fur market was Yiddish, the fur workers,
members of a Communist union, were Jewish, the very union
hoodlums who beat up nonunion shop operators were Jewish; there
was a synagogue on the second floor of a fifteen-story fur center
building to which mourners—workers and bosses—could go before
and after work to say Kaddish for the dead, and which had a Saturday morning service that was over by 8:30 punch-in time.

The tall buildings were filled with more or less permanent manufacturing corporations. In this business, it was said, everyone went
bankrupt at least once, and yet there was no way of doing business

without giving credit. The aim was to pass more "paper" than you received. You paid someone off with someone else's paper. If someone had somehow conned you into taking too much paper, you begged him—in this business men really went down on their knees —to settle for even fifty cents to the dollar before he had himself legally declared bankrupt.

On the ground floor of the buildings, with separate entrances, behind big plate glass windows where were displayed bundles of skins, were the skin dealers. They bought fur skins at farms or auctions in Idaho, Canada, Europe. They bought at ten dollars a skin and sold to manufacturers at fifteen. They bought big when prices were low and then put in cold storage until prices went up. The best of them knew furs, where to look, what to look for, and they got a better price for their merchandise because they had a reputation for quality. The dealers often were brothers-in-law or cousins of manufacturers and in hard times depended on their relatives to continue buying from them.

It was not unusual for a man to be a manufacturer one season, a dealer another, and a fur factory worker another. There were small timers, jobbers who rented back rooms and made coats with non-union labor and materials and sold them cheap to retailers and even manufacturers. There were men who thought themselves stylishly dressed who approached women hesitating before building directories and gave them a card announcing themselves as advisors and then piloted them to manufacturers who would give them 5 percent of a sale. There were older men in the jacket of one worn suit and the pants of another who were always going this way or that, fast, short of breath, selling this or that, the look about them of men sinking.

The doctor, in his topcoat, his hat, felt here—everyone out to make a buck, the smell of the money struggle like the smell of skins in the very air—that he was again making a mistake. What could the Cohens understand? Why should they offer their money for his parents, his sisters, and their families? That he was a cousin? That he was married to Eshka? Hadn't Joe blamed every Jew still in Europe for being stubborn? First you say they must be exaggerating their troubles, then, when plugging your ears doesn't help, you begin to blame them. Why should they help? No, he and his brothers would never be able to raise enough money. The fixer would again raise the price, would cheat them.

In the elevator were loud women; he took off his hat and held it in his hand. This whole industry, he thought, is only to put furs on the backs of rich women.

He got out at Cohen Brothers Furs, the firm of Ben and Jack in which two of the sons of Itcha Cohen were junior partners, Sam and Jonathan. Joe was the most successful of the Cohens; he sold furs to movie stars, socialites, the wives of politicians, but the doctor would not go to him.

There were two small fat Jewish women at one of the several tables in the thickly carpeted showroom; a tall thin model wearing a mink coat was standing listlessly before them; Ben, his hands on the fur at the model's shoulders, was showing how one could arrange the large coat collar. He was a good-looking curly-haired man, he wore a fur worker's starched long linen gray duster over a white shirt and tie. The end walls of the long room were all mirror, and one saw oneself over and over, smaller and smaller, he standing at the entrance, Ben smiling, a real warmth and interest showing beneath the wide professional smile.

"Doctor," he said, coming up to him, shaking his hand with both of his. "Is something wrong?" he whispered, leading him to a chair at a further table.

"Nothing's wrong. I'd like to speak to you and Jack."

"I've customers," Ben whispered, "but that'll take only a little while. In the meantime, will you give me the pleasure of letting me have you shown the place?"

The doctor had never seen Ben at his business. He was the youngest of the Cohens, younger by two years than Eshka. The doctor had always thought him a blowhard, a compromiser; he called all women but his mother and sisters "dearie." Hadn't he married a plain nagging woman years older than he because she was a bookkeeper and American-born, though America for her had been the Lower East Side and the fur market? They had two children, the girl, Lazarus's age, was slow and unhealthily fat, the father treated and dressed her like a doll. And yet here he had a competence and confidence that was almost graciousness. He gave an order to one of the "girls" in the office to get Mr. Jack, he answered a phone; he smiled at the doctor, maintaining that link, working on another.

Jack, big and strong, came out of the factory with young Sam, both in dusters. They greeted him so warmly and respectfully that he wondered, From where do I get my credit? They showed him the cold-storage room. They had 100 coats in stock. Jack, no boaster, hardly a talker, pointed with his sewn-together fingers and said, "Coats." Sam, gentle, showed him a coat of white mink. But it was Ben who, steaming in to get another coat to show the ladies, told him how much it was worth, in what magazines it had already been written up.

They passed into the factory. Standing at high tables by the street windows were the cutters, who, with razor-bladed instruments, prepared matched skins for the operators behind them at a raised bank of fifteen sewing machines. Behind the operators were the big nailing tables where the sewn-together furs were stretched. There were, in the up-and-down whirring noise of sewing machines, the wild tumbling of a machine to treat furs, in the dust and smell, forty workers. And among them—how had he forgotten?—were cousins, in-laws; there were Bereziners and even some East Bronx neighbors whom Eshka had pressed upon her brothers. "Hello, doctor!" He treated the families of ten of the workers here. They stood to shake his hand. And, for a moment, the work stopped, Jack, the factory boss, allowing that. But then, as they moved off toward the design and lining sections, he, by a look and not a word, set the factory back to work.

Ben was there to say, "Jack's the best cutter in the business, and I'm the best matcher."

"And Joe?" the doctor asked, ironic.

Ben laughed and said, "Ach, Joe, he has style!"

They sat in the private office, a small room with a large desk, a leather upholstered sofa built out of one wall and low cabinets and some closets at the others. One of the closets opened into a mirrored bar above a refrigerator.

Sam poured Scotch. The doctor took his neat. Like Ben and Jack, he drank to mark the occasion.

He sat in a small straight armchair facing Ben behind the desk.

Jack and Sam were on the sofa. Jonathan entered after the doctor began. He shook his hand and poured himself a drink.

The doctor told of his visits to his senator and congressman, to Visas. He told of the fixers, of the man who could sell him Cuban passports. He wanted to borrow $5,000.

"And the rest?" Ben asked.

"We've borrowed on our life insurance."

Ben could not refrain from shaking his head. "And if, God forbid, something happens to you?"

Jonathan said, "There's your father and mother, your sister Judith, her daughter, your sister Nuissa, her husband and two children. That's nine thousand seven hundred and fifty dollars plus ten percent—almost eleven thousand. Of which you've raised nine."

"We need a margin," the doctor explained.

"I'll call Joe," Ben said.

"I . . ." the doctor began, but understood then by the suddenly too smooth smile on Ben's face that it would be useless to say he would prefer them alone to make the loan.

There was a phone in the private office, but Ben went elsewhere. Jonathan too left. Jack said he would do some work in the factory while waiting, and, leaving, he touched the doctor's shoulder as if to indicate support.

Sam offered the doctor a drink, poured one for himself. He was a good-looking friendly boy, a reader, he went to plays and movies; he loved opera; he was overshadowed by his two brothers, the older one, David, the younger, Jonathan. Surely, the doctor thought, Jonathan was not the one to need Irving's treatment. He was too bright, too self-controlled for that. Surely he had gone to Irving accompanying Sam or David.

Sam spoke of his sister Sara, who was attending Hunter College. She was a poised and beautiful girl adored by her brothers; they had raised her.

What courses should she take?

Did she want to be a school teacher?

Half an hour passed, their conversation failed, Sam smiled on from behind a thickening screen.

Now, one by one, the Cohen brothers began arriving: Sol, the smallest, who had a small manufacturing business; palsied, hand-trembling Sam, who had once been in partnership with his brother Joe and now worked as a commission salesman for a fur bleaching firm; Joe, the oldest living Cohen brother and the richest; and the nephew David, who was a skin dealer.

It seemed to the doctor that this kind of meeting was usual with the Cohens, that this private office was even common property. Didn't David, limping in in that remarkable jerking way he had, so that he seemed to be propelling himself forward, exploding even, open a cabinet, kneel, and dial open a hidden wall safe and take an envelope out and thumb through a wad of bills? Only then, the envelope in his jacket pocket, did he nod at the doctor. Then he gestured his brother Sam to pour him a drink.

The doctor, in this small, Cohen-crowded, smoke-filled room, the mirrored bar, the safe still open, felt he was in a den of thieves and felt in the air here the quality of dream and thick blood ties.

They were five brothers and three nephews. In each of them, even as in his wife, was some dark energy.

One recent Sunday the nephews had come to the East Bronx with a friend who was selling scrap metal to the Japanese. "Don't you understand what he is doing?" Saul had demanded.

So that now, when he was again asked to explain what he wanted, he spoke not of senator and congressman, of the impossibility of getting visas through Immigration, nor of the fixers—he could not teach them anything about that!—not of right and wrong, not of what anyone should feel, but of the refugees he had seen in Washington. And speaking, it occurred to him that, if there are only two kinds of people in the world, they are not the rich and the poor, but maybe those who listen and those who do not.

"In Washington, wherever you go, you meet desperate people. They beg you only to look at their snapshots, of their wives, their children. There's not one of them who doesn't believe in one last train making it out of there, in one last ship. There is no hope but that. Things are happening now, at this instant, such dark things, on such a scale, that they dwarf all our experience.

"These are my parents and sisters. I must get them out."

Ben, in the desk chair, looked about the small room for questions, and some Cohens shook their heads almost imperceptibly to his look, and some were nodding still, as if with what the doctor had said, and Ben stood and led the doctor out, even through the show-room swinging doors to the elevator, the doctor not willing until then to understand he was being dismissed without a decision, angry then only at himself that all these years he had never guessed that these Cohens, when they had something to decide, met not at his apartment or at family meetings, discussed only among them-selves, here, had a real mechanism for making their decisions.

"We'll tell you soon."

CHAPTER *Three*

1

O N A WEEKDAY afternoon, Eshka's brother Sam came up to the East Bronx and spent half an hour with his mother. He went then to Eshka's next-door apartment and sat with her over a glass of tea. He always wore dark conservative suits. In the fur market, walking slowly from one client's place of business to another, he looked out of place, but the street people made way for him, his slow stiff walk. When they looked at him they saw his brothers behind. They knew who he was, the Cohen family messenger.

When he left her, Eshka remained seated at the table crowded with mute faces and later, waiting still, hardly replied to her boys come in from school.

Mother Cohen gave birth for the last time when she was fifty years old, her oldest son, Itcha, then thirty-five, having already fathered one son by a first marriage and David by the second. It was her sixteenth birth, and, like the one before, the child was born dead. Her sons and daughters were gathered in the big house they were then living in in Berezin, but she who had brought them all into the world would have nothing to do with them and their father. For two years she would not go out. She lived in an attic room reading holy books, lighting candles, rocking back and forth on her heels, praying, served in everything by her older daughter Leah.

There were ten men then living in the house, and it fell to Eshka, eleven years old, to supervise the peasant girl the family hired for cleaning, to cook for the men, to shop, organize, do. She was a mother to her younger brother Ben, a mascot to her older brothers. She learned by her eyes and hands, by doing. She watched others do but once, and then she did as if she had for years. And what she did made such sense to her that she did it better than it had been done. She did by intuition, though her intuition was perhaps appetite. She had an appetite for games, singing, dancing, costumes, friends, for having a roomful of family at table and food taken together.

Mother Cohen came back to the world removed from it. And though neighbors spoke of the hours she would now spend in prayer and study, she would forget certain religious observations she had never forgotten before.

A few months after Eshka had her first period, she had her first migraine.

There is in the migraine something of the wild disorder of the epileptic fit. Only the thing has no final explosion and one does not lose consciousness and one suffers at the edge of what one can bear for days at a stretch. It announces itself with a changing of lights; one shakes one's head, and spots and colors only merge and confuse, and you close one eye and see normally with the other, and already pain is on the way. It comes from far, and it builds slow, and you wait for it, and you hear someone coming, and you think it's him. You are all alone with your pain, and no one can do anything for you, and you don't want to see anyone until the pain has reached its peak, is settled there, you flat on your back, and then you want someone only perhaps that he see and know how you suffer.

Kneeling on her chair at the heavy, glass-topped table, Eshka told fortunes with cards. First she would study your palm, then she would lay out rows of cards, rearrange them, study; she would gather up the cards, shuffle them, deal out several, and would, totally absorbed, read each. Family, friends came to her in the afternoon hoping she would be alone; she would study and read and, to a niece who was having marriage problems, she would say, "I see an unhappy bed." The niece would blush, and Eshka would smile and drop her hand heavy on her niece's as if touch were good. They came to her crying as no one would to Mother Cohen.

There were times when, turning over the cards, a flash would come to her and she would *see* something. She had once seen dark news and had sat motionless looking at the cards, through them, their faces, and had herself been so dark and still that someone had said of her, "The Queen of Spades." That nickname, like *schwartze* and gypsy, stuck, though after she once said she did not want to be called that, it was not again said in her presence, but was sometimes in people's minds.

She was, when it came to hers, fearless. Word came to Berezin that brothers had been arrested by the Reds in Bobroisk. She threw on coats, hats, boots, and gloves and tramped five miles through snow to Bobroisk and entered, almost frozen, the headquarters of the Red commandant. Sixteen years old in that time of summary justice.

"What," she demanded, "are my brothers accused of? What liar and thief has accused them?"

"They are profiteers!"

"Who is not a profiteer? We are all hungry! What are we to do, shoot ourselves?" But she wept then and begged.

Who were these Reds or Whites to her? They spoke Russian, her language was Yiddish. She was born in the Pale, not in Russia. She was a Jew.

Typhus came to Berezin with the civil war. The young girl watched a man she had earlier laughed at for his seriousness, timidity, and pride battle the epidemic almost alone. A little man barely taller than her, no heavier, who walked into dead houses and treated the sick and dying. He was deserted by soldiers assigned to help him do what he did, white with fatigue, every day: disinfect, burn, bury. She was ashamed at that time for brothers—she had overheard bits of conversations—who went to him, who was, in the heat of epidemic, not only doctor but sort of mayor, who had to sign or countersign every permission to enter or leave the town, and asked him for this or that privilege. Why not? she would ordinarily have thought, he was family, his brother was engaged to her sister, but she honored him even then and maybe already loved him.

So that, years later, when he made her wait several months, that was only several months more, she had already waited years. She had in America gone to public school for him, she had, for him, refused to work in her brothers' factories. And then she got him, and she gave everything, all of her, and never got in return more than a bit of him. As if, with her, he would always hold back, a reserve in him that was more than modesty, that was, she thought, his rigor.

The migraines would come before her period and stop with it. During her pregnancies they disappeared entirely. She connected them to loss of blood, to filth.

"Who am I?" she, who had never spoken to him in such a way, demanded.

"What is it?" he asked. "Lower your voice."

"You think I care if my boys hear? What are we to you?"

"They told you?" he asked angrily.

"Why shouldn't they tell me? *They* are not strangers to me!"

"Again a mistake!" he said bitterly. "So they've refused me?"

"Who's refused *you*? Your money's there in the envelope."

"Why," she demanded, "didn't you tell me?"

He was embarrassed. These are *my* parents, *my* sisters.

"I'm asking why didn't you tell me that you're planning to go away!"

He knew then that he was wrong not to have told her. But even then he wondered how does she know that and asked coldly, "Are you reading my mail now?"

"What did you intend to do? Just leave in the middle of the night and never even say good-bye?"

"Has there been a letter for me?"

"You understand nothing!"

He wondered where the letter was, what it said; he thought his sons might indeed be listening, and he was ashamed of the scene, he wanted to justify himself to them, but not now, calmly.

The bedroom venetian blinds were, when she had a headache, kept drawn all the day. A bright light, even a point of sunlight, would explode into moving pulsing bands of pain, her nerve ends were at her skin and even noise hurt. She saw from flat on her back in the dark room, heard the cries of children playing outside the ground-floor windows, cars braking at the corner traffic lights, trolleys screaming past.

Leah would come and have tea always ready for her, sugar which she sometimes craved. An icebag wrapped in a towel was at the base of her neck. Sometimes in the afternoon, Leah would begin preparing the dinner.

Mrs. Silver, the grocer lady whose brother Eskha had placed with Ben, might come in. She was not afraid, that one. And for her, as for her sons at their bedtime, she would save a smile.

She would hear her whispering with Leah.

The boys played their radio low.

She could see in the mirror of her dresser the short hallway to the dining room, the shorter entranceway to the apartment. Each time someone entered, she would look up and then look away, as if she were waiting for another.

Her mother would come in, heavy, formless, the back hunched, the large heavy-lidded eyes, coming slowly from, it seemed, so far. She stood over her silently. She might be lost in pain and would crawl out of it, and her mother would be there looking at her with such sorrowful and pitying eyes. When her mother was there, she would not moan.

After a day, she had no modesty. She would come massive out of the room like an animal out of its den, her large hanging breasts seen through her nightgown, would grope her way through daylight or electric light to the bathroom, pushing wildly past helping hands, to retch, to sit, to return then to her bed, to twisting and turning, the sour smell sticking to her.

One side of her head saw things, the other was gripped in an ever tightening and loosening vise. She knew she was being punished and thought the only way out was to be punished more.

The room was an attic room in the house in Berezin. She was locked in. The door opened, and doctors stood in the doorway looking down at her, on all fours, crawling like an animal in her own filth, and they shook their heads.

He had explained to her that he could give her only so much morphine. She had understood. During her headaches, he stayed away that she should not beg him for another injection.

He came and took her hand, but she knew he was going for her pulse. She pulled away from him. He asked her how she was.

She had no strength left to fight, no strength to hold back the tears, and she said, "Why don't you shoot me! Why don't you shoot me!"

Even as the hypodermic needle slipped into her pinched-up flesh, she felt relief.

She saw, before dawn, in mist, a heavily loaded horse-drawn wagon. Where was it going at this hour? It was far ahead on the dirt road and moved so slowly it raised no dust. It was, no doubt, a Russian river road, bordered by tall birch trees, and she must have been in an open automobile. Now she could begin to make out what she had wanted to be hay or steaming manure, but had known even from the first was not, bodies piled one on the other. She saw arms, legs, hands. What had happened in Berezin? What was she doing in an automobile? She saw familiar faces she could not recognize.

Surely it had been an epidemic that had taken them all. Ahead, to a side, she saw a column of smoke, flames licking up. The bodies were being taken to be burned.

She saw the driver's back and thought it was the doctor driving the dead to the fire, and she began to call his name, "Saul! Saul!" She did not want him to go on alone, to lift the dead, one by one, and drop them on the flames. She wanted to wake him from his leaden sleep, and she reached out vainly. The car was pulling away. She saw the wagon driver's face, he sleeping as she had thought, and she sighed with surprise and relief that it was only her nephew David.

2

The letters the doctor was expecting came. The United States had no official representatives in Poland, there could be no protection of American citizens, and Americans could travel there only at their own risk. The International Red Cross did not need his services in Poland. The American Joint Distribution Committee replied that he should have patience.

Lipshutz said: "There are more than enough doctors in Warsaw. What is needed is drugs and money!"

"Shaylka," he said, calling him as hardly anyone did, "you are thinking of your parents. We must do what is for the good of all our people." Nevertheless, he gave the name of a man in Istanbul.

At this time came remarkable news: two letters from France, one from Paris postmarked before the German offensive, and the other, four weeks later, from Toulouse. His youngest brother, Dan, whom he had not heard from in six months, who had worked at a job here and then gone there and never had work as an engineer though that was his education, who, in his rare letters in those uncertain years, had never asked for anything, had married! The first letter described his wife, Tanya, how beautiful she was (a picture was enclosed), how talented, that she had had French and English governesses in Petersburg. Was he crazy to think of marriage at such a time? The doctor was even offended that Tanya was indeed beautiful. The second letter said: "Our residence papers are worthless, I burned my hands in a factory making watches, and I still cannot work. Can you bring us to America?" Only it was not just him and his wife, but her parents as well. Money could be sent to Vichy France. Once again they would have to beg for visas.

Irving took charge of this mission; he wrote to Dan that to be able to present his case better, he and Tanya should file papers separately from Tanya's parents. Dan replied that they would not leave without his wife's parents. Irving was furious: Had she married him only to use him as a ticket?

No mail came from the doctor's sister Sonia in Russia.

From Palestine the doctor's sister Esther wrote for the first time in years. Her husband, she wrote, had been arrested by the English. The why was censored out. What had the firebrand done now? The news of what was happening in Europe made it imperative for Jews to join together and fight back now. What was she talking about? Why did she write now? Did she feel guilty that she had run away with the Zionist, leaving parents and sisters behind? He sensed it was not that, he sensed she needed something and would not ask.

One night in sleep he heard his orderly calling to him, "Doctor! Doctor!"

"Don't you see?" he cried. "I've got to rest, I've got no strength, I must sleep." But of course he had to get up, he had to return.

First they had run out of morphine, now there were no more disinfectants. How am I to proceed without? Someone brought him still bubbling boiling water. He almost wept with relief. He dropped his instruments into the water, and the water turned suddenly black with blood.

There were too many of them, there were no beds for them, they were laid out on the ground and writhed. He stepped among them, he bent and knelt to them.

His hands were filthy. There was no soap, no fire, all water was filth. What was he to do to disinfect his hands? In an open wound, amid scraps of clothing, skin, tissue, was a blood-blackened shell fragment. How am I to put my filthy hand into there? Do it! Do it!

Nor is there drink left to make them drunk. Nor are there bandages. Boil linen! Boil uniforms! Boil! Boil! Boil! How can we progress without bandages!

He tossed and turned in his sleep. Was someone calling him, was the phone ringing?

Where, Lazarus, are you buried?

"Your brother was wounded in the thigh and side. We were busy," the officer said laconically. "Some of our boys shoot themselves rather than be taken prisoner."

"But him? What happened to him?"

"We left him, he had a pistol."

So that he might have lived days and nights. Propped up against a tree, a canteen of water, a bit of bread. Only it was cold at night. He heard the howling of dogs, he cocked his pistol, he heard a sound close by, his heart was beating and jumping. When he woke, the pistol had been taken from his hand and long-coated unshaven Whites stood above him. Did they hate him more because he was young, a boy? Because he looked a Jew? He looking up at them, the boy, the Bolshevik, not saying a word, wide-eyed.

Where is he buried?

I walk among the dead.

When was that? When I failed. How long did I last? A month, two? All of it only a day. In the morning we discovered some sick, and by half-morning tens were prostrated with fever and aching, the rose-spot rash like a signature on their bellies. By noon, the town smelled of diarrhea.

Kill flies! Quarantine! Don't touch!

I said, "There's no quicklime, we'll have to burn the clothes, the bedsheets, and, rabbi, the bodies. You see, if we bury them, the disease will reappear."

The rabbi said, "That you will have to take upon yourself."

"Why do you say that? I'm only saying what is objectively reasonable and right."

"That you will have to take upon yourself."

I do. I do.

In the evening, after we began the fire, I too fell. Who carried on my work? No, falling, I continued. How long did I carry my body from house to house? My sisters are dressed in black and are reaching out to me. My mother's hand is cool on my head. If I am recovering, why do they look at me with such pity?

"Saul! Saul!"

Who is calling now?

I have walked a thousand times about a smouldering fire.

I am climbing stairs. I climb one flight, and there is another. And I climb another and stand a moment on the landing to catch my breath and I look up and down and am suddenly dizzy with all the distance I have climbed and all the flights of stairs that are still waiting. I carry my little black bag that is so heavy, and yet, do I have in it what will be called for? I climb, I climb. Here, at this next landing, someone has left his door wide open, light lies like a door aslant on the landing. A long man in a long threadbare black overcoat is seated alone in an empty room. His face is long, he is smiling. Does he know I am looking at him? Is this not Cousin Hunger? What is he counting on his fingers?

"Saul! Saul!"

He awoke. It was Eshka calling in her sleep.

So he was ready.

He had bought Cuban passports, he had his US passport stamped with a Turkish visa. He had bought passage on an Argentine freighter going from Newport News to Istanbul.

He was uneasy still about the fixer. The agreement had been to pay cash on receipt of the passports in the fixer's office. He had wanted guarantees. The fixer had laughingly suggested, "Do you want to receive the passports from the hands of the ambassador himself?" But when he had gone with cash to the fixer, the fixer had taken him to the Cuban embassy, and there, as if it were a normal transaction, a clerk had stamped and delivered the passports, the doctor forcing himself to check each that the photo correspond to the name, that the information be as he had given it, afraid every second that some official would appear and demand, "What's going on here?" And only when they were back in the fixer's office did he pay the fixer, the fixer dealing with him and his money in so off-handed a way that he felt that the importance of this sum of money had been superseded, that he was being dealt with less as a buyer than as someone for whom someone else has bought.

3

The Sunday morning of the week the doctor was to leave, Karp, the vegetable store man, paid a regular visit. He was a small sturdy man with thick strong fingers. He wore a suit and tie, he held a new cap in his hands. He sat uncomfortable in a straight armchair; he would have been more at ease seated low on the end of a fruit crate.

In his small wood-floored store, the unpolished rough planks swept smooth but stained dark with juices, with tracked-in rain and snow, the crowded trays and crates of fruits and vegetables, the hook-hanging bananas, the hook-hanging scale, housewives waiting their turn gossiped freely. He was brusque with them, but he gave credit and delivered his vegetables even five or six blocks away, pushing an iron-wheeled cart, the wheels almost as big as the cart, up cobblestoned Hunts Point Avenue, carrying packages up flights of stairs, refusing tips.

He came to visit the doctor as others go to play chess. There was in their never-unserious Sunday conversations the air and pleasure of a game. Karp's opening move was Vichy France, Pétain's recent law depriving refugee Jews of all civil rights. How many refugee Jews were there in France? Half a million? What would happen to them now? "By law he has denied law. Once the law gives in an inch, it can be forced open all the way."

The doctor nodded, and that pleased Karp. But today the doctor would not engage, and after a while Karp grew silent and studied him hard and then sat on ten minutes, as deep almost as the doctor.

For lunch, they had delicatessen: hot dogs for the boys, salami, pastrami, corned beef, laid out on the tableclothless table in the paper plates they had come in; soggy paper platters of pickles, potato salad, and french fries; soda; a sliced rye bread. It was a Sunday treat for his children and Eshka, and that way Eshka, who would entertain all afternoon, would not have to cook.

He would, this afternoon, speak to his boys. He wished it were as easy for him as for others to put his arms about his children's shoulders. To take them for a walk toward the river.

My sons . . .

Irving arrived with Mary. Harry and Leah came from around the block. Irving spoke of his efforts to get Dan to America. He had accepted an invitation to give lectures at a medical school only in order to meet the dean whom he might then ask to intercede for him. Only, why did Dan give in so easily to his wife? He had a future here. He was an engineer, America was the place for him. He had always been lazy and without will.

It was worse than useless, the doctor thought, to question and blame. It could lead to grave errors, they had so few facts. Why didn't Irving simply accept that Dan would not leave his in-laws behind? He thought of his brother's burned hands, he thought of red-hot liquid metal, of radium dials.

Harry, who here, for Eshka, would not smoke his pipe, lit a Lucky Strike. "Shaylka, what do you think, how will our Yankees do next year?" He was making fun of him and was not.

"They'll win," Saul said. "They'll win the pennant and the series. Not only is there DiMaggio, but there's Charlie Keller and Tommy Henrich."

"They're hitters, those fellers," Harry said, nodding reflectively over his cigarette as if it were a pipe.

Now the Cohens began to arrive. Ben, his wife and children, and Sol and his family arrived from the West Bronx crowded into one car, Fanny, Sol's fat wife, at the wheel. They went first next door, Leah already there, to greet Mother Cohen.

She had little alms boxes, *pushkas*, for orphans, old age homes. You could tell it pleased her that you thought of dropping a nickel, dime, or quarter in a *pushka*.

Sol, only as tall as Saul, touched him on the elbow to take him aside. They went into the doctor's bedroom, and Sol, first making sure no one was looking or could overhear—the doctor waiting, observing again the lax Cohen posture, the belly out, the wide necktie—handed him fifty dollars and said, "Extra. Extra to be of help." How could the doctor be embarrassed when the donor, at his thanks, was so pleased that he blushed and looked away?

When Sol left him—hiding his gift even from his wife?—the doctor marked the donation down in his journal that it be not forgotten.

Ben said he wanted to show him something outside. He put on his hat. Marvin and Harvey, Ben and Sol's sons, and Lazarus and Max were playing ball against the building wall, Max the youngest and not the weakest of the players, fat, quick, full of enthusiasm. Lazarus, bigger, would be tall, his coordination not having caught up with his growth, watched the exciting play; Max dived into it.

The players stretched from one corner of the building to the entrance to the apartment and office, each player occupying a sidewalk square. The girls were watching, fat and not handsome. The Negro superintendent, wearing overalls, was sitting on an overturned garbage can outside the spiked iron fence to the building yard, a cigar stub in his mouth.

Now well beyond the boys, Ben gave the doctor $100. "That," he said, "you should not be short."

Side by side they walked back slowly. They watched the way the boys played for a moment, the ball bouncing on the sidewalk, hitting the wall, and then bouncing into someone's square and he returning it up or down the line. The way the boys moved about jerkily in their squares.

Emma and Bill came. The doctor could reply to Emma with the same politeness with which she addressed him. Why had she come today? Did she think he would ask her again? Did she think he would curse her before everyone? Never mind! These people paraded through life, and all that was important to them was appearance.

The dining room was crowded. The visitors sat about the table crowded with platters of apples and pears, red and white grapes, platters of nuts and cookies, boxes of chocolate, the photographs under the glass, water already on in the kitchen for the first tea.

Emma spoke with Mary, Irving's wife, and Edith, Jack's wife, the women forming groups, divided, it almost seemed, into fat and nonfat. Emma, though heavy, was at the center of the nonfat. They spoke of carpets and sofas. Mima, Sam's wife, spoke to Fanny of her garden; Fanny, smoking, waited for a card game. Dora was thin but fit into no group. She had ulcers. Had Ben not married her, she would have surely gone on all her life being someone's ever conscientious and disapproving bookkeeper. She did not understand the Cohens: one and one made two; the way Ben added, it could just as easily be three or seven.

The wives found common ground only when the conversation turned to the children. They praised each other's children, finding qualities in each that reflected their esteem for the parents. Joe's son was, of course, a prince. Ben, whose daughter Elaine no one praised, said, though smiling, with more cunning than irony, "What's important is to arrange the match yourself, to keep an eye out for a smart poor boy."

"Marriages," Mary said, "are not made like that any longer!"

Ben smiled knowingly.

Jack gave the doctor an envelope in which the doctor would later find $100. The big quiet childless man indicated with his sewn-together fingers the twin beds of the doctor's boys and said with great embarrassment, "Never worry."

The doctor could tell that no Cohen knew what the others were doing. They came to him as if they thought what they had already taxed themselves was not enough, or not personal enough.

Sam took so long at it he was discovered, but only by Irving. The doctor noticed the look of shame on Sam's face, distaste fleetingly in Irving's expression. A suspicion that had long lain hidden flashed through the doctor's mind. What was really wrong with Sam, this slow, dark-suited family messenger? Irving had turned to wait outside. They were, of course, doctor and patient. His trembling hands. Was his heart already affected? One could only look so far into his eyes.

His contribution was twenty-five dollars.

Joe brought the doctor a new soft black leather suitcase with straps. They examined it together in the doctor's bedroom. The doctor thought it was a beauty.

Bill whispered to Joe, "So Mickey Mouse is really going."

Joe turned away impatiently. Still, months before, he had coined the name.

Sam and Mima. They had separate beds. All these years. Something, yes, in his eyes of a man who has to hide and be ashamed of his suffering. He lived in Rockaway to be near the ocean, he liked to garden. They were, of course, childless. What single adventure had cost him so much? Not even an adventure, just a sordid moment.

These heavy corseted women.

He saw them seated on the edge of a bed, Sam pulling with his weak hands to clip the corset to.

"What do you want to be?" Bill asked the boys outside.

Marvin: "I want to be a farmer."

"What kind of farmer?" Bill asked grandly.

"A horse farmer," Marvin said.

"A horse farmer? You mean a breeder!"

The boy simply meant that he wanted to ride horses. When Ben spoke of horses, his son thought him wonderful.

"And you?"

Harvey: "I'll be an airplane pilot."

"A fighter pilot!" Bill exclaimed, approving.

There was a photograph under the glass of the dining-room table of Emma and Bill in the lobby of a grand hotel in Quebec. Occasionally he sent the boys boxseat tickets to the Polo Grounds. The boys were sure he knew ball players well, and that he joked with them as easily as with their fathers.

Lazarus: "A doctor."

Max: "I want to be rich!"

Bill laughed uproariously. He was so tall, good-looking, and jovial the boys almost danced with pleasure about him. He took them for ice-cream sodas at the candy store around the corner.

A Packard pulled up. Young Sam, alone in the front, wearing a chauffeur's visored cap, jumped out of the car and, to the children's delight, bowed open the door for his brothers Jonathan and David and his sister Sara. She stepped out a princess after the princes, her brothers. Then Sam was sparring with the children, and Jonathan too, a loud free-for-all full of cries and laughter, one of the children ending up with the chauffeur's cap clapped on even over his eyes— "Where am I? Where am I?" David, still his sister's prince, now tilted at her side, smiling ironically at the melee.

Evening was coming on.
"Where are my boys?" the doctor asked.
Lazarus was outside. Max, Lazarus said, had gone off in the Packard with David, Jonathan, and Sam.
"Where has he gone?"
Lazarus shook his head.

Drew Pearson was on. The doctor sat in his wooden swivel chair at his office desk listening to the radio—the model of a heart on a stand before him, a pen and pencil set, the rocking blotter, piles of papers, bills, laboratory results—Cohens, Katzes, cousins standing and seated in the office and waiting room, the doors to the waiting room and apartment open, Drew Pearson on in the dining room too, only there a big card game going.

The battle of Britain was underway. Greece would be next. Rumania, Bulgaria, and Hungary were already bending to German demands and would surely soon be yoked to Germany. Roosevelt and Wilkie were vying to prove to the voters that this was not America's war.

Fanny had taught the women to play a joker's-wild card game called kaluchee. One could play with any number of people, one just added decks of cards to the game. When everyone at the table was playing, the dealer had to shuffle together three decks of cards. They played for pennies and nickels, but as the game developed quarters were used and dollar bills were changed.

The doctor's hand was idly playing with the model of a heart, opening and closing the auricles and ventricles.

Walter Winchell spoke of Father Coughlin, who was preaching to the nation: "This is International Jewry's war."

No one wanted to be the first to go. Things had not been said. Why had they played cards? There was present in all the apartment, in the waiting room and office, an image of him in hat and topcoat, carrying a suitcase. There were sudden deep moments of silence in all the apartment.

Mother Cohen came in to say good-night and, having kissed and been kissed by her sons and daughters, her in-laws, her grandchildren, she asked, "Where is David?" She looked around her and, not seeing him, went off with Leah to wait for him in her apartment.

He entered shortly, limping in his violent way, veering as if to fall, break, or push, tipsy, with his tipsy brother Sam and smiling brother Jonathan, with Max, seven years old, so full of excitement he was flushed to bursting. "Congratulations, doctor!" David said. "The boy is more Cohen than Katz!"

The doctor stepped forward and, in front of all these Cohens and cousins, slapped his nephew and then took his son's arm and led him to his bedroom and did not see, the blood returning to David's cheek, the surprise in David's eyes, the beginning of a smile.

"Where were you?" he asked his son.

"They wanted me to tell their friends that David was my daddy." The boy was nodding, regaining courage, and now hesitantly took from his pocket three ten-dollar bills. "David gave me ten, and Sam gave me ten, and Jonathan too."

He wanted to empty his pockets of bills and envelopes, throw all that money on the floor.

Emma and Bill had left. Cohens were getting up to go.

Jonathan said, "Do me a favor, Aunt Eshka. When David comes back from grandmother's, tell his fortune."

She had seen David in the wagon in her dream, and would not. She said, as if she were still angry at David, "What do I care about him?" And then turning, called to her husband, "Saul, I want to tell your fortune."

He was drawn by something in her voice, a silence fell over the room. A place at the table was made for him. And then he and she, surrounded by their many brothers and sisters-in-law—Leah there too, leaning over Eshka's chair—by nephews, nieces, cousins, were face to face over a deck of cards.

He had to pick three cards from the spread-open deck, and then three more. She shuffled the cards together, and again he had to pick out cards.

She said slowly, "I see you in a hotel room, waiting, lying on your bed. Waiting for whom? For a message, maybe. You are at your desk writing in your journal . . ."

She was silent so long, someone asked, "Is that all?"

"I see an airplane." She had gripped his hand and was looking above his head, beyond him. I see an airplane flying through the night, flying to America. That phone is ringing in the middle of the night. A cablegram for you. And now we are dressing, and I am phoning everyone, and cars are all coming here, and we all meet here in the night, and in these cars we all go to the airport, and there are a hundred of us. We are waiting now in the airport, for there are delays, Saul and Irving and Harry, and us all, the boys, everyone here and everyone else, and then coming from the end of a long corridor, carrying suitcases, we see your bearded father and your mother and your sisters and their children. And I tell you there is such a weeping and such a joy."

CHAPTER *Four*

1

IN ISTANBUL the doctor settled into a hotel room with a double bed, a fan over it, a wardrobe, a mirror, a small table and chair, and a sink and bidet. There was a set of doorlike windows opening out onto a noisy crowded market street. Jewish refugees and representatives of world Jewish organizations lived in this hotel. The representatives came from America, England, Switzerland. There were young Jews from Palestine here to arrange the illegal passage of refugee Jews to Palestine.

The refugees commuted to Ankara to plead their cases at the United States and South American embassies. The Turks refused to extend the validity of their temporary visas, *bakhshish* could help. The British asked how could they be sure that the Jew who escaped the Germans and wanted to go to Palestine was not a German spy.

In Istanbul and Ankara the doctor went in vain to consulates and embassies, trying to obtain visas. To fill out forms he had to engage a translator; the translator insisted he give money to this one and that, even the embassy concierge had to receive a gift.

In the office of a Jewish agency he was told the agency was negotiating with the Germans to send a medical train to Warsaw. "I heard that in America six months ago."

A Jew told him he could smuggle papers for him as far as Budapest, from there he could try to have them sent on to Warsaw and into the ghetto, but there were no guarantees and it would cost plenty.

He went a second time to Ankara and this time hired a lawyer, who took twice as much money as the translator and actually arranged for him to sit down with an undersecretary in the Hungarian embassy.

"You'll have to fill these forms out."

"But I've already filled out such forms."

The Hungarian shrugged.

In his dreams he saw his sister Nuissa climbing a staircase.

He walked in the market. In vast hangars were stalls where valuable rugs were sold, jewelry. He was beckoned to and propositioned. He saw the squatting beggars, hands outstretched, eyes running. He saw the porters bent ninety degrees under loads strapped to their backs and foreheads. Their arms hung free, they stared straight ahead, their eyes popping beneath the leather bands cutting into their foreheads.

In his hotel he heard that a ship packed with 800 Rumanian Jewish children that the Turks had not permitted to dock, that the British had not permitted to continue to Palestine, had, sailing in circles in the Black Sea, hit a mine and sunk with everyone aboard.

He felt sick every time he thought of the gradual chipping away of money that was not even his; he felt sick when he thought of being here and being no closer.

He stood waiting in a broad hot dusty Ankara street. His hands were sweaty, did he have the knack? What was he afraid of? He followed the undersecretary. "Sir! Sir!" he called out. The undersecretary turned, his eyebrows immediately rising.

The doctor said, "I have something for you."

"I've had enough of you Jews!"

He began to spend hours at the railroad station. A train ran daily from Istanbul to Sofia. Sofia was a transit point to both Bucharest and Budapest. Warsaw was beyond.

The people arriving in the soot-covered train had been traveling for days, most had crossed several frontiers. Men carried leather portfolios; they were come to do business, or had done business. Jews stepped down last, they looked out fearfully and, finding themselves met by representatives of Jewish agencies, stood straighter, and there was again in their eyes the hard pride of the rich, everything was owed them for they could pay for it.

He put two twenty-dollar bills between the pages of his passport. I am, he would explain, holding out his passport, an American citizen, a doctor tourist. I thought you might visa my passport here. He packed his smallest bag.

I will not allow myself melodrama, and I write to my wife (in English to address too my sons) only the routine letter: Don't forget to remind Harry to run the Chevy every few days, don't forget. . . . And I look at their picture—Lazarus, Max, Eshka behind. And I am off. It is about time! I am brisk, only shaving I have nicked myself and a drop of blood has stained my collar. Never mind. I have a copy of the AMA journal, and I shall sit with it, calm, a doctor on holiday. A guidebook. Why didn't I think of that?

The train is moving, I am alone in a second-class compartment. The locomotive is chugging hard, a trail of smoke wafts back over and sometimes across the train, and I see Istanbul, the domes and minarets, this market shantytown, from behind soot-covered windows. I open my journal, my red pencil in hand. I try to force myself to study, I am repeating to myself in the rhythm of the never-quickening train, "Yes, I shall do it! Yes, I shall do it!"

The train stops. Have we crossed the frontier? The delay drags on and on. The old familiar sweats return, I am nauseous, short of breath. I hear the heavy steps of officials in the corridor of my car, I hear doors sliding open, voices. They slide open the door of my compartment, little badges on their lapels, a soldier with a rifle waiting in the corridor. And as I hand over my passport—good-bye Lazarus, good-bye Max, good-bye Eshka, I am on my way—the two twenty-dollar bills inside that I do not have the courage or decisiveness to open to, am I not hoping I shall be discovered: Go back, little man! Go home, little man! So that when I am being led off the train, striving now—"I am an American tourist, I thought you would visa me here"—and I am shoved once and almost fall, I know that I shall have to try again.

This time I go first to Ankara. For fifty dollars, my passport is stamped; this will get me through Bulgaria.

I sit in the corner of my compartment waiting to be discovered, for I have learned that about myself: not only that my luck is bad, but that I am waiting to be discovered, I am waiting to be uncovered. They look through my passport and let me pass. But the relief I feel is no good, no good. It is as if I am only sinking farther and farther into a trap. I have crossed one frontier, there are two more to cross, there is Poland to cross. I am going home, I am going home to my mother and father. This is crazy! Still it is so! I am going back to them! The countryside flies by, it is getting cold, it is getting dark. I shall bribe! I shall bribe! I shall buy my way in and I shall buy their way out! Only they are aged, and there are infants among them. It makes no difference. I must go on. I sleep. Again I see Nuissa climbing stairs; she pauses, holding onto the handrail. What is happening to her? Her mouth open, she is gasping.

I am being shaken awake, I am unshaven, I feel untidy, the collar stain. I hold out my passport. They take the money! But what is this? I must follow this man off the train! "I am an American!" I protest. "I am a doctor!" Two men take charge of me, one is holding me, the other is going through my pockets! They are hoodlums and thieves! They must not find the passports! I scream and throw myself headfirst into one of them and a moment later, my eyeglasses cracked, my body aching, I am in the hands of uniformed men.

Later, an American official escorts me by train back even to the Turkish frontier, where I am taken in charge by Turks who tell me I can stay in their country only seventy-two hours. But I give one a bill, and I am stamped good for thirty days.

At my hotel, a letter is waiting for me.

"Father died of pneumonia. Cousin Hunger," Nuissa writes, "has moved into our apartment from next door." Pneumonia, I notice, is misspelled.

I see my mother, my sisters, their children, standing about my father's deathbed.

My own fine hairy hands are the hands of my father.

I have come from America only to mourn with my mother and sisters. All day long gaunt expressionless people file into the room. Once, one asks me, "When will the airplanes come?" My mother's face is tightly drawn, her eyes are gray like stone.

It is night. I have drawn the shutters, but the light is on. I pace my room, I toss on my bed. I find myself washing my hands. And then there is a knock at my door.

"It's me!" my nephew David says, limping in, his tie too off center, an unopened bottle of Scotch in hand. "They wrote me from New York. I've come to sit a little *shiva* with you."

"You can all go to hell!"

For in the instant of seeing him I understand that after the Cohens met with me they met more than once without me. And I always knew, though I kept it out of mind, that they have a nephew and half-brother in Warsaw, that they, seeing me prepare, felt they too must do. They retraced my steps, they bought their own passports. They bought, I'll learn this evening, a fake US passport for David so that when he would cross a frontier he would not be a Cohen or Katz, but a Gentile, he would have the best reason in the world to travel, the reason everyone understands: business! Business! All is business! All has always been business! It is all there is, the changing hands of money and things, and everything else is weakness and failure. They are the future, these Cohens. They know how to live with life! I know nothing.

Twenty years before, I said to his father, "There are no exceptions in time of epidemic." He laughed at me. "Sign the paper," he said. I would not. So he picked up the pen and he signed my name and he said, "Now, if you want, you tell them to arrest me, to put me in *chains*, ha! ha! ha!"

Why did I ever begin? Look where it has gotten me!

The son is offering me a drink. "What happened to your eyeglasses?" he asks.

I will not answer.

"Isn't there," he says, "some rule about not sitting on real chairs?" He sits on my bed. He will lie on it, leaning on an elbow. "Shouldn't that mirror be covered? Health!"

It is even in their blood, for what did he know of his father. He was ten years old when his father was killed, eleven when his mother died. In America he studied voice, he was the genius, the special one. Ten years he studied, and then one day he realized he would never be a great singer and so, from one day to the next, gave up singing, and now all that was left of opera in him was his tenor's barrel chest and his manner.

"What do you want?"

"They want me to go back."

"So? What is that to me?"

"What a band of idiots! You know how they reach decisions?"

"I saw."

"You saw nothing!"

"Why did they send you?"

"Who else? In all the family there's only me with culture! No one speaks Russian like me. They speak Russian like Jews. I speak Italian, German; I *improvise* other languages. So can you see them? In Ben's private office? With my cablegram?

" 'He's sending us three thousand skins!' Ben says.

" 'What if the Germans sink the ship?' says Sol. 'What will happen to our money then? It will all go down into the sea!' "

I am shaking my head, thinking I should be mourning my father, that my mother and sisters are starving, and that here this one is talking to me of furs and Cohens and money.

"Never mind. Tomorrow," he says, "I'm going to Budapest."

"Budapest?"

"To Budapest to buy more skins!"

And he never, I consider now, again, ten days later, turning over cards three by three, said he was going for anything but skins, never said he was going elsewhere than Budapest, never made a promise, though without phrasing it as such he did make a request: "Only I'm short of ready cash."

So that I began to understand that the Cohens had sent him off here to buy skins, and to perhaps see if he could save one of their own, and to perhaps keep an eye out on me, and to perhaps take charge, that even as they did not trust me to succeed, that even as they did not trust themselves to give a mission that was not a deal, they had not trusted David with all the cash he needed, and I wanted to laugh that their prodigal now wanted the money I had raised from them. But his regard was such—not steeled to laughter but ready to scorn me for mine, and something else: you have slapped me once, I couldn't care less what you think of me—that I for the first time began to study him.

"Why did they send you?" I asked again.

He said with that mixture of mockery, bitterness, and flamboyance, "Maybe I too think I'm expendable."

That he, I consider again, hardly seeing the cards, just mechanically turning them, losing control of the game as I have of time, place, my very body, should have at that moment caught just the right tone, the right look, the right ambiguity! What does he mean by that? I thought. How dare he say that! As if his saying that were putting blame on others. And then, Does he mean he is so because of his failure? And then I was faint and nauseous for the word is in me too.

And so through the night, waiting, sitting, we played two-handed pinochle, I too occasionally taking a drink and snapping the cards down, and my nephew just as fast, and it was a good game, and me winning 1,000, and then he a close one, and then me again. We talked only in pinochle language, and our minds were all numbers, quick calculations and the face images of cards, so that midway in a game we would know who would win and by how much.

When I would let him take the bid I would aim to destroy his every possibility, and he, on the defensive, would do the same, and as he, by playing out trump, would ruin my chances for aces or kings, as I would his, I would smile almost and say, "Son of a bitch! *Swolitch*!" But my eyes went bleary, and once I caught him looking at me with a smile that was but half-mockery.

Toward morning I looked up, and he was looking through my money belt of passports that I had given him, and my money.

Then I was alone.

I have never been so alone. I am sinking. It begins even the first morning when I have not slept and I do not shave. I am waiting for nothing. I am just there. The tall blank walls of the room, the idle ceiling fan, sunlight and dust filtering into the room, the low bidet. I go out into the streets, these fierce streets where I do not speak the language. My eyeglasses are cracked. I am a Russian, I am a Yankee, I am a Jew. I would buy a *yarmulka* and pin it to my hair.

I play solitaire. I turn over cards three by three.

When do I take a sheet from the bed and cover the mirror?—the room suddenly smaller, everything reduced. I begin to say the prayer for the dead: *Yisgadal vai yiskadash shmai raboh.* . . . I glimpse my father, but even then I know that others are dying, they interrupt me, they enter my room silently, women wear black and black wrapped tightly about their heads.

I have, I realize, failed again and am now without any recourse. My nephew has stolen from me my honor and my pride, he has stolen from me my money. I throw myself on my bed, I have only myself to blame.

I am naked, straddling the bidet.

What have I become? What am I? I am nothing. I wash my hands.

I turn over the cards, I keep my mind on the cards, I put red on black that I can then order each suit, I calculate my every play not to risk taking from the uncovered cards what I might next turn over from the covered. The backs of my hands, even to my knuckles, are hairy, black and silver.

There is a knock at my door. Someone says, "Your nephew is on the phone."

2

"I want Scotch whisky! No brandy, cognac, or vodka! Scotch whisky!"

The doctor nodded into the phone. He asked no questions. He felt now as if he had known all along that David would go in and would come out, what David would, though still had not, tell him. He shaved, he would not think. He went out to find Scotch whisky.

He saw from his window a long dusty black Mercedes push its way through the people-, porter-, wagon-, and cart-crowded street. David, wearing a long leather coat, a fine soft-brimmed hat, stepped out, and a squat flat-headed man David's age, and a moment later they entered this mourner's room.

"You can sit *shiva* for all of them," David said, his eyes burned red with dust, drink, and sleeplessness. "For all of them except him." He indicated his companion, who smiled broadly and introduced him-

self in Yiddish. So they were all dead. And yet even as he began to
know that, he knew there was more to come; that card had been
turned up, another and another would be turned up, and it was only
when he would have seen them all, in place, that he might *know*. He
saw the two men from far, through a mist; he was alone, a suitcase
in one hand, a medical bag in the other; he heard fragments of what
David was saying, and he was walking forward in the mist, on gray
that rose like dust with every step.

Money. David was speaking of furs, skins, money. Furs bought in
Istanbul had arrived in New York, money had been deposited in his
name in Budapest. He made it known he was representing a fur
consortium. He met Germans whose territory was Hungary, Rumania, and Bulgaria. He went to meet a German in his hotel room,
and the German showed him furs, took coats one after the other out
of trunks, spread them before him, and said, " 'Look! Look at the
label!' " And David was standing before the doctor, holding the
coat, staring at him with the German's pig eyes and insisting he look
at the label. " 'What's written here? Paris is it? Paris!' " David said as
if he were the German. "And in this other coat I read Vienna. And
Warsaw, Budapest, Berlin. Every city of Europe!" And David whispered then in his ear, " 'I have diamonds and gold too. But they, I
warn you, are expensive. Women sell their furs before their diamonds!' "

He was shaking out and spreading the furs on the bed, on the
floor; he laid coat on coat and was filling the room with furs, and he
said, " 'Look, this one is almost—ha! ha! ha!—in mint condition!' "

It was dusk. No one had thought to switch on the light. The
doctor was seated at the small table, an opened bottle before him.
David lay, leaning on his elbow, on the bed. The squat man, he too
with a glass, sat on the floor against the wall, his arm resting on the
bidet.

"All our lives," David said, "we're only moving backwards!" He
was looking at the doctor, and he laughed soundlessly.

"Backwards!" he said and shrugged, and whatever it was he knew
he would not explain just as then, telling of what he had seen, he
never stopped to reveal what he had felt, except sometimes when he
laughed, ha! ha! ha!

"I was walking in those walled-in crowded streets, those *rush-hour* streets of filth and people, half a million sick and starving people in ten times ten city blocks. Everything they eat comes from the other side of the wall. The children are great smugglers. And there are 'operators' too. That place is three dimensional. Every Jew walks on roofs and knows the cellars, and the sewers to the outside are the ghetto's lifeline. Some days so much flour is smuggled into the ghetto that there's no bread—ha! ha! ha!—for good Christians! But it's never enough. What can they buy with? Poles come from the other side to buy wedding trousseaus, to furnish their apartments cheap.

"A car pulls to a sudden stop in a ghetto street. A leather-coated German holding an iron bar jumps out and lunges at a Jew, whom he hits once across the side of the head. These leather-coated angels screech in in black Mercedeses and then screech off as if they have other pressing business. Still, they murder only a little in the streets, little exceptional murders! Though every day men are rounded up and marched off to 'work camps.' Trivial the street murders! Though Poles do their share. No, a much superior ally is the louse!

"The Germans allow no antityphus serum into the ghetto. You can bribe the Germans, you can bribe the Poles, but you can't bribe the lice, though people with money scent themselves with precious Lysol and camphor to drive them away. You smell in those streets the dead and filth, and every now and then, exotically, you have a whiff of Lysol! You see in those streets the horse-drawn wagons carrying the dead and a horse-drawn trolley carrying the living, and starving old bearded Jews trading scraps of linen and mothers wheeling baby carriages filled with rags for sale. And beggars. And *rickshas!* A German tourist or, yes, an 'operator,' riding a ricksha harnessed to a panting boy.

"Rush-hour streets? Those people live in a day what we live in a year. If one lives a year in a day, how many days—ha! ha! ha!—can one live? If a man requires three thousand calories per day to live normally, what happens when a Jew can legally obtain only one thousand?

"I was, I said, walking in those streets, and Jews made way for me as if I too were an angel of darkness. They didn't dare look at me. I have nothing of the tourist about me! I had things to do, family to find, precious gifts to distribute! Passports!

"He," he said, impatiently indicating the squat man, who, seeing he was being spoken of, raised his head, gave a profile, his expression grave and trustful, "when I finally found him, a day later, looked at me suspiciously, wouldn't believe I was who I said I was. So I began to undress before his startled eyes. I got to the money belt, and, standing in my underwear, I presented him a Cuban passport, he not even realizing for a minute that this was why I had come, and finally he began to smile, not at the gift but in recognition of me, as if only a brother, only an American, only an American brother could be such a schmuck, and he showed me like a card-player playing out, not a winning hand, but a better one that was still nothing, shrugging them out, an identity card in his name with a Star of David stamped on it, and then from another pocket another identity card with his picture but another name and no Star of David, and then an American passport in a name like Levy, and then another American passport in the name of John Smith. I had dollars too in the belt. That impressed him. Though I must say, from the moment he saw my passports and knew I was who I had told him I was, he had a tender look for me. Tender. And in that place his tender look too was exotic! But that was a day later. One day and night later.

"I climbed tens of staircases, winding staircases and back and forth ones. There's little light in those pits; at a landing, left like garbage outside a door, you see a heap of rags—no, it is a body. Suddenly a descending mass of men is rushing past, something terrible about them, you flattened against a wall; half of them, you then see, are dead. These are the body collectors, and on their backs are the dead.

"I climb and climb. There is, in these staircases, the stink, and then, toward evening, the smoke. From every apartment smoke seeps into the stairwell. Jews with no other place camp on a landing. They burn papers, rags. You climb in a fog of dark, stink, and smoke.

"The room in which I found your mother must have once been a reception room, or maybe, for all the people in it, for the smoke, for the flickering candlelight, it only seemed that long. They lined the walls, they squatted on the floor, they stood in groups. The sick were stretched out on piles of straw and newspaper. I'd swear that, as I entered, a tall old Jew standing with a boy was teaching the boy his bar mitzvah portion, the old Jew's finger crooked to explain a point. But the instant I entered, all life there turned to ice. They stared through me. Those big dead eyes, and the blue of death in almost every face. And the only movement was the enormous slow-dancing candlelight shadows, and, on the floor, some old Jews gnawing toothlessly on bread.

" 'Katz!' I exclaimed.

"The Jews moved aside. She was seated on a chair in a far corner, her hands on her knees. She was skin, bones, and rags. I don't think the whole bundle of her could have weighed seventy pounds. If you were to touch her too brusquely, something would break. She wore a cotton stocking tight over the back of her head and ears, her face was shrunken about her features, wizened and dark as leather. She was looking straight ahead, but she saw nothing that you or I could see.

"I said, 'I am your cousin David Cohen, I am the son of Isaac and Anna Nissnievitch Cohen.' I had approached her, and now I knelt before her and began to repeat softly, 'I am the son of Anna Nissnievitch Cohen.' I don't know how much she understood.

"Names! I worked soothingly on names. 'Berezin. Starobinetz.' I asked, 'Where is your daughter Nuissa?'

" 'She is dead.'

" 'Where is Judith?'

" 'She is dead.'

" 'And the children?' I asked, for I did not know their names.

" 'Dead.' "

Sometimes he whispered, sometimes he almost sang. His round drinker's face was fiery red, he saw everything, then and now, the doctor's clear attentive and helpless gray eyes.

"One by one the candles in the room were extinguished. Some Jews, like me, sat propped against the walls. A Jew's shoulder was pressed to mine, and he too was pressed to another, and our feet touched the bodies of other Jews lying pressed together for warmth. And something in me made me begin again, made me turn and lean and look again into her face, the thin lips, the nose that in a fleshless face was large, the eyes, the head wrapped tight, the hands that lay so still on her knees. 'Where is your daughter Nuissa?'

" 'She is dead.'

" 'And Judith?'

" 'Dead. All dead.'

"By this time my hand was holding hers. 'And the children?' I asked again.

" 'Dead.'

"I insisted: 'All of them?'

" 'I taught them an address: Irving Katz, Professor of Dermatology, Columbia University, New York City.'

" 'Who did you teach?'

" 'Judith's Ruth.'

" 'Is she then alive? Where is she, Ruth?'

" 'She is an orphan. Sh!' she said. From the street below came a child's cry. This was the first of the nighttime street beggars. 'Mama!' This *holy* night. 'Mama!' For the nighttime beggars would not go away until alms were thrown down.

"I would doze and wake, and her hand would be in mine, and I would say names, your names, names from Berezin. I told her everything would be all right. And at dawn, when I awoke from a dream of praying Jews rocking back and forth, their prayer shawls over their heads and shoulders, and that misty air of a synagogue at morning service, and saw, in fact, some Jews standing and praying in this misty place, her hand was ice cold in mine."

The mist is smoke and the dust at my feet is ashes. I walk in ashes that rise and whirl about me. I see grim men I do not recognize. Where have they come from? They walk in the smoke in all directions.

I see my brother Dan. He approaches. Does he recognize me? He is in pain, there are tears at his eyes, his mouth is open as if he cannot get enough air. He shows me his hands. They are white and glowing, they are being consumed. "Dan," I call, "Dan," but he is moving off. I am searching in my bag for an ointment, I shall lose him in the smoke. I run after him, but he is gone and I grope blindly.

I am in Berezin. What has happened here? If it is typhus, there is perhaps yet something I can do. Briskly I enter a burned house, the ceilings have fallen, the stairs have collapsed, the roof has burned through. "I am a doctor!" I call out. "Is there anyone here?" I must clear rubble out of the way to make sure I miss no one.

I enter another house, and it is the same, burned and charred, and there is no roof, and though I look everywhere there is no one.

I go from house to house.

I stand before the porch steps of one and suddenly know it is mine. I stand in the center of the living room and all is burned and charred and I look up and there is no roof.

I go out into the street. I stand in the middle of the street, and I cry out, "I am a doctor!" And I see at the end of the town a white glow like the glow of my brother's hands, a great consuming white glow.

I have walked a thousand times about a smouldering fire. I walk slowly forward on still-smoking ash. My father is dead. My mother is dead. Nuissa and Judith are dead. Their children are dead.

"This one arrived in the morning as the others were leaving. He was an important man, you could tell that. He wore built-up heels to swagger on, a hoodlum's cap. He smelled of vodka and good times. He was a *provider*. That's right. It was he, and not you in America, who'd been keeping your mother alive, and someone, a *neighbor*, had gotten word to him when I had introduced myself. So I stripped. So he believed me.

" 'Ruth!' I said. And he snapped to as if now taking on the role of second-in-command—of whom? of everyone else?—as if the moment he had recognized me as his American brother it was known, agreed, contracted, stamped, and delivered that I would be taking him out of there to America. He told me the girl had been smuggled out of the ghetto and given to a Catholic group. She'd probably been sent with a new name to a Catholic orphanage. No, he didn't know under what name she was.

"The passports? He'd find a use for them. A shave? He'd find me a razor, a clothes brush. Did I want hot water?

"Your mother's body? He'd arrange the burial, he'd even arrange a *minyan*. All it would take was money. 'Money,' he volunteered, 'can buy anything.'

"The drive out? A Mercedes! We bribed here, we bribed there. We drank to stay warm, we drank just to keep going. Once, in the night, I thought I was driving a wagon, the reins in my hands. And it was pitch dark, and in the back were your mother and father, and your sisters and their children, and others too. And then I realized you were there too, in the back, and Eshka was there too. I was taking you all out.

"I must have been ripping the gears down wildly, for this one, this Louis said, 'Doveed, you drive like you walk.' And I looked up and—ha! ha! ha!—the only one I was taking out was him!"

CHAPTER *Five*

I N 1943, THE DOCTOR read in the *New York Times* reports
of the total destruction of the Warsaw ghetto. He had read previously
of the Germans overrunning all the villages and towns of his Russia.
And then there were reports of the existence of tens of death camps.

One Sunday, his brother Harry had a heart attack while driving
across the Whitestone Bridge, his son Eli at his side. He died almost
immediately.

And then the doctor's heart failed.

It happened just before the 1944 New Year, in the night, he in his
bed, after an ordinary day of sixteen hours up and about, up six-
story staircases, through hospital corridors, pulsing himself down to
be able to focus in on the sick. He felt piercing pain at his heart. He
reached for his medical bag. He found the nitroglycerin pills, but
felt only slight relief. Eshka was bending over him. "Call Shellin,"
he said, thinking first of his bachelor doctor friend. But already
sinking—the nitroglycerin would not help—he remembered that
Shellin himself had died of a coronary some months before. "Call . . ."
It was too late. He was suffocating, the flow of blood obstructed,
the oxygen only seeping through.

Still he came out of it.

In the small narrow kitchen, in the wall cabinet, over the shelf of
everyday dishes, over the next shelf stacked with newspaper-

covered dress dishes, on a shelf you needed a ladder to get to, were, also covered by newspaper, the Passover dishes. They were porcelain white and large, each plate banded by a single gold line. There were, in the high shelves over the icebox, silver serving platters that, each year before Passover, Eshka would—like the good silver kept wrapped in felt and stored in a small oak case—polish brilliant.

The glasses used for Passover were the same long-stemmed crystal Eshka used the exceptional times she made a formal dinner. There were tall water glasses, broad-cupped wine glasses, and very small and narrow liqueur glasses, the cup as deep as the stem was long. These glasses too had a single gold band almost at the lip, but the band was broad and the gold had not taken perfectly, seemed attached in flakes to the too-fine, irregular, and fragile crystal.

In the oak trunk in the doctor and Eshka's small bedroom (that, like the chest in the dining room for the fine glasses, like the small cabinet where wine and whisky were kept, Eshka kept locked) were, among heavy good bedsheets—mothballs, sachets of pine, lavender—some heavy tablecloths even eighteen feet long. When, hands washed, Eshka and the boys shook open such a cloth in the dining room, they let fall cloth as white as snow from wall to wall, from side to side. The table had been lengthened, there would barely be space in the room to serve.

There were seventeen place settings, each with, one on the other, grapefruit, soup, and meat plates, a salad plate to a side; the three stemmed glasses; six pieces of silver, for there would be fish and meat. There were heavy soft white linen napkins.

There were eight upholstered tall and upright chairs to the dining-room table set (two with arms); bedroom chairs were brought out, folding chairs from the hall closet.

In the center of the table was a decanter, of the same crystal as the glasses, filled with thick sweet red wine and the Passover observance plates, one with matzoh, one with bitter herbs.

"Wherefore," Max, the youngest at table, recited in Hebrew, singsonging as he had been taught, "is this night different from all other nights? On all other nights we may eat either leavened or unleavened bread, but on this night we eat only unleavened bread. On all other nights we may eat any herbs, but on this night only bitter herbs. . . ."

As if the posing of the questions was a starting signal, the answer came loudly from them all, a general recital that was as much mumbling as words—for some read Hebrew with difficulty and when in doubt mumbled through, and some read the English translation.

There were sixteen at table, and the seventeenth place setting, at Mother Cohen's right, she at the end of the table closest to the door, was for Elijah, the angel whose name is God is God and for whom the apartment door was left ajar during all the meal and for whom wine would be served.

Lily, Joe's wife, had phoned that their son Marty had been able to get a pass and was up from Philadelphia with his wife. Would it be all right if they came too?

"A pleasure," Eshka said with pleasure.

"Aunt Eshka," the new nephew, Louis, calling long distance, said, "I've got twenty-four hours."

"Come," Eshka said.

"I'm not alone."

"You have a buddy?"

"Aunt Eshka, I have my fiancée!"

Eshka said to Saul, "I want, this seder, to make meat blintzes too. I've just the time. And I want there should be carrot *tzimmis*. They are soldiers! And what kind of idea will she have of this family if there is no *tzimmis* on the table?" She knew he would allow anything for the soldiers.

Emma came early, alone.

She wore a black dress, a pearl necklace, pearl earrings for pierced ears. (It was Eshka who had pierced her ears years before, who was always ready to make a niece or neighbor a "gypsy" like her.) Eshka was in the middle of doing twenty things, but looking at Emma she sensed something that made her say, "Here, put on an apron!"

The kitchen was small, hot, steaming. Eshka gave Emma carrots to slice, and then there were onions, and there were bitter tears in Emma's eyes, and Eshka was now half in the oven and peering under a pot lid, the steam rising about her head, through her hair, was tasting, was giving Emma to taste.

"Go," Eshka said, "take off your dress, take off your corset. I'll give you a housedress."

Emma did, and for several hours she worked at Eshka's side in the steam and heat preparing food.

All the men wore hats. Some wore their street hats, most wore skullcaps. There were black paper skullcaps for those who had not brought their own. Louis wore his paper skullcap like a tent planted on the flat of his head.

"Why do you wear wings?" Mother Cohen had asked him, no one in the family having yet dared tell her that having been returned wounded from the Pacific a year before he had since forced his way into flight school.

"I'm learning to fly, *Bubba*."

"To fly?" She studied him carefully, this short squat grandson, and then began to nod her head approvingly.

His fiancée Rachel had come to America a girl from Poland. He had met her at a dance for Jewish soldiers. She was taller than him, but did not seem so—perhaps because she always stood timidly a bit behind him, or because he seemed bigger than he was.

The boys were interested in Louis's campaign ribbons. And before the dinner, when Louis had arrived and had been with Lazarus, Max, and Eli—Eli having recently finished basic training—Max had asked him what the ribbons were for.

"That," he said pointing, "is for the fucking Pacific. That is for killing fucking Japs. And that is for the fucking wound in my fucking calf."

At table he maintained a dignified, if not stiff manner.

Elijah's place was to Mother Cohen's right, and Mother Cohen herself had placed Joe's son Marty to her left. Big-nosed, thick-lipped, he was six foot two, a slope-shouldered, poetry-reading Harvard-educated nearsighted athlete. He had been an all-state high school football player, a champion boxer. He spoke no Yiddish; Mother Cohen spoke no English.

He was attending dental school under an army program.

" 'Slaves were we unto Pharaoh in the land of Egypt, and the eternal, our God, brought us forth from thence with a mighty hand and an outstretched arm.

" 'In ancient times our ancestors were idolators. But the Lord took our father Abraham from the other side of the flood. He gave him Isaac, and unto Isaac He gave Jacob, and Jacob and his children went down into Egypt. And He said unto Abraham: Know that their seed shall be a stranger in a land that is not theirs, and shall serve them, and shall be afflicted by them four hundred years. But that nation whom they shall serve will I then judge, and afterwards shall you come forth with great substance.' "

Mother Cohen prayed, and her son Jack, whose name was Jacob, prayed, and her son Joe, who was Joseph, prayed more or less.

Leah prayed, and Jack's wife Edith read, and Joe's wife Lily read, and Emma read more or less. Marty's wife Julie examined the text from a sociological point of view. Louis's fiancée read without any understanding, all her consciousness blushing that she would not be approved of.

Louis read and skipped, but when he came to the enumeration of the ten plagues God had brought upon the Egyptians, he read every word—pouring, as was the custom, a drop of wine into a saucer for every plague—reading "blood, frogs, vermin, snakes, pestilential disease," reading "boils" and thinking that that was for them all, every German, but especially that German brothers should see boils on the faces, hands, and bodies of their sisters, husbands their wives, fathers their daughters, sons their mothers, reading "hail, darkness," reading "locusts"—that they starve—and "the slaying of the first-born."

The hats, skullcaps, and books were put aside—there would be prayers after the meal. Eshka, Leah, and Jack's wife Edith served the cherry-centered half-grapefruit, the icing of sugar, and everyone set to with appetite, though Jack, smiling, raised his sewn-together fingers to remind the young ones of what was written in the book. "Slowly," he said.

Between Joe and Saul there had been, more than once, angry words. Joe had, when Germany attacked Russia, predicted the im-mediate defeat of the Communist armies and had said, "Anyhow, let's hope they kill each other off." But then the Cohens had heard for the first time in ten years from brothers in Russia, photographs of soldier nephews and cousins in belted blouses, and Joe had reluctantly accepted Stalin as an ally, though his real faith was in Mac-Arthur.

He had developed an arthritic condition that made turning his head painful. He had never had much of a neck, and now, as if to protect what he had, he dropped it into his body, and the whole of him had to pivot to look in any direction but his own. He was being treated for his condition by a Park Avenue physician who gave him injections that relieved him for a day at a time, and that gave him hope. Saul told him that his doctor was a charlatan and that, though he could not be sure what he was getting for his money, he was probably getting dope. Joe said, "Anyhow, all doctors are charlatans!" and continued going to his.

He had the happy ability of being able to forget the disagreeable when he could not avoid it entirely. But he kept coming back to the East Bronx, surely to see his mother and surely to see his favorite, Eshka, but also to deal with the doctor.

He was a rich man. His brother-in-law had never had much money and now was sick and would he get better? He thought he felt pity for him. He too was in his fifties, but except for his neck he was in the best of health, trim, active. He had invested in stocks and real estate. He was worth several hundred thousand dollars. He would be, no doubt, this American generation's family millionaire. His manner with Emma was warm and respectful that she should not take offense at his success.

Before dinner, he had asked Saul, "Do you need anything?"

"My health!" Saul had answered.

"What do your parents do, dear?" Joe asked Louis's fiancée.

Her family was in the furniture business.

"Wholesale or retail?" Joe asked.

She said blushing, "Retail."

Louis nodded.

"And your education?" the doctor asked.

"I've only done a year of college." Tears were almost at her eyes. Louis suffered for her stoically.

Eshka said, "I am a *graduate*—of P. S. Forty-eight!"

She served steaming chicken soup with *knaidloch* from a tureen on the table. The boys stood to see better how many dumplings each one got, how many were left. The soldiers were served especially plentifully.

"Such *knaidloch*!"

They were light, but just substantial enough. They melted in your mouth with the thick clear soup.

For Lazarus and Max, Passover was a new suit, was the night they were not only permitted but encouraged to drink the wine of blessings, and was the question, "Wherefore is this night different?" —the question opening up the book.

For Eli, only eighteen years old but a Phi Beta Kappa graduate of City College, a tall, solidly built, studiously hunched, nearsighted, deaf-in-one-ear soldier, Passover was only a splendid dinner. For my father, Eli thought, I'd have been a Jew or even a Hottentot. For my grandmother, I'll wear the skullcap. There is no God. I am an American.

Marty said, "There are things in the service—that God and the Israelites did—that are wrong. The ten plagues. Especially the killing of the Egyptian firstborn. And the way God gave the Israelites the substance of the Egyptians."

Eli said, "The magic too, the parting of the waters is childish."

Lazarus and Max were on the side of the young ones, excited by the argument. But the rebels needed no encouragement. Marty, in any event, was truly troubled. Some months before, when he could still have refused the place in dental school his father's influence had bought him, he had come to the doctor and had said, "I don't want to kill. But I don't want to make an issue of it."

The doctor had been embarrassed for this nephew whom he liked very much. All he had been able to say was, "A dentist, it is not the same thing as being a doctor, but it is not a bad thing."

Eli was speaking.

"What does he say?" Mother Cohen asked his mother, Leah. Leah translated as best she could.

"When I read in Exodus that just before their flight from Egypt, knowing they wouldn't return, the Israelites *borrowed* the Egyptians' silver and valuables, I can only think it was a dirty trick."

"What do you know about it?" Louis demanded.

"I know," Eli said, looking him in the eye, "that it was a dirty trick."

"That's enough!" Jack said to the two nephews.

But Mother Cohen was nodding her head approvingly, yes, let them go on, yes.

Marty said, "In the desert, when they had gone back to worshiping idols, Moses ordered the Israelites to kill their own sons, brothers, and fathers, and one in three Israelites was killed."

Julie said, "They were a tribe, and their laws were primitive. For modern people to honor the Israelites in all they did, to follow their laws or use them as models, is only ignorance."

Joe said, "So it's better to be a Gentile?" But he looked at Eli to take the onus off his son and daughter-in-law. "You college-educated people are always criticizing!"

"He's a good boy!" Leah said of her son. And though Eli shrugged impatiently at his mother's defense, no one would then continue to attack Eli, knowing he would be attacking Leah.

The long mirror over the long buffet held all the room, all the diners, and the table, and against side walls the stand-up radio, the tall chest, the windowed bookcase. The shawl-covered rounded back of Mother Cohen, her sparse hair parted in the center, the upright profiles of Joe and Jack, the doctor reclining almost in his tall armchair at the far end of the table. And the food that Eshka and Leah brought in past Elijah's place.

The mirror was gilt-framed and divided in three, the end sections narrower than the middle. Standing on the marble-topped buffet beneath it was the samovar.

After Louis had arrived in America, the Cohen brothers had met with him in Ben's private office. "You'll be a machine operator for Joe," Ben said, communicating their decision, "and then, if you show yourself a good worker, you'll be a cutter, and then a foreman. And finally, if things work out, if you are *enterprising*, we'll give you a percentage too—a small percentage, but a percentage."

Joe, thus, was Louis's boss, and when Louis addressed Marty, his boss's son, he did so gently. "You're an American, and you can't understand."

Joe said of the gefilte fish—served with red and white horse-radish, a carrot slice on each piece—"In no restaurant does one eat gefilte fish like this. Its stock is gritty, is fish, but it has something too of a cake. Such a gefilte fish!"

"Take more," Eshka said.

"Where am I to put it?"

"In wax paper. You can take it home with you."

"At the Westchester border," the doctor said, "they'll confiscate it."

"Darling," Eshka said to Louis's fiancée, "you must have another piece."

"Eat!" Louis, beaming, said to his fiancée.

Emma did not approve of Eli; a poor boy should be more prudent and respectful. This boy had still to get into medical school, would later need a well-off wife. He was, arguing with the Cohens, biting the hand that fed him. And looking at him, his obvious Katz intelligence and stubbornness, what had earlier troubled her—that she did not know with whom her daughter went out, did not know what she did on her dates—now almost reassured her; her daughter did not go out with poor boys. She forgot that she had come early, she forgot the deep pleasure she had had working with Eshka, and thought of herself again as a sort of patroness of these families.

She raised the threat of what no respectable Jew did. "Next thing you know, these boys will be converting."

"To what?" Eli replied immediately.

Emma looked about as if to say, See?

Marty said, "How could the Israelites expect to live in an alien land as if they were in their own? Anyhow, they killed too much, they killed too dutifully. Their survival is based on merciless war and murder."

"What does he say?" Mother Cohen asked.

The doctor knew that the answer he should have made his nephew before was the answer his nephew had surely now come to himself, and he said, nodding as if approving him, "You must always, all your life, make an issue of what you believe."

Marty, whose shoulders and body were that of a boxer but whose face was that of someone who hurts only himself, looked down at the table. Mother Cohen looked at him, her moist eyes forcing his gaze, he then raising his glasses and something very sad in his open clown's smile.

What shall we say of the brisket? That it was tender, brown, juicy, that no grain of it was too well-cooked when none of it could be red, that it indeed melted in your mouth. And if we say that of the brisket, what shall we say of the roast chicken? For it too melted in your mouth. And what shall we say of the meat blintzes, those baked pancakes enfolding chopped meat, fried for color—they melted, yes, in your mouth.

And the potatoes stewed with the juice of the meat.

And the carrot *tzimmis* sweet like a dessert.

Already only some months after his attack, the doctor's appearance had changed. He slouched in his tall armchair; sometimes, small as he was, he found himself standing less than erect. He was, for his condition, obliged to nap every day, to rest, to sleep ten hours at night. He took drugs. He conscientiously followed Dr. Konstam's instructions. Perhaps Konstam was right, perhaps in another few months he would be able to resume professional activities. Still his phone rang in the middle of the night, only now Eshka answered. "The doctor isn't well, you might call Dr. Konstam at this number." And he, drowsy with drugs, would see Konstam climbing *his* staircase, carrying *his* load.

From where he sat at the long and extended dining-room table, he could see himself at the table, could see almost all the room. These things Eshka had purchased or that her brothers had given her that he had never more than nodded at. The marble on the long buffet, the lace cloth on it—she, he thinking, observing without humor or criticism, having a need to lay lace over every bare surface—in one of the long buffet drawers she kept the everyday silver and, in the heavy drawer below, the everyday linens. The cabinet door on the left, which opened on the liquors, and in the cabinet on the right, among tens of knitting and crocheting needles, balls of yarn, the many drugs they had used to ease her headaches.

The bookcase—he could not see the books—the collected works of Mark Twain and Rudyard Kipling, leather-bound Russian volumes a patient had given him of Tolstoi and Chekhov, the thick broken-bound Hebrew-English Bible. The tall chest behind him where she kept the fine glasses. All the filled closets of this apartment, all the things crowded into this small apartment, and the mirror there, and her brothers and her mother—seeing her small shawl-covered rounded back in the mirror and seeing her small round leathery dark face, the heavy-lidded big moist eyes, she eating little, when called on, praising God for the fruit of the vine by touching the wine to her lips.

He said, "We too come out of the darkness. We too come from the other side of the flood." He spoke in English from his slouch in his tall straight armchair, the thin little man, his hand shading his eyes. "The Bible tells that in darkness we sacrificed even our first-born. But it tells too that God asked for other even of our father Abraham. I wonder if that does not mean that, as we moved out of the darkness, so did He. Today we read the story of Moses leading Israel from Egypt and you are struck by the cunning and blood-thirstiness of the Israelites. But they were still far from this side of the flood. And 'an eye for an eye' is the beginning of all justice.

"My dear boys," he said, looking from soldier to soldier, to his boys, to Lazarus and Max, "we are never far from the other side of the flood. Darkness is out there. Darkness must be battled with and must be destroyed! Yet darkness is in us."

Suddenly, Mother Cohen, looking to her right, through the short hallway to the apartment door left ajar, said, "Who is there?" Marty too looked to the door. The doctor leaned forward.

Marty put down his linen napkin and went toward the door, Louis already up and behind him. "Who's there?" Marty said, standing in the short hallway between the doorless kitchen entrance and the coat closet, the hallway mirror above the sewing machine console.

"Go!" Leah said to her son, who then shrugged and stood, the three soldiers, two of them tall, squat Louis, and Jack too had stood, waiting, the silence perfect, the sense in that crowded room that someone was indeed just outside the door, the boys holding their breath, expecting even a presence to enter and, invisible, drink the waiting glass of wine.

Marty opened the apartment door wide. "There's no one here, *Bubba*," he said.

He checked the door to the doctor's office and Mother Cohen's rooms. It was locked. He walked down the three steps to the street door, which also had been left ajar. He stepped into the street.

The street, he reported a moment later, was empty.

After the dinner, after the last of the prayers, the doctor stood, his small narrow gold-banded stemmed liqueur glass in hand.

"Let us pray for the allied forces, that they bring light to Europe.

"For David, who is in England.

"Jonathan, who is in England.

"Ruth, who is in Poland.

"Sonia in Russia.

"Dan in France.

"For Esther in Palestine.

"Your brothers in Russia."

And Jack was then naming the Cohen brothers, and Eshka and Leah.

"Their sons and daughters."

And they were naming them.

"All the cousins."

Even Emma had joined in, murmuring names, they all murmuring names.

"And you, my soldiers. Marty.

"Eli, son of my brother Harry.

"And you, Louis.

"Long life to you, Louis. May you flourish!

"And your wife-to-be.

"I drink to you, young lady, and to your children."

CHAPTER *Six*

1

THE DOCTOR'S TALL STRAIGHT ARMCHAIR was normally at a slight distance from the glass-covered dining-room table, between the locked tall chest where were the fine glasses and the venetian-blinded window. There he sat in the morning light, the venetian blinds angled to the sun, slouched, reading his *New York Times* virtually entirely, but not from first page to last. He read first the first-page articles that seemed most important, and then he turned to the obituary section, for his generation of New York City doctors had begun to die off. Shellin and Paperny were dead, Reisman had had a massive coronary. He read the *Jewish Daily Forward*. He went from his armchair to rest or read on his bed. Sometimes he went to sit at his desk in his office.

On cold sunny mornings of that spring he dressed warmly in hat, scarf, overcoat, and walked slowly the five blocks down Hunts Point Avenue to a little park—more asphalt than green—by the subway station where he could sit on a bench to catch his breath. He might stop a moment at Edelman's drugstore or speak a moment with Karp outside his vegetable store. In the park, patients of his might approach him. "How you doing, doctor?" He might have a conversation with a retired worker about the worker's health and children, his union, about the war. He watched the car and truck traffic, people entering the subway that roared just beneath the park, and if he did not feel pain he might begin to believe he was getting better.

Sometimes, sitting on the bench, the sun in his eyes, everything seemed slow, less urgent. There was money in the bank. He was receiving disability insurance checks of $400 a month. Only, the insurance company insisted on having him examined by their own physician as if Konstam and Paley, a heart-specialist pinochle-playing friend, were not to be trusted. And one day Mrs. Silver, the grocer, came and told him that someone was nosing around checking that he was not continuing his medical practice in any way.

He paid $80 a month rent for his apartment and $80 for his office and Mother Cohen's rooms (of which the Cohen brothers paid $35). He had been buying a $100 war bond every month for his sons' education. After six months of total disability, he would receive only $250 a month.

He had asked Leo his garage man to keep his Chevy for him. After several months, Leo came to the apartment and said he had a buyer for the Chevy. The doctor said angrily, "I never said anything about selling it! That's all right," he added before the other had a chance to apologize or explain. But he was not then up to making conversation.

Occasionally his sister Esther wrote from Palestine. He had not heard from his sister Sonia since before the Russo-German Pact of 1939. His brother Dan had written now and then until November 1942, when the Germans occupied Vichy France.

He had pain every day about his heart. He was often short of breath.

He played solitaire.

There were pinochle nights with Drs. Paley, Lesnick, and Alpern. Paley smoked a cigar, and Eshka would go visiting and come back late and air the apartment. They were all specialists, but sometimes during the game one of them might receive a call.

Dr. Reisman's first visit after his partial recovery from his heart attack was to the doctor. He was a fat man who when he could not sound like a sage smiled like an imp, his eyes really twinkling. They played two-handed pinochle. They spoke of the war, of new drugs, new medical techniques. "Perhaps two cripples can make one doctor," Reisman said. He too was receiving total disability.

The doctor had heard from the Zionist Lipshutz's brother, an army doctor in England, that penicillin cured respiratory and venereal infections. "It is a miracle," the doctor said.

Irving said, "You could receive patients."
He said, "That is not a doctor. There is no half-doctor. A doctor who cannot answer a call is not a doctor."
Irving said dryly, "No, he is a specialist."

He put on the radio news one morning and immediately heard a sound like that of the *shofar*, the ram's horn blown in the synagogue in short and long blasts, momentous and joyous, to usher in the new year, and his heart swelled and his pulse was beating fast. It was June 6, 1944, and the Americans and English were landing in Normandy, the radio reports direct, the sounds of landing craft horns, airplanes, machine guns, ack-ack. He stayed by the radio all day. He prayed for General Eisenhower, he prayed for all the American boys, all those Irishers, Italianers, all those tall Texans. He prayed for his nephews David and Jonathan. He prayed deeply for his brother Dan, wherever you are. Do you hear the ram's horn?
He stood by the table, the broken-bound Bible open, and read the Psalms of David.
They are landing now on the beaches of France,
They are parachuting behind the German lines,
Thousands of parachutes.
Our armies are landing on all the beaches of Normandy.
And the sky is dark with ten thousand airplanes.

He sold his car for $700.
His monthly checks were down now to $250. He insisted Eshka record every housekeeping expense so that he could determine where they could economize.
He sat at his office desk in front of his model of a heart. He studied it, the little veins of it, his hand touched it. Would he never recover?
Behind him were the patients' files he had laboriously prepared. Each time a patient came to him, he could see on an index card, entered in his minuscule script-print, what his weight and blood pressure had been, his complaints and illnesses, what drugs had

been administered. He had a fluoroscope machine that had cost $2,000, an electrocardiograph machine. He had cabinets full of drugs, cabinets full of surgical instruments. He had done every kind of medicine!

All this equipment, these fine hairy hands, which were not being used.

Forty dollars a month rent for this office.

To wake every morning with little biting pains at your chest, to wake short of breath. Never mind. Do your exercises. Prepare your day. Wash and shave and dress and make your walk. But making your slow walk, to feel that people are looking at you, and can't I stand straighter, and can't I walk faster?

I am spied on.

Though neighbors still come for free medical advice.

I am short of breath and short of money.

How shall I make ends meet?

One evening a man rang the office bell, and Eshka could not convince him to go elsewhere. He insisted on seeing the doctor and pushed his way into the apartment, the doctor having risen pale from his armchair.

"Doctor, I'm sick." He was fifty years old, flushed, his collar open. The doctor did not remember ever having seen him.

His children were at their bedroom door—Lazarus who wanted to be a doctor, but where would the money come from?

"If you aren't well enough to go across Hunts Point to Doctor Bernstein, I'll call him for you."

"What kind of doctor are you?"

"Call Doctor Bernstein," he said to Eshka. But the man got up then and left.

I want to die, the doctor thought.

2

Eshka wore a foundation of corset and gartered girdle. She wore stockings and a slip beneath her dress. She went regularly to the hairdresser, she wore lipstick and sometimes used perfume and rouge. She wore pendant earrings and on each hand some rings, she wore a bracelet watch and a bracelet of thin silver bands, she wore a necklace and a brooch. She had thick lips and a thick nose, her legs were slender. She was short, heavy, and wore medium high heels. In the winter she wore a dark brown caracul coat and a pillbox hat just barely cocked. She had a collection of costume jewelry that filled ten wooden candy boxes. Everyone brought her pieces. She would take a niece into her bedroom and place her before a box and say, "Take one," and when she had, she would give her earrings to go with it.

On warm spring days she would sit with her sister Leah and sometimes with Mother Cohen on folding chairs at the corner outside the apartment. Neighbors would join them. There would be six or seven women talking, knitting. A Bungalow Bar ice cream tricycle would come slowly ringing by, and the children would materialize: "I scream, you scream, we all scream for ice cream," the doctor had gently mocked.

She called her son Lazarus "the scientist" because he was attending the Bronx High School of Science. Max she called "Dostoevsky" because he wanted even then to be a famous writer, and because she had seen him, twelve years old, lying on his belly on his bed reading *Crime and Punishment*, tears in his eyes. Of course, there was other reading going on in that bedroom. She found copies of *Beauty Parade* and other picture magazines under piles of shorts, though she never mentioned that to her boys or husband.

The boys did not understand that her brothers were giving them twice as much money as before, not for movies and extras, but to help them all out. She said, "You'll have to buy your own clothes." But they had already spent everything on phonograph records of *La Traviata*, *Aïda*, *La Bohème*, or on their stamp collection.

Max and some friends were caught stealing pencils and erasers in the five-and-ten-cent store. She thought it funny; her husband would not speak to Max for a week. Once Max stole a dollar from her purse. She chased him around the dining-room table and, when she caught him, laid him like a baby across her knees and gave him a spanking.

In September 1944, Mother Cohen went into coma. There was then in her rooms and in Eshka's apartment a steady stream of visitors. In the day, in Eshka's apartment, there were always people seated at the dining-room table taking tea, the phone rang often. The Cohen brothers stayed overnight, sleeping in Leah's apartment and on a cot set up in the boys' room.

Leah and Eshka nursed their mother. In the evening, as the light in the sickroom faded, Leah lit candles.

The sisters took turns sitting up at their mother's side through the night, though Leah would not sleep farther away than on the sofa in the doctor's waiting room. Sometimes during the night one of the brothers might enter the sickroom, and then he and the sister would sit quietly, or the sister would ask if he wanted tea, or they might whisper a few words.

Jack appeared in the doorway tall and so straight he seemed stern. Ben would sit leaning forward as if waiting for his mother to sit up and say something. Small Sol, his too-long mouth turned down at the ends for tragedy; Sam, his hands trembling.

The flickering candlelight.

Her hair, no matter how her daughters combed it, was dead. She had no control of her body, her breast rose and fell faintly; still, the features of her face were composed and peaceful.

One night Eshka could not sleep and entered her mother's bedroom, and Leah was sitting up straight, her eyeglasses off, crying. For an instant Eshka thought her mother had passed on, but no, she was breathing still. She put her hand on her sister's shoulder. "What is it?"

Leah only cried more. Then, in the flickering light, their mother motionless except for the faint rising and falling of her breast, a high school graduation photograph of Marty on her bedtable, Leah, between sobs, told her sister, "Two years I lived in the same attic room with her. I'd wake in the middle of the night so cold I couldn't move, and when finally I could see in the dark, I'd see her sitting almost naked on the edge of the bed, staring. 'Mama! Mama! Cover yourself!'" Eshka's arm was tightly about her sister's shoulders, her cheek to her cheek. "Two years of dressing her and feeding her and cleaning her, for she did nothing.

"I've never told anyone, not even my Harry: Eshka, Eshka, she tried to kill herself with a knife. She tried to throw herself from the window!"

Eshka felt a bottomless emptiness in her. I have heard this before, I have known this, or something like this, before, or not yet.

"Two years. She came back like from only having been away. She told me then, 'We shall see such miracles.' She told me over and over in the cold night, and the sound of the wind, 'There shall be such miracles!' "

Eshka sensed a presence behind and turned and saw her brother Jack standing tall and pale in the doorway, his sewn-together fingers at his lips.

"Mama! Mama! Tell me!" Leah cried, reaching to her mother— the faint rising and falling of her breast, the features of her face composed and peaceful. "What miracles?"

Mother Cohen died toward evening, without a struggle, ceased to breathe on one long hoarse breath, two of her sons there, and Leah and Eshka and the doctor called for from next door, and the caught breath in all the apartment, and the brothers making way for the doctor and Eshka, and the doctor leaning over Mother Cohen, his ear to her heart, his brow at her chin, and then straightening up and his hand at her pulse, but he already shaking his head, and then letting go her hand, stepping back, and Eshka stepping forward, touching her hand gently to her mother's cheek, Leah crying now and tears in the brothers' eyes, and little Sol sobbing, and the doorway already crowded, and a wailing rising to Eshka's throat, a rising wailing that caught them all so that those who had rote prayers were rocking then in prayer, and even the American-born daughters were crying like their mothers, "Oi! Oi! Oi!"

Her sons and daughters, her grandsons—many in uniform—and her granddaughters, her cousins, nephews, nieces, and her East Bronx neighbors, and her landsmen from Berezin, Bobroisk, and Nishkovitz, and close friends of her sons and daughters, and representatives of the charities she had kept coin boxes for, and members of the synagogue she had gone to, all marched behind the hundred-bouquet-bedecked hearse carrying her silver-handled dark polished coffin. They were 300. They marched from her apartment down the middle of cobblestoned Hunts Point Avenue, trolley and car traffic coming after, to Bruckner Boulevard, where five limousines and seventy cars were waiting. The men and women wore hats. The women wore heels and had difficulty walking; they were dressed in black and wore no lipstick.

In their midst was old Starobinetz, Mother Cohen's first cousin, tall, mustached, with a walking stick, and about him his sons and daughters and their sons and daughters. There were the Brooklyn cousins, the Friedlands, about their proud chief Herman, who owned a bar and grill. There were the New Jersey cousins, the Feldbaums, their secretary of state, Frank, who had, in fact, been elected a state senator, walking now with the Friedlands, now the Starobinetzes, now the Katzes. There were Mr. and Mrs. Horowitz and Mr. and Mrs. Epstein, and there was little Mr. Matter. Karp had closed his vegetable store, and Mr. and Mrs. Silver had closed their grocery store to attend the funeral. Drs. Reisman, Konstam, and Alpern came with their wives. Irving and Mary, of course, were there, as were Emma and Bill. Lipshutz, the wall-eyed Zionist, was there, big-headed, big-chested, marching as if at the head of troops. From the fur market came workers in the Cohen businesses and well-dressed business friends of the Cohens, who had perhaps been taken once to the East Bronx to meet Mother Cohen. There were in the parade long-bearded, earlocked old men who seemed to have come straight out of the old country. They wore threadbare long black silk coats and tall black hats. The leather of their black shoes was worn and paper fine. They walked praying in a faint rocking stoop.

There were five limousines and seventy cars in a lights-on procession down Bruckner Boulevard to the Triborough Bridge.

And Eshka, at her husband's side in a limousine, Leah there too, and on the strap seats her boys and Leah's daughter and son-in-law, he in uniform, thought already, an hour before each of her brothers would throw a handful of earth on the coffin lowered into the grave, before the cantor in his tall regal miter and black-bordered white shawl sang the *El Mole Rachamim*—God Full of Mercy—that grief was turning mellow, was ripening. She saw the *shiva:* the apartment crowded and the movement from apartment to doctor's office to her mother's rooms, where the brothers would twice a day for ten days say the Kaddish, the mourners overflowing even into the waiting room, the mirrors covered by sheets or towels, the chairs leaned away, and only wooden vegetable crates for sitting, and people lying across the beds talking, and the fruit on the big dining-room table, the cakes, the tea. And the stories would begin. The brothers would speak, and the orator Lipshutz would fill the room with his stories, and then every one of them would have a story to tell of Mother Cohen, and now no one would weep aloud, but there would be tears and smiles in everyone's eyes. They would sit, talk, and nod, and mourn what was passing out of their lives. The brothers would speak of their lives in Russia, and memories would intersect, and there would be overlapping stories and parallel stories.

"What can you know?" Ben would demand of all the young ones.

"What can you know of what we have seen?

"What can you know of the cold?

"What can you know of chicken?

"What can you know of the taste of chicken? In Russia we ate chicken that was chicken as chicken should be chicken!"

3

One Sunday, after his brothers-in-law and their families had left, the doctor saw his son Max with a ten-dollar bill. "Where did you get that?"

"Uncle Ben gave it to me." The boy was afraid for his father's anger that he would take the money from him. He said, "It's mine! It's mine!"

The doctor slapped him.

So you are out of the running. You are no longer a doctor. You are becoming only a bitter little man without even the breath to scream.

Lipshutz's brother was flown home from the Ardennes, a pale shadow of a man. They sat at an end of the dining-room table and talked of this and that, but never of the war, nor even of medicine, the doctor seeing in the way Lipshutz studied his hands even what he had seen and done.

Ben said, "Take it as a loan. You'll keep every penny marked down."

"Thank you, I cannot do that. How could I even hope to pay you back?" And what was so right and reasonable a response left him, he realized when alone, no room at all.

A letter came from a cousin who had been in Poland in 1939 and had been marched by the Russians into Russia. He was now, with the Russian troops, back in Poland. His salutation was: "Listen." His first sentence was: "I am alive, my wife is alive." Then came a list of the dead. Cousins, cousins, cousins. Faces glimpsed, memories of Berezin. Thirty-five names. Name, deported to Auschwitz. Name, deported to Auschwitz. Name, dead in the ghetto.

Karp came one day and sat silent. He wore a suit, but was not shaven. He took from his pocket to show the doctor a war department telegram: his son had been killed in action in Belgium.

Early one evening there was a phone call from Mary: "Irving has had a heart attack."

It was the end of winter, but there was still snow in the streets and he had to wait for a taxi. He took his son Lazarus with him, and by the time they had crossed the bridge into Manhattan and arrived downtown, Irving was dead. In his tuxedo. He had been dressing for a medical society dinner at which he was to have given a speech. Mary was still in evening dress. The doctor sat weeping at his tuxedoed brother's side, the noble face of his brother, not even a last good-bye.

He held his brother's cold hand and recited in Hebrew:

"My brother, you were dear to me,
"Your love for me was more marvelous
"Than the love of women."

I am not a doctor. I cannot provide for my wife and sons. I cannot comfort the widowed wives of my brothers. I am of no use to anyone.

Still, it occurred to him one day to call the office of the dean of Columbia University Medical School. He would speak only to the dean.

No, the dean said, no one had mentioned to him that a letter might come mistakenly addressed to Irving Katz at Columbia. The doctor explained that he had a niece lost in Poland, and it was his good luck that the dean had indeed heard of Irving and was patient enough to hear him out.

In the middle of the morning there was a knock at the door, and the doctor put down his eyeglasses and newspaper and went and opened the door on a uniformed telegram boy. Through all his body there was then a rush and pulsing as if his body knew what his mind would not yet dare believe. He found a quarter tip for the boy and walked back with the message into the dining room. Eshka was there, her hand now on his arm. He said, "My eyeglasses, please." He slipped them on and then tore open neatly an end of the sealed telegram envelope. And even as he read the few words, he was sobbing. "My brother is alive!" he said and repeated. The words rang through the small apartment. "My youngest brother is alive! Dan is alive!"

They called everyone.

What a joy there was in the Bronx and Brooklyn, in the fur market on Thirtieth Street in Manhattan; Ben, in the middle of a sale, suddenly thinking of the doctor and tears coming to his eyes, explaining to his customer, "It's my brother-in-law, the doctor, his brother in France is alive."

They came from business that evening to the East Bronx. They looked at photographs of Dan and the one photograph they had of his wife. "She is beautiful," they said. And, "Look how intelligent are her eyes!" And, "There is something truly aristocratic about her lips." And her every feature was admired and loved. But of Dan there were photographs as a boy; with his sisters Nuissa, Judith, Sonia, and Esther; with his brothers; that brown-tinted photograph of the brothers lying in a field of tall grass, Harry, Irving, and Saul in army uniforms, Lazarus in civilian clothes and beret, and Dan in student uniform. Dan's so-wide and happy smile. There was a photograph of Dan too in a beret. There were stories of him, how good-natured he was, what an appetite he had. And yet he was barely taller than his brother Saul, even as thin.

The Cohens offered money. The doctor said they should call David in Germany, that he should go to Dan and Tanya and bring them food, clothes, and money.

"He's only an army translator," Joe said. "How will he do it?"

"He will do it."

The doctor was studying the photograph of his brothers and himself. He said, "We went to pose outside and the photographer suggested we go beyond the garden to a field of high grass, but there an idea struck him and he asked us to lie down in the field." He closed his eyes and said, "We lean on our elbows, though Lazarus is reaching back, his arm across my shoulder. I am wearing my visored cap like Dan's student one, Irving and Harry are bare-headed, and the sky is already darkening and you can see that we are happy."

Perhaps, the doctor thought, he could become an internist, have an office in the professional building on Southern Boulevard and several times a week, for several hours at a time, have consultations. He would have to study and pass examinations.

And one day in the normally heavy mail of drug advertisements, insurance papers, magazines, charity appeals, came a forwarded letter, its presence felt even before seen, the living thing burning in that pile, and he gathering it all up and dropping a letter and bending for it, and taking everything back to the dining room, and then holding only that letter, reading again the crossed-out better-than-real first address: Dr. Irving Katz, Professor of Dermatology, Columbia University, New York City.

CHAPTER *Seven*

"BERLIN, where I was a translator and where I lived two years, was rubble, piles of bricks, twisted metal, and charred wood. It was men missing limbs swinging through the rubble on crutches. With a package of Luckies you could buy a Leica. I could have become rich then in Berlin. But I'm not an acquisitive man.

"You think I am? You think this means something to me?" David asked, leaning forward in his deep black leather armchair, spreading his arms as if to encompass everything in the large luxurious apartment, the pearly nighttime view behind us of the East River bridges, the East River Drive far below, the lights of the city, the dark of the river. His hair was snow white, his face was full round red and cherubic.

It was March 1974 and I was staying in his apartment, and every day he would be up when I would get up—sometimes drinking still, his eyes red—and he would make me one of his specials, an omelet with Worcestershire sauce. "Is it not delicious? Is it not remarkable? As for its ingredients, does a magician give away his secrets?" And then, until nine-thirty, when the doorman would call that his driver was waiting, he would sit with me as I ate and drank coffee, and

would look at his *New York Times* and sometimes talk and sometimes get up from the table to go look in on his younger son Gregory, twenty-three years old, closer to three than two hundred
pounds, who slept during the day and listened during the night to
pop and rock.

My career was midway and failing. I was in New York to "see
people."

"So your father wrote me that I was to find her and marry her and
get her into America. I went from camp to camp. The underground
resistance heroes had already begun their trek home. Only the Jews
were left in the camps.

" 'They can't,' a British officer in charge of one camp explained to
me, 'sleep except behind barbed wire. They can't sleep except in
barracks with a hundred others. They're afraid of the outside.
Though they do move about from camp to camp.'

" 'Why do they do that?' I asked.

" 'Who can tell what's in their minds? Perhaps they hear rumors
of better food or conditions. They've no baggage, you see. They just
pick up and go.'

"They lay on their bunks, the lucky ones, the ninety-pound survivors, their big unblinking eyes. Women like men had almost no
hair. They had no shape, no age.

"I stood by the bulletin board. They went from camp to camp
only to look at the bulletin boards. Name-of-person is looking for
her husband name-of-person. Name-of-person of name-of-town is
looking for her daughters name-of-person and name-of-person.

"There were three hundred thousand lucky ones, three hundred
thousand pilgrims still wearing the camp uniform, or at least a part
of it, the striped shirt or the striped pants, the relief clothes on top,
shuffling from camp to camp. Unblinking they read the names, the
messages: 'I am alive. I am going back to Poland to look there.'

"It was a time of pilgrims, holy pilgrims! You'd approach the
bulletin board and you'd see the ageless unblinking survivors about
it, and they'd reach their palms out to you and implore you, Name-
of-person! Name-of-person!

"I found her in a dormitory in a camp hospital. She was seventeen
years old. She had tuberculosis, she had high fever, they were treat-

ing her with aspirin. It was, sonny, the most chaste moment of my life." He smiled. "And maybe of hers, too!

"I had an army ambulance come; I had a Doctor Goldberg of Brooklyn to shoot her full of penicillin. In my house in Berlin, she began to flesh out.

"She would have made a fine New York Jewish wife—I've never opened a door for a woman who expected more than the door would be opened for her. For whom it had never!

"She said she would go to Palestine.

"I said, 'You're going to marry me, and I'm going to get you into America.'

"She said, 'I had no papers, no letter, no photographs. Sometimes I'd wake in the middle of the night grasping to remember, to hold on to, the face of my mother. As if I could lose even the memory of her face. Do you know one of my dreams now? It's that you don't believe I am who I am.'

"She said, 'I went from camp to camp looking for someone who might know me. I looked for my Aunt Nuissa, for my grandmother, for cousins, for someone who might see me and cry out my name, Ruth! There was no one.

" 'I met a group of French ex-prisoners. "Where are you going?" I asked, hoping they were going in my direction.

" ' "We are going home," they replied.

" 'I met a group of Dutch ex-prisoners, and they were such decent-looking people and I wanted to continue on the road with them, and I asked, "Where are you going?"

" ' "We are going home," they replied.

" 'I met Poles, Hungarians, Greeks, and Austrians, and everyone was going home.'

" 'Palestine,' I said, 'is a desert. How is it your home? The English won't let you in.' She smiled the way she did when she stood in front of a door.

"They were shadows! Three hundred thousand shadows! They lay in barrack bunks in camps in which they had lost their wives and husbands, their children, all their children. They had lost mothers and fathers. They had lost their homes, their every possession, they had lost their very villages and nationalities. The Hungarians had sold out the Hungarian Jews, the Poles had sold out the Polish Jews, the Rumanians the Rumanian Jews, the Austrians even like the Germans, and the French too! They had nothing, nothing at all.

"And she said, 'I met a group of Frenchmen on the road, and they had a baby carriage full of provisions and they looked happy even though they wore camp clothes still, and shoes too big, and I said, because I liked their looks and they seemed to be going in my direction, "Where are you going?"

" 'And one of them answered, "We are going home."

" 'I met a group of Dutch men and women, and one of theirs was being pulled along in a cart because something was wrong with her leg, and I said, because I thought they were such decent-looking people and they seemed to be going in my direction, "Where are you going?" And they didn't speak an answer, but sang it, "We are going home! Come with us!" they said. "Do come!" ' "

"They lay in barrack bunks in camps, and no one in all the world wanting them, not even America, Canada, or Australia, except a token few, and Bevan in England saying in reply to the Zionist demand that England open the door to immigration to Palestine, 'What! Shall we drive all Jews from Europe?' and from some corner of their very nearly propertyless minds, their blanked-out, memory-less minds, came an idea that had been in the backs of all their minds, the minds of their fathers and forefathers, an idea taking on the force of *all* memories. Do you understand? The dead wife, children, father, and mother, of whom there was no trace, no grave but an unidentified camp site, no picture, no letter, no fixed smile to remember a person by, no handwriting, no message, no nothing, nothing but that they too had had this idea, so that everything was transformed into this one flame: We shall go home!

" 'You have no one there,' I told her, forgetting your Aunt Esther. 'In America you have an uncle, cousins, a family.'

"She answered, 'I am going home.'

"Three hundred thousand shadows without whom Israel would not have become Israel. And once again there were train movements of thousands at night, secret shipments of men and women packed again almost like cattle. And they boarded ships that could barely stay afloat and ran the English blockade of patrol planes and boats, and escorters and destroyers, and would not give an inch, even when caught, fought the British pitched battles aboard their floating wrecks, fought bare fists against billy clubs and, yes, British guns, and even then were not subdued, refused to obey orders and had to be carried off. And shipped back to Europe or Cyprus, they tried again, in the night. Until they got their way and landed in Palestine, your by-then eighteen-year-old cousin wearing French perfume—that's what she wanted as a going-away gift—when she arrived home.

"Arrived, those unlikely pioneers, just in time to take up rifles and fight off armies, and learned to live in the desert, to transform it, and they gave up their very languages, their German, Hungarian, Polish, their French—the language of Victor Hugo and Zola!—as easily as one gives up dirty linen, and they learned Hebrew. A dream they haven't finished paying for yet.

"So she left, and I was left with my drinking friends and my whores and caviar, which we got by barter from the Russians, and whole sheep from farmers and bribes and spies and trading penicillin—ha! ha! ha!—for the clap. And the free world and the other."

He would rise and at the bar freshen his drink. Sometimes, sunk deep into his armchair, he would close his eyes—only a dim, dark-shaded lamp on a table and a weak light at the bar on, and the night lights behind us of the city, the bridges—and I could not know if he was sleeping. Sometimes he would rise suddenly and in one limp be across the den and at the kitchen refrigerator, where he would stand, the door open, and take or just look: leftovers of smoked sturgeon and salmon, of tongue and salami, open cans, a plastic bag of week-old bagels, diet cola.

A light flashed on the phone that his son was using his line. "Sh," David said, reaching for the receiver. He listened in and his round cherub's face grew redder and redder.

"Parasite!" he spat into the receiver and hung up violently. And threw himself back deep into his chair, and drank, and the light was still on, and again he picked up the receiver and this time he cried, "What pills, what poison are you buying now! Hang up, Goddamn it! Hang up!" The light on the phone went off.

He looked deeply at me and said, "You're a spy in my house."

He said, smiling not pleasantly at me, "Do you know what she asked me? And think of your father in his hotel room in Istanbul. She said, 'Tell my son Irving.' Ha! ha! ha!"

He said, "You remind me of your father, you're a little man like him, a failure. When I look at you, Max, I even see your father." And then a thought seized him and he intoned philosophically, drunkenly, rabbinically, "And will you one day see me in my son?"

His eyes now were closed, his hand loosely holding his glass at the end of the thick-cushioned arm of his chair. In the morning when he would be driven to his office downtown, he would wear dark glasses. The light on the phone had gone on again, but this time he did not move.

He asked me, not even bothering to look my way, "Do you believe in God?"

"I long for God," I answered after a moment.

"Schmuck, yes or no?"

"I long."

He laughed.

"After Lazarus went off to college," I told him, "my father continued to read every day the *New York Times*, the *Jewish Daily Forward*, his medical journals. I remember seeing him more than once standing, rocking back and forth, his broken-bound Bible open at the psalms before him, he having read in the obituaries of the death of a doctor he had known.

"He wrote letters to his niece and sister in Israel, to his brother in France, he organized the sending of food and clothing packages. He never heard from his sister in Russia. He wrote once a week to Lazarus.

"Lazarus wrote that he was pledging a fraternity. My father answered him dealing with the advantages and disadvantages of belonging to a group. He said he must always make his own decisions. He wrote: 'If you are accepted, you must never close your mind to those of your comrades who will not have been accepted.'

" 'Dear Lazarus,' he wrote, 'your English professor's question is a good one, What is morality? The question can be even more precise, How is one to live one's life?

" 'Dear Lazarus, once again your English professor has asked the sixty-four-dollar question, Is there reason for optimism?

" 'We have seen the miracle of penicillin.

" 'We have seen the birth of the United Nations.' "

It was the middle of the night, and David was laughing softly.

We Grow Rich

PRINCIPAL CHARACTERS

THE COHENS:

The brothers:

Jack (Jacob) Cohen, married to *Edith*, childless, partner in Cohen Brothers Furs with his brother Ben and nephews Sam and Jonathan.

Ben Cohen, married to *Dora*, father of *Marvin* and *Elaine*.

Sol Cohen, partially deaf, the smallest of the Cohen brothers, married to *Fanny*.

Sam Cohen, married to *Mima*, lives in Rockaway. His hands are palsied.

Joe Cohen, stiff-necked, married to *Lily*, father of Marty. He is the most successful of the Cohen brothers.

Eshka Katz, Cohen sister, married to the doctor, mother of Larry and Max.

Leah Katz, widow of *Harry* Katz, mother of Anna and Eli.

The "boys" (the orphan sons of *Itcha* Cohen):

David, who limps; he has a skin business.

Sam, who is gentle, married to *Margo*.

Jonathan, who takes the family into the shipping business; he is married to *Sheila* and is childless.

Louis, squat man, married to tall gentle *Rachel*.

Sara, sister to the "boys," married to *Mike*.

Marty Cohen, son of Joe, married to *Julie*.

THE KATZES:

Saul Katz, the doctor.

Dan Katz, the youngest Katz brother, who lives in Paris with his wife *Tanya*.

Esther Katz-Nissnievitch, who lives in Israel.

Anna, daughter of Harry and Leah Katz, married to *Fred*, who was a brilliant law student but who went into his father's fur business.

Eli, Anna's brother, a biophysicist.

Larry (Lazarus), older son of the doctor and Eshka.

Max, son of the doctor and Eshka.

OTHERS:

Emma, a rich Nissnievitch cousin married to *Bill*; they have a daughter.

Herman Friedland, self-important chief of the Friedland clan, brother to Jack Cohen's wife Edith.

Dan Weber, who becomes an associate of Jonathan Cohen.

Artie Luria with whom Ben opens a new business.

Stanley, retarded son of *Rose*, the sister of Ben's wife Dora.

CHAPTER *Eight*

1

THE SURGEON SAID there was one chance in ten that Jacob Cohen would live. But he lived.

Jack's brother-in-law, the doctor, first diagnosed the case. It was in 1949, and Jack had driven with his wife Edith to the East Bronx for an ordinary Sunday visit to the apartment of his sister Eshka. There were there, as on most Sundays, his brothers Ben and Sol and their wives and children, his brother Sam and his wife, and his widowed sister Leah.

They sat at the big glass-covered dining-room table and drank tea and ate cake and fruit, and after a while, removing their jackets but not their vests, Jack, Sam, and the doctor began, at one end of the table, a game of three-handed pinochle.

Jack was six feet tall and broad and solid. He had, like most of the Cohens, little neck, and his head was perhaps a bit smaller than it might have been for such a body, but there was a nice regularity to his features and he was, for a man fifty-seven years old, not bad looking. He wore eyeglasses for reading and wore them now to play cards.

The trigger and middle fingers of his right hand were sewn together and were as one, but that had happened forty-five years before and was not a handicap. He was a partner in Cohen Brothers Furs and ran the factory there from his place at the cutters' table where he, who did nothing fast, cut furs with a razor instrument fast enough and with the greatest precision.

In the middle of a game, Jack paled and broke out into a cold sweat. "What is it?" the doctor asked.

"Nothing."

But the doctor then kept his eye more on Jack than on the cards, on the lines about his mouth, on his hands. And after the next game, the doctor stood and said, "Let me have a look."

They went to the doctor's bedroom.

Jack wore high shoes and had to unlace them down to the bottom eyes to remove them. He took off his vest, shirt, and pants, folded his pants neatly, and then lay with his long johns open on the doctor's bed. The doctor touched the inflamed place below his waist, traced it to its limits.

"Any bleeding?"

"Yes."

"It's serious," the doctor said and had himself become pale.

Jack nodded. He had thought it was serious, he had thought it was what he now knew it was. He even felt a little relief that what he was now to do was out of his hands.

The doctor had sat down at the head of his wife's bed. He was lost in thought, he seemed fragile. Jack began to dress. The doctor did not seem aware of Jack during all the time that Jack, sitting facing him not two feet from him, carefully laced up his shoes.

What is he thinking? Jack wondered. Bitterly, he thought, Why doesn't he just tell me how much time I've got left? And he became afraid, and he thought his fear was disgust that the doctor would lie to him, would offer him hope when he knew he had none.

The doctor looked up as if coming back from a great distance. He smiled gently at Jack and reached across to him to tap his two fingers, the trigger and middle, the way Jack did when he had a point to make, mockingly, warmly, on the back of Jack's hand.

Then the doctor was brisk again, stepping into the dining room only long enough to get a phone directory, saying nothing to the brothers and sisters at the table there, the wives, Jack's wife Edith. He called the home number of the great New York surgeon of that time.

He excused himself for calling on a Sunday. He said he was the brother of the late Dr. Irving Katz. He wanted his brother-in-law to be looked at by him urgently.

Yes, the surgeon was obliged to offer, the doctor not only a doctor but brother of a well-known doctor, he would fit the patient into his schedule for the following morning.

All the Cohen brothers except Jack, many of the nephews, their wives and children, gathered that same evening in Ben's apartment in the West Bronx, and Ben, worried as he was for his brother, was nevertheless pleased that he was his family's host. For two decades, the Cohens had gathered Sundays regularly in the East Bronx, but in that time Mother Cohen had been alive and had lived in rooms adjoining the doctor's office. And Leah had lived around the block with her husband, son, and daughter; now her husband, Harry, the doctor's oldest brother, was dead, her son had left home, her daughter was married and lived in Brooklyn, and she herself had moved to a small apartment where she could hardly entertain. Yes, even the space in the East Bronx had been reduced. Then there had been, like an anteroom, the doctor's waiting room, there had been Mother Cohen's rooms, Leah and Harry's apartment. Now the doctor's office and Mother Cohen's rooms had been taken over by another doctor. And the doctor himself, for all his intelligence, took less and less an active part in the family. It was only to be expected. He was ill, he had not practiced medicine in five years. He no longer had to take money from his brothers-in-law only because they had set his wife up in a liquor store. Besides, how could he be central in the family now? Then he had had a role, but now the major questions facing the family concerned business.

Of course Ben would never set up his apartment as a rival to his brother-in-law's. Who could take Eshka's place? In all the world there was no one like Eshka! Though, he had to admit, his wife's *kugel* and gefilte fish and, above all, her chopped liver were not so bad after all. A Friday night chicken dinner in his home was—who would deny it?—a not-so-bad second best! And yes, there were some even now who would have preferred to visit in his apartment than in the East Bronx. That apartment, the wonderful, unmatchable dining-room table, the doctor himself—that was the past. Whereas he, respecting the past, held the door open on the future.

Sol, the smallest of the brothers, wore, like them all, a double-breasted shoulder-padded suit. He moved in the crowd of family and, facing a nephew, would say, "Ach, who should think such a thing should happen to us!" Then he would wait as if the other might clarify things.

Sam, who worked at the cutters' long table at his Uncle Jack's side six days a week from eight-thirty in the morning to six in the evening, and sometimes from earlier and often to later, said, "I've seen him stopped, just standing there, his eyes tightly closed."

Squat Louis blamed his half-brother for having married a big loud aggressive woman, and he demanded, "Why didn't you say something?"

"Ach!" Sam, who was always mild, exclaimed. And he was too hurt to explain that he had, that Jack had said it was something he had eaten, but Louis understood anyhow and, regretting what he had said, touched Sam's arm.

"He can be wrong, too!" Joe declared. "I tell you, you send him to a surgeon and the surgeon will find something to operate on! We need other advice, a specialist's advice!"

Voices were raised.

"Who is a pessimist?"

"Which specialist?"

Ben had for each of the orphaned children of his oldest brother a paternal feeling, but for Jonathan he had something more. And when, not long before, Jonathan had proposed that the Cohens invest in a Liberty ship, Ben had been his most active and intelligent supporter and had, when the $200,000 necessary had been raised, put such restricting conditions on Jonathan's overseeing the family's investment that even the brothers who thought Jonathan too ambitious had been agreeable to it. Jonathan was fair, blue-eyed, and good-looking. Now again Ben looked to this nephew.

Jonathan had listened to other opinions, and he said, "It can only be smart to call another doctor. I'll call my wife's uncle, Professor Tishman."

"He's an allergist!"

"He's in a position to advise," Jonathan said calmly.

"Call," Ben said. "The doctor himself would find no harm in that." Ben went with his nephew to the bedroom.

The allergist wanted to know the name of the surgeon. Jonathan told him and then sat and listened. After, he reported: "The surgeon is the best. Normally he takes appointments two months in advance. And if we're afraid of an intestinal malignancy, every day gained can increase our chances."

They returned to the living room. Ben announced soberly, "He too says our surgeon is the best money can buy."

Jack could not sleep. But though the big man knew his wife lay awake in her twin bed, he would not even turn over, would not disturb the quiet rhythm of their breathing. They lay on their backs in the dark, the venetian blinds drawn, a dim glow at the windows.

"Why didn't you tell me?" she had asked just inside their small apartment, not expecting an answer. And later: "Would you like something to eat?"

He was, still in jacket and vest, sitting quite still on the living-room sofa. He did not smoke, he hardly drank. He shook his head. He was looking at the radio-phonograph console at the wall between the two windows. He had given the doctor's boys, Larry and Max, ten dollars to buy records for him. They had bought, he strained to read the titles of the few albums in the console space for records, the Grieg piano concerto, Paul Robeson's *Songs of Free Men*, the Rimsky-Korsakov *Scheherazade Suite*.

Ben had come down from his apartment in the same building two floors above. He had sat close to him. He had, because Jack would not be at business in the morning, asked him business questions: Who was working on what? Moskowitz, the matcher, would be in, which bundles of skins should he be given? What work was ready for the operators? Ben was, in fact, aware of everything that went on in the factory.

Ben stood. "You don't? . . . Everybody, you know, is upstairs?"

"No."

"Good-night."

He had, this last month, been reading a popular edition of *An American Tragedy* that Edith had long had in their bookcase, but this evening, the night-table lamp on, he could not. He began to look through a *Life* magazine, and when Edith, in her bed, closing her book, asked if he were reading, he realized he was looking at nothing.

So the night began.

And he thought now that day would not come. They would lie here in the dark, each in his twin bed, each on his back, and the night would grow longer and longer, and there would be no end to it.

He would die.

He wanted to cry out, to break something in his hands, but the spasm passed and his hands had not moved. He wanted to say something to Edith, to bridge the silence, but did not. And then the pains came.

They came from the left and the right, from above and below, they came from every angle, and his center was like a pincushion into which pain shot, and now a nerve shot the pain to under his arm, to an eye, his temples pounding, he still not having moved, not to worry her. Then the pains were diminishing, but that was little better, he was nauseous, sick in the bowels, he wanted to sit on the john, there was a pressing weight in his bowels.

"What is it?"

"Nothing."

Later he went into the living room, lit a lamp, sat in his pajamas, robe, and slippers on the sofa, out of the circle of light and, head in hands, elbows pressing into his thighs, closed his eyes and tried to see his pain, grief, the place of it. He pressed his eyes shut tighter and tighter and even saw his bowels coiled and slithering, swelling, contracting. He saw then a terrible ball of gray and red matter that was bowel and something else. He put his hands to there, his fingers pressing in as if to burst through the skin and rip out the mess. He could do it. The strength, anger, disgust was in his hands.

He stood. He stretched his arms up, and his fists pushed against the ceiling.

Cancer! He would say it. Cancer!

He went to the encyclopedia in the bookcase. What do *neoplasm* and *metastases* mean? The thing came from where? It attacked here, but could communicate through blood or lymph to some other place. So it was like a weed that you could cut out here but that was already growing there. Why did the cells multiply like that?

A worker in the factory had had a cancer and been operated on. He came back once to visit. His suit was too large for him even in the shoulders. He swam in his suit, he swam in his shirt. Could this happen to him? It was happening now. In his bedroom closet he had ten suits. He saw himself standing at the open door of his bedroom closet.

He looked at a cross-section of the abdomen. It was all tied together, stomach to liver, stomach and liver to bowels. Pancreas, gall bladder, spleen, kidneys—everything hanging together, and the malignancy was spreading within.

He should have asked the doctor to tell him more, to explain his condition to him. And then it flashed through his mind that the doctor had, in fact, told him something secret.

2

Like all people who go to sleep in the same bed or room as someone who is suddenly no longer there, Edith slept restlessly. She was open to the darkest thoughts, she wondered whether Jack would ever return from the hospital, how could she live alone in this apartment? It was the kind of self-questioning one cannot allow oneself to engage in, each question like bad luck. How dare she even consider his death? And yet, and yet, it was right; they had had bad luck since the beginning, why should it change now?

No! No! No!

She loved him. He was good, he was an honorable man. He despised himself when he did not live up to his own standards. He distrusted words, he rarely spoke. When he did, it was because he had weighed his words. He had a terrible temper; he controlled it. His strength had frightened and embarrassed her. She had softened him.

Of all the Cohens, save Sam, Jack's stuttering and palsied brother, he lived the most quietly, he dressed the most conservatively. He was the only one of them interested even a little in culture. She had insisted they speak only English at home, and his English was better than his brothers'.

He was good to her family, the Friedlands. He had helped her brothers financially more than once. He loved the sons and daughters of his brothers and sisters more than those of her brothers and sisters, but was equally generous to them all and would become formal rather than show a preference.

There was no one like him!

And she had brought him nothing but bad luck! After the death of their infant son there had been two miscarriages, and then a third, in the eighth month, and that had been the end of that. She had thought herself better than him, better educated, more cultured. She had thought her misfortune greater and more punishing than his.

She was weeping. "Jacob! Jacob!" she called.

In the morning, she dressed carefully as she did whenever she went to Manhattan. She wore a corset and girdle, though she was hardly heavy, a slip. She wore a fine dress, nylon stockings, medium heels. She wore her three-year-old mink coat, a turbanlike hat, and a silk foulard. And she drove the Buick slowly and prudently, as Jack had taught her, in the rush-hour traffic to the Triborough Bridge and then to the semiprivate pavilion of Mount Sinai Hospital on Fifth Avenue and 101st Street.

The operation was scheduled for 10:00 A.M. It was 8:30 and she was allowed to go up and see Jack for a few minutes.

He was already under sedation. She bent to him and kissed him, she lay her cheek against his, unshaven.

He said, "They shaved me up past my chest." He said, "All the insurance policies are in the black metal box. The rest is in the bank vault."

Shortly before ten, Fanny, Sol's wife, dropped the doctor and Eshka off at the hospital entrance. In the lobby, the little doctor, removing his hat, greeted Edith briefly and then, showing an identification card, made his way past the reception desk, the visitors' elevator opposite, up some steps, through swinging doors into a corridor.

Eshka had accompanied him, not only because Jack was her brother, but because the doctor was unwell. He had had a heart condition five years and this last month had seemed particularly pale and short of breath. Leah would manage the liquor store for her.

She sat down with Edith on a sofa in a window nook of the lobby from where they could see both the entrance from outside and the reception desk. She took her knitting from a bag and set to work. She would have read the *Jewish Daily Forward* that she had folded in her large purse—which stood with Edith's on the low table before them—but she knew that though Edith read that paper too at home, she would be uncomfortable at being in public with someone so old-fashioned.

Edith was active in Hadassah, where she met other women like herself interested in helping Israel. Hadassah paid for the building of hospitals in Israel, supported orphanages, planted trees. Eshka had all her life been too immediately involved in life to have the time to even consider being active in a charitable organization, though she did keep in her store, perhaps in her mother's memory, near the cash register, *pushkas*—coin boxes—for a Williamsburg Talmud Torah, for victims of polio, Jewish orphanages, a burial fund for the poor, and would, after a sale, drop a penny or two of the register's money into a *pushka* that the customer might drop in some silver.

"What are you making?" Edith asked.

"A dress for Shirley." Shirley was Joe's daughter and, as Eshka was, of all his brothers and sisters, Joe's favorite, Joe's daughter, now married and a mother, was hers.

She felt the approach of visiting hours by the growing number of people waiting in the lobby, the little groups that formed. Many came with flowers, boxes of candy. Probably for them surgery was past and now their loved one was recovering. Or not, it occurred to her, for they would bring flowers and candy regardless.

Behind her, beyond the window, was Fifth Avenue, and across the street was the park. It was a fine sunny day, brisk and not too cold for this late in autumn. There were benches on the avenue at the gray stone wall of the park; the shade trees were bare.

She thought that the Christmas season was approaching and business would be good. But it would not matter. In December the store might do more than $15,000 business. In the previous years, December business had made her confident. But she knew by now that these good months could not cover the bad ones. The $15,000 business was discount business. She sold cases at 10 and even 12 percent off. The markup on whisky was 22 percent. On a $1000 business she earned only $100. And rent was $350 a month, and Leah drew $50 a week, and she $75, and the salesman $110! And there were no percentages off there!

She thought of the changes the store had made in her life. It had occurred to her only recently that she did not like to sell whisky. It was against the law to sell to drunks. But she did good business on dollar wine with Negroes who she could tell would be sick-drunk an hour after buying. And there the markup was 40 percent.

Maybe it was the Jewish word that had confused her—*shikker*. One was *shikker* at weddings, one laughed at a *shikker*. A drunk was something else. The word for Negro, *schwartze*, which, for her black hair and black eyes, for something free and easy in her nature, had long been one of her nicknames, also helped. She was selling wine to *schwartzes* who would be *shikker*.

She did not like the bargaining. Her brothers had decided to buy the store in the heart of the fur market that she profit from all their connections. Still, some furriers bargained to get their whisky cheaper than anyone else. What they wanted was to be sharper than anyone else, to beat the other person down. If she gave 12 percent off to one, how could she not to the other? If she did not give off what they asked for, they went two blocks away to another store.

She went to work every morning at seven in the downtown-bound rush hour. She arrived home every afternoon after five all subway-tired. She walked from the store on Thirtieth Street near Sixth Avenue across town to Lexington rather than take the Seventh Avenue line up to Times Square and the East Side shuttle. She hated to walk in the underground maze of the shuttle, she hated the fast pace of the walkers, which became hers; she saw too many drunks in the subway dark and dirt, too many blind and crippled beggars. She thought that freaks came to parade in these long dark corridors, Negro albinos, men talking to themselves. She saw more than once a double-leg amputee who wheeled through the crowded subway cars on a roller-skated platform, his face appearing among the standing people at the height of a child.

Sometimes she took the Seventh Avenue subway up to the Bronx to a Negro neighborhood where she could get the Hunts Point Avenue trolley. Regularly she took the Lexington Avenue local all the way home, for even at four-thirty the homeward-bound rush hour had begun and she might be able to squeeze out a seat on the local. In good weather she walked the several blocks from the subway station to home up Hunts Point Avenue and stopped maybe for five minutes in a yarn shop.

Her husband would be sitting in his armchair by the venetian-blinded window of the dining room of the ground-floor apartment reading the *New York Times*, perhaps doing the crossword puzzle. He was alone in the apartment most of the day. She would smile up at him if he were standing at the window.

She might, if there were nothing special to do, suggest they play pinochle. But that was his game and hers was gin rummy, and he would insist that if they play they play gin rummy, and they might for half an hour.

Max would come in from his high school downtown. Larry was away at college. Max, at dinner, would speak of his remarkable friends, of the writer-genius he was reading. Like many of the Cohens, he was full of energy, an exaggerator, an optimist, if not a boaster. He spoke of the school newspaper of which he would be, he insisted, editor-in-chief. He was fat, sensitive. Sometimes she looked at him and saw him as he had been when he had been an infant and child, when things had been simpler, when she could pick him up and hug him tight.

Her fingers flew over her knitting, the needles clicking softly.

At noon her brother Sam shuffled in. He wore neat dark gray. There was something distant in his manner that made him seem severe. He had been the second Cohen brother to come to America, and for many years he had shared a room in lower Manhattan with Jack. He lived with his wife in an apartment in Rockaway by the sea. He had bought a large house there that he had transformed into a rooming house. Summers he rented small apartments, to the doctor and his family, to Friedlands, to landsmen.

In the company of his brothers, he would find a quiet corner and sit there and watch.

At twelve-thirty, Ben, Sol, and the nephews Sam and David arrived in a taxi. They entered the lobby in a bunch, Ben, tall, stout, leading, but David's wild limp giving all the group an air of impatience and rush.

"Of course," Ben said, nodding as if what Edith had to tell him, how Jack had been in the morning, that they had shaven him to above the chest, that the operation was not yet over, the doctor still not back, was to be expected and were good signs. He took things in hand.

"So we'll have lunch." He would take Edith and Eshka in the first shift.

"I'll go with Sam," Eshka said, that he would not be overlooked. She would have to walk at his pace. It pained her to see him trying to walk faster than he could. He ate so slowly they would take twice as long.

"I didn't in—in—in—vite you," Sam said and smiled. He had blue eyes, his face was always a little red, his hair was turning silver. "I'm not hun—hun—hun—gry," he said.

"We'll bring you a sandwich," Ben said.

In a delicatessen, Ben insisted they eat well. He would feel badly if his sister-in-law and sister did not choose the best the menu had to offer. All Eshka wanted was her favorite, hot pastrami on rye. Edith said she had no appetite.

"Eat darling," Eshka said.

"A little then."

"A minute steak," Ben insisted and, at her nod, called over the waiter.

Eshka's sandwich was good, thick with meat. Midway she wanted her coffee, black.

The squat nephew Louis had arrived in their absence. Edith's brother Herman Friedland arrived and took his place at his sister's side. He was the leader of the Friedland clan, and though he was only a partner in a bar and grill in Brooklyn he condescended, though not extravagantly, to all Cohens who were not chiefs.

It was after one-thirty, and no one wanted to go out to lunch because they thought the operation would soon be over. At two they began to make phone calls.

Ben called his place of business and spoke with Jonathan, whom he had left in charge. He made a point of speaking too to Pearl, the secretary, knowing that she would more warmly than Jonathan communicate to the forty workers in the office and factory that there was still no news.

Eshka called Leah at the liquor store. She told her who was at the hospital, asked her if she had gone out to lunch, told her what she had eaten. She would have told her to come here, this is where she should be too, but she was afraid that the hired salesman did not ring up all his sales, and she would have been guilty before her brothers, who had laid out so much money for her, had she told Leah to close up early.

She put on her coat, the old brown caracul she wore when she dressed up, and went to take some air across the street. She did not dare go far afraid that she would not see Ben if he came out to call her. It felt good to be in the sun, to feel the open space of the park; it would be nice to walk in the park.

She walked on the sidewalk by the park wall, but in her mind was walking on paths within the park, the bare trees, the hard bare earth, the unoccupied benches. Somewhere within the park was a pond, and there might be some birds there.

We live in brick, cement, and asphalt, she thought, and forget even what fields are like, and right now what would give me pleasure would be to stand by a pond and look at some ducks.

She smiled at herself. She felt she was "playing hooky."

It was a long time for her husband to be standing. Could they bring him a chair in surgery?

The bare shade trees here were planted in small squares of earth, and a section of the sidewalk, between the trees, was of small garden cobblestones. In the summer, she sometimes wore sneakers; at the beach she went barefoot.

"Aunt Eshka!" It was her niece Anna, Leah's daughter. She walked proud and straight-backed, briskly, as her mother, but was a little taller and was nearsighted and sometimes seemed hesitant, as if afraid of falling.

"How good of you to come," Eshka said, hugging her.

Anna was six months pregnant. She had had two miscarriages. That summer, at the beginning of this pregnancy, she had come for a Sunday dinner to the rooms the doctor, Eshka, and Leah rented in Sam's house in Rockaway and had begun to bleed. The doctor had ordered her to bed.

Her prematurely bald husband Fred, a lawyer who had gone into his father's fur business, said with the conviction of someone who knows there is a logical solution to every problem, "We've got to do something."

The doctor said, "We've got to do *nothing*. She must not move, and above all she must not be examined."

"We can't stay here." They had stayed two months, and it was a family joke.

"The operation isn't over?" Anna asked, really to show that she was thinking of Jack, and she looked up at the enormous face of the hospital.

Eshka looked up too, the hundreds upon hundreds of windows, and shaking her head, it occurred to her that Anna had come here from Brooklyn because she too loved Jack. She took her niece by the arm and they walked together.

Eshka said, "So will it be a boy or a girl?"

"Whichever," Anna said, smiling now.

"Let me feel." She stopped in the middle of the sidewalk and put her hand on the swelling. She said, nodding her head, knowing she was embarrassing her niece and that she was yet happy to be with her, "It's a boy!"

But the wind had become cold. It was not yet three o'clock, but one could feel the approach of evening.

"Where have you been?" Ben said to Eshka, his dissatisfaction, she knew, was that there had been no news and that even he was now worried.

He went to the reception desk. Mr. Jacob Cohen was still in surgery.

They were a large group in a window nook of the lobby—Edith; her brother; the brothers Ben, Sol, and Sam; Eshka; the nephews David, Sam, and Louis; and Anna. They had made twice as much room for Anna as she needed, and though they were silent and their mood was dark, no one did not have a warm smile for her. Eshka had taken up her knitting, but every now and then she would look up, fingers stopped, the needles crossed.

They were then—the little doctor coming through the swinging doors, his overcoat over his arm, hat in hand—all standing and moving, the brothers behind Ben, the nephews flanking, everyone giving way to Edith on the arm of her brother, but the look on each face that the news he would receive concerned him immediately, flesh of his flesh. Eshka alone saw how white the doctor was, and she took him by the arm and led him back to the sofa in the darkening window nook.

Ben hovered over him. "So?" he asked impatiently. Louis took his uncle Ben's arm to calm him. Louis trusted the doctor absolutely.

The doctor looked up at Ben. The doctor had shaven that morning, but already there was a stubble on his face, the stubble hairs white. His collar had lost its stiffness.

He said, "The cancer was generalized."

Anna was weeping. Edith had sat down, her lips parted.

"He took out everything he could see. Now it is out of our hands."

Eshka realized then that *he* was in pain. She too had tears in her eyes. "What is it?" she said, bending to him, her hands on his shoulders.

Louis was delegated to drive the doctor home. It was dark when they arrived. Louis had to help the doctor out and he stood behind the doctor at the dining-room table as the doctor caught his breath.

The doctor said, "In such surgery there are a hundred calculations and decisions to make, and in the midst of it the hands alone, the very fingers, decide. It's a battle between the surgeon and the disease for a human life. What the surgeon does is so forthright! One must accept one's losses, one must not fool oneself, one must give up on and remove contaminated organs. Beyond surgery is radiation. But we cannot shoot X-rays randomly into the body. And the scene of the battle, the terrain, is alive and has its say. There is, I believe, a will in the very terrain that medicine can do nothing about, and that the person himself is perhaps not aware of."

Then the doctor went to bed. His pain was not his heart and was not new, but now it had settled into him.

Ben held it against the doctor that he always saw the dark side of things. Ben thought education and too fine an intelligence could remove you from the realities. You thought too much, you became confused. You saw something happen, you made theories about it, you buried it in words, and finally you forgot entirely the fact you had seen and all you had left was words.

One had to work, love, and hope. Those were laws. Always work, love, and hope. And so, when the surgeon appeared shortly after the doctor had left, he rushed to him and asked, "So, professor?" This was an important man, a man in a hurry!

"He has a chance!"

"What chance?" Ben insisted.

This is even a psychologist, Ben thought, seeing the sudden smile in the surgeon's eyes.

"A chance in ten," he said and was gone.

That's already better, Ben thought. We are pushing the door open wider. To Edith, he said, "Did you hear?" She had, she did not understand Ben's mood. And yet his hope was contagious.

The internist Jack had seen approached the group.

"So?" Ben said.

"There's no reason to be overly pessimistic."

"The surgeon says he has one chance in ten."

"Yes, that's what I'd say, or maybe a little better than that."

A nurse came down to say that Edith could see Jack. Ben insisted that Edith be accompanied, and he obtained that. Herman Friedland, always one for rites, rose and made a gesture of giving his sister into Ben's care. And Ben took her on his arm to the elevator and the seventh floor.

They entered the private room, the private nurse they had hired to stay the night rising, and there was Jack, and it was all Ben could do to keep the tears from his eyes.

What have they done to you, brother!

There were needles and tubes taped into his nose. He was being simultaneously administered intravenously, from upside-down hanging bottles, blood plasma and a clear liquid food; there were drains from his body to below the bed. He was without color, and Ben thought they had taken all life from him except that he breathed, his throat rasping terribly. Each breath seemed to be a cry of pain.

Edith was crying softly. Ben was silently reciting prayers, forcing out of the man prone before him the image of his brother strong and rising from this bed and paraphernalia.

"He's doing well," the nurse said.

Ben was astonished. What could she mean? His heartbeat? Surely his heartbeat. His heart was beating strong!

He had not noticed, Edith had knelt at the bed and amid all those tubes and connections had taken her husband's hand in hers. "I am here," she said, addressing the unconscious man. "I am here," she repeated, reaching into the dark.

3

The day before Jack was to enter the hospital, he found himself walking on the Lower East Side near Orchard Street. He wondered what he was looking for. Was he looking here even for Berezin? It seemed no farther from here to Berezin than from the Grand Concourse to here. Was he looking for his life?

He stood outside the tenement in which he had shared a room with his brother Sam. He wore a suit with vest, an overcoat, and hat. Looking up at the building in that narrow familiar street, a man pushing a cart up the street, he looked like a landlord, but he was only counting the fire escape landings up to locate the room he had lived in.

He had often thought he was grateful for everything he had, for his brothers and sisters, for Edith, for America, that he had been able to work and make a living and then participate in the success of a business. But he thought now, If I should have been grateful yesterday, I should be grateful today. If yesterday my life was good, then it should seem good to me now. But all I can think of now is my wasting away and my death. I am fifty-seven years old, and I have been marking time all my life.

He stood by the East River. It was a gray day, and there was a cold wind, but here, at this walk by the river, bound by the steady almost silent traffic on the East Side Drive, you could watch the wind come across the surface of the water, you felt the spray in the air, you felt the ocean close, you could almost see the bay opening out into the full horizon of the sea, into the fullness and entirety of sea and sky.

Can I say that my life with Edith, and my life with my brothers, and my love for my sisters and for my mother, was nothing? Was marking time? No. And yet I have been marking time.

He was almost at the Brooklyn Bridge. He saw its thick heavy webbing. Its dark towers were massive against the sky.

Now lying flat, his eyes closed, his body too heavy to ever move again, it seemed, he saw a hand holding a razored instrument cut a line in his body from groin to chest. He saw a bright overhead light like a white sun that was yet a spider's web. He saw hands fold open the skin of his body. He saw himself lying on a surgical table, the open wound from groin to chest, the skin, clear tissue and muscle pulled and clamped open. He saw men in white, and white masks, bent over him.

He was running in a field and was sinking. It was a field of summer wheat, and the ears of wheat were full. He was running in a field of golden wheat, only he was sinking and his hands, which had now and then brushed the soft grain, were now within it, and he had to push the grain aside as if he were swimming through it, and then his head only was at the surface, and then only his eyes, and then he saw only the golden swaying tips of the ears of wheat against the pure blue of the sky, and then he was within, sinking.

He heard dogs. He was running in a field and was then sinking into the field, his arms swimming. He lay panting in the field and, looking back, saw long and lean dogs racing and leaping forward, and they were almost on him, and he could almost feel their teeth biting into him.

He knew they were cutting him still. Yet, not far from him in this surgical theater, was a magician in top hat, evening clothes, and cape. Smiling broadly, he bowed and snapped his hat flat and held it up so that you could see it had no thickness at all. Then he shook it open, and with a fluttering of wings three white pigeons were launched into the air.

He saw hands. He saw long fingered hands and sleight-of-hand hands. He saw a cupped hand into which golden grains of corn were being poured. The grains overflowed his hands. He saw the little doctor.

"So you are here too," he said.

He saw his own hand. What were they doing to his hand?

It was smaller, a boy's hand, and they were cutting open the skin of his index finger and then the skin of his middle finger, and now they were sewing the fingers together. "No!" he cried. "No!" But they held the twelve-year-old's hand, and there was his father, squat and *yarmulkaed*, two sons run off to America to avoid seven-year service in an army in which they would be only Jew and dirty Jew, and he having decided to cripple his sons rather than lose more. Sol had had his eardrums punctured and still was crying and moaning, and two other brothers had been smashed to have hernias. There had been a shouting and screaming in the house, and brother had held brother, and his mother's eyes had been wide, and then she had been beating her fists against a wall. I want no more sons! I want no more sons!

He was running in a golden field and was sinking and his hands, which had now and then brushed the soft ears of wheat, were now within the grain, swimming it aside, and now even his head was below the surface of the grain.

He heard dogs.

He was running and sinking and he looked over his shoulder and saw dogs leaping high in the pure blue sky.

He saw his hands cupped and golden grains of corn were being poured into them, were flowing over them.

The doctor sat down at his side. His head was bowed. What did he want to say?

He was bending to the tilled earth, and with one hand he made a cup in the soil. The other hand was full of grains of corn, and he dropped a grain in the cup and smoothed the earth over the grain, and patted it that he would know where to water. He moved on a step down the line and bent and made another cup in the soil, and dropped in a grain and covered and smoothed, and straightened and moved down the line, and bent and cupped. And moving saw the first grains he had planted thrusting up through the soil, and he, planting still, saw each grain thrusting up, and now the first was a stalk with stiff leaves, rich green, and the first was knee high and the second was almost, and down the line. And he was far now from the first, and the first was tall as him, and fruit thrusting out from it, and there were lines and lines of rich green corn, and he was walking back now between tall rows of corn.

When he came out of postoperative unconsciousness, his wife Edith was leaning over him, she was wearing her turbanlike hat; she had removed her eyeglasses and there were tears at her eyes. And she was repeating his name: "Jacob, Jacob, Jacob."

He saw her newly, the way one sees when one is calm and detached. He saw the thick flesh of her cheeks, the parted lips, the woman almost fifty. Her eyes were gray, and without her eyeglasses she had the nearsighted person's look of permanent helplessness. Her eyes were wet, webbed, blurred, and he wondered what she could see.

The nurse was standing behind her, beaming.

He was thirsty, but he was reluctant to speak. "Are you thirsty?" Edith asked. The nurse wet his lips.

He saw the upside-down bottle that was feeding him intravenously. The window shades and curtains were open, it was a wide window. He saw the twilight sky, the dying reds still silhouetting clouds. He saw the dark tops of Central Park West towers. The room too was filled with twilight. He saw on the wall opposite the head of his bed a framed reproduction of a painting of what he immediately recognized, in spite of the growing obscurity of the room and the style of the painting, as a field of grain in the wind.

"Look," Edith said. She nodded in the direction of a table in a corner of the room on which were several bouquets of flowers. There were flowers, he saw then, everywhere in the room, there were flowers on the inside window ledge, all the colors dark in the obscurity, and for an instant he had the impression he was in a garden of red, violet, blue, yellow, and orange flowers at twilight, the wet fragrance rising, and then he smelled something rotten and he closed his eyes.

I will need all my strength.

"How long?" were Jack's first words, to the surgeon, his gaze flickering down to indicate the rubber attachment from his body to a receptacle on the floor.

"In about a month we tie you together and you'll function normally again."

One visiting hour, he asked to be left alone with his sister Eshka.

She said, "The dogs are the disease. They were running after you, and you were afraid of the pain. The fields are the fields of Russia. And you wanted to eat this other food. You wanted to take the ears of wheat into your hand and eat them. But you were sinking, and that was your disease. The magician one never knows about. The planting is that you want to work with your hands, that you want to make things grow. The last dream, the one you did not tell me, the one in which you are running in a field of grain and are sinking and are repeating to yourself, 'I must rise, I must rise,' and you then running and rising, running and rising, becoming big and bigger, and your steps giant steps, and the dogs now leaping high into the sky like a dance about you, is that you've come back from the dead.

"Tell no one," she said.

4

Ben's day began at six, his wife Dora already shuffling about in the kitchen. She was thin, a little stooped; she was a worrier. She worried about her daughter, about her son in the army stationed in Italy, she worried about her sister's retarded son. She worried about Ben's business. She kept her ears open to know who owed him money. She knew what those men were worth! She kept the books for Eshka's liquor store, she knew how much money was going down the drain every week. David, she knew, owed money right and left.

She spoke to Ben from the sink, washing, wiping, and putting in place every dish as she finished with it.

"Yes, yes, princess," Ben would say. "You'll see, it'll all turn out for the best."

His daughter Elaine would get up well after his departure, often too late to even bother going to school, though her mother would have shaken her awake well before then. She would sit at the kitchen table all hunched over herself, fat, puffy, irritable. Dora would serve her breakfast as she had Ben, and would say cuttingly, "What else do you want, *princess*?"

Six days a week, twelve hours a day, Ben was downtown, selling in the showroom, matching skins in the factory (leafing through bundles of mink—this skin to this pile, this other to a pile of darker or more thickly furred skins—so that the skins to make up a coat would be all equally dark or light, luxuriant or fine), cutting skins (razor slicing parallel lines that the skin would, in a coat, lie large and flat), speaking on the phone—in the office, in the private office, in the showroom, in the factory, a phone even in the storage vault.

He had to keep an eye on each department, on Pearl the secretary and Rose the bookkeeper, on the tall Gentile models that they should keep busy even when there were no customers, on the Italianer Marie in lining (she had good ideas too for styles, but let her do only styles and who will do lining?), on the shipping department chief Solly (who wanted to be given a chance as an operator—"Next year, next year," Ben had been answering for years), on the other "boy," Gus, a cigar-smoking good-for-nothing who bet on horses, the numbers, on boxing matches, and baseball, who was always asking for an advance on his pay, and how could you refuse him when you knew he was his widowed mother's only support? He would, he knew, sooner or later have to give his wife's retarded nephew Stanley a job, he would be good only for sweeping up and delivering.

He had to see that the nailers, good workers and fast, always had something to do, that the sixteen sewing machine operators, the five cutters, the presser, were earning their salaries. Of course, when Jack was there everyone kept busy, but the place, from large mirrored showroom to factory, from office to lining, to shipping, to private office, was really his.

He lunched generally at The Traders. Here one ate sandwiches, but the sliced pastrami or corned beef was an inch thick. One could eat in a hurry or take one's time. It was a dark place with a bar, and it smelled a little of beer. One sat with others in a booth, the waitress keeping the cups always filled with hot coffee. Even Joe liked this place and went there now and then.

Ben would walk in, and three hands would rise in greeting, and voices would call, "Ben, over here!" And he would smile and greet and make his way to a booth. He sat with men his age who told him of their children. Some of their boys went to Harvard, Yale, MIT.

Max Blue, a little cigar-smoking furrier who commuted every day from Stamford, Connecticut, had political connections. He had been asked to go to the White House and had taken the president's measurements to make him a mink-lined coat. When he had made the coat he had returned to Washington with it, and the president had tried it on in his presence and been so pleased with it he had invited him to stay to lunch.

"So we ate, good simple American food. And then he offered me a cigar. And he said, 'Well, Max, how do you think I'm doing?'

" 'Mister President,' I said, for I always called him Mister President, 'I think history will regard you as the people's president.'

"The president nodded at that and he said, 'Max, that's what I think too.' "

Ben thought that this was in fact the generation of the people, of the little man, the self-educated man, of the immigrant. It was the most democratic generation of all time, and today's poor man might be tomorrow's millionaire, and the son of this manufacturer who worked twelve hours a day, six days a week, was going to a good college and might become a judge or a governor. Ben respected every man for what he or his son might become.

Joe had been in business forty years and had a steady Connecticut and Park Avenue clientele. Ben's business had begun to flourish during the war, and his clientele was still moving out of the Bronx and Brooklyn. They started coming about ten in the morning, and at about three every showroom table was occupied, the models modelling, Ben and Jonathan selling, selling, coats over their arms, laid out on the carpeted floor. Even Sam came in, in duster, from the cutters' table, to make a sale. Then they were all smiles, confidence, certainty, and an hour or two later relaxed a moment receiving some friend's brother-in-law or cousin come with a valise full of hand-painted neckties. Sam was impressed with the artwork, and he bought one with a willow tree on it, and Ben bought one with a peacock, and Jonathan bought as a joke for a friend one with a naked woman. "Who loves neckties like us!" Ben said, tying his on before a three-faced full-length mirror. And it was true. He would never forget buying his first American necktie, silk, blue and gold. The touch of it, the luxury of it.

Ben had discovered on Madison Avenue in the neighborhood of Mount Sinai Hospital, where he and his brother Sol visited Jack every evening after leaving Thirtieth Street, a fine and quiet restaurant, the Peachtree, and many evenings, after visiting hours, he and Sol, and whichever other brothers, sisters, nephews, and nieces had visited Jack, would dine there.

One evening, Ben went from Mount Sinai to the Peachtree with, among ten others, Artie Luria of Beverly Hills. Ben had known Artie's father and, when he had died, had helped out the family. Ben did not know how to have friends, only relatives. The boy became like a nephew. He would invite him home for Friday night chicken, he took him more than once to visit Mother Cohen in the East Bronx. Artie joined the marines, Ben cut out and saved his picture from the Sunday rotogravure section of the *Jewish Daily Forward*: "First Jewish Boy Wounded on Iwo Jima." When Artie came back from the war, he went fast from salesman to retailer. He opened a shop in Beverly Hills, where he sold fur coats manufactured by others in New York.

At first he needed credit. Ben sent him tens of thousands of dollars' worth of furs. Now his business was that good, he often did for Ben what almost no furrier did: he paid cash on the line. He was trim and wore $200 suits. He had that kind of sunburn that in the fur market was called $1,000 tan.

They sat at a big oval table and ordered shrimp cocktails or hot soup, for the walk over from the hospital had been cold. Some of the men ordered Scotch with their appetizers so as not to keep the others waiting.

"Edith, dearie," Ben asked, "where do you think Jack would like to go for his holiday?" For at the hospital Jack had announced that, after the closing-up, putting-back-together operation, he would go on a holiday and, though it disturbed Ben that he had not first mentioned that to him and Sol alone, they who always shared all their projects, he thought his thinking of the future a good sign.

"He wants to rent a cabin in the mountains."

Ben nodded. "It's a good idea, it's just what he needs. We'll make reservations for you at Grossinger's."

The decision would have escaped Edith, but she said, "No, I think he wants to be quiet."

"Ah," Ben said, "then we'll make reservations at Fleischman's. Maybe we'll all come up for a weekend."

Edith was pale, and there was a tremor in her voice. "I think he really wants to rent a cabin in a quiet place."

"Ah," Ben said, "I understand. Only what if you're snowed in? What if he suddenly needs a doctor? We can't let him go where there's not even a telephone." Sol was gravely nodding his head. Jonathan was smiling at her that she should agree.

"So how's business?" Sol asked his sister Leah. He knew this was the best month of the year and thought he would encourage her by asking.

"Ach, business!" she answered, refusing to give him the satisfaction of reporting sales. What was important was Jack's illness, was that the doctor was in bed, was that she, knowing like a twin when her sister Eshka would be sick, felt that something was beginning to go wrong with her.

Besides, her daughter Anna had said to her, "Mama, if it's a boy, we've decided we won't use papa's name. Harry's not . . . well, it's not American enough! It wouldn't be fair!"

"So how are the ships?" Herman Friedland asked.

Jonathan did not reply immediately, wondering if Herman's question represented more than idle curiosity. Herman and his brothers could probably raise $50,000. He smiled and said business was all right.

Sol said, smiling at his joke, "At least it's not sinking!"

"Uncle Sol," Louis said, "what do you know about sinking or sailing? The closest you've ever been to the ocean is up to your thighs at Rockaway." And he made the funny splashing gestures of a man wading and afraid of the waves, Sol first blushing but then laughing, accepting, yes, that is the way I look in the water.

Artie asked Jonathan's wife Sheila about her painting. Sheila was the family's second artist; Dan, the doctor's brother in Paris, was married to an artist. But whereas Tanya painted flowers it was a pleasure to put on your walls, Sheila painted garment factory workers at their machines. Ben thought Sheila's choice of subject strange; she was small and very pretty, neat and clean, she came from a well-to-do family. But barely listening to the conversation that followed, almost everyone with something to say about art, it occurred to him that hanging a picture of unhappy people on your wall might even, like charity, if the painting were well done, be a good deed.

"Great artists are madmen!" Herman Friedland said.

"Is that so?" Sol said credulously.

"Madmen!" Herman repeated, nodding his head emphatically.

"Some are, some are not," Jonathan said.

Sol looked from one to the other.

"Edward G. Robinson," Artie said, "has a collection of paintings worth millions."

Except for them the restaurant was empty. It only made Ben feel more at ease. Besides, he liked the look of the empty white-clothed tables, the uninterrupted distances the waiters had to cross to serve them. He too would have a pêche Melba. At home he would already have fallen asleep in front of the television, he had opened the top button of his pants. He was glad Louis was there and would drive him home. He would offer Leah money to take a taxi to the East Bronx. She would refuse, of course. They would compromise on her taking a taxi to her apartment from the Hunts Point Avenue subway station. He saw her standing alone on a subway platform. Ach! He would force her to accept money to take a taxi even from here. He was midway through the dessert and had closed his eyes with pleasure and fatigue.

Artie said, "Benjy, don't open your eyes. I want to tell you about a dream. It's a desert. An enormous desert. But now they're building something there. They're building high, they're building a skyscraper in the desert. What are they building a skyscraper in the desert for? Ah, look, they've planted palm trees, they're growing high. It's a hotel in the desert, but the desert is already an oasis."

Sol said, "A hotel in the desert? Why will anyone go to a hotel in the desert?"

But Ben, smiling, played the game, kept his eyes closed, pêche Melba in his mouth.

Artie was laughing. "Why, Uncle Sol? Because that hotel in the desert is Eden! It's where you'll go to be young again! It's where you'll go to be full of life again! Benjy, do you see it? The sidewalks are made of gold! Do you see the other hotels? It's a city! Look, it's night. Hundred-foot-high neon lights announce Frank Sinatra, Joe E. Lewis, Judy Garland, and Jimmy Durante. I mean you'll go from one hotel to the other, and in each there'll be million-dollar entertainment. And in each there'll be gambling, the fastest action in

America, and all of it legal and all of it on the up and up. There'll be winners and losers, only everything over in the space of a night, of a holiday. And even the losers will be able to say they've been to Eden! Do you see it?"

Ben opened his eyes, and Artie was smiling at him in a certain way, and Ben knew that some corner of this dream was being proposed to him. He saw Leah pale and thin-lipped and knew she would accept no taxi money from him this night. He said, "Hmmm."

CHAPTER *Nine*

1

Tʜᴇ ᴄᴏʜᴇɴs ɴᴏᴡ had Diners Club cards. And some of them lived three or four evenings a week as if they were rich.

Jonathan went to nightclubs. His sister and brothers all had children. He had begun to wonder whether he could be a father. At Cohen Brothers Furs he drew $300 a week.

One afternoon every week he went from the fur market to the Battery office where the Greek, their partner, ran their Liberty ship and ten others. Business was good, but, Jonathan soon realized, was better for certain ships than others. He remarked that certain ships had better-paying contracts than others, used less fuel, and paid lower ship chandler bills. He brought this to the attention of the Greek. The Greek explained, protested, argued. The Greek owned 49 percent of their ship. They could buy him out or sell out to him. He would, of course, buy cheap or sell dear.

At the Blue Angel, Jonathan met other men his age, veterans and avid. There was, to be sure, nightclub entertainment. Eartha Kitt and Harry Belafonte were among the stars whose careers began there. But Jonathan, like the other regulars, went only at the end of an evening into the long rear entertainment room separated from the bar and lounge by a velvet curtain.

"Yes sir, Mister Cohen sir," the hurried maître d'hôtel said and ushered Jonathan and his party through the dark crowded smoke-filled lounge to an empty table. There he sat back to back with someone from the dress business, or who had been in the fur business and gone into construction, or who was an artists' agent born in Russia, Poland, or the Bronx, his wife, like Jonathan's, a graduate of Julia Richman High School.

There he met his friend Sam Gold, who had made a million selling scrap metal to the Japanese before the war and had been a procurement colonel during. Artie Luria came there when he was in town. There he met Dan Weber and his heiress wife. Dan was tall, thin, American-born, Columbia College–educated. He had been a navy officer during the war; he was now in his father's fur business. He had a quiet waiting smile.

Bob Henderson, publisher of *Top Secret*, used the place as an after-hours office. He was tall, silver-haired; he was the first to wear pink shirts. He went from table to table sowing and reaping his brand of news.

He had been in the dress business. One of his models had worked for a "girlie" magazine in her off-hours. He had looked into girlie magazines and then bought into them, and soon he had five. In one, he ran an article on callgirls; sales shot up. In another, he ran two scandal stories. He then started *Top Secret*, which now had a circulation of more than a million. It exposed Joe DiMaggio, Thomas Dewey, and Henry Ford.

Who knew what was true? The men who gathered there had been born in ghettos, they had seen the world and what it was made of and now wanted their share. And they thought that Bob Henderson was something of a crusader when he said, "I've got something on every one of those sons of bitches!"

Starlets came to him begging to be exposed.

"Why, Bob Henderson!" a woman passing by said. And then, as he looked up, "I thought you were dead." She wore a tight sequined dress and walked off the way a fish might walk on its fins, the real activity in her twisting bottom.

"The same to you, honey!" Bob Henderson called out.

He drank too much. He had become a very rich man, but even now there were several million-dollar libel suits pending against him.

When, late in the evening, Jonathan and his party went into the long rear room, they were given a ringside table—the tables in that room barely larger than ashtrays. There one was packed table to table with the tourists, all pointed, in smoke, in bluish shafts of spotlight, toward a platform. There the minimum charge per person was $5, and even if one only signed that amount away one gave a good cash tip to the waiter and never shook hands with this maître d'hôtel without palming him at least a $5 bill. But one knew that the singer on the program was being paid $1,000 a week, the comedian $500, the magic act $350. Nor was it a surprise to see Walter Winchell in the audience, or Joe Louis, or Errol Flynn. The stars were everywhere.

The songs were full of wit, sex, and money, New York songs. The singer's lips were full and lustrous in the light, her hair powdered with gold or silver. She was slender and taut, a tigress. The comic was queer, or played queer, and any queer joke was good for a laugh. There was a Frankie-and-Johnny routine done in the dark with glowing scarves like worms—Oh Frankie, Oh Johnny, Oooooh Frankie, Oooooh Johnny—that was a sensation. Now and then the owner brought in an opera singer, but Yma Sumac with her weird jungle voice was better yet. Now and then you would see in the audience a fabulous woman with a nothing escort, and you knew that a star was up for sale. Her very name was Christian or Gentile.

In Los Angeles, Artie explained to Jonathan, "Vegas is racket money going straight."

Artie introduced him to the president of the Hotel Eden Corporation. The president said, "From what I hear, your whole industry's like musical chairs, and every time the music stops another furrier falls on his ass! And those bankrupts drag you down with them. You keep struggling to stay afloat, and they drag you down at fifty, thirty, or even ten cents to the dollar. There's only one way, I've heard, to catch your breath."

"What's that?" Artie asked.

"A fire! Ha! ha! ha! A good fire on a Saturday night when no one's around, and then you collect from the insurance a hundred cents to the dollar on everything you paid fifty or thirty cents to the dollar!" He smiled at them as if he knew them better than they knew themselves.

Still, there was truth in what he said. In the fur business, every time there was a fire there was one chance in two that the furrier had started it.

2

The East Bronx apartment of the doctor and Eshka was for a last time the center of the family. The doctor's brother Dan and his sister-in-law Tanya came from Paris and slept in Leah's small apartment close by. Everyone came but Jack, who was away on holiday and whom no one had told of the seriousness of the doctor's illness, and the doctor's older son Larry, who was away at college and whose studies, Eshka knew, the doctor would not want to be interrupted.

Bereziner landsmen came. It had been years since the doctor had treated them; the association itself was disintegrating. The members were all fifty and sixty years old, their children were grown up and Americans. Epstein, the Communist laundryman, came; he was divorced from his wife of thirty years, Fanny, who had sung Russian and Yiddish songs at a hundred meetings and parties. Mr. Matter came, the dear friend Dr. Lipshutz, Karp the vegetable store man, Mrs. Silver the grocer. Heavy Dr. Reisman came, twice impotent, once as a doctor, once as a friend, sat lost in the crowd and shadows of the dining room trying to catch his breath.

For the lights were switched on only late. For the apartment was smaller now than when there had been the doctor's office and Mother Cohen's apartment next door. And the sounds of the dining room carried right into the doctor's bedroom, and in the dark one was quieter.

They sat in the shadows in the dining room about the big glass-covered table, the photographs under the glass for the whole length and width of the table. There were platters of oranges and apples on the table, and cakes and cookies, and tea was served, Eshka's sisters-in-law helping her, or Mrs. Silver, or Emma, who was often there. For Leah was at the liquor store from eight in the morning to seven at night.

Eshka did not know who did the dishes, who prepared the tea. She had to prepare soft food for him for his gums had begun to

bleed. She had to have food in the refrigerator for her son, for any
guest who might be hungry. In the narrow steaming kitchen she
might find Dora or Fanny cooking a chicken. When had the sister-in-
law come? Who had bought the chicken?

Money came from her brothers in new twenty- and fifty-dollar
bills. What am I to do with this? "Why do you give me this?" It was
Ben's face that appeared for an instant through the emptiness, and
he was hurt and did not understand.

Leah brought her from the store checks to sign, orders to approve.
It was January, and they had to replenish stock. Who would do the
inventory? She gave Leah the power of attorney. The doctor had a
$20,000 life insurance policy she would not think of. She owed her
brothers $30,000 for the liquor store.

She washed and cleaned him. Everything had to be organized, the
basins of hot water, the clean bedsheets. He had always been small
and thin, and now he was losing weight. If she made too brusque a
gesture she might hurt him.

He had already begun to let pile up unread medical journals; now
he no longer bothered with the *New York Times*. Then he was
always more or less in pain, always more or less under the effect of
morphine. He did not complain, he had nothing to say, but sometimes, his eyes tightly closed, his sharp breathing would reveal his
pain. And she would stand watching him, thinking, Why don't you
cry out? Once when she had had a migraine she had begged him to
kill her, and he had then, as always, waited and given her a shot
only when she reached the blinding peak of her pain. Why don't you
too curse and reach? Nauseous with guilt she would rush to the
young doctor who had taken over the office next door and say, "Doctor, please!" And he would find time to come in and give him a
shot.

He turned yellow, and then deep glowing yellow, his liver attacked. She alone could really measure how far gone he was, his
yellow body under her hands, that she cleaned now with alcohol
and dried by blotting, his arms and legs mere bones, and his head a
small yellow skull. In the fleshlessness of his face, his nose turned
down over his lips like a beak, and he was, his head only out of the
covers, resting on a pillow, like a bright and terrible yellow bird, his
eyes watching.

Cousins, in-laws, friends stood about his bed. Each read something else in his regard. Karp, the vegetable store man, knew it gave the doctor pleasure to see him. Jonathan stood with his wife Sheila at the foot of the bed, and that was the week that he was spitting all day, hawking up phlegm into a shallow curved aluminum spitting cup, that he could not sleep for the phlegm rising, or not quite rising, and sometimes there was blood in the phlegm and he looked without alarm every time, and in the night more than once he had, reaching, overturned the cup on his bedclothes and said nothing, this so clean man, and now, as he hawked up, Sheila stepped back and he saw her doing so and whispered with a smile, though in that skull-like face that too was nasty, "Don't worry, I'm not spitting at you."

She was not the only one to feel ill at ease here. The wives of nephews and cousins came wearing furs, perfumes. And this apartment had begun to have a hospital smell. And when a man dies we blame him even for *that*, as if every time we *lose* it is our fault, as if we, blameless, will go on living forever. These sons and daughters had always been afraid of what he might tell them, and who likes to look at a dying man? And when they had stood three minutes at the foot of his bed they were afraid even of his silence.

Squat Louis stood often at the foot of his bed, ill at ease as he was the one time a year he went to synagogue, an obligation not understood, deeper than understanding. David sat on Eshka's bed, immobile as stone. Emma was in the apartment several hours almost every day, and only in the last week did she go in to see him.

In Max's room, Eshka read, typed in the portable machine the doctor had used in his office: "He is dying. He is turning yellow."

She said to the fat boy, "What are you writing? What are you, a scientist? How dare you write this! How dare you!"

"Mama, he *is* dying."

"Don't mention it!" Her mouth was in a shout, though her voice was only a hoarse whisper. "Don't you dare mention it!"

Now the doctor could not control his urination. And now the doctor could not control his bowels. The excrement that eased and caked about his body was black. And still there was sometimes something about his regard that made her think, He is waiting.

She had been afraid to call Larry home because the doctor would be angry that he had interrupted his studies; now it was jealousy and another fear that kept her from calling. She thought that if the son came the father would die.

The eighteen-year-old acne-faced big tall hunched boy was a premed sophomore at a small co-ed college in upper New York State. He lived in his fraternity house, he drank beer, loved and admired his friends, and still made Dean's List every semester. He had little success with the girls, but threw himself with an awkward passion into intrafraternity football. His friends called him "the heap."

The doctor had written him weekly letters almost until now, and though the son had seen something in the handwriting, he was not prepared for what his younger brother Max, meeting him at the railroad station, playing Cohen—the one with the practical information, who lived easily in and with the world—told him. "Dad's dying." The big boy had then the bloated look on his face of shock and then of, What am I that I am told only now? of anger but of hurt, acne, and self-denigration.

"He's turned yellow," Max said.

"What the hell do you mean, he's turned yellow?" He had tears in his eyes and was raging.

"I mean he's turned yellow."

He was in that in-between state of adolescence and manhood. He wore a suit and tie, a tweed coat in the lapel of which you could see traces of tens of pinned-in buttons, buttons backing his college football team, announcing his fraternity, his political loyalties. So he went in, dressed like a man, prepared to see a yellow dying man, but saw the almost glowing birdlike face—he could not have weighed even eighty pounds!—and saw images behind, the father who had sat by the dining-room window reading the *New York Times*, and saw images behind, the father he had accompanied on his afternoon calls, the Chevy, the long wait in the car, and then the father coming out of the apartment building his black bag in hand, The Doctor.

He was almost a man and would not let the sobs rise.

"Lazarus," his father said.

"Yes, Dad."

"It's not easy."

"What did he say to you?" Max asked his brother in their room.

"He said, 'It's not easy.'"

Now the doctor's eyes never seemed to focus in. His breathing became pained. All day and all night long one heard his pained breathing everywhere in the small apartment. Sometimes he breathed as if he were suffocating, sometimes his head was thrown back as if he were being choked. The sharp deep inhalation like a moan, the quick expiration, and then the next sharp deep moaning inhalation. At the dining-room table tea was served, and one listened and almost counted, and one waited.

In some deep place in her, Eshka, seeing the terrible changes in him, the lessening of him, the pain, the isolation, wished him dead. Why go on? Why suffer more? Aie! If she could only let herself go, if she could only cry out her pain and bitterness. She would be alone. She *was* alone. She had always been alone!

Still, if he had called her then, she would have forgiven everything. But he never called. He breathed in in that deep inhalation that was blind to everything, that was so concentrated only on empty air, as if even as he had shrunken into the thing in the bed, the world and everyone had shrunken into the well of air at his open mouth.

She lay in her bed, the night-lamp between their beds on, and he was breathing like that, the sharp deep moaning, and she could not sleep. She sat up, and his head was thrown back and to a side, and his eyelids were open and in his yellow face there was only the whites of his eyes. This was not her husband! This was not the doctor! She stood and raised and spread her arms as if in imprecation, and then swooped him up, bedcovers and all, into her arms, the childlike weight of him, and then was rocking him in her arms, moaning, "Ooooh, ooooh, ooooh." His breathing eased, and she was weeping as if he had spoken with her, and she wrapped him to her. But before morning he began to choke again.

And her world was splitting in her head, and now she had no thoughts but sat with her hands clasped to her head.

3

His brothers had told Jack that the doctor was not well, but that his illness was not serious. And after his second operation, Edith drove Jack in their Buick to Fleischman's "in the mountains," where Ben had made reservations for them. And that they should not be too lonely, Jack's nephew Sam and Sam's wife Margo spent a week at the same hotel.

The women wearing fur coats and hats, snow pants and boots, the men wearing ski shoes, winter caps with earmuffs, Jack wearing his town overcoat, Sam a mackinaw, the foursome went walking before lunch when the sun was almost melting warm on the snowplowed driveway of the hotel. Jack held Edith's arm that she not slip, and Margo said she was falling, and so the four of them held arms and Margo made a game of not falling, and they laughed. But Jack wanted to walk more, and so another day he and Sam left earlier and alone. The snow under their feet was packed hard. From time to time a car passed going to or coming from the hotel, or the post-man's old car, the snow-chained tires rattling pleasantly. In the dis-tance were gentle rolling white hills, and here and there, off the road in the deep fields of snow, was a farmhouse or a large red barn. Sam thought it a joke that he, twenty years Jack's junior, and Jack now recovering from major surgery, was always the one to suggest they turn back.

A sportscoat and tie was dress enough for dinner, though Friday and Saturday nights one made an effort. After dinner, Jack and Sam might play pinochle. They played a nickel a point, and though nickels still meant something to Jack, that was no money at all to Sam.

Jack had taught Sam to be a cutter and since that time, for twenty years, had worked almost elbow to elbow with him, both wearing dusters, standing on raised wooden boards that made standing eas-ier on their feet, at the long high cutters' table at the bank of tenth-floor windows. If one nephew were closer to him than all the others, it was Sam, and when Sam had had a son, Jack had felt even the joy of having a grandson. Yet, he sometimes felt in this so discreet and gentle nephew a different density, a different blood from his own.

He did not understand Margo; she was too frank for him. She wore enormous rings, bracelets, diamonds and gold, she wore lip-stick, eyeshadow, false eyelashes. She was big, heavy, she had a slight tense hunch, and she walked about as if always alert to grab for something. She said, "Jonathan goes to Hollywood, and we go to Fleischman's! Ha! ha! ha!"

Jack spoke little even to Sam, though now and then on their walks he might say, noting something, a word or two, and in his mind Sam would translate. Once Jack looked up at the telephone line and said, "Even the telephone," and Sam nodded. Yes, there is electricity and even the telephone, there are snowplows. What a remarkable and fine country this is! Sam smiled tenderly at the quiet of his uncle and gave up on the deeper resonances.

Jack suggested one evening that Sam find a gin rummy game, that he would watch. There were many gin players here, family men who did not play poker but who went so far as to play Hollywood gin rummy, which tripled the stakes.

One evening Sam lost $100, and the following day Margo seemed happy as if her husband had done something large. Sam told Jack, Ach! he would stop playing cards, but even he seemed half-pleased with himself.

After Margo and Sam's return to the city, Jack and Edith went for long walks, and Jack was sometimes delighted to have forgotten Edith's presence at his side and then to discover her there quietly with him.

He did not know what he wanted, he wanted to sweat. One afternoon they walked so far that returning they were caught by the sunset, and they quickened their pace, and the heat of their pace chilled them, and now they were like children hurrying home, only they felt silly arriving at the brightly lit hotel, the guests already at tables playing gin rummy, and glimpsing themselves in an entry mirror, there was something silly even in their appearance, Edith in her seal coat and babushka and he in his earmuffed cap and city coat.

They drove north, snow-chains on, at twenty miles per hour, stopping overnight at village hotels. At Lake George they stopped in biting cold to watch gaily dressed ice skaters; they saw solitary men way out on the ice, huddled on crates, fishing through the ice. They drove through rolling hills and small quiet villages straddling a river, the road ran parallel to the frozen river. They drove across wooden covered bridges and were in Vermont, in rolling hills at the foot of bigger hills, spotted with big red barns and orchards of old apple trees and low stone walls separating fields.

They rented a house at the edge of a village. There was water, electricity, and heat, and though the house had not been heated that winter until then, there was a big stone fireplace. And when they had been out shopping or walking and returned at quick-falling sunset, they were returning to the making of a fire and to the making of dinner, to the quiet taking of dinner before the fire.

So there was the fire, and Jack had to prepare dry newspaper, kindling wood, and then branches and thicker limbs. And one sat in front of the fire after dinner and watched the flames and embers, grew sleepy watching them, and felt the heat at your head and the drafts coming from behind, Jack's city overcoat over his shoulders and Edith with her seal coat.

In the middle of the night, Jack got up, put on his shoes and overcoat, and went outside to pee, and stood, the night cold and still, looking at the stars. It seemed to him that the stars were in their place, each of thousands of stars in its place in the clear dark sky. And another night when he saw the Milky Way, the flow of stars, and when he saw a shooting star, and then another, he thought still of things in place, everything moving, flowing, even burning out in its place.

Often he went tramping alone through the snow in the bare-treed forests. He saw a fox one day and both stopped, a hundred feet apart.

He told Edith he would cut wood.

She said, "You're still convalescing."

He said, "I'll work slowly."

He bought a bucksaw and an ax. The ax was a small thing in his hands, against his overcoated body. The handle was of hardwood, was curved well and polished, the iron hammerhead and blade was wedged tightly in. He had used axes whose handles' polish and smoothness had been worked out by the up and down gliding of generations of hands. No matter. This ax felt good in his hands.

He found his place to cut wood, not far from the road—where he could leave the Buick—a fallen oak tree, trunk, limbs, and branches. This hard wood would burn slowly. He sawed branches and began to load the trunk of the Buick. He had no need to use his ax, but when he had a trunkload of wood he went to a long limb a foot across and spit on his hands, which were smooth and tender, and began to cut, and it was as if forty years had not passed. What he had learned doing came back to him doing. Now, with these strokes, he began to sweat, and his breathing grew deeper, and he paced breathing to stroke, to what had to be done to the wood. He cut from over his right shoulder and over his left, the ax biting deeply, at the angle he wanted, into the hard wood. And heat pulsed into him from his hands, as if with each impact of blade, wood, and hands, into his arms, across his shoulders, through his body. And when he had to stop for faintness and he leaned his body on his ax, he was surprised that all was stillness, that the echo of his strokes was not ringing in the air.

Edith bought apples that were just beginning to wrinkle and were savorous. She bought fresh eggs, good cheese. Her hands, too, grew red and cracked. They visited historic places. These country villages gave one an appetite for history. This village church was as it had been then, and these white board houses, and these stone walls, and the fields, river, and hills. Edith read every bronze marker with the eyes of a school child discovering her heritage. He had a city hat with him, and when they went history-visiting, he brushed his coat and wore that hat.

They would buy a cottage, a house, land, something here.

He called Ben from the general store.

Why isn't Ben happy that I am happy?

"What is it?"

"Ach, Jack! The doctor, he is in coma. He is passing away."

And suddenly the roar and clamor of the city was all about him. It rang in his ears, his hands were fists. The Buick! The Buick!

He walked on these empty shoveled-clear narrow sidewalks as if ready to ram his way through crowds. And already questions were forming. I have been lied to. They lied to me about the doctor, who did not lie to me.

4

The man is in coma, and he is no longer he whom we knew. And yet, though he cannot be aware of our presence, we gather about him as if it were he and as if our presence about him now were meaningful. We come to console her who will be the widow, and the children. And we come that others will not leave us to die alone. We sit with him as he takes leave of us.

Ben sat through the night in the straight armchair between the dining-room table and the window where the doctor would sit whole mornings and afternoons reading his newspapers. The apartment was inadequately heated during the night, and Ben sat in his jacket and tall wide-brimmed hat.

The bathroom light was left on, the door left ajar, the light reflecting dimly in the dining room in the long mirror, on the glass surface of the table. In the boys' room, Larry and Max slept in one twin bed and Jack lay fully clothed on the other. The doctor's brother Dan slept on a folding bed. David was in the armchair across from Ben, he slept lightly, restlessly, almost as if alert.

Eshka was in the doctor's room, probably lying sleepless on her bed, the night-table lamp between beds on. The sound of the doctor's pained breathing filled the apartment.

Ben might doze and, waking, see one of the boys, in pajamas, standing a moment in the doorway. Or Eshka might come out of the bedroom and sit a while at the dining-room table, her head in her hands.

Ben remembered the night watch here and in the apartment next door for his mother. Then all the Cohen brothers had been here through all the nights. And Eshka and Leah had relayed each other at Mother Cohen's side. There was something darker about this death. This rotten disease! And Eshka, aie!—this death was eating her alive.

He thought, This is an honest man, this is a fine man. But how shall I put it? For all his good deeds, for all his merit, he has always lacked something. You could never say of him that he was a simple man or that he was good-natured. His life was too full of pain! We buried our mother and then we talked and talked, and we almost sang, our memories were so strong and good. But this man gnaws at us.

If you took him to dinner, you could always sense he was thinking it wrong to spend so much money for food. Not, doctor, only for food, but to be served, to eat in a fine place, and that it makes me feel good to eat with my family and friends, and better yet when I am host, and best of all when I can wave a waiter over and offer you exactly the best!

He is, yes, too proud a man, the doctor. This Katz pride that made him think Katzes better than Cohens, so that even having chosen one, he broke the engagement and kept it broken almost a year! A tall man's pride, though he was little! What a complicated man. He was, yes, like a judge.

He himself had in his pocket five addresses of doctors and cancer clinics that he had collected as insurance for his brother Jack. Well, maybe two or three were frauds. But how could you be sure without trying? The doctor thought all chiropractors charlatans, he thought any doctor a Cohen would go to a charlatan. A month ago he had taken his courage into his hands and stood at the foot of the doctor's bed and begun to suggest that the doctor be seen by another specialist, a scientist, than the ones he had seen. The doctor had had his spitting cup in hand, and had spit, and had said curtly, "You stick to your business and I'll stick to mine." The doctor had no hope; that was it: All hope in him had long ago busted.

In the small narrow kitchen, Ben lit the gas and put water on for tea. He sat, wide-brimmed hat on, at the small kitchen table. He saw the street, for here no one had bothered to pull the shade and he had not switched on the light, the streetlights unevenly lighting the cobblestoned street, glinting off the trolley rails, storefronts across the street.

He emptied his pockets onto the table—there was light enough, the gas on low, hissing—the ring of ten keys, the penknife, the pens and mechanical pencils, the alligator wallet stuffed with bills and cards (every pocket of his stuffed, though the broad heavily shoulder-padded suit he wore, cut loosely, hung smoothly on his big body). The slit-open envelopes with statements, receipts, checks still folded inside, calculations, addresses, phone numbers noted on the envelopes. Every key represented a host of responsibilities. He had put on his horn-rimmed reading glasses and was squinting at a number. Whose number was this? He sat in the dark adding up checks received, remembering them customer by customer, writing down sums—the real sum and not the tax-declared sum. Every week he had to meet a $12,000 payroll.

What had he forgotten? What was the problem?

Dora said Elaine should have tutors. She said, "She's fat! fat! fat!"

"I," he said smiling large, "am fat, fat, fat."

Yesterday David had taken several hundred dollars from the safe. Who kept count of his debts anymore? He drove a cream-colored Packard convertible. Who needed such a car? Why had he gotten married, why had he had children, if he couldn't stay home?

I arranged that Jack should have a month's holiday, but I feel it in my bones that he blames me for that!

And what is this story? The doctor, Emma says, will be buried in her burial plot. As if we wanted to fight to have him buried in our plot. He has asked her to be buried next to his brother Irving, and Irving was buried in Emma's plot. What a family! Didn't they ever think they would die? The doctor's brother Harry is buried in our plot, and Irving with the Nissnievitches. What an idea, one brother here, another there. So Joe comes to me with Emma's message and says, "I'll pay my share, he's to be buried next to his brother Irving in the Nelson plot." As if that's all one has to do, pay one's share! As if there weren't questions to be asked, thoughts to be thought. One day—had Joe thought of this?—Leah, God grant her long life, would be buried at Harry's side in the Cohen plot, but Eshka, God grant her long life, would be buried with the doctor in the Nelson plot, and those sisters who had lived their lives like twins, who had married brothers, would be cut forever from one another!

And so there would be the sons, half-orphans! Larry would return to college, he was a smart boy. But medical school was something else again—it cost $1,000 a year just to attend, and then there was the expense of setting up an office, and these were poor boys. Though a doctor as a son-in-law—Elaine was only his first cousin —would not be a bad thing. As for Max, still in high school, he would help his mother in the liquor store and then, if he showed himself as smart and able as he seemed, he would have a future in that business or another. Ah, there would be businesses and businesses for a smart fellow!

Aie! The water was boiling. While the tea bag steeped, he pushed his hat further back on his head, he felt better, surer.

Jonathan was hedging. Yes, that was the problem, that was what was bothering him.

For $20,000, Cohen Brothers Furs would have an option on 50-percent ownership of all the luxury stores in the Las Vegas Eden Hotel: furs, jewelry, leather goods, perfumes. Jonathan, they had decided, would go out there and, with Artie Luria, their fifty-fifty partner, set things up. But now, every time Ben mentioned Las Vegas, Jonathan put him off. Ben knew what it was, the *prince* wanted to go deeper into ships. But how could they invest in Vegas *and* in the ships? The $20,000 was only for the option! They would have to spend $50,000 before they would see even a penny coming in. Jonathan had always thought he was better than them all, he had always looked down on the fur business!

Dan, wearing his overcoat over his pajamas, entered the kitchen. He did not speak English; they spoke Yiddish.

He had come to America the first time five years before, he having lived in Occupied France with false papers, working here, hiding there. Who would ever forget the reunion! At La Guardia, a hundred of us there, and all the delays, and the doctor a sick frail man, and then the younger brother entering the hall, and a silence over us all, and a way opening up through us so that the two men, brothers who had not seen each other in twenty-five years, were suddenly facing each other. Magic! Magic! Ah, there was magic in their lives. About Dan would always be the glow of magic!

He was small like his brother. But this was a good-natured fellow, you could see it in his face. He was an engineer, but had worked as a salesman and had become a businessman, was manager of a copper and aluminum works that employed twenty men.

Ben poured the water out of the pot for him, put new water in and put that back on the gas.

Their knees touched.

Dan's pajama pants were attached by a string, old-fashioned. He would give him something of America before he left, an electric razor.

They were about the same age, they had memories in common of Berezin.

David leaned into the kitchen and said, "It's five, I'm going home." As if the hour were his reason, that now that five o'clock was passed the doctor would live another day. And indeed, though the doctor was breathing as before, something had changed, the mood, as if the hold of night had eased.

Outside there was almost simultaneously the roar of the Packard motor and the squeal of the tires, and the cream-colored car flashed into their line of vision, U-turned wildly, and was gone.

"Ach!" Ben said, shaking his head with one intention. And Dan shook his head with another.

"He was the first to find us, you know. In Paris. We had nothing. We were thin as nails. We lived on the fifth floor, and one evening after dinner I started taking the garbage down and I saw this American climbing up, and he had a duffel bag over one shoulder and was dragging another with his other hand. I didn't recognize him— how could I? He was a child when I last saw him.

"He said in Yiddish, '*Nu vos?* You can't give me a hand?' And I still didn't know who he was. I took one bag, and it was very heavy, and I dragged it up after him.

"He said, 'I bring you also regards from the doctor!' I think that was important to him, he put everything under the sign of my brother as if he were nothing but a messenger. Even to, when opening those two wonderful duffel bags, complimenting himself 'for the doctor's sake' on the well-balanced diet he had provided, piling cans and stuff on this table and then that chair: powered milk and eggs, Spam *and* cigarettes; chocolate, salmon, *and* nylon stockings, sugar, flour, *and* Nescafé. How good was your Nescafé! Though, it's true, when he took us out the following night, he brought Tanya an *armful* of flowers and said, 'This is from me!' "

"I didn't know," Ben said softly. "You know," Ben confided, "we made him come back from Germany. He really wanted to stay! But since he's back, nothing has gone well. His business is not good at all."

"He's too large," Dan said. Ben nodded, that was true, but it was more than that.

It was dawn, and Leah was crossing the cobblestoned street. She was short and heavy and wore a heavy seal coat. She wore eyeglasses. But you could tell she had been a pretty girl. Also there was pride and purpose in the way she walked: No one had called her, the doctor had lived another night, she would prepare breakfast for everyone, cook perhaps for those who would be at the apartment for lunch, help her sister with whatever had to be done in the dying man's room, and then subway downtown in the rush-hour crush to open the liquor store. Ben could tell that it pleased Dan too to, unobserved, watch her crossing the street.

This next night no doubt was to be the end.

His breathing was like cries of pain, all that was left of him focused only on the air at his mouth. The shrunken yellow body. The whites of his eyes only.

He was become so little like us, some of us began, even as he continued to breathe, to think of afterwards. Already Max felt he was become more a man that his father was dying. What new step forward was waiting for him at his father's death?

"It's not easy," his father had said to Larry.

Yes, but I am strong, Max thought.

Sam, the doctor's palsied brother-in-law, sat quietly in an arm-chair, tears sometimes at his eyes, and listened to the doctor's every breath, and Jack stood restlessly here or there in the apartment in pain and anger all this time, and if a nephew or cousin spoke a little too loud he glared or hissed him into silence.

Jonathan too, though he wanted to avoid Ben, had things to do, was no doubt in the middle of taking the most important and daring step of his life, came early to the East Bronx and sat listening to the doctor's every breath, breathing with him.

So this night there were many there, breathing with him, as if a call had gone out. There were, as well as his wife and sons, his brother Dan, his sister-in-law Leah, his brothers-in-law Ben, Jack, Sam, and Sol, his nephews David, Jonathan, Sam, and Louis; Joe's son boxer-shouldered Marty, sat on. The wives were home, waiting. Leah's daughter Anna, in her ninth month of pregnancy, lay sleepless on her bed in Brooklyn looking at the telephone. The doctor had saved her pregnancy. Had he ever thought of her child during his sickness? Such a thought, she felt, would be a blessing.

It was 1:00 A.M., and Marty still had not been able to get up and drive home. And suddenly there was a change in the doctor's breathing. Some of the men seated at the big dining-room table stood. Jack said, "The boys."

Young Sam stepped into their bedroom and said, "Come, boys." They had not undressed; they were groggy, puffy.

Dan went to the doctor's bedroom. The boys followed. And then Leah, Jack, and Ben. And then all the others, standing in the small hallway outside the doorway in a tight group.

The doctor's inhalation was a cry without end.

Eshka held his hand and looked at him; his eyes were only whites. And then he stopped, and she held her breath, and there was a terrible silence, and he was gone.

Ben thought it would have been appropriate that the doctor's friend, the wall-eyed Zionist, Lipshutz, say a few words at the funeral service, but a year before Lipshutz had become unwell and had settled in Israel. The fur market synagogue rabbi, who had not known the doctor, would have to do.

In the crowd in the funeral home suite in which the doctor's open coffin lay, Bill, Emma's tall American-born husband, whispered his feelings of loss to this young man or the other, and then told a joke or two. The doctor's face was filled out and powdered white, the eyes were closed. His thin silver hair was neatly parted and combed to a side, as he had combed his hair. But though the features and intervals of his face were as they had been before his sickness, this face was as far from the face of the well man as from the yellow face of the dying man. Yet, in the line of mourners who approached the coffin and stood a moment at its head as if at his bedside, many wept. Eshka had chosen that he be buried in one of his everyday suits.

The fur market synagogue rabbi, a small man who wanted to please the Cohens, begged a minute of Eshka's time. He would, he said, make the eulogy. She said, "You will make no speech!"

Ben, who was watching, caught the rabbi's eye and gestured him aside: "You'll ask for a minute of silence."

"The family Katz-Cohen," the rabbi, standing on the raised platform in the chapel, looking down then at the dark polished now-closed coffin, said after some prayers, "requests a minute of silence and prayer for the departed soul of Doctor Saul Katz."

Things were already so returning to normal that some family members arrived only during the minute of silence, and Anna's husband Fred, who had been a lawyer and was a furrier, who had in his way honored the doctor, said bitterly after the minute, "That was a furrier's minute of forty-five seconds."

Ben stood under the funeral home awning directing mourners into limousines and cars. There were pushy types who wanted to get into the cars of important mourners. One had to be large and firm. He glimpsed the little vegetable-store landsman Karp making his way through the crowd to tall acne-faced Larry. What is he going to ask him for? he thought. And he stopped listening to his then-petitioner to see what Karp wanted, and he saw the little man put his hard stubby hand on the college boy's shoulder, and saw the college boy's embarrassment, and he heard Karp say, "Ach, doctor!"

The sauerkraut-making neighbor, fat Mrs. Kreindel, turned and her eyes glistening said, "Lazarus is the doctor!"

All about the boy, his face bursting with red and acne, neighbors and former patients of the doctor, and doctor friends of the doctor, were looking at him and smiling and touching him and nodding their heads. And Ben felt a cold fear passing by him, and a surge of relief as if he had, by this, been saved some terrible mistake.

When they arrived back in the East Bronx after the funeral there was a basin of water on the doorstep outside the apartment, and they washed their hands before entering, and on the dining-room table were fruits, cakes, and cookies, and the rooms had been aired, and everyone wanted to put aside the past. Herman Friedland, backed by smiling Friedland brothers, approached Ben and said, "So, partner?"

"Ah," Ben said, "are we partners now?"

"What is this?" Herman said, quickly sensing trouble.

But Ben was not concerned with reassuring Herman, and thinking, So Jonathan is already raising money, so he is already doing what he would do and not what we even decided to do, said, "Just a moment, please." And he began to make his way toward Jonathan. Jack stood in his path, and this was too much, and he said, "You've looked at me enough. Come."

So the three of them left the dead man's apartment and drove in silence downtown to their business. The place was closed for the funeral except for Pearl, the secretary, and Gus, the shipping department "boy," there to answer the phone and receive deliveries. Louis and Sam arrived almost at their heels, and Ben, leafing through the mail, understood they had followed them to back Jonathan, but no matter, he would bring them all to their senses.

Do you know what's wrong with you? he would say, pointing at Jonathan. But Jack, who had not been back to the place since his operation, walked through the office and storage vault to the factory all empty and gloomy, and they trailed after, and Jack was at his place at the cutters' table and Ben was near a large nailers' table, and Jack turned and, pointing his two fingers at Ben across the raised bank of operators' sewing machines, Jonathan, Sam, and Louis behind Ben, warned, his words echoing in the large empty place, "No more of your lies!"

Sam, who had come to step between Ben and Jonathan, stepped back now as if to leave, but squat Louis held him by the arm.

Ben removed his eyeglasses. "What lies?" Ben asked.

"Why didn't you tell me he was dying?"

"Brother, you were recovering from an operation."

"I was *ice skating* while he who saved my life was dying! I was on *holiday* while my sister was in pain!"

"Brother, I was thinking of *your* health."

"Big shot!" Jack said like a curse. "I spit on your lies!"

"What lies?"

"You were thinking of Las Vegas!"

"What about Las Vegas?" Ben demanded, and now he too was angry for Las Vegas was for everyone, was for Eshka and Leah and for the orphans.

"He was dying, and you lied to me, and you were making plans to go into business with snakes!"

"Who is a snake? Is Artie Luria, whose father was our friend, who has been like a son to me, a snake?"

"To whom are you giving twenty thousand dollars?"

"Is that all? I've given money to New York State judges that we should have a liquor license for Eshka. I've given money to union men that our workers should not go out on strike. I've given money to policemen and hoodlums. Am I worse for it? And where have you been until now?"

"To whom are you giving twenty thousand dollars?"

"To the owners of the hotel!"

"They are snakes and bloodsuckers!"

"They are the owners of the hotel!"

And there they fell silent, the time clock ticking.

Jack was pale. He did not want to go on. This was his dearest brother, these his nephews-like-sons, this was his place. He said softly, "Ben, you do as you like, but I cannot go with you."

Ben knew that Jonathan was not at fault for Jack's anger, yet he blamed him. Had he and his nephews been as one, they would have already drawn Jack back into the fold. But they were fighting among themselves.

Jack moved as if to leave. Ben said, "Wait, please, I'm not finished." He turned to Jonathan and said, "So?"

"I want to buy another ship."

Louis moved from the shadows closer to Jonathan.

"I know that. There is no fault in that! I know what you want! But what have you *done*?"

"I'm raising money."

"You're raising money *behind my back*! You're raising money from the Friedlands. Did you ask Jack if you could ask his brothers-in-law for money? Did you ask us if that is what *we* want? Jonathan, all of us, we chose Las Vegas!"

"Big shots!" Jack spat out.

"Do you have other *partners*?"

"I've spoken to others."

"We were a family," Ben said.

"Do you know what's wrong with you?" Ben asked Jonathan, who took every blow open-eyed without complacency. "You've never in all your life made something with your hands. You're a smart boy, you've always been a smart boy, but you've never made anything with your hands. You never worked in the factory. You're not interested in making things, but in making *it*. Me, I'm a whole man. I sell what I make, and what I make I make from A to Z. I buy the skins. I select and bargain for the best. I handle them, fur side up and then skin side up. Do they have to be treated again? It's me who decides. And then I match them. And I tell you, I don't match when I'm not in shape. I have to see like an artist to do good matching, and I wait until the light is right, and then me here and Moskowitz there we match, and our hands fly over the skins, and our decisions are good. I know the skins before I know the coat. And when the customer comes in, I show her the models that'll go good on her, and I show her the skins that'll go good on her in the models I've chosen for her. And I know who she is, I know what her husband does, and she tells me about her children, and I'm interested. So we fit her. So now, in the factory, we stretch the skins, we pull them this way and that, and then, as they're pulled tight, we nail them out until they're stretched dry. Now we treat them again. Now they go to the cutters' table, and the slices the cutters make are sewn together at the operators' machines, and then skin is sewn to skin. And during this time Marie has been cutting patterns. And now we lay out the back, and now the front, and now the collar. So now the customer comes back and she tries on the coat, and we make the alterations if they're necessary, and we choose the lining and the buttons. And I tell you, I know the skins, and I know the woman, and I know the labor. It's my labor that has gone into each coat. It's my thought, imagination, decisions, and worries.

"But you, you're only a broker. Only a broker! Now that means something, that means something deep! And I'm not boasting, though I could! When I sell a coat it's not like when you sell a coat, no, not even if you get more money for it. When I sell something I've made, and I get a good price, it's a healthy feeling I have, it's like breathing in fresh air. When I take money into my hands for a coat I've made that is a good coat, and I've gotten a good price, and the coat goes good on the customer, I'm a happy and whole man. And it's not the money that makes me happy and whole. It's that I've made something good and am being paid good for it.

"Jack, I know what you think. We've stood together there at the cutters' table so many years I know the words passing through your mind. I hear them. You think I haven't heard you now saying to me, 'Ben, the doctor, *he* lived a meaningful life. The doctor, *he* never thought of profit.' And I say, Amen! Only, my life too is meaningful! And the big difference is that I enjoy life, and I enjoy making, and I enjoy profit! Is that wrong? Is it wrong to enjoy making things and selling them and being paid for them? And having an appetite? And wanting to live?

"Jack, we built this business together, you and me here in the factory, and me in the showroom. We worked twelve hours a day every day six days a week, and sometimes we worked Sundays too, and once union hoodlums tried to beat us up because we were working a Sunday, and we sent them running. Back to back. Didn't we? We did. And in that time there were hard times and harder times. And once, you'll remember, I traveled through America with trunks full of coats trying to raise money. Aie, I was alone in strange cities, in hotel rooms in strange cities, with those trunks, and in some cities I knew no one and went from fur business to fur business, from stranger to stranger, and people could be hard, as they are, but I tell you here and there I was received like a man. Here and there were kind people. And more than once they took me home with them saying, 'What is a Jew to do alone in a strange city?' And they took me into their homes, and served me *first* at their table, and asked me about my wife and children, and were good to me. And we became friends.

"I am loyal to my friends! And when I give my word it is for good! As for the other, the blood loyalty, it is *holy*. When have I ever hurt a brother or sister? Are you not, Sam, my partner? Jonathan, are you not a partner? What have I not done for you? Louis, we brought you out of the dark! This factory, when I die, will it go to my son? He will be like you, a partner! Aie! I have gas on my heart! We are not uncles and nephews, we are closer than brothers, we are all twins. We are so close you would have to kill one of us to tear us apart!"

Louis whispered to Jonathan, "Whatever you decide."

Jonathan told them to send Pearl and Gus home, he would close up the place, he wanted to think.

Outside it was getting dark, it would be cold.

In the East Bronx, Cohens, Katzes, Friedlands, Starobinetzes, Nissnievitches would gather for the evening prayers. Jonathan had not known his parents, he had known only Katzes and Cohens, he had only and always known rooms full of them. He had known Sundays in that apartment in the East Bronx, with the big glass-covered dining-room table, and the fruits and cakes on it, over one's own photograph, and the pinochle players at one end, and maybe Eshka kneeling on a chair, leaning over the table, reading someone's fortune with cards.

Dan Weber, the furrier's son, had raised $50,000. Sam Gold, the scrap dealer, would buy in for $25,000. The Friedlands had agreed to put up $35,000. He had arranged a bank mortgage of $100,000 on the family's 51-percent interest in their Liberty ship. With that money in hand he could borrow an equal amount from another bank and buy a second Liberty ship.

He wanted to speak to his wife. He had made it a rule never to speak to her about his business worries. He called her. She was preparing to return to the East Bronx. His voice echoed lonely in the large empty place, and her voice was far.

"Darling?" she said softly.

He said he would see her shortly.

Not even Louis, the only one in the family he had been able to count on for a man's help, could help him now.

Las Vegas could be, even as Ben thought, a gold mine. He could swim in that world as in this. What he had done, he could undo.

He saw himself arriving in the East Bronx apartment, saw himself nodding at his Uncle Ben that everything was all right.

He closed the place door by door; he gave the protection agency signal.

He drove toward the East River Drive, but then did not enter it. He drove south on the dark river street to the pier on Nineteenth Street where the Liberty ship he had been negotiating to buy was tied up.

He sat in his car, the motor and heater on, looking up at the hulk of this unloading almost empty ship tall as a six-story building. It was night now and worklights were strung out all over the ship, some parts of it more in shadows than others.

He lit a cigarette.

The ship was long as two city blocks. It looked hollow and old. Still, it could pick up 10,000 tons of what you had to sell and take it at ten miles an hour 5,000 miles to market. It could carry coal, wheat, or ore. It could carry general cargo crates. With its booms it could do its own loading and unloading. It had a thirty-five-man crew, a radio operator to keep it in touch during its two-week or month-long voyages.

He cut the car engine and on the pier stepped his cigarette out. He climbed the almost ladder-steep gangway; his hands would be filthy, his topcoat. The captain was ashore, the night mate shrugged him past.

The ship's building did not interest him. He had seen the cramped crew quarters, roaches in the captain's cabin. Nor did the almost still engines interest him. He walked on the sometimes oil-slicked main deck, stepping around coiled ropes and steel cable. The booms were raised for unloading, the deep holds were open. The bulwarks were rusting. One had to chip and paint every day of every voyage just to keep up with the rust.

Between open holds the sailors had stacked the wooden lids that covered the holds. When the ship was loaded, the wooden lids were laid into metal frames, and then a tarpaulin was pulled tight over it, and that was roped down and then shot tighter yet by blunt wooden wedges. The booms were lowered into their locks and the ship was low and neat for the sea.

You sent a ship out to sea with thirty-five men and a cargo of 10,000 tons, and you sent that ship to Antwerp and from there to Marseilles to maybe pick up another cargo and go from there through the Suez Canal to India, and from there to Japan, and from Japan, with new cargo, across the Pacific and back to America.

5

The season had changed, it was full spring, and Sundays Ben, Sol, and their families went house-shopping on the Island, stopping to visit nephews and nieces already settled in outposts even as far as Massapequa and Manhasset. Anna and her husband Fred were buying in Woodmere, Louis had bought in Lawrence, Marty in Great Neck, Marty's sister and her husband in Saddle Rock. David had bought in Amityville, five minutes from his sister Sara. Her husband had obtained through Cohen contacts an Oldsmobile agency in Freeport, and everyone but Joe—whose rank, no one would argue, even demanded Cadillac—bought Oldsmobile. They were powerful cars and were so sprung and cushioned, were, even coupe and convertible, that long, that there was a feeling about them of ships. The interiors were roomy and comfortable and had so many little decorations, conveniences, and controls they were like living rooms. The driver had only to steer and keep his foot on the gas.

In these living rooms, Ben and Sol sailed the Island, north to south, east and west, looking for houses, for these two brothers would live together even if Jack had chosen not to. In a morning they looked at two developments, in the afternoon another two. The wives had not graduated from walk-up apartment buildings to buildings with elevators to now buy a house with stairs. Not for them two-story houses or split-levels where you never knew what floor you were on. It would be ranch or nothing!

"So what do you think?" Ben would ask of Leah and Eshka when they went visiting houses with them.

One day, Dora said to Ben, "What's wrong with you? You're showing them things they can't have."

Ben's face clouded and he replied, "Ach, you think my sisters are like yours! You think my sisters could be envious. It's you who are wrong!"

But afterwards he made a point of making the lunch stop something different and special each time. A restaurant with a view of the sea. Seafood! And he made sure that Eshka's boy, Max, had everything he wanted, two desserts if he wanted—and the boy was inventive, ordering one dessert combined with another—for he was, it was true, half an orphan, and he was going most mornings and evenings to synagogue to say the mourner's prayer for his father.

And so they sailed. Until one Sunday they found their dream ranch house, a harbor in Far Rockaway of twenty houses, brick and wooden shingle and picture windows. Then everyone had to come and give his opinion. One said there should be three bathrooms and not two. Or at least two and a half. Another said Ben should arrange a den or playroom in the basement, but Ben had seen that a den was an added option to the house and he consulted with Sol and the real estate agent, and because they were two they got their dens for 15 percent less.

Three bedrooms, two baths, a big living room with dining area. A

big kitchen. A den, a garage. Front and back lawns. Aie! the pleasure of wall-to-wall built-in closets and sliding closet doors!

Far Rockaway was fifty minutes to downtown, but only fifteen
from their brother Sam in Rockaway, five from their nephew Louis
in Lawrence, ten from Anna in Woodmere. The Amityville nephews
and nieces were half an hour away. Eshka and Leah would maybe
take an apartment together out here. It would be like the Bronx,
only bigger, and in cars, and with trees, and the ocean little more
than a walk away. Yes, the ocean! Louis had become a fisherman.
He spent Sundays on the ocean and Sunday evenings came visiting
with a string of fish. The aunts did not say anything, but it was
fifteen years since they had had to clean their own fish. Louis
bought a twenty-foot boat and joined a yacht club. The best people
of Lawrence and Cedarhurst belonged there. His friends were businessmen and doctors, but these were good-looking young doctors,
they had been officers in the navy, air force, and army, they invested
their money, they were as friendly and confident as businessmen.

What a pleasure for Ben to walk on *his* property, *his* land. To, in
his pajamas, go out at night when no one was up, for the back
windows of his neighbors' homes were only 100 feet away, and pee
on his land. Once, in the night, peeing, he heard on the other side of
the bushes his brother laughing softly. "Are you there, too?" Ben
asked, smiling.

"Yes," Sol said, but continued to laugh.

"So? So we're peeing together. What's so funny?" he asked, he too
beginning to laugh.

"I'm peeing on your bushes!"

"Son of a bitch!" Ben said, and it was a joke he told and retold.

There was a time when the homeowner thought he was typical.
And his brother Sol was typical in his way, and Sol's fat cigarette-
smoking card-playing wife Fanny was typical, and his own thin
worried Dora was typical. And not only typical, they were funny.
"If we were to write up these stories that have happened to us and
send them to Jackie Gleason, he'd pay us a fortune. Listen, when Sol
can't sleep at night, he gets up and puts on his bathrobe and his
shoes without socks and goes for a walk. One night, he gets lost. Aie!
He's lost in Far Rockaway in the middle of the night in his pajamas

and bathrobe, and he can't find among all the streets and houses his street and house, and a patrol car pulls him up, and he's mumbling to himself, 'For this I spent a fortune! For this I moved out of the Bronx!'

"And he's a little deaf, and they keep saying, 'Okay, mister, where do you live?' And Sol gets angry repeating, 'Don't you speaka the English, I'm lost, I tell you!' "

"That's an Italian accent, Uncle Ben."

"So? So in the middle of the night, there's a call from the police station, and Fanny sleepwalks to the phone, and the policeman says, 'Mrs. Cohen, there's a man here who says he's your husband.' 'Whata you talking?' she says."

"Come on, Uncle Ben, that never happened."

"And I'm Jackie Gleason next door. And we all go down to the jail, and it ends up everyone taking coffee around the sergeant's desk.

"We could do episodes of Sol and me deciding to do all the plumbing and home repairs. Or when we decide to go bowling like everyone else. And Fanny and Dora getting worried and not believing we were at the bowling. And Louis'd be a character, he'd be crazy Louis!"

Ben would come home at night and eat fast, and open his belt and the top buttons of his pants while filling up, and holding his pants up with one hand, his *Jewish Daily Forward* in the other, go into the wood-panelled den to his big leather recliner, lever it into position, mount it, lie there then stomach up, legs stretched out and spread, and watch his favorites. "It's all about us!"

"Are you watching?" he would phone from his recliner to any number of nephews and nieces. The weekly program "Marty" got him in the heart. Aie, Marty, when you go out on a blind date, I love you.

And one day the Cohens realized they were rich, at least on paper they were rich. Three months after Jonathan bought a second Liberty, the Korean War began and overnight ships doubled in value. Within a year, Jonathan headed corporations that owned or operated six ships. The Cohens spoke then of tonnage, charters, government contracts. The world was suddenly smaller than it had been, or they were larger. Ben himself was carrying on the Las Vegas venture; he was often in telephone touch with Artie, who shuttled from Beverly Hills to Vegas to supervise everything.

"Pink mink?"

"First we'll open the fur salon in Las Vegas with it! And then you in New York and me in Beverly Hills, we'll open the following season with it! It'll be in all the papers! Benjy, it'll be worth a fortune just in publicity! Pink mink stoles, pink mink capes, pink mink jackets, and big pink mink flowing coats for movie stars and royalty!"

"Not over the phone," Ben said, for though everything Artie said made him smile with confidence and hope, he knew that such a decision had to be weighed carefully.

Artie took him at his word and the following day was in New York, and like boys they stayed in town for dinner, and Artie showed Ben samples of the mutation, and they began to plan and estimate dollars and cents, and there was a chance it would be big, and it looked good, it looked good.

6

Eshka had once, reading a fortune, seen such dark news and had herself been so dark and brooding that someone had said of her, "The Queen of Spades."

She woke alone in the bedroom she had shared twenty-six years with *him*. She woke in the middle of the night thinking the telephone on the night-table between their beds was ringing.

Larry was away at college.

Every day after school, Max came to the store to do deliveries and help out.

"Yes ma'am," the well-dressed man said, having shown her his card. "It's the barber's boxer brother, little Sally, who got his brains busted in the other night, and now he's lying in a coma in the hospital of the Holy Cross, and the family's not got the money, and so I'm taking the time from my business to make a little neighborly collect."

"Of course," she said, opening the cash register. But the following day, her salesman told her there was no barber in the neighborhood with a boxer brother.

She had clients who owed her one and two hundred dollars, and after you had gone three times to collect and each time they made you wait and each time they lied to you in such a way that not calling them liar you felt somehow their accomplice, they offered you some money now and the rest later. But they were smoking their cigars now, they were selling coats now, and she had been made to wait on a straight chair in the office for they did not want her in the showroom.

"They are smart alecks!" Ben said with disgust. But her sums were too small for him to make enemies over.

She sat knitting in the store all cramped over herself. Leah too knit, and sometimes one sat behind the desk and the other at its side, knitting.

She passed a delivery entrance and saw two men beating up another. She did not know what to do. Were they union men? Were they hoodlums? "Stop it!" she commanded, approaching. And then she saw they were beating up Gus of Ben's shipping department. "Hoodlums!" she screamed. She was carrying a small umbrella in hand and a big purse, and she lowered her head and went in swinging with both. She broke her umbrella, but the hoodlums were running, and Gus was looking at her from a bloodied smiling astonished face.

Ben spread his arms to give her a medal-winner's embrace, but then said she should not again risk her skin for a gambler. "He welches," Ben said, and Eshka did not understand. "He doesn't pay his debts."

"Ah," she said, "he's a smart aleck."

She and Max were invited to dine with this brother and that nephew in so many expensive restaurants she thought there was a whole other New York City she had never had an idea of before. Jonathan's mother-in-law was Eshka's age, but was slender, well-dressed, she wore the same gold charm bracelet as her daughter. Eshka liked to be served, but wanted to joke with the waiter. She was ill at ease for her clothes, her manner, her weight. She knew that behind the waiter was a busboy, and behind the chef were assistant chefs and dishwashers, and even if they were Negro or Puerto Rican and even if there was nothing wrong with hard work, *something* was wrong. She joked to Jonathan, he forcing a smile, the mother-in-law affecting not to hear, "The food is delicious, but it only gives me gas."

Larry called her one Saturday night from the city. He had come in with college friends. No, they were driving back early in the morning, he had called only to say hello.

"I see," she said.

Her niece Margo invited her and Max to dinner one night. They went to her Riverside Drive apartment, and the doorman rang to ask if they could be allowed in, and Margo and Sam were out. "We'll wait," she said. They waited outside the lobby and for a while in the street, and then she said to Max, "Maybe I confused the dates." Margo called the following day to apologize, but it was no good, they had forgotten her.

Everyone thought her moving to an apartment in Far Rockaway with Leah a good idea. But Ben also had projects to get Leah re-married, and Eshka sometimes wanted that, that she who had never leaned on her would stop counting on her.

It was evening, and there was such a crowd outside and inside the second-floor funeral home suite that there was hardly room to move. All of the Katz-Cohen allied families were there, even the most distant cousins, for this was Emma's daughter, Cynthia, and she had committed suicide. The family of Cynthia's husband was small and proud and kept its distance as if they had been offended against; Cynthia's child, of course, was not there.

"What can it mean, such a beautiful girl?" small Sol Cohen, his thick lips turned down at the ends, asked. And as his interlocutor nodded sadly to his question, he added, "So well off, too!"

So soon, Eshka thought, come back here. Only this time at a distance, almost a spectator. Mourners who the last time dared only to bend to me on the sofa and kiss me and look at me and murmur maybe a few words, this time hold me by the arm and stay with me. Larry, I say, is Dean's List, and Max, Max is here.

She wore a black-feathered hat and the black dress she had worn here the last time. She stood with Leah. Was Leah thinking of Harry's funeral seven years before? It is all repetition, she thought.

Where is Max? Among the nephews, they buy him suits.

Joe and Lily were passing. He could not turn his neck, he saw only what was directly before him. It was so fitting an ailment his wife had to smooth the edges about him, giving soft smiles to those who might be offended that he did not say hello. She lived in his shadow, from time to time she made him face where he ought.

"Let me alone!" he would say.

"Your sisters," Lily said.

"Ach, Eshka!" he exclaimed and held her in his arms. "What," he asked, "am I to say to Emma?" Emma was his client. He was like a big boy. "Eshka," he said, as if he were suffering, "I can't bear these funerals."

She said, "Let Lily say for you." And she kissed him on the cheek as if, she realized, forgiving him.

What am I forgiving him for that he has not done? What is happening to my sight? She saw things darkly.

She saw her nephews in a group. Marty, I forgive you. That you came to me in the liquor store one lunch hour and across the counter whispered to me that you would put both Larry and Max through school. But you others are with greyhounds now, and you are princes now.

"Ach, Sam," she said, holding onto the arm of this quiet brother who always wore dark clothes, his face red for the networks of tiny capillaries even at his skin, the little hair he had black and silver and slicked back with water. His hands shook, he stuttered. He stood quietly with his sisters. Mima, his wife, approached. She was stouter than Eshka and Leah, was corseted and girdled hard, and was a little short of breath. She was a busybody so ready to help you could not hold it against her.

She said, "You can't tell a thing, they've dressed her in a high collar."

The father of the suicide, Bill, was so tall he was head and shoulders above the crowd. A vain handsome man, he was pale and preserving his dignity. She realized she felt nothing for him, no pity or guilt that she felt no pity.

"Come," she said to Leah and Sam. They began to make their way through the mourners to Emma, receiving here almost as if in her apartment, but Emma turned then to her and Eshka saw in her the young mother of twenty years before whose father had committed suicide, saw the proud woman in pearls whose husband was nothing, saw the woman whose only child had now hung herself, and she saw in her large eyes, the raised black veil, the parted unlipsticked cupid lips, that she longed to throw her arms about her, that she longed to weep, and then felt a stiffening in her that she would not. She, like Emma, went through the motions, embracing her, thinking her oneness was behind her with her sister and her shuffling brother, and then turned as if to leave the room, but was faced with the coffin.

It lay on an altar in a glowing, flower-surrounded alcove.

She stood, her sister and brother behind her, on a line of cousins that moved ahead a person at a time, the person at the head of the line at the head of the coffin, the raised head-lid lined with crushed satin. Then there had been her husband, false, false, except for the suit. To see him made up like that! But here, now, there was in her a growing fascination, and her hand slid along the body of the perfectly smooth and polished dark coffin, she already seeing without seeing the long-haired fierce girl, the scornful lips, the closed waiting eyes, the fascination of the covered burns at her neck, seeing darkly then, approaching a heavy veiled woman on a sofa again, the woman turning, Emma, but something terrible about her, she was hat and veil and body and no limbs, and Eshka was staring even then at the face of the suicide, and her hands flew to her eyes.

Then she was being supported by Jack and Ben, and that too was already seen, and her legs could hardly hold her up, but she was deep in fascination, everything darkening still, everything fitting into place. Emma stared wide-eyed at her, everyone was looking at her. Not repetition but rehearsal. It had all been rehearsal, and now it was her moment to cross the stage. Where is Max? And there was fascination there too that she desired him at her side and desired too that he not be there. Again fierce pain ripped through her body and her black eyes glowed.

7

What do we know of our bodies? Ben thought, his own immersed up to the neck in Elaine's bathtub, the pink-tiled and pink-carpeted bathroom filled with steam, steam filming the mirrors, condensing and dripping on the mirrors and tiles, the water's heat no longer prickling his skin, and his body relaxing entirely, the hard-worked arches of his feet, the fine calves, the strong thighs, the fat belly, and *tzitzkas* like a woman's, or almost, the shoulders that he always kept straight.

It was the morning of the day before Rosh Hashona. This evening the new year celebrations would begin, ushering in ten days of prayer, of mourning the dead, of taking stock of the year, of what had been done and what was to be done. It was a period for reflection, renewal, and resolutions. And he thought this long hot bath a sort of preparation for that, a sort of purification by sweat. The thing was to keep the hot water running, the steam rising.

In the house there were phone calls, there were perhaps visits, he heard almost not at all. And no one dared disturb him. His mind was free of *now*. The night before, at his place of business, he had emptied all his pockets of all papers and bills, of slit-open envelopes, notes, phone numbers. He had arrived home and put his keys and cash away in a drawer; this day he would not even drive. He said to Dora, "Princess, these are holy days and days of prayer, and I want peace and calm in my house."

Ben believed.

He addressed God every Friday night and Saturday morning at synagogue. When he was troubled or worried, he prayed; when something good happened, he remembered to thank God. He believed God took all his prayers into account, but that once a year, at Yom Kippur, ten days hence, God listened and watched in another way. That was the day of atonement and pardon, the great fast day of truth.

He read Hebrew with ease though he had no dictionary and knew the meaning of words only in the context of prayer. Sometimes a word came to his mind whose meaning he could not remember. Sometimes it would be only a syllable, the first sound of a forgotten or undiscovered word. And he would caress the word or sound as if to coax the meaning from it. Long ago he had learned that each letter in Hebrew had a numerical significance, words and names were also combinations of numbers, and two different words might be numerically equal and that would mean something. He had long ago heard that God's real name was hidden and that one who knew the name would be like David before the armies of the Philistines.

There were times he thought he was on the verge of knowing the hidden name, and he was sometimes convinced that one day that would be given him for already there were sounds in his mind secret only from his tongue, and once when he had felt close he had had a vision of a red desert.

He increased the flow of hot water and lay back.

What do we know of our bodies? What do we know of our insides?—and yet we live and die of them! What do we know of the cause of disease? What do we know of resistance to disease? Where is the seat of resistance? Sweat! Sweat!

Eshka was undergoing tests, what would they show? Why did she not accept my invitation to spend the holy days here? Why does she refuse me? Why does she stay in the stinking Bronx in that small dark apartment with those chairs and that table, and the mirrors, and every furnishing, which contain still that man's death, which exude it like contagion! It is the apartment, I know it, and it is the stinking subway and that store!

What do we know of our bodies? What do we know of our juices and intestines? We know that in some people the spring of life is busted! And who can explain that? And how do you repair that? He felt the powerful beating of his heart. What do we know of our bodies?

He thought his was half woman's. He thought he would pee like a woman, leaning forward. He felt the rumbling of gas in his big belly and thought, I spoil my body as a brother spoils a sister, and it occurred to him that he was brother and sister. He felt himself soft and melting in the steam, and he thought that he loved with all his heart and body as a mother loves, and he found himself in the posture of giving birth. Aie! Unnatural! Unnatural! He leaned forward to make the hot water pour.

Sweat! Sweat! Sweat out a year's dust and worries! Sweat out the debts people won't pay, the aggravation of lies!

I'd have myself beaten with birch branches! Aie! I'd sweat off the fat, too! I'd sweat off the mother fat! I am too fat! How can you fight when you are so fat!

In the afternoon, his nephew David came by with his older boy. David never went to synagogue and his boys, of a Christian mother, would they even be bar mitzvahed? David drank all the time as if he had no business to go to, no home. He spread darkness about him, but no one would dare face him but Jack, and Jack did not understand. The darkness was part of David, just as was his heart. "I want to speak to you," he said to David, and they walked outside on the lanelike sidewalk that had only recently been finished. The red-faced limping nephew was fifteen years his junior, but his presence was dense and he was now tight-lipped, and Ben felt suddenly they were walking on a tightrope and they could fall. And he knew: He comes to me even that I do not speak to him of his business that he is destroying by neglect and gesture—he would buy for $10,000 when all he needed he could buy for $1000—of his debts—he would lay down $20,000 for 50 and then forget the missing 30—nor of his wife, who drinks now as much as he, who sleeps through the day and does not bother to dress, nor of the children, of what would happen to them. As if Ben had not to speak but only to know. "David," he said, for there was nothing else he could say and surely this would be a good thing, "why don't you come to synagogue with me this evening. And you'll bring your boy."

But though David did not say no, he began an hour later to speak of the zoo, the Bronx Zoo, he would show the animals to his son, and they were even then gone, in the Packard, in a roar.

Louis came by with his friend Dr. Jerry Maxwell. "Come on, Benjy," Dr. Jerry said, "you know very well why I'm here. We can never catch you except on a holy day."

They went into Ben's bedroom, and he took Ben's blood pressure and a sample of his blood and urine, and Ben told him he peed frequently, and Dr. Jerry looked at that and shook his head in mock seriousness and said, "Join the club, Benjy! It's the prostate. One of these days you might have it taken care of. I'll tell you one thing, when you do you'll feel like a new man."

The large Inwood synagogue was crowded that evening with well-dressed men who wore town hats and their own prayer shawls. They were men who had succeeded in business and moved out of the city. Some, like Ben and Sol, had been born overseas. They were home-owners and modern, and yet they had not forgotten how to pray. Their synagogue was not as orthodox as the synagogues they had been members of in the Bronx and Brooklyn, nor was it reformed like those on Fifth Avenue or in Lawrence, where Jews did not even wear hats and prayed in English. Here they prayed like their fathers, but now and then made concessions to the times. The rabbi, a man Ben's age, spoke, like them, English with some Yiddish and, now and then, to make a point, used a Hebrew word of great meaning.

This evening, at the end of the service, the rabbi gave a sermon to direct the thoughts of his congregation during this holy period. He said Abraham, the father of our people, was Love, Isaac was Justice, and Jacob was Truth. They are ONE, and that, the rabbi said, is our Star of David.

"We go through life behind the *Shield* of David and like the superimposed triangles of the shield, Love and Justice become one with and are the Truth. But we are men of the world, and sometimes we fail Love or we fail Justice, and sometimes we misread the Truth. And so we come to God every year, ten days from now, at Yom Kippur, to acknowledge our guilt and make amends."

Ben, listening, thought of David, and the idea of the Shield of David struck him forcefully. There was such a reverse to it, it could even be true! No matter, he sensed now that David, not just the nephew but his very troubles, was tied to them even by one of those knots full of mystery that God himself made.

8

She was dressed, her suitcase was packed. She was early, she boiled water for tea. She wondered if she would ever see this her kitchen again. The oven, the broiler below, the four gas rings. All these years of cooking in this kitchen, spaghetti and salmon croquettes for the boys. The cakes, five thousand cakes. The whole apartment would smell of cake, and the boys would be in the doorway like flies about sugar.

He liked broiled lambchops.

The dumbwaiter that was no longer used for the garbage, the refrigerator opposite, where the icebox had been, so that half the time I still call the refrigerator the icebox. The Passover dishes.

I sit at the dining-room table, I look across the room at the long inclined mirror over the buffet.

What did we know of money? A doctor earned one dollar a house call and then two, and made more money than a garageman or a vegetable-store man, though not that much more, but *more* because his work was more important.

A man who does not pay his debts has no respect for men. If money is nothing, then what people do to be paid for is nothing. And if what we do is nothing, then we are nothing.

The doctor came in from his office for lunch every day, and the boys came home from P.S. 48 down the street.

Summers, when mother was well, we went to the country. Fridays were special, all day, even when we got up in the morning, because we knew *he* was coming in the evening. There would be Saturday together, and on Sunday we would already be different, knowing he was returning to the city in the evening.

His heart broke, and that was all the staircases he had climbed and all the times he had answered calls in the middle of the night. But it was not his heart that killed him, it was money. For the money coming in was not his, and he could not even hope to pay it back.

He saw Larry go off to college, and then he let go. The other boy is mine. What will happen to him? That he is black-haired like me? That he is Cohen and grasping? That he feels. That he feels and feels and feels.

Where shall I die?

She heard a car stop outside.

"Do you want some tea?"

"No," Jack said, but they sat down. Edith wore a brown bellboy hat, her old mink coat. She sat leaning forward, her hands clasped before her on the glass of the table.

They heard the roar of the trolley outside.

Jack put her suitcase in the trunk of the Buick; Edith wanted her to get in the front, and she did. They drove down cobblestoned Hunts Point Avenue. At Bruckner Boulevard they turned left, and now the road was smooth. She felt Jack's hands tight on the wheel as if on her shoulders. She smiled. She said, "Jacob, you want to kidnap me to the country."

They had taken a private room for her at Mount Sinai Hospital, and the window gave on the park, on the Central Park West skyline.

She had walked with Anna on the sidewalk seven stories below so short a time before.

Jack waited outside.

Edith opened the package she had brought for her. It was a sky blue nylon nightgown.

"It's beautiful," Eshka said, holding it up. Then she began to cry, and Edith, who was a reserved woman, was crying and held her, and they sat down on the bed.

Jack knocked on the door.

"Just a minute."

When Edith let him in, Eshka was sitting up in the bed wearing the new nightgown, smiling hard.

The boy was seventeen. He adventured on his bicycle through colored neighborhoods. From his high school downtown, he was drawn to skid row, where disfigured drunks staggered and begged in the shadows and roar of the Third Avenue El. He read a lot, he went to the movies, he masturbated. His father once said in quiet anger to him that he would be a businessman like the Cohens, and the boy felt as if his father had given up on him. He wrote his first long story, "The Resurrected Christ," in which a bum was Christ. He was asked to read the story aloud in his English class, and his teacher and classmates were moved. He wrote about the dying and death of his father, his spitting, his growing yellow. The summer after the death of his father, he decided to hitch his way south, to see chain gangs and suffering. Jonathan shook his hand as if going off alone were a manly thing.

Now he went from Hunts Point Avenue to high school every morning in the rush hour. In the afternoon, he worked at the liquor store. In the evening, he visited his mother at the hospital and then, almost every evening, went out to dinner with family.

With Sam and Margo he went to the Viennese Lantern. There you are Wiener schnitzel and cream-filled pastry while listening to costumed gypsy violinists. Margo was loud, she jangled her jewelry. At their home, their four-year-old boy stole the change Max left in his overcoat.

With David and his tall wife, he went to the Russian Tea Room, where you ate caviar or smoked sturgeon, shashlik, blini, where you drank "vwodka." Louis and his wife sometimes accompanied them, and sometimes Sam and Margo, but Jonathan rarely went out with David, for when they were together David would almost certainly make a scene at his expense. He needed no excuse to make a scene, his limp was the beginning of a scene. He attacked the American-born cousins at table or not at table for being American-born. He attacked the college-educated ones. He mimicked their accents, their wives' accents. Louis mimicked his accent mimicking theirs. Everyone laughed, uneasily.

Max had to be up before dawn.

He lived alone in the three-room apartment.

What must I not forget? Every day there was something not to forget, some errand to do here or downtown for his mother. He received his mother's salary and sent money to Larry at school. He wrote his brother, two years older than him, "Like they say, money doesn't grow on trees, ha! ha! ha!"

With Ben and Sol, he went to the Peachtree. Others came along, they were a party of ten, twelve.

"What can you know?" Ben said to Max whenever Max entered a conversation that Ben thought did not concern him. "What can you know of unions? What can you know of Communists?"

"Murderers!" Louis exclaimed.

"What can you know of hardship?"

Ben's son, Marvin, in the army stationed in Italy, had sent his father a case of Italian mineral water. In every restaurant Ben went, he wanted to drink only mineral water.

"Sean O'Casey," Marty said to Max, "you should read him." Tone-deaf, the boxer-shouldered cousin intoned in what he did not even think was an Irish accent: "Innnishhhfaaalennn Faaare Thee Waaal."

Intoned in the noise of family at table, of different conversations, and "What are you going to eat?", his own competence proven only by how fast he decided, how well, that he ate with pleasure and dispatch, as if it were thought that no boy who could eat with such pleasure and dispatch could be all bad.

At the Blue Angel with Jonathan and Sheila, he met Bob Henderson. "Young fellow, I'll give you a start." In that smoke-filled, crowded, noisy, dimly-lit, velvet-lined antechamber.

"Who," Jonathan asked Max another time, "is a man in the family?" Max considered. Joe was the richest. "Uncle Joe."

"Close."

"Uncle Ben?"

"There are only two real men in the family: Louis and me. What makes a man?" he asked and left Max with the question as if one day in the future he would quiz him again.

With Jonathan and Sheila he went to the best restaurants and the most exciting nightclubs. Wherever they went, people came over to their table to say hello.

"Call for you, Mister Cohen," a waiter said and plugged a telephone into a wall socket. It was a radiogram from a ship at sea: "Storm here, can we change course to proceed to————?"

Jonathan dictated his reply: "Proceed at own discretion."

You are here eating your dinner, and 5,000 miles away a ship at sea is in trouble and the captain radios to you.

"My reply covers me before the insurance company," Jonathan said. "But it means proceed to original destination."

"I want to work on a ship this summer."

"Yes," Jonathan said smiling, understanding even the nuances, "that's good."

There was the first of the three operations. He sat at her side in the dark seventh-floor room, the winter sunset behind the Central Park West skyline, she tied and tubed to her bed, and her pained breathing, and the face pinched, and the black hair spread and dry, and he scared, scared, scared, all those lumps under the bedcovers you don't understand, and the eyes shut not like someone sleeping but like someone about to fall, and you not knowing what to do, only, Be a Man! How? What? Anger doesn't help. You cursed God for your father, but you never believed. Act as if it doesn't scare you! You make notes! Ben and Jack join you; you stand, but Jack puts his hand on your shoulder as if to say, That's all right. And the three of you stand, one at the foot of the bed, one at a side, one at the window, and your closeness is silent, watching over her every breath, until it is late and the nurse tells you you must leave.

They are all waiting in the lobby, the uncles and aunts, the cousins, and everyone makes much of you if only by his regard. How is she? And then you are walking in their midst down Madison Avenue, and you are suddenly aware of the biting cold wind, and you are shivering, and you enter the Peachtree blinking—the white tablecloths, the muffled sounds of diners finishing their meals, glassware, silverware, the warmth. Which is real? She is still there, as she was, pinched face and pained breathing and black hair spread and dry, but you are already feeling warmer. She is tied to her bed by tubes. Can both places be real? What are you going to eat?

In the summer he sailed as an ordinary seaman on a Liberty carrying 10,000 tons of coal. The carpenter's father was an able-bodied, his brother was an ordinary. They were saving to buy a farm. The carpenter was big, slow, quiet, and very strong, and when the boatswain was drunk and insulting one time too many they fought, and the carpenter hugged the tall lean slugging boatswain to him and swung him over the side of the ship and banged him back to him, only against the bulkhead between, smashing ribs, until the chief mate came down from the bridge pistol in hand.

In Antwerp, the drunken red Indian able-bodied bought a Polaroid camera that jammed half the time. Max drank too much, and his girl was forty years old and fat, and in the hotel room there were *three* single beds pushed together, and he was lying waiting on one, and she came crawling across to him, her breasts enormous, swinging, the nipples the size of half-dollars like his mother's.

He arrived in New York the day after they had put his mother back together again and closed her up, her second operation. It was too early to visit her, and he had $500 he had earned in his pocket, and he went to the fur market, where everyone made much of him, and then was anxious to get uptown to see his mother for freshman week had already begun at Columbia, where he had been accepted.

9

"Beautiful!" Dr. Reisman said when he came down from surgery.

"What does that mean?" Ben asked the potbellied fleshy-faced sick man. Reisman smiled at the profane.

Dr. Konstam, who had come late, said, "Nothing is changed. These next months will show."

But one was pompous and impotent and none of the Cohens had ever liked him, and the other was a little Jewish doctor from the Bronx who had an accent thick enough to butter your bread with. And Joe had his doctor. And Louis had his doctor friends. And Ben had addresses in his pocket.

It was at that time that Jonathan sold the Cohen interest in their original ship for three times what they had paid and that one morning Ben, Jack, and Joe each received in the mail a certified bank check for $90,000, Sol for half that, and Sam for half that again.

Ben kept his check in his pocket all week. This is America! It was like those TV quiz programs where people won $10- and $20,000 in an evening, everyone cheering. "This is America!" Ben said, showing the check to nephews and nieces. "Look! Do you see?"

"Dora," he asked, "do you see? Now do you believe?"

He showed the check to Eshka in her hospital bed as if the check were a sign for her too.

Herman Friedland spoke to his sister Edith, and Edith said to Jack, "My brothers invested all their savings, why don't they get checks?"

"Did I ask them to invest?"

"Is it fair that the Cohens get rich and my brothers get nothing?"

"This was not their ship."

"Where are their ships? They too have sons and daughters!"

"Enough!" he said, and she shut up.

Jack was tired of complaints, involvements. He had so little pleasure from his family. He worried for Ben's daughter Elaine. Why didn't Ben take charge there? She was a good girl, but so fat she never went out. She was nineteen years old and went shopping and to the movies with her mother, or sat at home in Far Rockaway with her mother. What kind of father was he? The girl was unhappy! Sol's children were bright enough, send them *away* to college! The boy went every morning to Brooklyn to study to be a rabbi, and Sol was not against it, for that way he would not be drafted as a soldier and in the afternoon he could give him a hand in his place of business. "Be men!" Jack wanted to say. Sol would only smile and shrug. And besides, who had been a man? Had Joe been a man thirty years before when he had gone into business for himself, leaving Sam in the street? It was nothing to be a man one day out of three, but to be a man every day, everywhere!

This apartment was too small. Couldn't Edith see that? The bedroom and this living room with its carpeting and sofa and too-soft chairs and too-expensive lamps. Couldn't Edith see that her brothers would get along without her, and Hadassah, and the Bronx, because how could he tell her that she must give it all up. Yet he would. When they were away on their land in Vermont and he thought of returning to this apartment, to the subway to work, to his place at the cutters' table, he became short of breath. I suffocate here.

"Why so far?" Ben had asked. "Aren't there any farms in New Jersey or in New York State?"

"I like that place."

"How are we to visit you?"

"You will come to see me or you will not."

"Of course we'll come to see you."

"To see *me*," Jack said.

"What are you talking? Who shall we go to see if not you? But you better have two bathrooms!"

Two bathrooms! What do I need? I need a roof. I need food. I need heat. I shall have a garden, I shall have chickens. I shall cut wood. I need *that*, and I must get out, and *that* equals my health.

But Edith.

But Eshka.

It was a four-hour flight to O'Hare. Jack and Edith had driven to Far Rockaway, where Eshka was staying in Ben's house. Fanny had driven them off to Idlewild, Dora and Elaine standing on the sidewalk, the ranch homes, the gray morning, the slender bare young trees, tears in fat Elaine's eyes, she, like her mother, still in nightgown and robe, hunched over herself, hugging herself.

It was the first time Eshka had flown. She sat by the window, Edith at the aisle, and during takeoff watched the ground flying by, dropping below, far below, the four motors roaring. But then they had to change seats, for Eshka did not feel well, and Edith accompanied her each time to the washroom.

By the time they arrived in their hotel rooms in Chicago, Eshka was having sharp pain. She was in a sweat, and she lay on a bed, her eyes half-closed. Jack called the clinic while Edith unpacked for Eshka. The doctor, Jack was told, could not change Mrs. Katz's appointment and did not see patients except at the clinic.

The hotel doctor read the letter Jack had with him from Dr. Konstam and, without examining Eshka, prepared to give her an injection of Demerol. Jack watched, the doctor bending, his sister in pain, her head turned away, Edith standing pale, the open valises, the hotel-room mirrors. He accompanied the doctor to the door, paid him, turned, and could see that the pain was already easing and something eased in him.

Eshka was asleep. Edith said she would go across the street to the Art Institute. She put on her turbanlike hat, her old mink coat. Jack stood with her at the door and put his arm across her shoulders and said, "Be careful."

When she returned, it was almost dark and Eshka was awake.

"What did you see?" Eshka asked.

Edith looked better for the air she had taken, the museum visit. "I saw El Grecos, Van Goghs, and such a beautiful Renoir."

Ben called and wanted to know everything, how was the flight, the rooms? Joe called. And David.

They had dinner in their rooms.

In the night, they left the door between rooms open. Eshka again had pain, and in their night clothes Jack and Edith circled her bed, and Edith put a damp cloth on her forehead and held her hand, and Jack again called the hotel doctor. Again the doctor gave her an injection of Demerol. Jack stepped into the corridor with him and asked him what he thought of the clinic.

The doctor was not wearing a tie, he was sleepy, and was about to answer angrily, but he remembered to look at his interlocutor's face, and he shrugged even as had Dr. Konstam—What do you want me to say?

After his operation, Jack had been sent to the hospital X-ray laboratories. Seeing others in night clothes like himself, or in plain hospital robes and pajamas, arriving from elevators and passage-ways, converging, some in wheelchairs, some walking slowly, hold-ing their bodies as if holding themselves in, walking close to the walls as if afraid of falling, Negroes too—and that was a surprise, though he knew there were charity wards in the hospital—he had felt the beginning of nausea he had thought he had passed beyond by surgery, and had been able to fight only by closing his mind to everyone else—that is not me, I shall live. But now, here in this clinic waiting room, he was with his sister—this is my sister. And only by looking, by being present, could he be present with her.

There were others here, pale, accompanying the sick. The sick were emaciated, their clothes were too big for them. One man was jaundiced bright yellow. She was looking at them and feeling her hollow sallow cheeks, her moving teeth.

I shall lose my hair and I shall lose my teeth.

One by one the sick were called and each, with each accompanying husband, wife, brother, sister, son, or mother, rose almost breathless with expectation. And they too, when it was Eshka's turn, hurried, Jack holding her by the arm, Edith following.

"Yes!" the thin little doctor said after he had looked through the X-rays they had brought, a glow almost in his eyes as he stared at Eshka. "Only you must believe. You have to believe I can cure you, and when you do believe it, then I shall cure you."

His treatment, he explained, was hormones and enzymes proven on monkeys. There would be three stages of treatment, and the first would require twice-daily visits. There would be pain, and during the periods of treatment she would not be allowed to relieve the pain.

"Do you understand? Do you want me to help?"

She raised her hands to the level of her breasts and opened them palms up.

"Say it!" he demanded.

"Yes!" she said. "Help me!"

He gave her her first injection.

Jack wandered quietly through the museum, he wore a suit with vest, his high shoes. He carried his topcoat folded over his crossed arms.

In the airplane she vomited at her seat.

Edith wanted to take her to the washroom, but Eshka was too weak and nauseous to move. Edith asked the stewardess for damp paper, and she cleaned where Eshka had soiled. Jack stood in the aisle with the stewardess as Edith, wearing her eyeglasses, her turbanlike hat pinned to her hair, bent and cleaned and passed them one by one the soiled papers, which they put into a plastic bag. She cleaned Eshka's dress without wetting it too much and then sat again at her side and moistened her hot forehead and lips.

Louis's friend Dr. Maxwell had influence at Idlewild, and he, Louis, and Ben were waiting in the evening cold at the foot of the airplane gangway, and a wheelchair and an attendant, for the stewardess had had a message sent ahead. They crossed the asphalt in a group, bending, asking, pointing, and at the terminal were met by Sol, David, and their wives. Eshka was wearing her brown caracul coat, a hat with a feather, and she had put on lipstick and powder, and she had little strength and she looked about and, though one of her boys was away at college and the other was everywhere every day and how was he to get from the Bronx to Idlewild, she asked, "Where are my sons?"

Ben led Jack by the arm out of hearing distance of Eshka and said, "The place in Texas, I have excellent reports." Jack stared at him. Ben firmly made himself clear: "We go on with Chicago, but just to make sure, we look into Dallas, Texas, too."

In Dallas too, at Hopper's Cancer Clinic, there were waiting rooms; there too were emaciated men and women, and now you noticed the dark about their eyes, the flesh about their eyes sunken and brown, their eyes glowing in their dying frames. Their cheeks were hollow, their gums were going rotten. A man was coughing into a handkerchief, and you thought, *It* attacks the throat and lungs too. You saw a man with stained bandages over lumps at his neck, and you thought, *It* attacks and suppurates anywhere on the skin. *It* attacks, you thought, sitting in the waiting room at Eshka's side, and Edith at the other, the innards and everything. In women, *It* begins with one breast. *It* attacks the very bones, *It* attacks the very blood of children. And you sat there in your high shoes and your suit and vest, and your hat and topcoat on your knees, and you had closed your eyes, but you saw men hobbling and crawling, converging on this place.

Here there was no burning-eyed doctor. Dr. Hopper was young,

good-looking, fair-haired, American through and through. He sold
them twelve quarts of stuff Eshka should take eight tablespoonfuls
of daily and gave them a diet for Eshka to follow and, shaking hands
on parting said, "Don't forget, absolutely no tomatoes!"

How could they say anything to Eshka about this clinic in Dallas
when she had to continue in Chicago?

In the airplane returning to Idlewild, Eshka rested and then
dozed, and that eased Jack, and when Eshka awoke, Edith asked,
"What were you dreaming of, dear? You were smiling."

"Was I?

"I was thinking of Ringling Brothers, Barnum and Bailey. You
know how that was? Mrs. Silver would put big display-window
posters in her grocery store, and they would give her complimentary
tickets. She has no children, and the tickets were, every year, for my
boys. So we would play hooky from school one weekday afternoon
—the tickets were never for weekends—and go down to Madison
Square Garden. The seats were way up, but that brought us closer
to the acrobats. They were our favorites, the men and women who
flew through the air 'with the greatest of ease.' And when it seemed
they would have to fall, were falling, and suddenly—you wouldn't
even see him coming—someone would swing in hanging upside
down and catch the falling one by the wrists!"

At home, Edith said she could not again go to Chicago. Jack
would not argue. These days Edith did not want to leave the apartment. "I'm cold," she said. "I'm always cold."

Leah had to be in the store. If Leah were to accompany Eshka as
she wanted to, who would watch over the salesman? Max went to
the store every day after school, but he would read or would joke
and talk with the salesman, and the salesman would tell him to
make deliveries, and Max could not change that without saying,
"Okay, I'm the boss. Okay, I take charge of the store."

A nurse was hired to make the trip to Chicago with them.

Again, for three days, Eshka was not allowed to take anything for
the pain. Jack would not leave her alone with the nurse. At night,
though the nurse slept in the bed twin to Eshka's, he brought his
bed close to the communicating door and left the door ajar.

He lay in his bed and thought that already everything was different. She suffered more, she moaned. Edith was not there, the stranger at Eshka's side made it worse.

In the airplane she was sick again. The nurse wanted the stewardess to clean. Jack said to the nurse, "Get out of my way!" He sponged the stuff up with paper. Eshka whispered almost into his ear, "I don't want a wheelchair, I want a stretcher! Let me be carried off! Let them meet me on a stretcher!"

So when they arrived, in the cold dark evening, there was an ambulance waiting, and surely Ben, Louis, and Louis's friend Dr. Maxwell knew it was for Eshka, but what, Jack wondered, is my brother-in-law Herman Friedland doing here, and why are they looking with such apprehension at *me*?

Ben pointed Louis to Eshka and, followed by Herman and the doctor, came up to Jack and said, "It's Edith, she's in the hospital."

Edith had had a stroke the day of Jack's return. She had reached for the kitchen wall-phone, but had only been able to remove it from the hook. A Friedland nephew trying to reach her had called the phone company and then gone to the Bronx and had himself let into her apartment. Jack was driven directly from the airport to the hospital.

Edith's face was pasty and bloated. He said, "I am here." Her left side was paralyzed, she could not speak, though she tried, and muscles about her mouth and in her neck grew taut and she dribbled at the mouth. She had passed her right hand through the protective bars of her bed, and she was slowly moving it. Jack realized she could see him only in a blur, that no one had thought of her eyeglasses.

He turned to Ben and Herman and his nephew Sam, who immediately stepped forward from the crowd of in-laws, brothers, nephews, and their wives at the walls of the room, and he was tapping his two fingers furiously into the palm of his hand as if to drive them through his hand, and he could not speak for the anger and bitterness in him.

"Eyeglasses!" he spat at them, and there was a commotion among the visitors, and Sam was already hurrying off, and Jack turned back to his wife and did not that evening recognize anyone else.

So now he sat at Edith's side on the fifth floor of Mount Sinai

Hospital, and Eshka, who the doctors said would have to be operated on a third time, was on the seventh.

He sat in his suit and vest, his high shoes. Her head was turned
toward him, and sometimes she just looked wide-eyed at him and
sometimes she seemed to forget his presence and would stare at the
fingers of her hand, would move them as if discovering them, as if
fascinated they could still move, terrified they would cease.

It grew toward evening, and the sun was setting behind the Central Park West skyline. A Friedland brother-in-law and his wife sat
with him, a dark quiet vigil, and the waiting brooding presence of
Eshka two floors above.

"It's an epidemic," Sol said to himself at the big Peachtree table.
"It's an epidemic," he repeated, and then shrugging said, "I have no
appetite."

"Eat!" Ben said and addressed by look his command to everyone
there, to Max, Leah, and Anna, to Dora and Fanny, to Jonathan,
Louis, Sam, and David, and their wives. "Eat!"

Emma went even to Ben's house in Far Rockaway to visit Eshka,
and she often went to visit her at Mount Sinai. She wore a black hat
with veil, a dark mink coat, a fine black dress, a pearl necklace, and
no lipstick.

Her son-in-law did not want his son, her only grandchild, to visit
her as often as he did, and then he did not want him to visit her at
all. "I am not doing this," he said to her on the telephone. "*She* did
it. She wiped us all out. I don't want my son to hear her name."

Twice she went out to her son-in-law's house when her son-in-law
would not be home and commanded her grandson's nurse to give
him to her for the afternoon. She received a court order forbidding
her to do so again.

"What do I care! Put me in jail!"

Her son-in-law hired a Negro guard, who refused to let her into
the house. She stood on the doorstep, her taxi waiting, the Negro
waiting impassive behind the chained door, and would have cursed
the house itself had her grandson not been somewhere inside.

She sat with Eshka and said as if she were speaking for them
both, "They are all bastards!"

She gave Eshka earrings, brooches, bracelets. When Eshka was not in pain she might try them on and look at herself in a mirror.

10

Ben could not put off leaving any longer. He should have been in Las Vegas days before. Almost a year they had been preparing for this opening, it was tomorrow night, Artie had been calling every day, it was not fair to put everything on his shoulders. Besides, he would be gone not even three days.

He stood combing his hair at his big dresser mirror in his bedroom. He had curly brown hair, it was not even beginning to thin. He had been going regularly to the Turkish, he had dieted off thirty pounds. His daughter Elaine, still in her nightgown and robe though it was noon, was watching him from just inside the doorway, hugging herself as if cold. He took several minutes to choose a tie—he had a hundred, and every one of them a beauty. He asked Elaine's approval of his choice.

"Papa," she blurted out, "you're so good-looking!"

"It's your turn next," he said. And her eyes grew bright.

But Dora whispered to him before he left, "Don't come back with any scabies!"

"Scabies?"

"You know what I mean!"

"What you say is dreck!" He spat out the word meaning shit, his stomach tightening that she should speak to him like that now.

His nephews Sam and Jonathan arrived from the city to accompany him to Idlewild. They had not brought their wives, they were even as serious as he: Edith was in coma, and Eshka the surgeon had opened and almost immediately closed.

Jonathan was a man. "Leave with a clear mind, Ben. I'll take over for you in the showroom and office. Sam'll run the factory."

Ben thought, he offered that for me. For us, for the family. For Jonathan had more than enough to keep him busy. His office alone had ten employees. He was one week in Japan and the next in Rotterdam or Bremerhaven.

They checked in Ben's airtight metal cases full of furs, a new leather suitcase. He carried the super pink mink coat long as a gown in plastic over his arm. They still had half an hour. Jonathan said, "I'll buy you a drink."

"Yes," Ben said, approving.

Jonathan raised his glass. "Health!" he proposed, and Ben and Sam at the dark airport bar drank with him, each of them thinking of Eshka and Edith and of Jack waiting. Then Jonathan raised his glass again and said equally firmly, "And success to you, Ben!"

Yes, Ben thought, releasing his seat belt, the airplane rising still, I am tired of people who don't believe, I'm tired of people who give up, of complainers, of people too fearful to do, to be. And it was like a sign that he was right in his impatience when the stewardess, bending across the empty seat at his side to take his order for his first-class complimentary drink, asked him, "Are you the famous Mister Cohen, the furrier?" For a second he thought he was.

"That's my brother, dearie."

He sat looking out his small window at the clear sky, the white clouds below, and from time to time and sometimes large views of it, the earth, America. Farmland, roads, highways, the smoke of cities. As a boy and young man he had loved nothing so much as riding horseback across fields. This was a hundred times more wonderful, so special, he understanding Louis then who flew, sailed, and drove fast. And he sensed before he realized the timelessness of flying West.

He thought of his son Marvin overseas in Italy doing his army service. He had flown to Israel on leave. He thought proudly of his son deciding on such a trip, the adventure of making it. He saw him in an airplane like this one, at a window like this one.

Jack had no children. Jonathan was entirely out of the business, Sam did not want to be a bigger partner than he was. The boy had had a college education, he would start his active life as heir to a flourishing business in New York, to an interest in a business in Las Vegas, to an important interest in the ships. His thoughts tangled pleasantly in images of himself and his son walking out briskly to lunch together, and doing things together, and a big green lawn.

He shrugged himself alert.

Immediately on arriving he would have to hang the coats out and still would need a presser. There would be tens of things to do when he arrived. Rehearsals with the models. They would need someone like Marie ready with a magical needle and thread. Yes, I should have thought of that already. Artie won't have. He's a good boy, but what does he know of making? He would have to call New York, Marie herself would have to be flown out!

The seat belt lights went on.

It was nine hours after he had left New York, and yet the sun was only now setting. Then he saw the desert. He had never before seen the desert, and it was undulating and red, dark in its hollows and deep red toward the sun, and he had that feeling of returning to the source that one has when one recognizes one's dreams.

At the foot of the gangway, photographers, models, and factotums were waiting with Artie.

"Benjy!" Artie shouted joyfully.

The discharging passengers gave him room ahead and behind.

"Ladies and gentlemen," Artie announced, "Ben Cohen, the father of pink mink!" Flashbulbs exploded, factotums applauded.

"Mister Cohen, what do you think of Las Vegas?"

"Beautiful! Beautiful!"

"A picture of him with the girls!" The models came smiling and posing about him.

There were limousines waiting, they had to hurry for a small reception Yaglin was giving for Ben, but Ben exclaimed, "The coats! The coats!"

"Goddamn!" Artie exclaimed. "The coats, go get the coats!" he demanded of a factotum.

"No sir," Ben said, "I'll go get them. I've taken them this far and I'll see them hung out in the vault."

So they all trooped in to check out the coats. And Artie took Ben aside as they waited and whispered, "You didn't forget your tuxedo?" Ben smiled and punched the big fellow on the arm.

Artie had taken a suite for them. He opened the bathroom door for him and Ben stood agape. It was big as a living room, all tile and marble, and there was an enclosed steam bath in the center.

"Who is Yaglin?" Ben asked.

"You've never heard of him? He's a sort of banker."

His wife was a countess. She spoke with a harsh accent. She was fifty years old, but dressed, moved, and looked like a star.

The showroom he thought too small, the private office too big. Who needed so big an office? To impress whom? One did one's selling in the showroom. Never mind. It was 7:00 A.M., and he was freshly shaven and wearing a clean white duster over his shirt and tie. He had sent one of Artie's "boys" for coffee, and he and the sleepy models sat at a showroom table sipping coffee-to-go.

"Of course," he said to a model named Georgia, "you, dearie, are from Georgia?"

"I'm from Brooklyn," she said, and they all laughed.

All morning Ben rehearsed the models. He wanted them to have the feel of the coats—in New York he had his models "rip" coats, tear down to the skins old coats for remodelling. He wanted them not to look natural in the coats, capes, jackets, stoles, but enhanced. Each of the models, like each of the coats, had a personality. There were, all together, fifty pieces, each had a personality. The super pink mink should tower over everyone, over even all the show, and so it would have to be Georgia for that, and, "Dearie, can't you get heels higher than that?"

"They'll spike the carpet, Mister Cohen!"

"Never mind the carpet!"

In the afternoon Marie arrived from New York like a plumber with his kit. She had even brought an iron. Ben kissed her and declared, "Where in the world is there another like you!" She was a small mousy girl, but she was quick to laugh, and she sat right down at a corner table and threaded her needle and was at work.

All day long, Artie kept coming in with people to introduce. *Women's Wear Daily* had sent their man from Los Angeles, *Harper's Bazaar* and *Vogue* had sharp women there. A Chicago furrier wanted the Chicago and Midwest option on their pink mink. Artie had arranged that starlets would come to the opening, and a movie star's agent had promised that *she* would be there.

Then it was five o'clock. There were red and pink roses on every table in the showroom, there was a white cloth–covered caterer's table in a corner, and guests were already arriving, the president and vice-presidents of this hotel corporation and the other, their factotums and guests, Artie's clients from the West Coast, reporters, agents and their starlets, and the movie star, flashbulbs exploding, and Ben and Artie entered from the private office and they were wearing pink tuxedos, and the girls came in almost running behind them, tall, and wearing pink mink capes that were like wings, and already people were applauding.

Pink champagne was served and would flow.

Artie told the story of the fabulous pink mink mutation, of the unbelievably careful selections that permitted its breeding. Then he introduced Ben, who introduced each fur piece, the model walking in as he had rehearsed with her, and he turned her around and raised and lowered the collar and pushed the coat further back on her shoulders and pointed out the most important characteristics of the piece.

But then he stopped the show and said, "Artie, I can't be natural wearing this thing. Marie!" She was standing ready in a corner, and she brought him a duster dyed pink, and he put that on over his tuxedo, and Artie guffawed at that. The last coat shown was the $25,000 super pink mink, and women in the audience ooohed as it flowed across the length of the showroom, and Georgia swung it around her like a cape, making it seem even twice as commodious as it was, and everyone applauded, and now the models came forward for applause, and then Artie and Ben, and then Ben took Marie from the corner and plucked her a rose and applauded her. The movie star came up to Ben and kissed him smack on the lips, and then the starlets, and everyone was coming up to congratulate them, and he recognized the countess, and he felt so at home here and such a gentleman that bowing to her he reached for her hand and kissed it as one should a countess's.

11

From the cemetery plot where Jack watched his wife's coffin lowered into the ground, he seeing as if through the heavy coffin lid Edith lying paralyzed still, one side of her mouth drooping still, her eyes staring helplessly at him, Jack went to stand, like stone, at Fred and Anna's two-door Ford, unable a while to fit himself into the car. They drove to Far Rockaway, where they would sit *shiva* in Ben's house—that arrangement not inconvenient to Edith's brothers the Friedlands, who lived comparatively close by in Brooklyn.

People were still arriving. Jack saw Eshka's boys Larry and Max talking with cousins in a corner of the crowded living room, every lamp lit, a painting of flowers above the sisters-in-law and nieces on the sofa, everyone talking, smoking. And he made his way across the room, the conversations stilling, and he whispered to Larry, for he was older, though loud enough for them all to hear, "What are you doing here?"

"We visited mom this morning," Larry replied.

"What are you doing here!"

For their mother was being treated in a nursing home in Brooklyn.

Every room of the house was filled with mourners, conversations in the bedrooms, the overflow next door in Sol's house. The close or older mourners sat on crates and folding chairs, the mirrors were covered. But there were snacks, and if one was really hungry there were cold chickens in the refrigerator, pounds of tongue and salami and loaves of sliced rye bread. Dora's retarded nephew Stanley sat at the end of the kitchen table flush to the wall reading a comic book. He wore thick eyeglasses and seemed studious. No one paid any attention to him, but each time someone sat down at the table to eat a sandwich or a piece of chicken he pressed himself to the wall.

The Inwood rabbi said consoling words to Jack, who wanted to understand, but there was too much noise, and though this man's face was good he had no patience, and he suddenly turned and walked off into Ben's bedroom.

Three nephews there ceased talking. At the door, one asked, "Should we turn off the lights, Uncle Jack?"

He had thrown the first handful of earth on Edith's coffin and had then, as he was supposed to, only like a blind man, led the mourners from the grave. Tony, the White Russian from Berezin who had swept out the place of business for twenty-five years until he had retired years before on Social Security, who had never learned to speak English and whose every speech began "sonofabitch," had pushed through mourners to him and had then stood lopsided looking up at him, shaving scratches, his tie not flush to his collar, gobbling his words, sonofabitch-gibberish, and Jack had said, "I'm sorry." "Mister Jack," he had said, and that had sounded like an appeal from far, but then he had been able to go on only with sonofabitch-gibberish. "I'm sorry," Jack had said. What did he want to tell me? Jack wondered now. What?

He should have carried the coffin, his shoulder under a corner of it, and his brothers and hers. He himself should have filled in her grave, his grief was imprisoned in his knotted hands.

Ben found him standing by the window in the unlit room.

"Buy me out," Jack said.

"What?"

"I want to be out of the business."

"What are you talking? You have nothing to do with Vegas."

"Not Vegas, not ships, Thirtieth Street."

"But that's what we made together!"

"Buy me out."

"No matter what you say, no matter what you do, you'll always be my partner there fifty-fifty."

The cold gray afternoon was dissolving into snow.

"Buy me out," Jack said.

12

The nursing home in Brooklyn was a barely remodeled four-story brownstone in what had been a fine residential area. Now some houses were boarded up, and Negroes were living in some, and Jews still in others. The nearest subway station was a ten-minute walk and was inside the Negro ghetto. Among the ten or so women in the home there were five women cancer patients. They were being treated by a team of medical doctors who had observed that women with cancer who became pregnant often had remissions of their disease. The doctors had consequently developed a line of cancer treatment based on hormonal changes experienced by pregnant women.

Eshka's room was on the ground floor, but there was a high stoop outside and the ground floor was considerably higher than the wide empty street. In the morning at eight-thirty, at lunchtime, and at three o'clock children passed by going to or coming from a public school not too far away.

Now and then she, seated in an armchair by the nearly floor-to-ceiling window, glimpsed visitors arriving by car, or by foot from the subway. She might notice in a way she never had before their street clothes, their hats, purses, their ears and cheeks red from the cold.

Her bed was against a wall, its head pointed to the big window, its foot almost at the door to the room, her view from the bed of the more somber back of the room. There was a door there that opened on a small passageway where her bathroom was. Beyond the bathroom was a narrow steep service staircase. Almost opposite to the entrance door was a side window, which, giving on the very close blank wall of a building twin to this one, never received the sunlight directly. Surely this had been a sitting room. There was, by the dead window, a blocked-up fireplace with a high mantel.

She could read little. Often she had trouble with her eyes, or trouble focusing her mind, and much of the time she could think of little but her body. Every day her son Max brought her a *Jewish Daily Forward*, and some nephews and nieces brought her magazines and novels. She would have liked picture books, reproductions of paintings. She put the postcards family sent her when they went on trips or holiday on the empty mantel of the fireplace.

The front hallway was just on the other side of the wall at her bed. She heard all the comings and goings, the daily arrival of the doctors, the brisk voices of the nurses, the visitors, who were allowed to visit at any time of day. Two or three times at night she heard the arrival of a doctor and once, very early in the morning, an ambulance to remove the dead.

Her hair was falling out in tufts.

She had thick lips and black wide-spaced eyes and a wide forehead. When she had been younger, she had worn her hair straight, pulled back, almost flush to her head, and that had become her very well.

Because of her treatment she was administered limited dosages of narcotics, and some days she suffered so she could hardly remember anything. Yes, I opened the door from my pain and saw this one sitting there, glimpsed that one offering me a box of candy. But nights of pain were different, for there was no one of hers to call on and this place was nothing of hers.

She paced the room in a crouch, her hands at her scar, or wringing her hands, or her hands clapped to her head.

And then the picture postcards on her mantel infuriated her. And she began to fear that this place where she was was beyond the ken of everyone she knew. They came here, yes, but they left at the beginning of the night, they did not *know*. And she was not who she had been, and she feared that one day they would notice, and then it would not matter so much, *she* would not matter so much. And then they might not recognize her in her at all. And then they might begin to forget to visit.

Nights, pacing the long unlit room, from the big window that gave on the empty street-lamp lit street to the door hidden in the dark to the small passageway, feeling the cramps in her bowels, even in her head, the pain whose beginning in the bowels could no longer be remembered, was, ever since fifteen minutes of it, a dull throbbing headache and a dull leaden ache in the rectum, and the occasional fierce cramps, she thought she was forgotten and she could hardly breathe. She put her caracul coat on over her shoulders over her robe and found the door to the passageway. She passed the bathroom and climbed in the near pitch black the steep stairs, pulling herself up with great difficulty, to the second floor. She walked there in a corridor in the middle of the night, her coat over her shoulders, in a crouch, listening to the sounds coming from the different rooms, and was so careful, slow, and silent she was not discovered.

"You know what I want?" she asked Max one Sunday afternoon. "I want a hot pastrami on rye!"

But Leah only was there with Max, and they did not have a car. Max went off looking for a kosher delicatessen as once in the East Bronx he had gone from drugstore to drugstore looking for a spitting cup for his father. He was gone more than an hour, and when he returned with the sandwich she was too sick to eat it.

David brought her gray caviar. They brought her bagels and lox, smoked sturgeon. In her room on the fireplace mantel were boxes of chocolate and wax-paper-wrapped leftover delicatessen. Sometimes a brother, son, or nephew might absentmindedly make himself a half sandwich.

David was separated from his wife, his business would be declared bankrupt. He had his children with him in his small Manhattan apartment weekends. One Sunday evening, driving them home to their mother, he had an automobile accident and his oldest son, who was at his side in the front of the cream-colored Packard convertible, was almost killed and would have a scar on his forehead the rest of his life.

Jack came every day to Brooklyn and sat quietly an hour or two. He no longer went to business.

Eshka awoke from a nap one afternoon feeling her breasts full to bursting, and rays of sun reached even to her half-closed eyes. And she was twenty years before, waiting for the infant child to be brought to her. But then she opened her eyes and opened her nightgown and her breasts were dry and withered as before. She lay still in her bed, and in the evening, when her brothers, sisters, and son came from downtown, she said, "They are making me into a guinea pig!"

"Eshka," Leah said softly, "you will get better."

"You think so!" she almost shouted.

"Eshka, darling," she said from tears, "you will get better."

"You *too* think all I have to do is get up and dance!"

But her sister was shaking her head so sadly and the bitterness went out of her, that what Leah was telling her was even simpler, that she was saying she would not survive her. So there was that as well, that what I touch is touched with death.

Sometimes she sat by her sister, or stood by her, and found her hand gripping Leah's arm tight, or an arm around her. And in the back of her mind was an image of Leah and her in their mother's small apartment behind the doctor's office, the middle of the night, the death watch, and Leah revealing secrets to her, their mother in Berezin locked in an attic room.

There were entire days that she felt milk full in her breasts.

The store would be sold. Who would pay her debts to her brothers? Of course, the debts were in her mind only. Of course, her brothers never even would think that money was owed them. But it was a back door into manhood for sons not to be able and not even to be asked to pay back a father's and mother's debts. Who will pay for my funeral? They will pay for that too! Will my boys one day bring money to Ben and say, "Here, that we should pay for our mother's funeral." If they do not bury me why should they even visit my grave?

What kind of son would be away at school when his mother is dying? She thought then of the doctor and was contrite; he had not allowed Larry to leave school.

These are my debts before they will be their debts. They were his debts, and they are my debts, and they will be their debts. We leave them our debts. As we leave them the seeds of our deaths!

"Don't touch me!" she said to Max. "Don't touch me!"

What am I doing here? Why am I not at home? Why are we not at home?

Some nights Max slept in Joe's apartment on West End Avenue near Columbia, some nights in Ben's house in Far Rockaway, and some nights in the East Bronx.

What is happening to my house? Who is cleaning it?

What is this writing business? Will you write of me? With the notes you make? Will you write, "*She* is becoming yellow"? What can you have to say? What is there to say?

What will become of him? Who will take care of him? Who will pay his debts?

She saw the dark-haired boy seated at his bedroom table writing with a pen, typewriting, pacing. Will you write of me, "She is dying"? Will you write of yourself, "I was ashamed of her"? Will you write, "She left us her debts and the seeds of her death"? Will you write, "She lay dying five hundred days and nights and during that time we visited her sometimes? And there were times she asked us for things that we then forgot." Will you write, "When she was sinking, sinking, sinking, one of us was away at summer-session college and the other was a summer sailor"?

No matter. What are they to me? Flesh of my flesh? Of this flesh? *This* flesh never gave birth! This flesh will forget even what it was.

In the night, when I have pain, and the pain is fierce cramps in my bowels that becomes as well a dull headache and is as well a leaden pressure at my rectum, in these pacing nights I am alone and I prowl in this building, and this is my world, these sick old women —visited, yes, Sunday afternoons!—who wake coughing in the night, who die in the night, alone, no one at their side, who are taken silently off before morning and it is as if they had not been. That is me. I am them.

So that I know I am dying and know I am *transforming.* I am new, or less, or more than I was. I am with them and not with *mine.* I see myself in these withered women who, if they had husbands, children, or grandchildren, it does not matter now, for all that is left is the deserted forgotten husk, abed, unable even to rise, and that is me, though I have a force still unspent, a secret and surprise.

13

They woke in Far Rockaway in the dark and dressed, and Ben went to start the car and warm it up while Max finished his coffee. Fred arrived, Anna half the time not bothering to get out of the small Ford, her nightgown on under a suburban coat, the baby bundled in the rear. She too went every day or second day to Brooklyn. Fred pecked her a kiss, she drove off as if still in her sleep. Louis arrived. Sol came last, hurrying from his house, buttoning this or that, the Oldsmobile backed down to the street, everyone boarding, Ben closing the garage door.

All but Max wore town hats, they filled the car even to the roof.

Louis drove, and shortly they were on Rockaway Boulevard in the early morning mist. For five miles here the road ran by inlets and filled-in bay, the flat empty limit of Idlewild Airport on one side of the road and empty muddy fields on the other. The mist rose from the land and hung there. Idlewild was becoming a great airport, and even at this hour there was air traffic. In the heated enclosed car they would first hear, when it was almost just over them, and then briefly see a giant airplane dropping out of the mist and then passing, dropping still, fading and disappearing.

Here, at this hour, their thoughts were still in touch with their dreams, as in those minutes after waking when one can still catch the thread of last dreams, and like sleepers they pressed against each other, their chins buried in their coats.

Here, every morning, Eshka was with them.

Where is she in her room now? What is she thinking of now, what is she feeling now?

Even the in-law nephew Fred, for he too visited every day or second day, and he had known Mother Cohen, the doctor, and Sundays in the East Bronx, and thoughts of her were thick in the car.

It was only on the Belt Parkway that they began to think of business.

Jonathan had deposited $50,000 to have a place on line to build a giant tanker at a just-opened shipyard in Japan. It would be his turn in a year. Two months before that time, he would have to pay the balance on half a million dollars and then, when work began, another half a million. The ship would cost $2 million.

Where would such money come from? It gave Sol vertigo to even think of such obligations. This was speculation! Tankers were an entirely different business.

For tax advantages, Jonathan owned some ships under Liberian registry. David would open the office in Liberia. No one liked the idea. Where were they sending him now? Why was it always him?

"So where are you tonight?" Sol asked Max, for he wanted to have his turn too, that Max should eat at his table and sleep in his house.

Still Ben worked in the factory and still he sold in the showroom. But now he hired famous designers to make his styles, now he met fashion magazine editors, and he, like Joe, had advertisements in *Harper's Bazaar* and *Vogue*. He and Joe went fifty-fifty in rare leopard skins. And he had a new clientele for that. Movie stars called him Benjy and asked for the loan of leopard or the super pink mink; he escorted one to a film opening at the Strand. He was almost six feet tall, he was curly haired, his clothes now were the best, and he looked good and yet prosperous even in single-breasted.

Every evening, when he had locked all the doors of his place of business and given the burglar alarm signal, he drove with Sol and Louis, and generally Max, and often Fred, and sometimes Leah, to Brooklyn.

He would sit at his sister's side. He would ask her how she was, what she had eaten, what the doctor had said. No detail was too insignificant for him, her temperature, blood pressure, blood sugar. Who had visited, when, how they were, what they had said. He searched in his pockets for newspaper articles he had cut out for her to read. He brought a box of candy for the nurse or gave her money.

She might have, five other visits or not, waited all day for this visit, to explode all her pain on this brother, the other with the corners of his wide mouth turned down for sorrow, the son nothing but a visitor, and Ben would look her in the eye and say, "It will be all right. I promise you."

"What will be all right? The pain will be all right? My *tzitzkas* that are full of pus?"

"*Everything* will be all right!"

And he would sit with her until after eleven o'clock.

"You have not eaten?" she would say.

"We had a bite," he would lie.

He met movie producers, impatient young men making a fortune in television. He was the furrier. He was invited to cocktail parties where he met lawyers, and maybe some great doctor specialist, and talent agents, and a man who seven years before was only just getting out of the army and now owned an electronics corporation that was listed on the New York Stock Exchange. People came to Ben with deals and wanted to introduce him to this one or the other. He might ask, seeing some man whose manner was sure and elegant, "Who is that gentleman?" And it occurred to him that he must be that to them too.

"Come, Max, I'll buy you a cup of coffee."

They went around the corner from the liquor store up to Childs. The tables were already set for the heavy lunch business, but now there were only some women Gimbels shoppers sitting here and there over coffee.

"I want you to take over the store, Max. I want you to take it over now. Your mother and Leah, they're not saleswomen. You have to be a go-getter, and how could they be that? I wouldn't even want it. But you, you're a man now. We'll get rid of the salesman, and Leah will stay in the store while you go out into the market and make contacts. We'll give you every help, and if you do well, it'll only be a beginning. After, we'll find a place for you in the fur business, and if you do well there, then—I've spoken to Jonathan—there'll be a place for you in the shipping business. So I'm speaking of one hundred and a quarter a week right away, and after, well, the sky's the limit!"

Ben was so convinced he was offering the boy not only a future but the only way for him to act as a man that he did not even consider there might be resistance. The boy's mother was in Brooklyn. He would never say so, but who was paying the bill? The liquor store was losing, who was paying the bill? Here was a chance for a smart boy to take his place in the world.

It was a sunny winter morning, and sunlight came down between the tall buildings and through the plate-glass windows of the restaurant and warmed Ben's back and lit the boy's dark round face, like his mother's.

For he is not my son, though I love him too. My son is in Italy, and my business will be his, but who is to say that this boy will not be the Louis of his generation? Or even the Jonathan, to lead us all into a new and profitable venture.

But the boy, fully in the sunlight, and the restaurant heated, was sweating even at his hands. His mother was dying, he would be on his own. His mother was suffering and in pain and would die, and he was going to Columbia and would be a writer, and what Ben was offering him was only what his father had said to him, "You will be a businessman like the Cohens."

Ben saw his trouble and explained, "Success, Max, is the key to all the world. When people know you can serve them, do them favors, make them gifts, then you have esteem. And success begins with making a living and taking care of your own. That is the beginning of everything. It's as simple as: Either you have something to offer people or you do not. You're not like some of your cousins who've gone to Harvard to study philosophy and now are in their fathers' fur business and have to be psychoanalyzed to understand how they got there and what they're doing there! No, you have no father. You have to make your own way."

"Uncle Ben, I want to be a writer."

The boy was only a boy. Ben smiled leniently. "So you'll run the store and write at night."

It was hard too for the boy, now shaking his head, for he loved his uncle. He would have wanted to make him understand what he himself did not. There was something inflexible in the boy that had

been born in him in the East Bronx but that had come from further
back, that was his father's life and more, the lives of his father's
brothers and sisters, that was his mother's life and her dying now,
that was the Cohens, that was: As my father was a doctor so shall I
write. He said, "I want a college education."

"So night school!"

"That's not college. I'm going to *Columbia!*"

In Brooklyn Eshka was in pain, her store was sinking, her will was
breaking, and the boy thought only of *Columbia!*

"Who do you think you are? A prince's son? Who's paying for
your *Columbia?*"

The boy understood nothing about debts, nor did he hear the
scorn in Ben's menace; he thought only how unfair it was of Ben to
say that, and he said, "Excuse me, Uncle Ben. I've got to get uptown
to school."

"So go."

Her voice had nothing gentle, it rasped, and her accent was un-
familiar. Her hair was red. Her skin was tanned and lined, her
mouth was wide, she had high cheekbones and her eyes were quick
and hard.

"Where do you live, countess?"

"We live in Chicago, but I travel a great deal."

She wanted a leopard coat. She was his age, tall, broad at the
shoulders, and her neck was long and strong. She wore her clothes
better than any model. There was something about her like scorn,
like devil-may-care, that someone picked up for her.

She said after the fitting, "I have nothing to do tonight. Will you
take me to dinner?"

"My pleasure," he said gallantly.

In the taxi going to the Central Park South hotel, he remembered
Sid Caesar and Jackie Gleason episodes. He smiled at himself. Should
he not take off his horn-rimmed eyeglasses?

They went to a restaurant she knew just a short brisk walk in the
cold away. She held his arm.

He ordered wine. A colored man played piano.

"I bet," she said, "you're a good dancer."

He smiled without false modesty.

She said she was going to Paris.

"In nineteen twenty," he said, "coming to America, we crossed Paris, but we were too many and too poor to stop."

What a woman! he thought, getting dressed in the sitting room so as not to awaken her. This room too was not lit, but its picture window gave on Central Park, and though they were on the fifteenth floor (she had told him that in this hotel there was no thirteenth floor) it was touched with city light here like moonlight.

He wore boxer shorts.

He thought that down there at the corner of the park, no matter that it was one in the morning, no matter that it was cold, a couple might even now be hiring a carriage, the horse's steaming breath, for a ride through the park. The driver would lay heavy blankets over the legs of the passengers. He too might one day hire a carriage and take the countess for a drive through the park. The best of life was generosity and gesture.

He thought, Can this—that was so good, that was better than anything I have had in all my life—be wrong?

Dora, he said to himself, is dried up.

Jack pushed through the swinging doors of the showroom, and though he was dressed as if for business, he had forgotten to shave that morning. Ben was in a clean and starched duster, and he left the customer he was with and went right up to his brother as if to embrace him and welcome him home.

But Jack whispered harshly, "We are our sister's torturers!"

It was not yet five in the morning when Ben was awakened by a phone call from the nursing home in Brooklyn. He woke Max and then went outside and across the lawn to tap at Sol's bedroom window.

The three of them drove off without shaving, Ben at the wheel, his brother at his side, his nephew in the rear, on empty roads into the Rockaway Boulevard mist.

They dared come to her still with their problems.

Nieces went to Logan's in Brooklyn for dress sales and then stopped by to see her.

Sara was pregnant a third time. She did not want another child. But she would have it and hold it a reproach against her husband and even against her brothers David, Sam, and Jonathan, as if they too were responsible for her martyrdom! "Aunt Eshka, what do you think I should do?" She was a fine-featured proud pale and slender woman.

Joe's tall and quiet daughter, Shirley, wept at her bedside that her husband was unfaithful. They had two children. "He won't leave you," she said, tired, tired, tired.

Joe said he was very tired, and Lily needed a holiday. He was thinking of maybe going to Florida for a few weeks. "Go," she said gently.

She dreamed of Joe riding horseback across fields, she could remember the odor of this older brother come back from journeys, his cold hands framing her child cheeks. He had left Russia when she had been a child, and she had thought of him on horseback all the years until she had seen him again—handsome and prosperous in the crowd waiting at the dock.

Ben told her Max had refused the store. She understood debts perfectly, and she felt that *she* was a debt that would be unpaid.

I wake with pain in the middle of the night and I cry out, "Saul! Saul!" The nurse comes, she tells me as if I did not know I'm not allowed another injection. Must I beg? My eyes are shut tight and I cry, "Why don't you shoot me now?"

I am alone in the dark, alone with my pain, my body, my smells, and the pain is intense, burning, tearing, in my bowels, nor separate from the throbbing in my head, there are lines of pain across my eyes like cracks in glass, nor separate from my rectum where the pressure is dull steady and ugly, and half the time I want to retch, and I spit on the floor of my room. I am wearing my robe, I put my caracul coat on over my shoulders. I remove his wristwatch that I have worn since his death, and my rings, even my wedding ring, and I wrap it all in a handkerchief and put it in my purse and lock it away that they do not rob me. Though what does that matter now, what does anything matter now? I am standing as tall as I shall ever again stand, and I am in a crouch; and I have hardly begun, and pain robs me of my breath. The streetlight enters my room and shows me the way back.

I enter the dark. My hand is on the bannister, I begin to climb the narrow steep stairs. I was here yesterday or the day before, but tonight I am climbing *through*. Even as he, I have climbed these stairs in the middle of the night.

I am crawling up these stairs even as he, but I shall not come down. Step by step.

This steep step I pull myself up is for our leaving Berezin, that we had to flee from there leaving everything behind, and our brothers and their wives, and their children whom we never knew except by photographs. This step is for the first year in the Bronx, when I had to learn the new language and when he kept me waiting. Yes, that for all the time he held me off. This step that I crawl up now, my body spineless, the force only in my wrists, is for my daughter whom he could not save, who died in the night as we all die in the night! This steep step is for Warsaw and his parents who wrote him, Isn't it enough that Harry who has no profession has married a Cohen? This is for his sisters who should have been mine. This step is for the heart attack that came to him in the middle of the night like another call! This is for the first pain that sprang across his chest, and this for the choking and suffocating, and for the gasps drawn from him. And for the waking every day hoping the strength has come back. And for the knowing it would not. For the money he had to take. This step is for my brothers, that they gave him money. This steep step that I am pulling myself up now is for the taste of bile that came to him even before the disease. For the disease that ate the *rest* of him away as I am being eaten away now. This is for his spitting. That he watched himself turn bright yellow.

She was on steps she had not climbed to before, and the stairway turned sharply, the steep steps become angular and twice as hard for her to climb, reaching, sitting, pulling, lying, crawling, slipping back.

This is for the store. For the money owed me that businessmen made me wait for, that they wanted to settle for. For every 10 and 15 percent off I was forced to give them. This step is that they sent me to Chicago. And this step that they sent me to Texas. This step is for Ben! And this for Joe, who goes away. For my son who went to summer school and is now at school. For the other, who will not take my hand, who will not pay my debts, and, dear God, who will pay his?

What have they ever brought me? What gifts have they ever made me?

This step is for Leah, whom I have touched with my disease as he touched me with his.

She had arrived at the door of the roof and she was moaning softly with the pain and her fierce fury and she opened the door and the cold air flew at her and she saw her mother seated on the windowsill of the attic room in Berezin, hunched over herself, ancient and small, the snow-covered steep-roofed houses, the whole village below her. She closed her eyes and knew the doctor was standing watching her, and then the strength was leaving her, and You do that to us, and You do this to us, and still You have no pity.

She crawled half out into the cold damp city night, the dirty moonlightlike lit night, the sky thick and not a star, and she knowing the hundreds of buildings like this one in this ghetto, and the pain robbed her of her breath.

Who will pay his debts? The boy's face rose before her. We leave them our debts and the seeds of our deaths. Do we leave them the way we die too?

We die alone, we die alone in the dark, and yet we do not. We do not die alone, we leave them the way of our deaths as well as the seeds of our deaths.

We do not die alone.

She had pulled herself up to sit with her back against the doorway, she had pulled her caracul coat close about her, and her arms were crossed at her chest holding the coat close. She had no strength left.

She felt she was poised over all of low flat endless Brooklyn. She was filled with such a pity for herself and everyone else, who had come to this threshold, who would come to this threshold, and tears came to her eyes and she was weeping gently and the tears were streaming down her face, and then she began to pull herself back into the building.

Now she never left her bed. All we saw of her was her head and sometimes her addict-thin and infirm arms. She was darker yet, her skin was brown, her flesh was eaten away, and her features seemed larger, sharper. Her black eyes were very large and bright in her brown emaciated face, and they seemed as deep even as they seemed to see.

So that she would never be alone there were three shifts of private nurses, and weekend substitutes, and we would arrive and kiss her and greet the nurse and whisper questions to the nurse we would have asked Eshka before.

Ben had not wanted it known that she had done what she had. But Dora and Fanny had known why their husbands had gone off so early, and Louis, and Anna and Fred had come to Far Rockaway at the usual hour, and Ben, Sol, and Max had already been gone. So most of the family knew of it, and if no one spoke to Ben of it, still they looked at Eshka thinking of that. And if some thought it is our fault she did that, some thought it is their fault, and some of the younger ones thought suicide too is a solution, and euthanasia.

Ben came to Brooklyn every evening, and later he would come before work in the early morning too, and he struggled to be one with her, but what could he say to her? Could he reproach her? He could no longer reach her. He stood now among his brothers, nephews, and cousins, and not at their forefront.

The doctors decided to administer her more morphine.

She was settling into this final stage of her illness, her change. She had no strength, no appetite. She grew used to using a bedpan and very soon was hardly aware of that even as of her loss of strength and appetite; needs and habits, she discovered, simply passing away.

Her every breath was deeper, prolonged. She watched her breath as it came in, as it passed her throat and filled her lungs, watched it as it flowed back out of her body, across her lips. Concentrating so, she suffered less and differently.

She knew she was going now. And she was only sometimes aware of those, though they were many, who came to share her wait. They came in the morning, in the afternoon, and many came in the evening and stayed into the night.

She dreamed. She saw long files of people crossing the snow, her mother, wagons and wagons. She lived with the very images of those mysteries—Where do we come from? Where do we go? And the image of one was her mother and men walking in file across the snow, and she could not see an answer to the second in her death, her death had nothing of an end to it.

"Where is my son Larry? Tell him to come home."

She realized it would not slough off from her, it would not pass away from her, and she wondered if by saying good-bye it would be easier.

Emma came in the early afternoon and sat at the side of her bed and said, as if a joke, "So, tell my fortune." Eshka did not reply, for she had seen her fortune.

A niece entered the room. "No," Emma said impatiently. "Leave us alone."

She said to Eshka, "He's hired a colored bodyguard for my grandson. The bodyguard meets him at the school door. I sit in a taxi just to glimpse him."

She was wearing a black hat with a raised veil and was a proud handsome heavy and corseted woman, and she was sitting straight, and no one but Eshka was there, and when Eshka would be gone she would have no one, and if she did not speak now she would never. She wanted to go on enumerating her griefs, but though all she knew was that Eshka had tried to commit suicide—as her father had, as her daughter had—she sensed that something had changed in her, had ripened in her. She could tell her now only the untellable. She wanted to confess.

"Eshka!" she reached. Her eyes were red; Eshka had nothing to say. And Emma thought even as if Eshka had heard her confession, She has cut me off! And gathering her gloves and purse, she began to know her perfect solitude.

Eshka's brother Sam, his palsied hands trembling, sat silent hours at her side. She smelled the salt ocean on him, and the tides, and heard the never-ceasing sea sound.

She smelled turned-over fields, she could almost taste the dew. That was Jack at her side.

One night she asked, "Where is Sol?"

The small brother was astonished to be called.

She looked up at him and smiled. He waited, but her eyes had closed and, later, when Ben asked him, "So, what did she have to say to you?" he answered with embarrassment, "She smiled at me."

Larry was in his last year of college. It was almost spring, and he had received rejection after rejection from medical schools he had applied to.

He said to his mother, "I can become a psychologist, a chemist, why not? If I want, I can go into business too. Why not? That's where there's money. Why do I have to be a doctor? I take this money, and it's not mine, and I feel everybody watching me. And I've done my best, I'm Dean's List ten times over, and I'm still nothing!"

Eshka had been, the nurse told the first evening visitors, lightly moaning since she had come on duty some hours before.

The brothers were all there except Joe, who was in Florida. David, who was delaying his departure for Liberia for her, was there with his brothers Sam, Jonathan, and Louis. Tall, boxer-shouldered Marty and his wife were there, Anna and bald Fred. Her boys were there. Leah was there. The room was dark, the shaded night-table lamp was on the fireplace mantel.

She opened her eyes slowly. She saw David, whom she had seen long ago in a dream on a wagon in the place of her husband.

"The children," she said.

"What is she saying?" her nephew Sam said, afraid.

"What children?" Marty asked of Eshka, leaning over the shoulder of another, his big nearsighted eyes.

"Every debt of ours will be paid by our children."

She was leaning up, her eyes open wide, something of the revealed skull in her brown drawn face.

She saw a beautiful boy, fair-haired, light- and smooth-skinned. He was boy-just-before-man, on the verge of the big growth, and that growth firm in him, and that even in his regard, a humility as if in awareness of that in him. He wore a small visored black cap like students wore in Russia in her day, and when he smiled he smiled with the smile of the doctor.

She gave Larry his father's wristwatch.

She gave Max her wedding ring.

She asked that Leah stay with her, and that quiet older sister who lived alone moved into the room with her. Leah took over from the nurses the brunt of their activities. She fed her sister and kept her clean. She slept only when her sister slept, she was like the walking shadow of Eshka.

CHAPTER *Ten*

1

We buried Eshka, we wept, we sat *shiva* for her in Far Rockaway.

Joe was at the funeral, he came every evening to *shiva*. The stiff-necked brother walked with Ben around the block, they were quiet as brothers are quiet, Joe said Florida was a good place to live, he would buy land. Florida was sun and the sea. He meant he wanted to build a house with high walls, and he wanted to hold on to everything he had, and he would build walls thick and high. And Ben understood. He had been hurt as never before, and he could speak of his hurt only this way.

Jack spoke to no one. He brooded over Ben.

David went to Liberia, his children would live with their mother in California. Who, Ben thought, will teach them to love?

Eshka had taught love reading fortunes, teaching children low words in Yiddish; her smile, laughter, and energy had been love. Sundays in the East Bronx had been love! Giving money, playing cards, eating nuts, oranges—the fragrance of just opened oranges!—taking tea, her cakes.

He thought, Who will teach them all to love as we have always loved if I do not teach them to love? What will hold us together if love does not hold us together?

Max came every Friday evening to Far Rockaway. "Eat!" Ben

insisted and reached from the kitchen table and swung the giant refrigerator door open to offer him more. Dora had served hot chicken soup and chicken, or boiled beef, but he brought out like gifts bottled gefilte fish, or tongue, pickles, cranberry sauce, cold *tzimmis*. He gave him ten dollars every time he visited. But after dinner Max would not sit and watch television with the others in the den. He might go down to the basement, where Ben stored some few pieces of furniture from the East Bronx apartment, and the dishes and linens, books and papers.

"What does he do down there?" Dora said, as if he were doing something unclean. She really wanted to say, "Does he think he's too good for us?"

For her sister Rose and Rose's retarded fatherless son Stanley, to whom Ben had given a job as a delivery boy, came every second weekend from Brooklyn, and they crowded the den sofa with fat and pouting Elaine.

"Sit up straight, Stanley!" his mother would say, frowning, show-ing Ben and Dora her good intentions, that she would change her son if she could.

She was thinner even than Dora, she had Dora's posture. Neither sister had a belly to speak of, but they carried that forward, and he thought, Aie, these sisters, they are pregnant with ulcers.

Rose never looked Ben in the eye, she was always shuffling out of his way, but she fawned on Elaine. Sometimes he would pass Elaine's bedroom and hear Rose talking softly to her.

"Princess?" he called.

"Papa?"

"Come give me a kiss."

Elaine was twenty-one years old. She had gone briefly to a junior college, she was attending a secretarial school.

Dora said, "You move her out here to the sticks. Where's she supposed to get dates!"

He was in his recliner, his belt and top pants buttons open, his feet raised, his shoes unlaced. They were watching Jackie Gleason.

"Princess," he asked his daughter, "why aren't you using my Ar-thur Murray tickets?" He had bought her dancing lessons.

"I'm afraid to go out alone at night," Elaine answered.

In the basement, he asked Max, "What are you doing down here?"

"Just looking," the boy said. He was standing at an open dresser drawer filled with papers, photographs, letters.

Back in the den, he demanded, "I buy a phonograph machine, where is it? Come on, where is it?"

He switched off the television and sent them moving about.

"Hello, Anna! Come on over! . . . Yes, right away! . . . Of course it's important!"

Sol, watching television in his den, saw Ben and his family leave their den, and by the time the phonograph was set up in the living room, Sol walked into Ben's house. He wore his weekend plaid cap.

"So?"

"Sit down," Ben said.

Anna arrived.

"Okay, the rhumba," Ben said. "Come on, come on, everyone stand."

Anna wore a three-quarter–length car coat, pants, and sneakers. She was nearsighted, and when she was surprised her mouth would drop open and she might not know, like being out of focus, whether to be angry. She began to laugh. "I left Fred babysitting so I should rhumba?"

Then she was cracking up and Max coming out of the kitchen from the basement was smiling to hear her, she was almost like a sister, her mother his mother's sister, her father his father's brother.

"Honey!" she said to Max.

But Ben would not let her move off, she was his assistant, and the music was playing, and Ben was already rhumbaing in place, and though she still had her coat on and her big bag over her shoulder, she began to rhumba with him.

He knew how to move his shoulders and hips, he had a dancer's confident smile. He was wearing his heavy dark horn-rimmed eyeglasses, and he rhumbaed away from Anna doing little things with his hands close to his chest, encouraging her by his smile to do something special, and she went into a slow turn, but was too self-conscious to do it very well, and he, dancing, nodded appreciation and went into new movement, now doing bigger things with his shoulders, and his whole body swinging around in a circle, bending and bobbing from the hips, and Anna dancing in place, watching him, and all of them watching him as if he were really terrific, and he called out impatiently but happily, "All right, what are you all waiting for!"

And they all—Fanny and her daughter had come in too—began to dance except Max, who had his father's privilege of standing by and watching.

Dora and Rose were shuffling in place, and the funny thing about Dora was how serious she was about that which she would never be able to do well, getting the steps right, one-two, one-two, and Rose maybe thinking she would do it better than her lucky older sister, and Stanley, the most nearsighted of them all, scared of doing wrong, scared of being caught cheating and so looking at no one's feet but his own. Fanny was a good dancer, she could still do a leg-kicking-out *kazatchka*, only she weighed 200 pounds, and she was dancing energetically now opposite her daughter, and china cups and saucers were tinkling and the very walls were shaking, and Sol was dancing alone, his eyes half-closed as if to better see himself, and quietly doing funny things with his hands and hips and half-smiling at himself. Elaine was dancing for and with her father all the time, directing her steps at him, her hand, shoulder, and bust motions at him, her smile full of trust and her body loose and mus-cleless.

They drove in caravan on the Island parkways to Amityville to see Sara and her new baby. Fred knew the way so he and Anna led in their two-door Ford, then Ben and his family in one Oldsmobile and Sol and his—Fanny driving—in another. It was a four-bedroom split-level with two and a half baths and in the back lawn was planted a ribbed metal eighty-foot-tall radio tower, for Sara's husband Mike was a ham and communicated with hams all over the world. He had said he would try today to raise David in Liberia.

Sol stood staring at the tower. He asked, "What if it falls?"

They had stopped on the way for toys for the older children and for cakes. They had bought chocolate layer, cheese, and mohn cakes, coffeecakes, and they were all carrying packages, and there were other Oldsmobiles there: Louis, his wife and children, had come from Lawrence, and Sam had come from the city to see his sister with his wife Margo and their boy. And Jonathan and Sheila arrived just after Ben and his caravan, Jonathan then taking gift packages bigger than suitcases from the trunk of his sky blue Oldsmobile convertible. For Sara's three-year-old daughter, Jonathan had bought a baby doll that cried, drank from a bottle, and wet its diaper. Margo exclaimed, "It's a hundred-dollar doll!"

Sara received in her bedroom.

Except for the short staircases, this house was like all the others: the sofas, low tables, lamps, carpeting were the same, the black ironwork ornamental railings defining areas. Flights of little children flew down from one level to another.

Like Fred, Mike—a strong bullish fellow—had married a favorite of the family and was American-born and college-educated. But while Fred's father's once important fur business was failing, bald Fred working ten and eleven hours a day at his father's side to keep it going, Mike's business was flourishing and had been Cohen-started and he had more to prove to the Cohens. He kept expanding his business as if to bury the gift of the Oldsmobile agency.

Now he drew all the men to his den radio shack and explained what the various switches controlled. Red and green instrument lights were on and blinking, static came in loud. Mike sat down and fine-tuned and then began repeating into a microphone: "ACX here, do you read me JWY-five-seven-two?"

"Sh!" Ben said to the others.

"Hello, Monrovia, do you read me?"

Even the wives had bunched about the den doorway.

Now Mike was speaking to his correspondent in Monrovia, where it was the middle of the night. The correspondent telephoned David.

"Hello, David!" Mike exclaimed triumphantly.

There was a pause, everyone was waiting breathlessly.

"Schmuck!" David exclaimed.

"Ha! ha! ha!"

"Ha! ha! ha!"

Sara, pale but smiling, had come down from her bedroom helped by her brother Sam.

Sol too was given the microphone. He asked with real interest, "So how's the weather?"

Ben asked Sam, "But where's the baby?"

"She doesn't want to see it." It had been a Caesarean, Sara had been in critical condition several days. Ben said he would see the baby. Aie, what a red little thing.

The uniformed nurse was watching television. Have the blinds been drawn all afternoon, and the child left neglected in the television glow and low noise?

"Koochie koo! Koochie koo! She doesn't take my finger!" he said in mock unhappiness.

Why didn't Leah come out for the weekend? What keeps her in the Bronx?

He woke in the night to pee. Some nights he woke twice. It burned at its tip and back into his body. It was winter still, but he went out onto the back lawn, the sky was milky with low thick shapeless clouds, a dirty glow in the clouds that was the streetlights and protective night house-lights, and Idlewild Airport two miles away and the city twenty miles, and the airport noise, the expressways, the city, or their echoes, or their resonances.

He noticed a mushroom almost at his slipper. He was surprised and pleased to see it here, as if he had begun to think that this place was not really land—he had seen them filling in marshland with dump trucks off the Belt Parkway, and he wondered if this place were that too. He squatted down to the mushroom, tilted like a hat, delicate in the winter grass.

Every weekday morning, Louis drove Ben, Sol, and Fred fast through the Rockaway Boulevard mist.

Once they glimpsed in the mist a half-shrouded and then disappearing cabin boat; every morning at a certain place airplanes appeared out of the mist and then, landing, disappeared into it. The mist rose from the land as from the water, and once when the car skidded no one said a word as if this place were unattached and unreal.

Here Ben thought of his brother Sam, his purple splotched face, the tiny blue capillary ends that one saw at the surface of his skin, the tightness like paralysis in his every movement but the trembling of his hands. He thought of Mary, the doctor's gentle and widowed sister-in-law, whom he had glimpsed in the chapel at Eshka's funeral. She had worn a hat and veil, but the veil had only barely shadowed her almost luminous pallor.

Leah lived alone in the East Bronx, and every morning she subwayed to the liquor store and every evening she subwayed home. How many times had he seen her in his mind, waiting alone for a train at a subway platform, small, heavy but compact, hatted, eyeglassed, the straightness of her back?

They passed on shortcuts between cemetery walls, they rose on highways above cemeteries so crowded they seemed like cities, and then only minutes from the Midtown Tunnel there was a bridge that rose steeply above fields and fields of cemeteries, the city appearing suddenly, thrusting up all vertical before them, the clusters of skyscrapers, the skyscrapers above skyscrapers, the mirror face of the United Nations building, the pointed tower of the Chrysler Building, and at this place every day Ben, even as he reached into his pocket to be first to have coins ready for the tunnel toll, felt his heart begin to beat powerfully—I am alive.

The first thing he did this Monday morning after opening his place of business and putting on his clean starched white duster was to call Artie, stopping at a hotel in the city, and tell him to come and see him that afternoon.

Artie, he had learned, was passing paper. Business was generally bad, and Artie, like Ben, was obliged to pay cash every month on the Las Vegas place.

Artie strode not walked, he was tall, bronzed, and wore a belted camelhair coat.

Ben went to him from a showroom table where two clients sat looking on, and he looked deeply at Artie and then hugged him.

"Is he your son?" one of the women whispered to him. He almost answered yes.

And later, sitting at his desk in the private office across from Artie, Sam on the leather upholstered sofa—Sam made all soft by what he knew Ben was going to say—Ben thought, They are all my sons, the orphans David, Jonathan, and Sam, and Louis, and the orphans Max and Larry. And this one too is my son.

"I'm sending you ten coats on consignment, Artie."

Artie, who had been in a comfortable slouch in his armchair, drew himself up. "Ben, I didn't ask you for anything."

"Yes, but I'm sending.

"Artie, I know you're in town to get coats."

"Not from you I'm not. Ben, I won't give you my paper."

Sam's eyes were wet. He stood at the bar, his back to them. He could never speak to anyone of this—who would understand?—but it made his heart swell and made him love men.

Ben said, "What's a friend for?"

He dialed Dora. "What's for dinner, princess? . . . Aie! It will never be as good reheated. No, princess, I've got an out-of-town customer I've got to speak to. I'll try to make the eleven o'clock train."

The workers had punched out when Ben walked back into the factory. There were some fluorescent lights on in the shipping department area and over the cutters' table at the windows; the city sky was dark.

No matter that clients rarely came in after five, Ben would not close up before seven and often not until eight. These were the hours of doing a little matching, a little cutting, of looking things over, reminding yourself of things, of catching up, of laying out work for tomorrow. Marie was still bent over something in her little section. He never paid her overtime. Some weeks he just folded an extra fifty into her pay envelope, and every Christmas who got a bonus like Marie!

Ben matched, standing on the cutters' raised wooden platform, Sam some feet away at his side. Since Jack had stopped coming in, Ben had had to virtually take over the factory too.

Sometimes he sensed Jack close by. He thought now that Jack was walking in the cold dark streets below. The big man, his coat collar up, and something hawklike about his regard. He thought, He is pacing the street wanting to come up. Come, brother! Come!

Artie was in a showroom in this building or another, or was he already in The Traders, where they were to meet later? He could almost see him talking earnestly over drinks with some manufacturer.

Solly, the chief shipping clerk, came up to Ben. "I sent Stanley out on a delivery in the neighborhood two hours ago and he's still not back."

"So?" Ben said and turned back to his matching.

There was something about Solly—that Ben had remarked even the many years before when Eshka had sent him from the East Bronx to him for a job, he smiling at his bandy legs—that seemed undeserving. He worked fast and was never idle. When Gus or Stanley did not work fast enough, or were out, he would do the sweeping. Sometimes he too would go out on deliveries. He was only forty years old, but his hair was thinning and graying and his back was bent.

Leah called. She said Stanley was in the store.

"What's he doing in the store?"

"He lost the coat he was delivering."

Of course, Ben thought, when the anger and surprise had subsided, the boy had gone to the store as if Eshka were still there. Then, when Eshka had been alive, he would come in after his hotdog lunch at a stand around the corner and say, "Hello!" And Eshka and Leah would answer. He would come all the way down the store, the length of the counter, and lean on the end of the counter and look at the shelves upon shelves of differently labeled bottles, and maybe Eshka would say from her desk, "How's your mother?" The boy would blush and stutter out an answer, and then just remain there a while, and then leave like someone who does not want to overstay his welcome.

Leah, who never interceded, met Ben before he had come halfway down the counter. "It's all right," Ben said, brushing past her.

Max was standing behind the counter at its end, but Ben ignored him. The boy was seated at a side of the desk, his rounded back to Ben. Ben waited until the boy turned to him. His red teary face was a grandmother's face, and Ben thought poverty and fear is like age.

"What are you afraid of?" Ben asked. "That I'll hit you?" Because he wanted to.

The boy had gone to the service entrance of the address, and a man there had said that delivery boys were not allowed into the building, that he would have to leave the coat with him.

"But who'll sign the receipt?" the boy had asked.

"I'll sign it."

Stanley had given him the coat and taken the receipt, and then coming back had begun to worry that the man might not deliver the coat, and had gone back to the building and the man was not there, and the elevator operator said he would take him up, what floor?

It occurred to Ben that he had thought Jack was pacing the streets, but it had only been the boy.

"I'm insured, that's not the issue. The boy was cringing, he was looking up at me as if I were a god, and I could have said, 'You can't work for me anymore.' I could even have said, ha! ha! ha!, 'I will never again invite you to come to my house in Far Rockaway!' And maybe he thought I could take the money he had lost from his mother, or maybe that I could somehow even turn his mother against him for ever and ever!

"Leah was watching me. You know, I send customers for the store to Leah. For there are customers, tens of them! Like us, brothers who want to buy a business for a sister. Or a father for a son-in-law. They come together in a group from Queens or Brooklyn to look the store over. And they ask Leah how business is. Do you know what she answers? 'Business,' she says, 'is not good.' Ha! ha! ha! She wears black in there.

"No, I'm not a hard man, Artie. I couldn't hurt the boy."

"A hard man! Of all men I've ever known you have the greatest heart!"

"But what I think is some men are more deserving than others. And it's not just being a hard worker. It's what you have to offer others. And you can work and work and work all your life and still have nothing to offer. And another man can have a great vision and be worth a dozen workers! You know, when I sell, and this is why they buy from me and why they keep coming back to me, I'm selling youth. Because, you know, we need great visions."

He was seated now naked on a wooden bench in the Turkish, the steam so thick he could barely make out Artie, his long body all bent over itself on a stool only some feet away. They had checked in and undressed, each with a locker and a little basket for valuables, and Artie had turned his back to him and dropped lenses out of his eyes. And Ben had been surprised, You wear glasses too!

He saw through the steam in a soft blur.

It was good after a long day and evening—and Artie had reluctantly listed for him a hundred depressing figures—to be naked in this heat, to sweat it out, to sit with your thighs thick and nothing constraining you at neck, waist, and crotch, and no shoes, and not standing on your feet.

Other men were distant in the steam, sometimes he could hear the murmur of a conversation.

"How far back do you remember, Artie?"

Artie looked up.

"I remember," Ben said, "when I nursed at my mother's breast. I remember from before!

"Who was that actor you introduced me to?"

"Sam Jaffe?"

"Yes. And the movie he was in?"

"*Gunga Din.* He's an Indian waterboy who saves all the English. Din! Din! Din!" Artie said smiling.

2

Jack was a big man and strong. His shoulders were sloped like a wrestler's, his arms, wrists, and hands were strong, and his thighs. He had always been fastidious, now he was filled with loathing.

He blamed himself that he had brought his sister Eshka into the hands of fakers and torturers in Chicago, Dallas, and Brooklyn. He blamed himself that she had not died in her bed in her home. He blamed himself that he had been in Chicago when Edith had been broken and alone on the floor of their apartment. He blamed his brothers for their lies, that they had fed Eshka hope when there had been none. And now Ben was slim and wore $150 horn-rimmed eyeglasses.

He hated the city. Many times he found himself walking, his hands fists, in the red and green neon-lit Times Square area among the freaks, the colored *chazerai*, the whores, their lipsticked lips open, their blued eyes.

He sat with Leah at the kitchen table in her ground-floor East Bronx apartment. There was little light in this room, the window gave on a vacant lot where boys sometimes played ball.

She was diabetic. She ate wheat germ and read Gayelord Hauser. Going to the bathroom, he passed her bedroom door and glimpsed her with her skirt hiked up about to give herself an injection.

He took her sometimes to a vegetarian restaurant on Southern Boulevard. They had little to say, there was something severe in her as in him. Some Sundays he drove her to Woodmere to see her daughter and grandchildren. She would not stay overnight, and he would drop her off alone at her apartment.

He thought, She is too proud to impose herself on or be a burden to her daughter. We are all alone, there are missing links between us.

The view from the kitchen of his brother Sam's fifth-floor apartment showed, between low buildings, the boardwalk and the beach, the gray misty ocean that you had only to raise your glance to. They played two-handed pinochle at the kitchen table.

He visited Mary, the widow of the doctor's brother. She kept a small yellow and gray bird in a handsome cage. She was a gentlewoman, she blushed easily. She and her husband had entertained infrequently, and when they had the meat might be burned, or the vegetables. She had been born in a small town in upper New York State, and the doctor had invented a reputation for her as the only one in all the family who could make real American apple pie: "Ah, Mary's American apple pie!"

Jack had not called before coming, and Emma was there. Emma was in black, and pearls, and her veil raised. And Mary's eyes were red. What was wrong? What had he really come for?

They both understood better than he, and he had not liked Emma's smile, and he thought, She is a spider weaving her web in corners, and Mary smiled at him from so far she had not even had to blush.

The Friedlands, his wife's brothers, called now and then. They had spoken with him to get information on the money they had invested in the ships. Did they now think that Edith had left them money that he was holding back? He saw the money look, the give-me look, in his orphan nephew Max and despised him a little for that.

One morning, he called his brothers-in-law and Sam's Mima, who had a summer boarding house, and he said, "Come, take!"

The sofa, take! And the gilt-framed mirrors, take! And the coffee table, and the dining table. Take the twin beds! Take the living-room rug! Take the porcelain vase lamps.

He drove his Buick.

He saw Edith lying half-paralyzed looking through the hospital bed bars at her still moving hand. Her nearsighted blurry eyes. She moved each finger, slowly.

He saw the doctor, yellow-skinned, his yellow bird's hand touching his: "You will live of the disease and I will die."

Eshka was crawling up the stairs of the Brooklyn nursing home.

He saw the dark furry mass of the mountains.

He wore his earmuffed cap, his double-breasted navy blue overcoat buttoned to the collar, rubbers over the bottom parts of his high shoes.

High clouds were ill-defined by icy blur. The cold red winter sun was dropping behind the mountains, the cold red spreading now high in the sky and already the different nighttime cold rising. It rose in him too. It seemed to come up from the floor of the car, and his feet were as ice, and it was the night and it was all about him. And then, even as he saw his house lying dark against the snow-covered slope behind it, he saw another house as if emerging out of the first, taller by far and the roofs steep-sloped to slide the snow down, and a lit window way up in a roof, and someone small and hunched perched outside on the window ledge.

The house was one story, with a large unheated area that had been a barn and that he would use as a workroom and garage. The large kitchen was flush to the garage, and the living room was flush to it. Behind these two rooms were two bedrooms. Someone had once begun to build a porch off the kitchen and living room, a foundation had been laid, wooden floor boards had been put down and painted, but there was no roof and almost all the paint had flaked off and the boards were rotting.

He cut wood, in his overcoat, cap, and rubbers.

He would wake and dress and go to the kitchen and prepare his coffee in a five-and-dime-store aluminum percolator. There would be the rich smell of the coffee and the rasping of the butter knife across the toast.

He wore a sweater and so often forgot to remove his cap that he stopped thinking of removing it altogether.

He adjusted his eyeglasses and in a neat and painstaking hand began to make lists:

Clothes	*House things*
boots, waterproof	woodwax
mackinaw	floormat
work gloves	
woolen shirts	

He polished the kitchen table. He leaned into it, he felt the wood soaking up the wax.

It occurred to him that if he wanted chickens, now was the time to think of that.

Chickens
chicks, 12
chicken wire
wire tools
wood for lean-to
book

He bought a dozen week-old chicks guaranteed to be egg-a-day producers. He had to have special feed for them, he had to keep them in the house under a heating lamp. He arranged a cardboard carton for them in the corner of the kitchen and once or twice got up in the middle of the night and went into the kitchen, where that lamp was on hanging close over the chicks. And, of course, he was worried over their still forms, but reassured himself. When he would wake in the morning they would already be chirping and he would put his hand among them to change their water and fill their feed and they would flock to his hand and he would have to gently brush them away in order to bring out the water without wetting them.

So I shall have eggs, he thought. But shall I eat even a dozen eggs in a week? What shall I do with seven dozen? Let's say I shall have five dozen eggs to dispose of. At forty cents a dozen, that's two dollars, two good dollars!

He kept the house temperature at sixty, he wore long underwear, sweater on sweater, in the evening he made a fire of wood that he had cut down and cut to size.

He found himself recording his expenses. He thought it important that he knew where he spent every cent.

He sat before his fire and looked through *One Hundred Great Reproductions From The Metropolitan Museum of Art*. Or read a little of *An American Tragedy*.

He sat before his fire and could not read, he saw Leah about to administer an injection to herself in her thigh.

What's this? Why this chicken is a cock! Well, we'll need a cock to keep a little order in there. But this one too has the beginning of a cockscomb.

He was walking on neon-lit cheap carnival streets, and though he never looked but straight ahead he saw high heels and ankles, he saw hair too blond to be real, their blued eyes, their open red lips glistening.

It was night, and he was on a dark side street off Broadway. He was older, he wore his cap and overcoat, his back was hunched. He was walking in the middle of the canyon-like street. He did not walk straight, he did not weave drunkenly, but there was a pattern to the way he walked between the rows of parked cars that was familiar and yet unrecognized. His hands sometimes hung together low on his body as if he were hurt. Sometimes he looked up at the tall dark buildings, the lights dull in windows. Had he come from one of those cheap sidewalk-marqueed hotels?

He was seated before his fire, only the fire had died out, and the door flew open and in the cold draft David limped into the house followed by two women fat in cheap furs.

"What is it?" Jack shouted at his nephew. "Why have you left your wife and sons? Why have you come to disturb me here?"

But David was laughing at him, his round cherubic face red with drink, and when he leaned toward one of the women his listing limp brought him to her low, and he was implike and nasty, laughing and whispering up to her.

"Get out!" Jack said. "Take your *chazerai* with you!"

His fists were clenched and he stood, and he saw then David's father where David had been, his own oldest brother, wearing a rich fur coat open, and Jack grew wild with anger like bursting hate, but he was then stalking the nephew, and the women in furs were laughing because the nephew was even daring Jack, reaching toward him to tease him on, and Jack was confused, and there was heavy in him an image of chasing the limping boy through a house. He removed his belt to strap the boy, only, no matter what he did, he could not catch him, the boy would slip under a table or circle a chair, and once he thought, If I could only grab him by the ankle, and even then the ankle was before him, but he could not grab it, knowing he would be grabbing into something else, even darker, and the boy was lying flat on the floor and turned and smiled up triumphantly that this had been done, the leg broken that it would knit wrong, that it would knit one leg shorter than the other. "No!" Jack cried. "No! It's not true!" And he was, knowing it was true, strapping at the boy for a liar, only the boy squirmed away from him and he found himself before one of the women and she had opened her coat and she wore a sheer bright red dress and his anger went suddenly dull and heavy and he did not want to beat but to hold to him, the warmth to him, to bring the soft body powerfully to his, to thrust his sex in, to thrust up, the rod of him, the impossible but maybe still possible dream of him, but as he went heavily toward the furred woman her lipsticked mouth opened in a leer and he turned, half-falling, and he whipped the floor at his feet, and then was bent and moving all about the room, whipping at the floor, trying to kill the snake writhing on the floor.

He awoke at the table, and for an instant he did not know where he was, in what place of his life, as if he were still running and had found this place to hide. He heard then the long distant cry of a dog. He saw a vast expanse of snow, the animal wailing, the head raised, the cry that came up from the very bowels and filled the lungs and the mouth and the eyes.

One day he woke and dressed and put on his boots and went outside to feed the chickens, and the sun was shining, and though that was not unusual he felt for some reason that today was different. It was the snow. His boots passed through the snow as if below the brittle surface it were empty or almost. The snow had been melting at the touch of the sun, but the snow had also been melting, and soon would be running, at the touch of the earth.

The snow will grow dirty, and muddy, and then there will be only the mud. He could almost see the muddy fields. He longed to walk in them. His body, which had shrunk during the winter, was breathing in deeply.

> *Garden*
> rake
> hoe
> spade
> seed
> book

If I plant enough corn, I won't have to buy feed.

He drew plans for his garden—potato, tomato, string bean, squash, and eggplant squares. The corn too, for pollination, should be in a square. He had, even while it was muddy, to prepare the soil.

A farmer would sell him two tons of horse manure.

"Do you have a tractor?"

"No."

He would not look at Jack. Surely I paid too much for my land, and surely they overcharge me at the garage, but no one likes to refuse a neighbor, and I shall stand here until he looks me in the eye.

They loaded the farmer's tractor together, and the farmer drove it over and dumped it out in two great piles on Jack's land, and the powerful odor rose into the mist and hung there. One walked into that odor as into a place, and one stood in one's boots in mud and manure that were already forming one, and maybe because the odor had never been forgotten, he even almost at sixty remembering stable smell from when he was a boy, the place seemed rich and dark with giant life.

He worked at his slow measured pace, the speed only for the short thrust of pitchfork into pile, and then raising the ten or so wet pounds and swinging it to the wheelbarrow. And doing that ten times and then wheeling off through the mud to the farthest corner of the acre garden. Even the drip of the stuff was not unpleasant, though he was a clean man and would at the end of the day wash himself thoroughly. So there was in this work four stages, each with its own rhythm: loading the wheelbarrow, which was calmest, one's thoughts slow, patient, building; moving the loaded wheelbarrow through the mud, which was hardest; unloading, which was one rising effort and over; and then wheeling back the empty wheelbarrow.

Then there was the spreading of the manure from each wheelbarrow pile onto every square yard of the garden. Then the working of the manure into the soil to speed its mix, the spade turning of the soil and manure—and glimpsing the rich pink worms falling in the falls of black earth. He knew that he had a week of this work, of getting up in the morning and in the good weather or wet going out into his field and stepping the spade into the wet soil and lifting it just enough to turn it and moving on and stepping the spade in. And in such deep work he was not alone.

He went on digging, he thought of the next stage of his work, of smoothing the earth where he would plant.

He remembered a dream he had had of apple trees in flower, hundreds of well-spaced apple trees in line, and full limbed, and the pink-white flowers. He would plant apple trees. He remembered a dream he had had of rosemary bushes, lines and lines of round-trimmed rosemary bushes three feet high, and the bluish-purple flower right at the green pin leaves of the plant so that from a distance the bushes had a bluish haze and glow, and something else that meant much to him that he had forgotten. What was it? Yes, the murmur of bees. There would be rosemary, and it would flower, and there would be the murmur of bees, and then there would be the rich smell of honey, and he would watch it all, and he would have the honey, and what he did not use he would sell.

He placed a long distance call to Leah, but could not reach her.

He called Anna. The store, she told him, had been sold. Ben and Joe had sent Leah for a holiday to Miami Beach.

He was standing in his overcoat and boots in this general store at a wall telephone, and he was reaching to Leah but had gotten Anna and she gave him news of herself and Fred, and then of her boys, and then of Eshka's boys, and then of Sam, Jonathan, David, Louis, and then of his brothers, of Sam, Sol, Joe, and then of Ben. Ah, Ben! One day he would invite them all here. They would come in many cars. There would be a driver for Leah and a driver for Sam. He would show them his house, his chickens, his garden, his field of apple trees. He would take the men into the fields, they in their city clothes, ha! ha! ha! And Ben would be proud and erect as Ben had always been, and full of life, and enthusiastic. He told Anna he would call her again.

Then, driving home on the road that ran parallel to a small river that in this season was swollen and ran fast, he felt strange and parked his car and walked slowly across a muddy field and then down another toward the water and already he knew that he had been here before, that this had happened to him before, or to his. He wanted to take off his overcoat, boots, and cap, and his shirt and trousers, and his long underwear, and to enter the water naked and to be bathed clean. He saw himself lowering himself in a shallow place in the water, he was seated flat on the stony bottom, the icy water rushing across him.

3

The small airplane was already no more than a speck in the hazy summer sky. Ben stood looking after it like someone left behind. He was alert too for any car arrival, though he had not been able to make out where the road was in this expanse of flat dusty fields—the mountains north like a low even wall hazed faint and blue by the rising heat. He wore a light suit and hat, a necktie, he carried a one-suiter, a raincoat was folded over his arm.

"Taxi, mister?"

"No, thank you," Ben said, smiling. But the other pointed insistently to his taxi, which Ben only now noticed, a four-door prewar black Chevrolet standing tall close to the small airport cabin. One posed for photographs with one foot on the running board of such a car. Ben smiled again and this time pointed at his watch as if that would make it clear he was waiting for someone, and the driver did, in fact, nod reassuringly and walk away.

His handkerchief was dusty and wet where he wiped it under his hat brim and under his chin.

The taxi driver was in the front seat of the Chevrolet and seemed to be dozing. A man was riding off on a bicycle, and the airport cabin was locked. Had he seen the man lock the cabin and mount the bicycle?

It is the heat, he thought, and that though I know exactly what I am doing, have arranged everything down to the slightest detail, that my son is late. Still, I feel as if I am in the wrong place.

"That's better!" Ben said, folding his necktie into a pocket. He thought he would enjoy the breeze in the open Jeep, but it was too warm, and rushing at him that way it was almost hard to breathe.

"We'll go to the beach," the boy called across at him. "It's cooler there."

He was, like his father, a little short of six feet. But he was narrow like his mother and was a worrier, though he fought that in himself.

"What a city Rome is!" Ben said.

"I've been," the boy said, nodding.

"Did you see my shoes?" They were dusty now, but he loved them dusty too. "I lost a quarter of an inch in Rome! Moccasins! I've never worn such fine shoes." He almost had to yell to be heard.

He wanted the boy to be as large as himself. A man was made for the world.

They sat in the Jeep at the empty beach. Ben removed his dark glasses. The boy was looking at the sea.

"It's such a country!" the boy said.

Ben smiled and exclaimed grandly, *"Tagliatelli! Montebianco!* The way we walk before dinner on Via Veneto just to look at the people, such interesting people!" But his son was shaking his head impatiently.

"No, Dad, I'm speaking of Israel. Even the arrival. You come in over the sea, and it was dusk and you go deep into the country to circle, and you're circling over red desert that you've never in your life seen before, only you have!"

The boy told how he had, in the airport, felt he should immediately call to greet his cousins, whom he had never met. He went to an information counter and the woman there said, "Who are you to call Esther?"

"I am Marvin Cohen, Ben's son."

"I am Esther," she said and came out from behind the counter.

At the Hotel Plaza Athenée in Paris, Ben took for the countess and himself a two-room suite and adjoining room. They were big rooms and somber, the large windows opened out on the many-umbrellaed patio restaurant five flights below, the sounds, even during meals and tea, coming muted, the very gong with which a blue-and-silver-uniformed boy might appear in the patio to page a guest pitched low, to whispers.

There were velvet hangings from tall ceiling to floor at the sides of all their windows, and gauze that veiled and billowed out. When the door to the adjoining room was open, there would be a long corridor through all their rooms down which the countess would come, tall, so straightforward, with all that space about her, and there would be a stopped instant in which to watch her appear.

There was her bedroom and his, and her bathroom and his, and the spacious sitting room with a small bar. There were mirrors deepening the rooms, there were long-stemmed flowers that revealed the height of the rooms. All in this somber light, the gauze billowing, for the sun touched only small angles and not for long, and even on hot days the rooms were pleasantly cool.

He had asked her once, at the beginning, thinking of her husband, "Are you sure? I don't want you to do anything wrong."

She would phone him long distance at business. He would take her calls in the private office. He was so delighted to speak with her, he had asked, "What is it about me, countess?"

She had laughed. "You're an optimist."

He had nodded his head thoughtfully, but then had said, "No, I was an optimist. I would say the thing about an optimist is that he can afford to be disappointed. But now that is past."

In Italy, she had once begun, "You should know . . ."

"I don't want to know."

Now she took him to the Place Vendôme.

He said, "Another turn, countess?" For his mind was still absorbing: the countess on his arm, her flaming hair held to and covered for walking by a plain silk foulard, her assured way of walking even when they walked slowly, the mottled trunks of the full trees in the park in the square, the aged large-windowed fading red facades of these buildings, the cool dark arcades, the shops dark as if to better show the glow of the antiques inside. He could almost see the spacious apartments, the polished wood floors, the dim paintings, the wall moldings.

They walked on narrow side streets so full of life, goods, and variety, so much a world apart, that when they reached a corner and saw they were on one of the wide and familiar avenues of Paris, here almost at La Concorde—he having seen it at night, in a taxi, all the fountains and lights, and the stretched out lights of the city—he stood astonished and enchanted.

Passersby sometimes smiled at them.

They raced traffic across a cobblestoned street to pass through the pedestrian arches of the entrance to the Louvre. They passed from masterpiece to masterpiece, and they put on and took off their dark glasses.

The Mona Lisa!

This, he thought, is about people, about their lives. What history there is in art. Yet how little present we are. To Rembrandt we owe a special debt of gratitude.

"Cohen," she said mockingly, "what's in a Cohen?"

"Yes," he said. "We are, you see, the sons of Aaron, the brother of Moses." He was embarrassed to speak of the priestly mission given to a family.

And from the Louvre, and from The Handball Court—the Impressionists! Renoir!—we go to the fine dark shops of the rue Faubourg St. Honoré. How quickly and surely she looks through sweaters and feels and chooses for me a dark blue cashmere sweater! Cashmere! And buys it like a kiss so that I feel all good inside and long to give her a kiss in turn. What will it be—gold, leather, silk?

I buy her five silk foulards. A pair of earrings. Because I like to watch you turn your head—the length of your neck!—to fit them on. I buy you long gold earrings of a hundred surfaces to shadow your neck. I buy you a ring, a necklace, because they are *useful* to you, they are landmarks on your body. I stand and watch you brush your hair, your long straight body, the way you touch perfume behind your ears.

She buys me ties, gold cufflinks.

We sit on the sidewalk terrace of a café.

"I'm in love," I say, teasing. Her eyebrows arch. "Ah, countess, I'm in love with Paris!"

I say to her of the *fagellas* parading by, "I know them! I know them! They are dress designers! You think I'm narrow-minded. Not at all. They are talented and charming!"

"May I ask," a young man says, standing politely at our table, "where you bought your moccasins?"

"Yes!" I say. "Yes, of course!"

We go to the fashion houses. My name is not unknown. We are ushered in. Fellow furriers from Thirtieth Street see me so accompanied and bow to her like gentlemen; they too are in their way men of the world.

The models are Negro, Eurasian, flat! They are six feet tall, they walk like they were hypnotized. One's head is shaven!

We eat at Corniloff's. The waiters are cossacks, they are bald, arrogant, they stride. The sturgeon is enormous, the slices are like steaks, except they are really like butter.

How does one fish sturgeon? With a spear! Only with a spear! We shall go fishing sturgeon from horseback! Ha! ha! ha!

We throw thimblefuls of iced vodka back into our throats.

We eat at the Tour d'Argent overlooking all the city, the river Seine glowing below, the towers of Notre Dame opposite, and the restaurant lights are extinguished when we are served our flaming crêpes Suzette.

She takes me to Pigalle. Everything is neon, the street is crowded with people passing through and prostitutes standing in place like barber poles; they are lipsticked, their eyes are blued, they are mascaraed, they are wigged, their skirts are short, are slit, they wear net stockings and heels six inches high. Their busts are almost bare or their blouses are pulled so tight you see their nipples. They purse their lips and suck, and you see behind them the tawdry hotel rooms. And has she taken me here that I should take her into that filth? That we should see ourselves as they are? That we are nothing but that? Ah, but I know her, I know my beauty. It is not to hurt me but herself! She cannot bear to be what she is, the best of women! I do not give an inch! And when we have walked the gauntlet once, I say to her as coolly as you please, "It's as you like, we can walk back or we can take a taxi here."

She smiles and says, "Well, anyhow, you'll take me to the Moulin Rouge."

The French call that *cochonnerie*, and that too is part of their way of life!

I call New York every other day.

Sam says he has been looking through the safe and is worried. "Why do we have so much paper?"

"Schmuck, if you give paper, you have to take."

"Have we been giving so much?"

"It's the way the market is."

He tells me Jonathan is in Rotterdam.

"What is the great man doing?"

"Who knows? He won't talk business."

I call Far Rockaway.

Dora says, "So Rome?" Because she thinks my going for the styles even to Paris extravagant.

I tell her about our boy.

"How are Dan and Tanya?"

"I'm seeing them tomorrow," I lie. "Tell Elaine I've bought her Chanel Number Five."

"I'm listening, daddy." Her voice comes so unexpectedly it is as if it comes from my own mind.

"I'm here too," Sol says.

I call Dan. "Do you mind, I'm here with a friend."

This is, after all, Paris, and Dan is a man of the world.

"To Maxim's?" Dan repeats.

"It's the best, isn't it?"

"To Maxim's on a Friday night?" He does not speak English, we speak in Yiddish, and he says *erif yontif*. "It's a smoking I'll have to wear?"

I do not understand.

Dan says, "I have good news. Your nephew Lazarus . . ." Who is Lazarus? ". . . has been accepted at medical school."

"Larry! You mean Larry!"

Aie that is good! That is very good! Aie, how happy Eshka would be! Aie, how happy Eshka would be for the doctor's sake!

"The other is arriving in Paris this week."

"Max?"

"I have better news yet, but I'll wait till I see you."

What? Who could tell what a Frenchman and a Katz at that would think was good news? The arrival of another schlemiel in Paris, ha! ha! ha! How had the boy gone about it? I told him, "No! You don't learn the value of a dollar by spending what you chose not to earn!" Well, he is enterprising anyhow!

4

Still Jonathan had no child.

Whose fault was it? Was his wife Sheila too delicate? He had thought that a wife who painted was like a wife who played piano nicely. But she painted all day long, and money brought one up or down and art was become part of his world. He read history and novels, he listened to his wife's teacher, a small Jewish painter well known in New York who had made his reputation in the thirties painting garment workers.

Every day at business he had to deal with ship chandlers who gave 5 percent off to one but 10 percent to another, with ship stewards who accepted phony chandler invoices in order to have a percentage for themselves, with union officials who could strike his pier and lay up his ship for a week or a month—he with a $1000 daily operating expense to meet—or who could, for a price, favor, or deal, get his ship loaded when others were laid up. There were a hundred federal, state, and port regulations enforced by men sometimes ready to make a buck.

He had to do almost everything himself, his Christmas gift list was as long as his arm.

Sailors signed on and off a ship as if it were a bus or flophouse. If he bought a piece of expensive equipment, he could be sure that after one or two voyages it would be stolen by dockers or sailors, and the only way he could insure against such thievery and petty thievery—for they stole ropes, screwdrivers, paint brushes—was to grease the palms of the chief mate and boatswain, and then let them control how much loot the others took.

It was a world in which every man wanted *his*.

He had to deal with his creditors. With family too. Herman Friedland called him at his office. His Uncle Joe called. Sol called him at
home. "So," Sol asked, "what's new?"

What could he answer to his uncles who had brought him, his
brothers, and sister to America, who had raised them, who had
given him a job and a partnership and his chance, who had invested
and reinvested in his projects.

A lawyer called and said he was representing the Friedlands and
they wanted their money back now.

He had raised mainly from his uncles, from his brother Sam and
from Louis half a million dollars on a gamble, *his* gamble. He was
risking it all, everything, the ships he owned and the ships he ran.
Why take such a gamble? Why *again* and why *so soon*? What justification could he have? He would sink his family with him. He could
have backed out, he could have sold his fifty-thousand-dollar option
to have a giant tanker built for seventy-five, and he would have been
known as a dealer. What craziness had made him fight to put up the
first half million as if he really had or could raise the other million
and a half? Nor could he go to banks to ask, because they would
know he needed and would bleed him dry. Yet, he had thought it all
out and had given himself better than one chance in two that someone would sooner or later tap him on the shoulder and say, Look
here, Cohen, and come through with an offer profitable for the
offerer and that would make the builder big. Life is short was his
only justification, his only answer to why, and he knew it was no
answer at all. He felt he was empty at the core and knew he was
not.

He had headaches, depressions.

In whom could he confide? In his dearest brother Sam, who, if he
were to tell him what he feared, would turn pale and tremble and
put his hand to his heart? In Louis, who would want to rush head
first at enemies? Or in his brother David in Liberia, who every day
sent him cables of reproaches, fantastic suggestions, and who always
needed cash! cash! cash!

Once, a rare evening alone with Sheila in their apartment, he
realized he was sitting alone on the sofa with not a thought in his
head and not a book or even a drink in his hands, and that Sheila
was walking across the room with the quiet of a nurse.

Now, at his arrival for routine business in Rotterdam, he was met at the airport by a young shipping company agent. He sat at the young man's side in the small automobile during the drive to the city, and the young man asked him two or three polite questions and then let him alone. But arriving in Rotterdam, the highway touched the port and the young man proudly and unthinkingly pointed out distant construction and said, "Look, we are building a great port."

It was late in the afternoon and the summer sky was deepening red and the sea horizon was flat and one had to focus in on the tiny distant pencil-mark derricks and cranes, and then one realized that the entire horizon was covered with them, and then one could almost hear the dredging, creaking, groaning.

The city too, Jonathan saw during his stay, was being rebuilt, but it was the rebuilding of the port that fascinated him. Because of the port this small country was, as it had been before the war, the turntable of European trade, and the port was already twice as important as it had been. Shipbuilders had just begun to build 50,000-ton tankers, the port was projecting where it would receive 1- and 200,000-ton tankers. Rotterdam, he thought, had a *vocation* to be a great port, and that was the beginning of a meditation whose counterpoint, or underside, or night side was his wanting to let go, to let go of tomorrow as of yesterday, of Sheila, of all.

He matched his ship's captain glass for glass. They arm-wrestled, and though the captain was bigger and though Jonathan's hands were small (his fingernails manicured), his forearms were like iron, and the captain was sweating and Jonathan glared his broad smile at him though the bones of his hand were being crushed, and he downed him.

The captain insisted they return to the ship.

It was after midnight, but dockers were working still. The ship had transported 10,000 tons of scrap metal, there were five holds, two giant magnets craned from the dock to drop into the holds and draw out. Each drop was a crash, and with each crash the rust exploded into the air, and the magnet was craned out and swung with its jagged load to drop with another crash into the back of a waiting truck. The rust infested the very air. The captain had told him it was a disease, no matter how soon the ship would be at sea and they cleaned it off, no matter how many coats of red lead they would lay on the decks, the disease would take, the rust would reach the very core of the ship. Their hands were filthy with rust, and even inside the hot narrow passageways they breathed it. Doors were open, and crowded in one forecastle after the other, in narrow double-decker beds, were snoring undressed sailors and their whores.

They climbed to the captain's quarters. They cut thick slices of sausage and bread, they drank clear aqua vitae. Two whores came up sleepy and rumpled, and the captain offered Jonathan his "fuck-sil," only Jonathan said he would not dream of displacing him and go right ahead and glared his broad smile at him and did not leave.

First they watched the whores together. Then the lights were out, but the portholes were not shaded. The captain lay in a narrow bed head to head with one whore, but the other was halfway down, cross-legged, bent forward darkly. Someone was moaning. Jonathan heard an explosion from outside—it lightly rocked all the ship—of a magnet falling into the piles of twisted metal. He smelled hot breath, sausage, drink, and sweat. The whore halfway down had thrown her head back to catch her breath. He saw thickly wet lips. Her gaze met his.

Her head dropped forward eagerly, eating! eating!

And this is all there is. And this is all there is, and I am sterile, empty, and inviolate.

But standing on the dock, he thought that a city like a man can have a vocation.

He thought: Five magnets instead of two. Size! Size! Size! Not a thirty-five-man crew for a 10,000-ton ship, but a handful of specialists for a ship three, five, and ten times as big.

Speed! Not ten knots an hour, but twenty and thirty.

Why is there no permanent paint? Where can I find someone to manufacture permanent paint?

He had seen a barge loaded with railway cars. There were unused rails for railroad cars even at shipside. And if, as if with some giant hand, giant grip, I could load car after car onto a ship, railroad cars like bales of cotton, only each car filled with thirty tons of goods. Only entire trains, and fleets of trains, waiting to be quickly loaded.

He turned weak with what he had just seen. He would not think about it. He would let it settle into him.

At his hotel, there was a message for him to call Ben Cohen at the Plaza Athenée in Paris.

5

They sat at the kitchen table in the minuscule and crowded apartment in Neuilly—from the living-room window you could see distantly, above the Paris rooftops, the rising converging lines of the Eiffel Tower—and she said, "We want you, Max, to think of us as your parents."

The black-haired boy smiled and sipped from his bowl of *café au lait* and did not say what he thought, that he had heard this before, that Joe, Ben, Sam, Jack, and even Sol were to be his fathers, and their wives his mothers. He thought, She is being polite, sentimental, this is the way people (Jews?) are. And there were as well thoughts beneath the thought that controlled his mood—this offer has nothing to do with me. My father is dead, my mother is dead, I am free. And they died in great pain, and that disease stalks us, only I am young. He was made big in his own eyes by his knowledge and freedom. And like most of us who have begun to sense we have something to say, he saw all things only in function of that, only of him.

She was bringing to bear that she was forty-five years old and had had no child, the war had robbed her of that, that she had lived with false papers, and sometimes in hiding, four years, that she understood him, that people had been good to her and bad, and stupid and evil, and one had to know how to get around them and ahead, and that she was an artist, and that she could help him. There was something in her yet of a girl on the point of falling in love.

She wanted to know about him, his life.

He said, "Emma took the samovar that had been a gift from her mother to my mother, that was under the long mirror on the marble-topped buffet in the dining room.

"The night before the furniture was to be moved out and the small apartment closed, I invited two friends to the Bronx and we drank all the leftover whisky. We drank a decanter of sweet raspberry brandy my mother had made, the kind, the fruit not fully

dissolved, that I'd been allowed a sip of Friday nights in my grandmother's kitchen, where we would go to be with her when she lit the
sabbath candles, the candlelight glinting off her fingernails. And we
were drunk and we spoke about Jackson Pollock, and one of my
friends said that the white X's you see on the windows of big new
unfinished buildings are as powerful as paintings, wilder, the new
strength, and that was a revelation to me, and I wanted too to
whitewash X's on all the mirrors, the mirror in the small entry hall
above the sewing machine, and the long mirror in the dining room,
and her mirror in their bedroom.

"In the morning, my Aunt Mima came before the movers. 'Why
do you sell this? They'll give you *bupkas* for it! To me it's precious!'
And later she went off down Hunts Point Avenue with a filled suitcase and the dining-room mirror wider than she was tall under her
arm."

"Where did you live then?"

"Here and there. Mainly with Joe, weekends with Ben, and then
on campus."

He spoke of the Broadway area around Columbia, he told of Alexi
at the West End Bar. He was a white-haired Russian wine drunk
whose ties were silk and filthy, who would argue about Jefferson as
easily as about Tolstoi. He would interrupt his argument to go outside to vomit and then return and excuse himself and ask, "Where
were we?" At 4:00 A.M. when the bar closed, he might go, with a
certain dignity and challenge, from one student to another and ask
to be allowed to sleep on his floor, in his bathtub.

"We'd give him a quarter or a half-dollar," Max said, as if with
regret.

But he was thinking and would not speak of Terry. She was a
quick-moving lithe whore, and she gave him a topsy-turvy trip
around the world in a cheap Broadway hotel three blocks from Joe's
fine West End Avenue apartment. And he went again with her several months later, only this time she insisted on five dollars more,
and was hard for five dollars more, and this time her body was black
and blue with injection marks, and her flesh was shriveled and so
unclean that when she again gave him a trip around the world he
had to close his eyes and imagine the other Terry that it be all
right.

Nor did he speak of Barbara, who was tall and colored and took him to her room off Broadway on 112th Street, in one of those giant apartment buildings transformed into rooming houses, with corridors going in every direction, and at the foot of her bed was, crosswise, a small bed in which her four-year-old boy was sleeping.

"Don't you bother none about him."

This too was life, he was experiencing life, only in the middle of it he opened his eyes and saw the boy leaning up over the foot of the bed impassively watching them.

He would not speak of the restlessness he felt before he went Broadway nightwalking, the mounting excitement, the whip of it, hoarseness, stalking.

He had little tolerance for whisky or wine. He would have a bare instant of being high and then would be sick. Still he would let himself go.

She said, "Of course no one can replace your parents. But we want to."

After a moment, he said, "I write.

"Normally, I'd spend weekends in Far Rockaway with Ben. But this one Friday night I was writing and it was already late. Dora called. 'What's wrong with you?'

" 'I have to work, Aunt Dora.'

" 'You don't live normal. Who do you think you are?'

" 'Aunt Dora, I'm in the middle of work right now.'

" 'Why don't you work like everyone else!'

"I hung up on her."

Tanya said, "You were wrong," though he could see she was on his side.

Would he get around her the way he did his gentle Aunt Mary by being bigger than life? He had told Mary of how when he worked on a Liberty ship the ship was empty in a storm, and he stood lookout topdeck, a line strung around the funnel. The ship was like a cork in the high and wild seas; staring straight out he saw the sea raging and foaming a hundred feet above his head, and holding on tightly to the line behind him he wanted to yell exultantly. He had told the story so many times he hardly believed it.

She said, "I understand your wanting to work. I've never enough time for my painting. I have to take care of my parents, do their shopping. When I'm painting, the telephone never stops ringing. But you have to understand Dora, too. She's not happy."

"I worked two weeks this summer in Mike's Oldsmobile agency washing cars, sweeping up. I lived with Mike and Sara, and I got a cold and high fever and Sara was afraid for her young children and said I should go recover at Aunt Leah's. She drove me to the Long Island Railroad station. I stayed a week with Leah in her apartment in the Bronx two blocks from the other. She'd have kept me forever. I told her I'd get a driver's license. She said, 'Why?' She meant: How will an orphan student with only a poor aunt ever own an automobile? She made me cakes."

"Don't you see your brother?"

"Larry's going to be a doctor. I'm already what I am." He waited for her to ask what he was, but she only nodded her head.

She excused herself that she was not a good cook, but brought out from the refrigerator smoked herring and eel, sausage, radishes, butter. Dan came home for lunch early with bags full of food. He embraced his nephew and kissed him on both cheeks, his eyes wet.

Max went on telling: "Two months after my father's death I went to meet her at the doctor's office at Seventy-ninth Street between Madison and Park. I was approaching the street entrance, and she was just leaving. She was wearing her brown caracul coat and no hat, and she did not greet me or even answer my, 'Hey, you weren't going to wait for me!' I walked at her side, I took her arm, I said, 'So?' She only shook her head. We went down the stairs into the subway, and even there on the downtown platform waiting for the local, for we had to go to the store, she did not speak, but I was beginning to *know*. I think half of dying is knowing.

"I was sixteen when my father died, fifteen when I began to pray wildly for him. But now I was seventeen and she, standing in her caracul coat at my side, was condemned and there is no appeal."

He would not speak about the *Shma Yisrael*.

Mother Cohen had taught Larry and him that prayer one summer in the country, they in bed repeating the words, the small wizened back-rounded woman giving them each a nickel and bending to kiss them good-night on the brow. After, he said the prayer every night, and at his bar mitzvah when he sang the service from beginning to end, he sang *Shma Yisrael* like a clarion call. And after said the prayer every night, and if he did something wrong during the day, or bad, or questionable, he said the prayer, and if he wanted something he said the prayer, and at night if he did not say the prayer well he would repeat it until it came out clear. If he ever forgot to say the prayer at night he would awake afraid and guilty of what the omission might cause and would say the prayer many times.

Every night now he wanted to say the prayer. The first sounds would come even to his lips, and he would refuse. Every time he woke in a room he did not recognize he would want to say the *Shma Yisrael*, but would not allow himself to, and he had become stronger.

He told about Brooklyn, her room. About his waking in Far Rockaway, and it still night and off to Brooklyn and then to the store, and then to Humanities or Contemporary Civilization at Columbia, Emile Durkheim on suicide, Hannah Arendt on totalitarianism, and then back to Thirtieth Street and the store, and then to a restaurant, and then to Brooklyn, and then back again to Far Rockaway.

The cousins Jonathan and Max spent Friday together. They went to the Louvre where Max, though he had never been, walked in the manner almost of a proprietor. He had bought a beret, he wore a light-blue hand-me-down lapel-less jacket that had been in style some years before, and he looked, he was convinced, not only Parisian but Bohemian.

Jonathan went at his own pace in the crowded galleries, and Max would have to wait for him or would double back to him to dismiss all a gallery with a gesture addressed as much to the tourists about them.

Each painting had information for Jonathan. In Rembrandt he recognized the great psychologist, but also his feeling for men and their condition: Bathsheba, knowing David's will, had no power to resist, but at this moment after her bath she could almost see what would become of her, the scope of what she was doing, and was like someone forlorn.

"Where to now?" he said, putting himself in his cousin's hands, though there was in that a little of the general who will for once, briefly, allow himself to be led.

They walked. They did what Jonathan would never even have thought of doing: they bought bread and cheese, a bottle of wine,

and picnicked in the Luxembourg Gardens. He was wearing a summer suit, a batiste shirt, a tie; he removed his jacket and folded it
neatly over the back of the park bench. Now all was rich summer
greens, the blue sky, the leaf-mottled, somehow discreet park-facing
buildings, a dull orange roof, the sounds of children close, of water.

He said, "I'm glad we stopped here. I have weak arches." It was a
gesture toward his cousin.

The boy was going on to Provence, to Van Gogh country. From
there he was going to Barcelona and Seville, he would see bullfights
and the oppressed. Jonathan was smiling faintly, the boy was still so
young. Yet there was that in his projects that fit the moment, this
place, so cut off from the real struggle of life. He would have made
the moment last, the bread, wine, and cheese were good. For building, Jonathan thought, is step by step and every day, and building
big is different only in that you must keep your eyes open at all
times and know when to be patient—and be so!—and when to seize
the moment. And that is the active vertical direction of our lives, to
build big, while the horizontal . . .

Jonathan had arrived in Paris the evening before.

He had never seen Ben so good looking, so calm. Yet, even in the
exclamation-crowded first half hour together, he had begun to sense
such a darkness about his uncle that the questions he had gone over
in his mind before arrival—what does Ben want? Does he too want
to know where his money is? Does he intend to threaten me? Does
he, on the other hand, want to show off his mistress to me? (For
Sam knew of her and what Sam knew Jonathan knew)—were suddenly meaningless, as if he were entering another language of
feeling. And even his own vision, which had grown in him through
the last days—train cars, truck cars, containers, he organizing in his
mind the researches, the directions he would have to follow while
going through routine business, while canvassing for new routine
business, while waiting for the other things to happen, the call, so
that every instant of every day was filled with faces and getting
behind them, and figures, and estimates, and estimates made against
time, for business contracted today would be enacted in months and
prices would change, and with the construction of that vision, the
financial base for it, the associates he would have to have, the technicians, the very look of it, the number of ships, the port facilities, the

necessary gigantic port facilities, for it could never work if it were not gigantic, three or four giant ships at least, the when of it—seemed now not less great, but itself colored somber.

What he did immediately understand precisely was that Ben had not called him to put any weight on him, that Ben loved him, and that in some immutable way Ben had taken things into his own hands.

They had gone to dinner.

Jonathan's manner to women was ordinarily courtly, his manner to the countess was twice so. He knew all he had to know about her immediately. These women took and took and took. They bargained hard, they lied. They had the hard pride of winners. She was married to a financier he had heard of, a moneylender. He had nothing, he thought, against such people, but what did she want of his uncle?

Ben whispered to him when saying good-night, "Wait up for me."

"So? What do you think of her?"

"She's a very handsome woman, Ben."

"Ha! ha! ha! I know what you think. You think I'm out of my class. Never mind. There are things you can't understand. I don't blame you. All you see is her surface, I've seen her heart." His smile was so gentle, Jonathan had to smile in turn.

"In time, you'll understand."

For the next quiet instant Jonathan thought that perhaps he had been wrong, that perhaps everything would be all right, but then he knew that the darkness was something else.

Ben said, "You know there was a fire in Artie's place in Beverly Hills." Jonathan felt distaste. He hated these stories. "A hundred and fifty thousand dollars of goods. Everything went up in smoke. Seventy-five thousand dollars he owes me."

Jonathan had turned away, and now he looked at Ben and Ben was nodding.

"I gave him seventy-five thousand dollars in merchandise."

"Oh, Ben, what a rotten time to lose that money!" he said in exasperation because Ben should never have given that much credit and because he was in no position to help.

"Lose? No. It's bad money become good."

Jonathan felt weak. He asked no direct question, not that he was then certain of what had really happened, but that he sensed that not only would Ben not give him a direct answer but that the issue was already beyond that.

Ben was wearing a suit and tie and was in an armchair leaning forward, looking calmly at his nephew—his heavy horn-rimmed eyeglasses—his hands loose between his knees.

Jonathan felt he was sinking in darkness. Nor could he for his gigantic debts reach out to his own hopes. Everything was falling to pieces, and what does a man do? And then he thought, What can I do for him? And then, What does he really want of me? And behind all the questions an image of his wife was taking form, Sheila waiting for him in their New York apartment.

Max was sitting at his side on the park bench and was saying, "So they said I'd need a *smoking*. 'A smoking?' I said.

" 'A *smoking, quoi*! A tookseedo!' Dan said, and he said he had just the thing. He'd had a tuxedo made just for tonight, and he said he had this old tuxedo. It was my Uncle Irving's, and it was given to my father, and my father gave it to Dan. It's Brooks Brothers . . ."

Jonathan was smiling impatiently. He said, "Your heroes are underdogs. That's all right. Don't be one. Your heroes are tormented. That's no good at all. The thing is to be great. Don't interrupt, I'm not arguing. You could become a scoffer, a critic. They are nothing. Your Uncle Ben . . . You are not a man—and if you are not a man you are nothing—if you are not loyal."

The boy sensed his cousin was speaking of blood loyalty, of blood oaths. About them children were playing. Jonathan saw the boy through mist. In such a mood he could almost cry for the welling love in him or he could be hard as stone. The boy thought he understood.

"You mean I have to guard Ben's secret?"

"No. You have to live the secret."

He stood, he reached for his jacket. He looked automatically at his watch. But then he smiled gently and said again, "Where to now?"

6

Dan said to his nephew, "*Il faut bien rigoler!*"

"What does *rigoler* mean?"

The uncle, who had just passed him a handful of banknotes, winked and said, "Ha! ha! ha! To have a good time!"

Tanya was not back from the hairdresser.

Max wore a raincoat over his tuxedo and went to the Plaza Athenée.

It was a classic black tuxedo. The lapels were black-satin-covered and wide, and there was a black satin stripe down each pants leg. The suit had been tailored to Max in a hurry, but the fit was good. Though he had tried the suit on several times, he had only once or twice put his hand in a pocket. In the metro, he put his hand in a jacket pocket and brought out an invitation to the Russian Medical Society Annual Dinner of 1940. He had thought that the tuxedo had been given to his father by Mary after Irving's death, that his father had kept it without ever touching it. But no, he had worn it once.

He showed the invitation to Ben, who had been a long time in a bath and still had not begun to dress. He was nearsighted, but had to hold it almost at arm's length to read. He smiled, "Yes, yes, I remember. Your Uncle Irving was to give a speech. He gave your father his old tuxedo so he could attend."

His bathrobe was wine red brocade.

Jonathan and Max had removed their jackets, the high room was not air-conditioned and was pleasant, the gauze at the windows billowed.

Ben said, "Not even Rome can touch this city!"

His dressing, which he shared with them—coming in to talk to them while shaving, appearing then in shirt, black dinner pants, and gleaming shoes, his hands spread palms up for Max to attach the gold cufflinks, and then the tie, the equations of which Jonathan balanced and tightened, and then, hair combed, coming in touched with scent for the slow putting on of the white dinner coat—had something so luxurious about it as to seem celestial. Nor had his face ever seemed so freshly shaven, so youthful, never his hair so curly, never his eyes so bright.

Jonathan said to his uncle, "You put all the boys in the shade."

But then, even as Ben was confirming in the mirror, the countess's bedroom door opened and she filled the corridor, and though only Ben could see her approach, the nephews were both standing when she entered the sitting room.

She wore a tight-waisted long light-blue dinner gown, her neck and shoulders were bare. She went right to Max.

She had a thing with him—when they had first met she had insisted he was French, had admired his beret and lapel-less jacket—a complicity, an understanding: You too are free. And now she made him put on his tuxedo jacket and turn around, and she, who was so exciting, the breadth of her shoulders, and who had all the authority of beauty, money, poise, and even title, took for herself, as if through her compliments and decency with him, a touch of tenderness, like that a sister or a younger aunt might have.

"*Gutt shabas!*" That was Dan at the door, smiling so broadly all his face was a smile, he too in white dinner jacket, and Tanya behind all in pink billows and fluff, and a regularity to her face that was almost that of a porcelain doll, but too much intelligence and sensitivity in her eyes. She too was a beauty.

"Dearie!" Ben said, kissing her hand.

Dan had brought flowers for the countess.

Ben gave Dan, the Frenchman, a bottle of champagne to open. He raised his glass, and they all raised theirs, gaily but with a touch of solemnity for their first toast: "To friendship!"

Ben asked Max to retell his tuxedo story.

"You are wearing your father's mantle!" Tanya said.

"The Katz mantle," Jonathan corrected.

"What is the Katz mantle?" the countess asked archly, but not unpleasantly.

Tanya said to the countess, "I knew nothing of Dan's background. But when he showed me the photograph of his father and mother, I knew I could marry him."

"The photo," Max asked, almost seeing it under the glass of the dining-room table, "where they are sitting on a park bench in Warsaw in their overcoats, he in a bowler hat?"

Tanya touched his hand.

"Is it true," Dan asked, already believing, "that it was because of Irving that we could not get out of France in 1941?"

Ben looked to Jonathan, the secret was not his.

"Irving said to me, 'Not one cent for bribes and corruption!' " Jonathan said, tapping his finger in the palm of his hand like a schoolteacher. Dan smiled wanly. He recognized something of his brother.

"Did he say that?"

"He asked me to leave his office." Jonathan nodded, grinning.

"Irving and Saul were both proud men," Ben, who had begun to serve hors d'oeuvres—gray caviar, smoked sturgeon, thin slices of buttered toast—said. "Doctors! Intellectuals! They were the best of men! But you know, your father, Max, was the better doctor! He could have been a great doctor! What a diagnostician he was! He took one look at you, and he would say, 'This is what you have!'"

"Is that so?" Dan asked, for though he was still shrugging off the hurt of Irving he loved to hear of these brothers.

"Only he lacked confidence," Jonathan said.

"Yes," Ben agreed, "he was too scrupulous."

"Perhaps he didn't want 'confidence,'" Max said.

Tanya said, and surely what Jonathan had confirmed about Irving had reminded her of a bitterness, "To succeed in life, to get what you want, you *must* have confidence. It's like luck or health, and if it's not always pleasant to have it when others do not, you must still have no scruples about using it!" She felt she had spoken too harshly. She was not harsh, she was not tough, but she had learned how harsh and tough the world was.

She explained, "Not once, not twice, but three times I've lost everything. When I was a young girl in Russia, I had an English governess and a French. I began again in Berlin, and in art school I was first. Still, I didn't even know I was a Jew. That time all we could take was what we could fit into a suitcase. In France we had to *disappear*, we had to leave the little we had and *hide*.

"No," she said, the chagrin still with her, "I don't want to be unhappy. Do you know," she said, smiling tenderly, "it's fifty years almost to the day that my parents came to Paris on their honeymoon. They learned to dance the tango here."

Ben said gently, "Then we shall too."

They moved arm-in-arm down the wide corridors of the hotel, the men in white dinner jackets, except Max in black, and one woman tall in blue, her red hair, and the other no less handsome, but everything about her rounder, softer, in pink, and their walk was almost a dance about Ben, he the tallest of the men, so evidently, though quietly, presiding, so large, that the epauletted door captain and the uniformed boys made wide imperative gestures for them and speeded them on their way.

At Maxim's all was dark red velvet, gold and glittering crystal, all was quiet, aglow, and dim as if gaslit, the very air here was somehow different and separate. Everywhere people in dinner clothes were quietly celebrating.

"How do you like it?" Tanya whispered, putting her hand on Max's, he seated at her side.

"What I'd like," Ben said, "is a champagne dinner."

"I shall drink red wine," Max said. Ben laughed. "Dark red!" Max said.

"*Prince Noir*," the sommelier said, as if he had understood an order in what Max had said.

Menus were brought.

"*Soupes?*" Ben asked, reading a menu for them all. "*Coquillages? Crêpes? Oeufs Cendrillon aux truffes? Pâté de canard de Lucullus?* Scampi? *Suprême de turbot? Poulet aux écrevisses?* Or, *Canard aux pêches?* Well, what shall it be?"

They turned this way and that, they studied, discussed, asked. And finally, amid laughter and pleasure that was so perfectly the very expression of this restaurant that every table's gaiety was perfectly private, they ordered their dinners. Only Dan remained silent and imperturbable during the ordering. He deliberated his every decision and was so serious and studious that Ben pointed him out to their nephew as an example.

"So," Ben then asked Dan, "you told me there was other good news."

Dan became quietly radiant. "I've heard from my sister Sonia. It's thirty years since I've seen her. She's in Moscow, she has a son."

Her picture too had been under the glass of the table. She had been twenty years old, her hair cut short, head bent pensively, clearly a student, an intellectual, the kind who hides her beauty in severe clothes and dedication.

Dan had spoken low, and Ben understood that secrecy was involved, that probably it had been a great risk to some people just to communicate to Dan the news of Sonia's being alive. Still he said gaily, "And you kept this miracle quiet during all the time you ordered your dinner! Aie! That, darling, is what it means to be a Katz!"

Tanya said, "When Dan eats—you know the joke—the whole world can go jump in the lake!"

"No," Dan said, "only when I order. The eating takes care of itself. It's the ordering that is sacred."

Ben said, "You'll live to be a hundred!"

And the warmth of the moment was somehow prolonged and made palpable by the arrival just then of the food.

The scampi were giant, they were presented like a bouquet to the countess, pink with red and sea-salad green, they seemed even alive and asking to be eaten. As for the *Oeufs Cendrillon aux truffes*— that Ben, Dan, and Max had all ordered—that was out of chicken and out of the earth, but was touched by the gods, the scent of it magic. One had *langouste* and another *huîtres*, and there were plates within plates and the plates made a circle of their own on the round table, and there was movement of hands and food from one plate to another, and hands that came from behind and above as from velvet and crystal, for there was a captain for their table and two waiters to serve, and boys, and their champagne glasses were so nicely attended to that Ben had only to think of gesturing that the glass was filled.

"What do you know about truffles?" Jonathan asked Max.

"They're mushrooms."

Of course, Ben thought, they're mushrooms, I knew that.

"Pigs root them out of the earth," Jonathan said.

"Then oink, oink! Oink, oink!"

"They're worth their weight in gold," Dan said.

But Max had hunched down over his plate in his tuxedo and had scrunched up his face at the level of his plate and was oink, oinking, and everyone was laughing.

"What a boy he is!"

The countess waved her wand at him and said, "Dance with me!" He stood instantly, performing still, handsome, straight, even as tall as her.

Ben laughed and said, "Countess, countess, he doesn't know how to dance!"

"Be careful," Tanya said to Max.

She said to Ben when the countess had by the outstretched hand led Max off, "He is very low."

Ben did not understand and so smiled warmly.

"He's very high," Jonathan said.

"He is at zero," Tanya insisted.

Ben said, "He's a good boy, he'll be all right."

"Ben," she said, "he is very troubled."

"Who isn't?"

Jonathan almost reached out to touch his uncle.

Max would never be a dancer, but he impersonated one so well for the space of one dance, was so perfectly a man at ease in a tuxedo, that Jonathan wondered if Max had possibilities he had not thought of before.

"Will you write of us?" the countess asked when they had returned to the table.

Max said, "Even now I am."

"You better come with me," Jonathan said, standing. He took him to the *toilettes*.

He said, "You lean forward, you put two fingers into your mouth, then deeper, deeper, and you throw it all up. Do as I say!"

The boy, looking at himself in the mirror, did as he was told, things had already been swirling. He washed out his mouth and was ready to return, but Jonathan held him there.

"You've only begun. You've got to get it all up."

He stood then weak, leaning on the sink.

Jonathan said, "How does it begin, what you're writing? What's the first line?"

"It's about the river Berezina."

"What has the river to do with *anything*?"

"What you want is a first line that tells us that you know who you are and know what you've got to offer. What do you have to offer *me*? What do you have to offer people? Deeper!" he exclaimed. "Deeper!"

Tanya was concerned for the boy who sat now all pale and recovering and only tasted his *confit de canard*.

Max's *Prince Noir* had been served and it was dark and tasted, he said, of the past. Ben tasted it and nodded.

"It tastes of the past," he said warmly to his nephew.

"Of the past, thick as blood," Jonathan said.

"Then it's just what I need." The countess poured some drops from Max's glass into her champagne. The red fell like dye, and she drank it down.

Tanya said to Max, "It tastes of sleep and of dreams."

Even then the musicians were playing a tango as Ben had quietly requested. Tanya blushed.

"Dearie," he said, standing.

She went with him to the dance floor.

It was all so suddenly sad and beautiful there was a haze before her eyes, and all the other dancers were out of dreams too, and the steps sideways and the steps back, and the gowns swirling, and the men arched backwards. She felt so young, her father was her cavalier, and it was so wonderful she grew quite afraid.

Now came the *volaille* and it too was truffled and the farce was *foie gras*. It melted even before it reached your lips, its essence was spirit, it rose all about you, it flew, it flew!

"Never have I eaten chicken like this!" Ben exclaimed.

"Uncle Ben! Uncle Ben!" Max reproached. "I've heard you say that before!"

"Chicken! Chicken! What chicken we have eaten! We have eaten Russian chicken, and Eshka's East Bronx chicken, and Mima's Rockaway chicken, and, yes, Dora's Friday night chicken, and now we eat Maximum chicken!" he concluded, looking at the countess as if she were chicken.

"*Poularde*," she almost sang, correcting him, leaning forward, throaty.

"*Poularde*," he cooed.

And the birds flew between the diners' heads and hands, and the waiters reaching in, and the champagne flowing now from here, now there.

They danced.

The countess danced again with Max, and Jonathan with Tanya, and Ben with the countess, and then Dan with the countess.

Max spoke of the Jewish quarter where he had taken Jonathan

that afternoon to change dollars. "It's legal and illegal. You run no risk, but the moneychanger does. They're all named Max," Max said. "The Max we went to—in a small café, he always looking out the window—asked, 'Bist a Yid?' I hear Yiddish," Max said, "and I feel a little at home."

"He hears Yiddish, and says he feels at home," Jonathan said, "only who spoke with his Max? This Max doesn't speak the language."

"Why don't you speak it?" Ben asked with astonishment.

"He eats it!" Jonathan said. "He eats pastrami and changes money and is a Jew!"

"You are so American!" Tanya said of Max.

Jonathan said, "What's wrong with being American?"

"You think you can do anything. Ben," she whispered, "she is not a countess."

"Ha! ha! ha! Dance with me, dearie!"

And this too was part of it, dancing with Tanya, to catch the countess's eye so that each knew the other was really dancing with whom he would. And smiling down at Tanya to see the glow of the countess, for she had been dancing and dancing, and, before the end of the dance, by a wink at Dan—who was, after all, a man of the world—to change partners.

His hair was a little disordered, and the countess put her hand into his curls. "Ben! You are so handsome!"

"Darling, you are my fountain of youth!"

She laughed, but her hands framed his face and they danced like that.

"In nineteen forty-one, we went every day to the American consulate in Marseilles. Only we were hundreds, and they would process only five or ten an hour. And they made us wait *outside*! Do you understand? I'm not speaking of the rain or cold. Outside in full view of the German-paid police, who could take pictures of us, or insult us, or ask for our identity papers and arrest us if they wanted."

"How, countess," she asked as Ben and the countess returned to the table, "do you stay so young?"

"Darling, he is my fountain of youth," she said so naively and then smirked that all but Tanya laughed.

"Dearie, dearie, what is it?"

"You have never had to run! None of you has ever had to run and hide. You do not know!"

"We know! We know!" Ben said, drowning her. And he did know.

He knew and he knew. He knew even what he was doing, which no one else really understood, even the countess, his very partner. For he appreciated Tanya's concern, yes, she was right and was good to speak as she had, but she was wrong, and he appreciated what Jonathan gave him, his love as thick and real as blood, and he wanted to say to Max, "Yes, Max, we can even bring the past and the dead to life." Yes, ha! ha! ha! For we can do anything. For who—ha! ha! ha!—is to stop us?

He danced faster and faster with the countess, who alone in all the world could keep up with him, and suddenly she stopped him, breathless, and she removed his horn-rimmed eyeglasses and took his face between her hands and kissed him on the lips, the other dancers swirling still, all in a blur.

There is an end to dying and a fullness in death.

It is what I have observed and lived, and that is the beginning of what I have to offer.

Max was exultant walking alone in the close-to-dawn Paris streets, his raincoat over his tuxedo. He was certain of his strength, his mind teemed with people, he was a giant. But like a dog who follows the scent even without thinking, he found himself near Chatelet. The prostitutes here at this hour were few and old or fat; a dwarf too was pacing a corner. It was a cobblestoned street where during the day flowers were sold and in the streetlamp light flower dyes stained the cobblestones dark red and purple. He found an unsmiling girl thin as a board and went with her.

She was in a hurry.

She opened his pants and drew his thing out and looked at it and washed it with soap and water. He had removed his raincoat and now began to remove the satin-lapelled jacket, but she had already raised her skirt and positioned herself at the edge of the bed, and he did not remove his jacket or even his tie. She aimed him home into the dark between the span of the lace elastics of her garter belt, and he thought later, This too is what I am and who I am, and this is even what I want and deserve.

Ben awoke to pee and afterwards stood at the sometimes billowing gauze at the window, faint moonwhite lights on in the hotel patio below, the milky city sky and yet some stars.

His pajama top was open.

She slept, her breathing profound, her arm stretched toward his place in the big bed.

His boy had said, "I took a bus to the Dead Sea. It's the lowest spot in the world. It's such a bitter place there's salt even in the desert, and if you bathe in the sea your skin burns. And there, in that desert, on a desert slope up from the sea, was Ein Gedi. They've made an oasis in the desert."

"No," Ben had said without reflection, and then haltingly in Hebrew, "My beloved is the flowers in the vineyards of Ein Gedi."

Where had that come from, from what corner of my mind?

My beloved *is* the flowers in the vineyards of Ein Gedi.

Then he felt a sharp burning pain that reached in and back even to his kidneys. "Aie!" he cried, gripping his thing hard with both his hands.

CHAPTER *Eleven*

1

"THERE IS A CALL in me for the sea even if the sea has been for me only walking the boardwalk at Rockaway. It is the call for clean flowing water in the spring. It is the summer longing for cold mountain streams, and that is in us all.

"I showed you where I've begun to build a storehouse. I had to learn to mix mortar. You shovel the sand and lime together. With the back of the shovel you hash through the mixture. You circle the mixture shoveling, hashing, smoothing. In the hot sun, and the tool in my hands, and the mixture on the ground before me, and sweating."

They were quiet before the fire. A lamp was lit in a corner by the bookshelves, but the broad-planked room seemed lit by the fire, the light flickering and changing. They had never heard Jack talk so long and they—his two favorite older nephews, one Joe's son, the first of the American-born, the football player, boxer, and Harvard boy, and the other, Sam, the gentlest perhaps of all the family, who had worked at his side at the cutters' table twenty years—listened carefully even to his silences as if to his thoughts, for in the course of that day they had, though they had come here as messengers, begun to sense that *they* were somehow at issue.

They had driven up in Sam's red Oldsmobile convertible, they both wore sports coats. They did not intend to stay overnight, but they had glimpsed their beds made, twin beds, a child's room, it was a hundred years since they had slept in such beds. They were here without their wives, their children; there was such a deep silence about the house, they were disoriented. And Jack was changed. He was older, his hair was thinner. His head had always been too small for his body, his nose seemed even more than before to hawk down over his mouth. Living alone he had lost the habit of looking at himself, and his clothes were shapeless, his hands were earth-stained. When he spoke it was a little as if he were speaking to himself, and he did not hear everything that was said to him.

He had shown them his property, the field of spindly apple saplings he was even then working foot by foot. There were ten lines of twenty trees each. He had shown them the long narrow field where he had planted rosemary, and in that corner of the field he would have beehives. He had shown them the garden, there were tomatoes yet, though the season was too far gone for them to ripen, there was late corn on the stalk that they had picked for dinner. He had shown them potatoes prepared for winter storage, told them how important it was for them to be laid out flat and stored dry and kept dry. He had shown them the chickens, and among them four cocks. "I have killed one. The way I eat, it lasted a week. I don't like to kill, though four cocks do me no good." He had gathered the eggs. "Six eggs for seven hens," he had said proudly. "Though in two years I shall have to renew the chickens."

"That band of property," he had said pointing, "I can buy. The porch foundation can be used to make the living room larger."

Why is he listing for us? They felt, they did not know why, delinquent.

He wanted to explain, There have been moments in my life so piercingly lived before that I know we recognize our deepest needs and longings only through echoes and dreams. Mixing mortar I was thousands of years ago.

He said, "I'm speaking about a house. A house is midway between how we live our lives and the earth. But your houses are empty."

They had even known he would attack them. What does he mean our houses are empty? Is he speaking of our wives, our children?

But they had information he did not, and they were as loyal as they were modest, and they thought, He is attacking us only that we are the weakest link, but he is attacking all the family, all of us, the way we live. Nor would they allow that he had chosen to speak to them for they had been sent and not invited and that would have been too much like pride. Still Marty sensed something like that in the regret he felt thinking they would not sleep in those beds in that room.

Jack said, "We are responsible for the way we live our lives."

Marty wondered if Jack knew that he and his wife were in psychoanalysis and if he was attacking him a little for that. He said, "Nevertheless, Uncle Jack, it's important for a man's self-esteem to be a success."

Jack thought, What does he mean?

Sam spoke with a welled-up bitterness that was only partly that everyone always criticized Margo. "You want me to divorce her? Because she's big and doesn't give in? But she's smart, ambitious. And if she's loud, so was Eshka! Yes, there's much in her of Eshka! Her taste for earrings, and bracelets that jangle! Is that wrong?"

Though he would not tell even Marty that she too was in psychoanalysis, that she had once bought a dog for their boy and then had found the dog too much a bother and had yelled at the dog that it was ruining the carpet and stank, and they had gone for a drive in the open car and she had sat in the back, he and his son in the front, and when they had stopped the dog had been gone. "She jumped from my lap," she had said.

"Is it wrong that she's already reserved a place at the Dalton School so that my boy will not be a furrier if he doesn't want to be one, though will be if he wants, but always, no matter what, will be a gentleman! No, I wouldn't be ashamed to have my son in my business as I am in Ben's.

"Uncle Jack," he said, and there were tears in his eyes, "must we judge you as you judge us? You say we're responsible for the way we live our lives. Before whom are we responsible? Before you?"

"I think," Marty said, "he means before God."

"Or maybe he means," Sam said bitterly, "before the law."

Jack was shaking his head. He had dug everything he had said out of himself as out of the earth, and what he was hearing now was only words. He said, "We do justice on ourselves."

"Because, Uncle Jack, you left us when we needed you!"

Jack paled. He looked at them deeply for the first time. They were afraid of him as of hurting him. Sam was steeling himself to speak.

Marty said quickly, as if to begin with the least, what in fact had passed out of Sam's mind, "Mary's dying, she has a generalized cancer."

"Mary's dying," Jack repeated softly. He was weak and empty.

He thought, It is back. He thought, She was dying even then. Yes, in the long living room of that nice apartment, the grand piano, the books, the bird on a perch in its cage, and already It inside her.

"She was operated on for a breast cancer a year ago," Sam said, "and no one knew."

Emma knew.

"She confided in no one," Marty said, shaking his head. It had only then occurred to him. This dying of a cousin's widow had never seemed so important.

Jack sat down. She was in him now, this other grief.

"How are you, Uncle Jack?" Marty asked. "Do you feel all right?"

He felt the two nephews reaching to him. They had been here all day, all day he had been trying to tell them what he might have told them better by gripping them to him in his arms.

Boys, boys, we can make a life!

He asked Marty softly, "How is the baby Eshka?" For Marty's second child had been born just after Eshka's death and her Jewish name was Eshka's.

"She is fine. The boy is as good-looking as his daddy," Marty said. "Ha! ha! ha!"

Jack said, "The next time you come, you'll come with your families."

But Sam, whose eyes were wet, that of course as Jack loved him he loved his wife and children and wanted to see them here, that he had to tell all and that if he did not speak now he would not (knew that Marty had already decided, as if generous, that he would not hurt his uncle more), said, "Leah is undergoing tests."

The way he looked at Jack, breathless, the frozen tears, gauging his reaction, Jack knew he still was not through, and Jack felt the dark invading the room thick as night, and he said, "Are you telling me all?" Thinking, Tests is only a way to begin to tell me; thinking, Where is Leah right now?

"It's Ben."

That could not be.

He had stood, and his hands were on Sam's shoulders. "What is it with Ben?"

"He's in trouble."

He could breathe now.

"He wants to see you."

"What kind of trouble is he in that he must send you first?"

Sam wanted to say, He doesn't even know how much trouble he's in, but he saw his uncle's face.

"It's money trouble, isn't it? He needs money, doesn't he? What are you buying now? Are you buying more ships? Or are you buying gambling casinos? What shit are you buying now? Tell him I'm his brother and I'll not refuse him. I am here."

Long after they had gone and the fire had died, Jack still sat in his chair in the dark, and in his mind were a hundred rooms, and Mary was in one, her eyes glowing, and under her hospital gown her breast was gone and her underarm gone, and It was under her arm. And Leah was in another room. And there were doors and doors he would not open. There were corridors in his mind, and they converged into other corridors, and the corridors were full of people going toward machines.

Only It was here and It was there. Their hair would grow dry and would fall out. They would die in pain. How do we wrestle that? How do we live to be old?

Even then he was walking Leah down one of those corridors.

This room was cold; with every day the dying women were further and further alone.

He thought of digging and planting. He thought, if I do not reach my nephews, who will? He thought, When I spoke of mixing mortar was I not saying I was building my house? Was I not saying that what we want, what is in us, is house? It is a landmark up in our needs. Boys, house!

I offer you apples and rosemary, and spoonfuls of honey fragrant with rosemary. My hands, boys, have dug the honey out of the earth, my fingertips are burned to blood with mortar.

But no matter where you go, no matter where you hide, no matter that you build, the bastards come limping to you. Who will bring me good news! Leah is dying even now! And I want a woman.

He was kneeling into a woman who was rising to him. Edith! Edith! We shall have a son! He could have burst the house with his need.

Outside the night was clear, the sky was filled with an eternity of cold stars. And then, as if his appearance had interrupted them, nightbirds were singing. Surely there were multitudes of birds, and sweet nightingales, and he looking at the stars was comforted thinking eternity was made intimate by the birds.

But in the morning he went to kill the cocks.

He washed his hands fastidiously. He had a small-bladed knife that he sharpened on a whetstone. He wore his earmuffed cap and a full denim workshop apron.

He had to separate the cocks from the hens, and though they would sometimes, when he entered their enclosure, fly at him as if to show who was master here, they fled him now. He walked heavily behind the skirt of his apron, his heavy-fingered hands hanging low. The cocks and hens were shrieking now, half-running, half-flying into corners, against the netting of the fence.

There was an excitement in him too, to lunge, to do it. But he could not, as if there were a code written in him, as if he like the knife were only an instrument. His every gesture had to be right, every step certain. There was a moment of pause and every hen and cock was poised, one chicken leg planted, the other as if on tiptoe, the beady eyes that seemed to be looking elsewhere. His hand shot out, and he caught a cock by its stick leg and held it then out from his body upside down, the cock's wings beating the air.

At a distance behind the house he hung the cock by its legs to a tree branch. He caught the tense swinging neck of the cock and then slipped his gripped hand down its neck almost to the little head, the upside-down beady eyes, and with the razor-sharp knife he cut the thick artery of the neck. He kept the neck and head pulled down tight as the blood showered and then fountained out, the soul of the animal and thus we eat no blood, and with the knife hand he caught and stopped the beating wings against his body.

The bleeding had ceased, and the blood on the ground was congealed like a pudding, but as he let go of the dead animal the wings opened wide again and beat wildly.

He was expecting Ben but not Sol, though when in midafternoon he saw the two waiting for him on the foundation outside the house —in city topcoats and hats, little Sol peering through the living-room window—he was not surprised. Sol had always been closest to Ben, a complement to him even as Yiddish was a complement to Ben's English. Sol was pure mother-tongue, open-mouthed astonishment before all achievements as before all misfortunes. He was slow, simple, and half-deaf, for his eardrums had been punctured when he had been a boy and he had to keep cotton in his ears still. His arms were too long for his body, which anyhow hung forward a little, and his mouth was wide for laughter and sorrow. He too had been a wrestler.

Ben, standing straight, was lost in his thoughts.

Jack glimpsed in Ben's face that he was not thinking of him, of what he could do for him, but, as if in the city, as if in the place, already of other appointments, of lunch at The Traders, of a buyer from Chicago. They brought the city with them, the Thirtieth Street crowds, the cigar smokers, the men in a hurry.

They had brought him a Zenith portable radio. The antenna telescoped up six feet. "With this you can get all the world," Ben said.

They tried the radio standing on the foundation outside the house. "It's a very good radio," Jack said.

"So?" Ben said, smiling largely, looking all around.

What was it about him that was so different? Not that he was lean or that his hair, when he removed his hat, was fuller and curlier. He carried himself still like a heavy man, he stood poised and bent back as if from great substance. That his manner with him was changed.

Jack thought, He has sold us all our lives, only then he believed. He sold me when he convinced me to leave Joe's business and start a business with him, he sold me when we all rented apartments in the same building off the Grand Concourse even as when we every summer all rented rooms in the same hotel in Belle Harbor. He sold me every time we went to the same restaurant or movie! He sold me a thousand decisions, only then he believed, only then he was enthusiastic even for me, for my sake. Now he is here to sell me something he knows I will not buy but only give.

Jack gestured them forward to show them his land, to take them across his fields as he had more than once in his mind. Then, leading them, he suddenly stopped, knowing what about Ben was so strange.

"You're not wearing eyeglasses!"

"Ha! ha! ha! Science!" Ben said. Jack did not understand. Sol thought it a wonderful joke, and Ben held onto it a moment longer for effect.

"Apple trees!" Jack exclaimed, pointing his sewn-together fingers. "Two hundred apple trees!"

"They are baby trees," Ben said.

"They will grow large and sturdy. The tips of their branches will touch, and you will walk here in their shade. Next year I shall buy two hundred more trees, and I shall plant another field. You're wearing slippers, not shoes! Come!"

He walked at his pace, which was not fast, but they were not used to walking the land, and Sol was short-legged, and they trailed after him.

"That field too I shall buy!"

"What?" Sol called.

"I shall buy that field too."

"What can it cost, a field like that? A hundred dollars?"

"There I shall build for more chickens, a hundred chickens."

"A hundred chickens! Is it worthwhile?"

"Every chicken gives me something. Every day every chicken gives me an egg."

"That is something," Sol said, nodding his head, lost, in spite of himself, in calculations.

"I've planted rosemary there."

"Rosemary?" Ben said.

Jack broke a sprig off a plant and squeezed it in his hand under Ben's nose. "Ah," Ben said.

Beyond the field of rosemary were fields and woods that rose so gently that the distant mountains seemed to rise out of them.

"You will have bees?" Sol guessed. "Bees?" He took off his hat, he was nearly bald, and he was smiling broadly and he slapped his hat against his topcoat at his thigh.

"Rosemary," Ben repeated musingly. "All these years we smelled this in Rockaway in the pillows on Mima's sofa, and it was rosemary."

"We could make pillows," Sol said.

"It's very quiet here," Ben said.

"How is Leah? Is it only tests?"

Ben said, "He doesn't believe me. Sol, is it only tests?"

Sol nodded, his long lips were turned down at their ends.

"Ah, brother," Ben said, "we know each other so well."

"You'll stay for dinner?"

"Let us take you to dinner."

"No. Are you thirsty?"

"I could drink."

"There's soda water."

"No beer? Brother, how you loved cold beer!"

They were walking slowly back toward the house and road, Ben's four-door Oldsmobile pulled off the road at an angle, and there were comfortable distances between them.

"Sunday mornings we would go for a walk on the boardwalk, in the heat, and it would be a reducing walk for me and an exercise walk for Jack. But he, what a thirst, and he never had to reduce, he would say, and I would be waiting for it, when we passed the big delicatessen, 'So?' Then he would order a draft of beer and I would order hotdogs! I would order: 'Give me two heartburns!' Ha! ha! ha!"

There had been sun and now it was cool, and Jack, before serving them soda water, made a small fire.

"At home, we drink No-Cal," Sol said.

They had removed their hats and topcoats, they sat in their suits and ties, and facing the fire they sipped their drinks.

Ben asked, "Do you remember Judy?"

Jack's shoulders drew back as if, How could I not? Her father had been a skin dealer and friend. He had died when the girl had been young, and the mother and then the brother had run the skin business and the girl had gotten scholarships.

"Do you remember the conversations on the porch of the hotel at Belle Harbor? Waiting in rocking chairs for dinner time. Or in the dark after dinner. Henry Wallace! Do you remember how she insisted everyone vote for Henry Wallace? She's married to a surgeon in Philadelphia, they just had a little boy."

"That's good," Jack said.

Jack asked, "So, how are you?" But Ben only smiled.

Ben said, "I'm thinking of Weeks Avenue in the Bronx. Do you remember when Louis's first was born, the circumcision? I was on the sixth floor, and you were on the third, and Sol was on the fourth just a few doors down from Louis. It was a holiday time."

"It was this time of year," Sol said. "Toward Rosh Hashona and Yom Kippur."

"It was the first great-grandchild," Jack said.

"We went from the hospital to Weeks Avenue in taxis, in your Buick."

"The doctor's two-door Chevy," Jack said.

"Everyone was in my apartment except the children, who were in yours, Sol. And the mother and child in Louis's, with visits from the wives. And a report came that the baby was crying. 'The baby is crying! The baby is crying!' spread from one apartment to the other. Immediately the uniformed flyer went down, and he went koochie-koo, koochie-koo, but still the baby cried, howled, as you know babies can. He was already an officer, a hero, and he came running back: 'Doctor, the baby won't stop crying! Doctor, the baby!' So the doctor put down his pinochle cards and went to wash his hands. And then Louis opened doors that the doctor get no germs on his hands, and they had to take the elevator down for our little mother, may she rest in peace, came with them. But Eshka had gone ahead, she had arrived before them all. And the little baby was in her arms, the mother standing behind her, and she was rocking the little baby in her arms at her breast, and the baby was sleeping, sleeping so nicely.

" 'What did you do?' they asked. 'What did you do?'

" 'Sh!' she answered, smiling. 'Sh!' she answered smiling. Do you remember?"

"Like it was yesterday."

Sol was nodding his head.

The room had grown warm, the fire was flaming. Their bodies were at rest in their chairs, though sometimes one or another would cross his legs or stretch them. Outside it was growing dark.

Outside were the fields he had worked in the spring and summer, that had given in the summer and now lay quiet and bare and would soon be covered by the winter. And inside were these brothers, and Weeks Avenue, and July Fourth parades on the Grand Concourse, and the IND to the place, and the New Campus restaurant where all the growing-boy nephews ordered Boston cream pie for dessert and where there were live lobsters in the big plate-glass windows. The warmth, the memories, sapped his will. He was tired of his anger and bitterness.

Ben said, "Do you remember when we'd be in a hole, unable to pay our debts, even the salaries? And in those days workers made money just to be able to feed their families! I'd pack suitcases with furs and go off across the country to sell in every town and city! I'd be gone weeks, and then suddenly one day I'd enter the showroom pushing the doors open, and I'd open my suitcases, and there would be the cash!"

"I remember," Jack said, "when you arrived in America. You came out of immigration on the dock knit together, every one of you with a hand to support our mother. I remember your greenhorn caps."

"Even that first day," Sol said, "you bought us suits."

"I'd thought I'd never see my mother again. You gave me second wind. I knelt to our mother, and my arms about her, and hers about my head, and I was weeping, and when I opened my eyes I saw you, Ben. When I'd left Russia, you'd been a boy. Now you stood so straight, and you were looking right at me, and there was such warmth in your regard, such confidence and manly pride. You were beautiful. *You* were America."

"Ach!" Sol said, bringing them his own memories, "we were young then, just beginning."

For an instant the three of them could almost feel the force they had had then in their arms and thighs.

"Where's the bathroom?" Ben asked.

Jack was standing at the window.

"We did well for greenhorns," Ben said, returning. "Look how we've risen. We're farmers! Ha! ha! ha! I'm joking."

"Do you know," Ben said, "Margo's put a bidet in her bathroom. She told me she wants to have an antique bathroom."

"Antique?" Sol said. "An outhouse, maybe?"

These were jokes the brothers put together and made into routines out of their conversations during the every-day drive to and from the city.

"She'd like a gold bathroom."

"That," Sol said, "would really be to sit on a throne."

"I'd like a sauna in my bathroom," Ben said. "Louis spent *five* thousand dollars remodelling his bathroom."

"How is the place?" Jack asked.

He felt the pause that was: Why should you care? But Ben then spoke about bandy-legged Solly, and Gus and his bookies, and his wife's nephew poor Stanley.

"First we hired cousins, landsmen, neighbors. Then every orphan and stray cat had a place with us, and now, with the lousy union, they're suddenly *menschen* and *workers*, and if we want to lay even one off, they all go out on strike on us!"

Jack set the table in the kitchen.

"And the *goyim*?" Sol asked without prejudice at dinner.

"A neighbor boy taught me to mix mortar."

"Aha!" Sol exclaimed, as if that were astonishing information. "Aha!" he repeated. But Jack could tell that his little brother was already thinking of something else, was troubled that it was getting late and that Ben had resolved nothing. The ends of Sol's mouth were down, he hardly listened, he scrutinized his brothers' faces as if that might help him determine what was happening. He did not know how to take the initiative, Ben had always initiated for him.

Ben said, "What do you do for . . . ?" and he winked.

Jack turned away. He brings the city with him and he brings his *chazerai*. And he knows what he is doing, and why does he do this?

Sol said quickly, "Jack, Ben's going for an operation."

But Ben was immediately laughing. "It's nothing! Nothing! It's only the prostate. It's to make me younger! Why don't we all have the operation at the same time? Hm? It's a cosmetic operation. Doctor Jerry tells me it's like fixing a nose, ha! ha! ha! A couple of days' holiday in the *clinic*. The clinic, where they feed you well. Restaurant meals!"

"Brother ..." Jack began.

"Pretty nurses! Television! Not like that lousy Mount Sinai Hospital! Even the doctors. Here they're young and smiling, and they understand people, and none of them will ever say, 'The operation was a success, but the patient died!' "

He was not going to let him speak.

Yes, he would, if I were to get down on my knees, if I were to bow to him that he's done whatever it is he's done, that he is whatever he is, then he'd listen to me, then he'd let me offer to help.

"Brother!"

But just then a familiar pain that he had almost forgotten caught him in the lower body and his sight dimmed and he saw the sunset towers of Central Park West. He had paled but had not even winced, and his brothers were waiting still, and he felt a chill and recognized It then.

He said, "You're not lying to me about Leah?"

Ben said, "Ah, we know each other so well, we know each other's farts."

Sol said, "What's the matter with you two!"

"For you've lied to me before!"

Ben had stood, and now he looked at his watch and said, "It's late, we have a long drive back."

Sol would not get up from his chair before he looked at Jack. But Jack was slouched in his chair, his head almost sunk in his shoulders, and one hand was holding the other, the two sewn-together fingers like a lid.

"You were wrong," Sol said to Ben, who sat stiffly forward at the wheel of the Oldsmobile, his brights on, he rarely remembering in time to dim them for a car passing in the opposite direction. It was a two-lane road, and Ben was not used to driving on unlit roads. The road ran parallel to a twisting river they could not see, and some-

times narrowed, and Ben had to concentrate hard on the edge of the
road. "Schmuck!" he would exclaim angrily when the driver of the
other car would blink his brights at him.

"You never even asked him."

"You think I'd deprive him of even one apple tree!"

But Sol was shaking his head, no, that was not why.

"Did you see the lines in his face?" Ben asked.

Sol nodded.

"Did you feel his hands?"

"They were hard, they were cramped."

Ben was nodding in the dark, leaning toward the wheel. He said,
"He's let himself become an old man."

"It's living alone," Sol said.

"He made his decision all alone!"

"Still," Sol said, "if we'd invested our money in farms . . ."

"Yes?"

"Well, we wouldn't be where we are now. We'd at least have
something."

"We'd have dreck!"

"We'd at least have the eggs."

"The eggs!" Ben exploded. But then he laughed bitterly. "We'd at
least have the eggs! Ha! ha! ha!"

"Yes," Sol said, and his wide mouth broke into a grin, "we'd have
the eggs."

And then they were both laughing.

"And the chickens!" Sol said.

"Only why did he have to kill that lousy chicken *twice*!"

"Ha! ha! ha!"

"Ho! ho! ho!"

"Still, we'd have the eggs!"

"Ha! ha! ha!"

"Ho! ho! ho!"

2

In Los Angeles, Artie had been charged with arson and fraud.
Once again his picture was in the newspapers, though this time not
in the brown-tinted Sunday rotogravure section of the *Jewish Daily*

Forward: "First Jewish Boy Wounded on Iwo Jima." He was given bail, he was not allowed to leave the state of California. In New York, under the clock on Thirtieth Street and Seventh Avenue, at The Traders, furriers asked each other, "How much were you taken for?" Of course, there were heroes who had resisted Artie's pitch, and men of wisdom who had always thought him too slick. The newspapers said the fraud was for a quarter of a million dollars.

Furriers consoled Ben, but Ben smiled blandly at them and said, "Artie's as innocent as a newborn baby lamb!"

The Las Vegas boutique was closed. One day two hoodlums came to the place to remind Ben he owed rent. He called long distance the president of the Eden Corporation. He explained that the boutique was closed, that Artie was under indictment. He said, "You send your goons to me in my place!" He was in the office, and the goons were waiting in the showroom, and his secretary and his bookkeeper were pale with fear.

"You are bloodsuckers!"

Artie called. Ben sensed he was embarrassed and asked gently, "So what is it?"

"Benjy, I can't even pay my lawyer."

"What's his name? I'll send him a coat for his wife."

"Ben! Ben!"

"What's the difference, it's only paper!"

Insurance investigators came to speak with Ben. They called back and made an appointment to look at his books.

"What'll they find?" Jonathan asked Fischer, the accountant.

"It's complicated. Coats went out on consignment to Vegas and then on consignment from Vegas to Beverly Hills. Artie took direct from Ben in New York, and then, just a week before the fire, he took all the pink elephants from Vegas."

"I see," Jonathan said. He was in the private office of the place. He used it now almost as his office, he was there most of the day, every day.

When he arrived at the building, Bob, the uniformed Negro elevator operator, greeted him with quiet respect. "How is Mister Jack, Mister Jonathan?" he might ask.

Fischer sat opposite Jonathan, Sam was on the leather sofa.

"Salaries and operating expenses we can meet," Fischer said. "But we've got notes coming due. You've got to call and convince them it's temporary, to give you time."

"What are you talking?" Ben, wearing his starched duster, standing just inside the private office door, said. "I'm the one who signed, I'm the one who calls."

But some manufacturers were not in when Ben called. Some said they would gladly give time, only first they would have to speak with their partners.

"Anyhow," Ben said to his nephews, "I've things to do in the factory."

Joe said his wife Lily had raised $15,000 cash.

"That's worth thirty," Jonathan said.

Sam's Margo raised $10,000 on her jewelry. Sam had never been so proud of Margo, of her cleverness in buying jewelry, of the value of beautiful things.

Jonathan put the money in a safe deposit box.

Some friends called long distance and asked, "What's happening?"

Jonathan said, "Ben's in trouble," and then hung on.

Some friends said just like that, "I'm good for a thousand."

Pappas, the Chicago Greek who still paid his by-now forty-year-old son only $125 a week, was good for $10,000.

Marty raised $10,000 on his house.

Louis's home in Lawrence was already mortgaged, he borrowed money now on his cars and boat. He would have borrowed on his shoes. He said, "That's being rich! You own nothing, and you keep borrowing on that!"

Emma said she would make the loan, but her husband Bill insisted on a guarantor. "No," Bill said, "I want Joe. He's the only one of you who's really worth anything." Joe signed.

Joe's son-in-law offered $1000.

Louis said, "The son of a bitch!"

"Take it anyhow," Jonathan said.

Jonathan went out to Amityville to see his brother-in-law.

"Yeah? What kind of trouble?"

Jonathan was embarrassed for Mike. "He's probably going to be accused of collusion in arson."

"Yeah?" Mike said, as if, Did he do it?

"Mike, you got your agency through Ben."

"I already know that."

Jonathan's wife Sheila came to him with a check from her mother for $10,000.

At the Blue Angel, Bob Henderson whispered into Jonathan's ear the names of fixers, the unlisted phone numbers of judges. Jonathan had his own fixers; now he had the beginnings of a long list he would keep in his inside jacket pocket.

Dan Weber, who had invested in the ships with Jonathan, suggested he make a gift to a political party. He went with Dan to the Bankers' Club. He recognized the place even as he entered. This was Harvard, Yale, and Princeton, this was the high men's dining halls there become richer, denser. This was banking and seats on the exchange, this was grain, steel, shipping.

They ate with the lieutenant governor and other men whose attributes were so general that one even knew of Jonathan and said, "Oh yes, you're the Cohen who wouldn't sell his place on line."

So that Jonathan was immediately doubly on guard, one world thickening another, he almost having forgotten the other. Ships! Sending ships around the world. Big ships, fast ships! A land and sea network to speed shipping. Trains, trucks, *containers!*

"It's true that I'm having a fifty-thousand-ton tanker built, yes."

But the other just looked at him blandly.

Leah was in a four-bed semiprivate room at the Lenox Hill Hospital in Manhattan. It was an old building, and the windows of the room gave on a dirty gray courtyard.

Who had arranged for this room? Where is Ben? Jonathan thought.

"My Sonny! Why doesn't my Sonny come?" Leah had wept to her daughter Anna and Anna had later wept to a cousin and the cousin had later told others and now, in the hospital lounge, Louis whispered, "Son of a bitch! He's no cousin of mine!"

Max said, "He's in Oak Ridge."

"His mother's here!" Louis said.

"He's a biophysicist," Max said, as if that might make a difference.

Jonathan asked, "Where's Ben?" Sam winked at him, going

through the motions of believing in a joke that no one really thought funny.

"I sit with her," Max said, "and maybe she asks me who washes my shirts. It's when one of the Bereziner ladies comes that she's most interested. They speak Yiddish. She doesn't cry, she doesn't complain, she asks for nothing."

"You come often?" Jonathan asked.

"Every two days or so."

"You'll come to dinner with us."

Max explained, "Columbia's not far, and I haven't that much to do. And," he laughed, "I get free meals."

The Los Angeles County district attorney's office issued a summons that Ben appear there.

Jonathan went to the lawyers Dan had recommended him to. They were bright Jewish boys; they too had uncles, cousins, or in-laws in the garment business. And they never asked what would have sent Jonathan to others. Jonathan smiled his warmest, the steel and dare yet in his smile, and said, "He's never in all his life harmed a fly, the man's as innocent as a newborn babe."

They said he should not go to California.

Fixers said they knew fixers there. Each fixer had a name to sell him. Who were they going to fix? How sure a fix could they buy? Were they going to fix the district attorney?

Jonathan had given $5000 cash to a six-foot-tall smiling Irishman who, some years before, had gotten them a liquor license for Eshka and who now insisted he was making progress.

Jonathan sat in the private office with Sam, Louis, and their Uncle Sol.

Could they make a deal with the insurance company? What kind of deal if the fire was criminal? But Ben's goods were covered by Artie's policy *and* by Ben's.

"Settle," Sol said.

"Settle what?" Louis demanded.

"Settle," Sol repeated like enunciating a principle.

Louis said, "You mean that we should accept that he . . ." His face enflamed even to consider that unspoken prospect.

"Only to avoid scandal," Sam protested quickly.

Now, with news of the summons, Ben's creditors called in one after the other. One apologized, "It's because my daughter's getting married." Some did not have the courage to come up to the place themselves, they sent their sons just out of college. These were men Ben had known, ups and downs, thirty years.

A buyer wanted a 33⅓ percent discount for paying cash.

"Maybe we should declare bankruptcy," Sam said. He was Ben's partner; his future too was at stake, and he did not want to involve everyone else.

Anna came downtown to see Jonathan.

"Darling, why is your mother in such a place?"

Immediately there was offense and tears in her eyes. "Who's to pay for better?"

"What are you talking about?"

"No one's asked me anything. I arranged it. She has no money, we have almost nothing. My brother sent money!"

He took $500 in bills from his wallet.

"I didn't come for this."

"There'll be more. Take it!"

She did.

"I came for your niece. For Sara's daughter."

"Yes?"

"She's not well."

"What do you mean she's not well?"

"She should be seen by a doctor."

The way she said doctor, he understood. He smiled and said, "What kind of *doctor*?"

She took her courage in her hands and said, "She's autistic."

"Goddamn it, darling, what's autistic?"

"She doesn't relate."

"She's not even a year old. What do you want her to relate to?"

"She doesn't reach out, she doesn't focus, she doesn't grip your finger."

"Is that all? Ha! ha! ha! It could be a hundred different things."

It could be coordination, he thought later. It could be her eyesight. He read that such children were born generally of intelligent parents who did not want them. That such children rocked back and forth, back and forth.

The Friedlands' lawyer called Jonathan and in a roundabout way made it clear they were willing to settle out of court at a loss. Did they think that soon nothing would be left?

Dan Weber called him at home and asked, "Would you take a loss on your place on line?"

"Who's offering?" Jonathan asked even as he sat down, for he was drained empty.

Dan said, "I don't know who he represents."

They held on.

Dan said, "That they're interested now means you were right all the way, right about size, right about tankers. It means it's going to be big, someone's going to make a lot of money."

Why did he tell him what he could figure out himself? Did he want him to ask, *when* will it be big? Was he hanging on for that? Or was he standing by as a friend who knew even what he had to say?

"Let him call me and make an offer."

3

When Ben, in the heat and steam of his bath, opened his eyes and saw the single drop of blood hanging in the water at his thigh, he thought of the Bible. He thought, It's only an accident. He thought, I'll have to call the doctor. He thought, I'm disfigured. Can I go to synagogue like this? Better that I stand slowly.

He had laid out his clothes on their big double bed. He weighed himself anyhow and was satisfied. He called the doctor, who was not at home. He called the rabbi.

"What do you think, rabbi?"

"It's not a running infection, it's nothing impure. But to be on the safe side we won't call you to the Ark."

"That's what I thought," Ben said. Smart man! he said to himself of the rabbi.

The doctor came during the meal.

"So, doc," Ben said in the bedroom as the doctor examined him, "a fly in the ointment?"

"It's nothing, Ben, but you better rest. I'll call you in the morning."

Sol had come from next door. He was dressed and ready to go, he had his prayer book, his prayer shawl folded into a small velvet envelope. He could not hide his disappointment. When had they not gone to synagogue together for Yom Kippur?

Dora and Fanny were wearing dark clothes like winter, and Dora's sister wore so much that had been Dora's that Ben looked twice, the hat and veil, the dress. Elaine's clothes were more expensive than her mother's, Dora bought for Elaine what she would think too flowery or extravagant for herself. The girl wore a corset and a girdle, and half-high heels, and a hat with a veil and feather.

Fanny would drive them to within several blocks of the synagogue, and they would walk the rest of the way, the light autumn coats, and there would be families coming from down this street and the next, everyone dressed for the holiday, and on the tree-lined streets there would be little boys in suits wearing white satin *yarmulkas*.

He was resting against pillows on his bed in the half-dark.

He thought there was, nevertheless, a sweetness in their lives in Far Rockaway too. The dressing up and renewing. The hundred handclasps at the synagogue, how after the service men would circle around him to shake his hand.

He saw across the backyard the back of a neighbor's house, night was advancing from the sea. Airplanes, their landing lights on, were coming into Idlewild on an approach almost directly over his house. It was Yom Kippur only for the Jews. He could pick up the phone and put through a long distance call to *her*.

Joe did not go to synagogue although he fasted. Sam went to an orthodox synagogue off the beach like ones there had been in the East Bronx. The boys did not go to synagogue, though they too would fast. Or maybe Louis would fast everything but whisky. Everything changes. I have eaten pork. Am I worse?

The day before he was to enter the clinic for his operation she had phoned him. She was in the city with her husband, someone was giving a party for them. It was in a townhouse, crowds of guests circulated from the long living room to the small terrace and garden outside.

He stood by a column, a drink in his hands. She took his arm and said, "We'll take a walk, darling."

She had no bag, no hat. He had not worn a topcoat, he had left his hat behind. They walked quickly on Madison Avenue; as they approached a hotel, she pulled on his arm.

He did not like that, he did not like to hide, and this hotel was not first class. The room was too small, the ceiling too low. Her long arms, her uptilted thrusting chin. He did not like her urgency, as if they were running from something.

After, she said, "I didn't know. Do you believe me?"

He was dressing.

"What didn't you know?"

"That it's to my husband that Artie owed money."

"Is that so?" he said, nodding. All this time Artie had not told him so as not to trouble him. As if that could have troubled him. We are all children, he thought.

"Do you believe me?" she insisted.

"Sit down," he said. "What shall become of us?" he asked, smiling.

They did not touch, they sat quietly looking at each other.

But walking back it was getting toward dusk and it was cold, and she had gone out without her bag or hat, and he still had to get downtown, and he had to shake the moneylender's hand and say good-bye to her even as briefly.

He went into the bathroom. He had not drained the bath, and in the obscurity it seemed to him that the water had clouded with blood, and he stood motionless a moment and heard then a sound from somewhere in the house, and he cried out, "Who's there?"

"It's only me, Uncle Ben," came the fearful reply of his wife's nephew Stanley.

Ha! They had not even thought to buy a seat for the boy at the synagogue.

He switched on the light, the water was as bathwater is, he pulled the drain. He peed, there was no blood. It would pass, it would pass.

"Do you play gin rummy?" he asked the boy, who sat reading a comic book at the kitchen table.

"I don't know how."

The kitchen was brightly fluorescent lit.

"Never mind."

He had put his hand on the boy's shoulder, the boy's body was tense. He ran his hand through his sandy hair, "Good boy, good boy. You know, I've never meant you any harm. Do you want the television?"

But when the women returned, Dora was angry that the television was on. "It's a high holiday. In every house everyone is begging pardon, and there he is in the den watching television."

"What's the difference?" Ben said from his bed.

"I know the difference," she said.

He shrugged, he felt, in fact, as if he had not even begun to fast.

There was blood on every doorpost and the angel of death was passing from door to door and Ben heard screams and then a terrible wailing.

He woke in a sweat, it was the middle of the night. I must make amends, he thought. I must not put my workers in the street. There's Marie. There's Sid and Julie. Some of the workers are too old to find new jobs. Who will give a job to Stanley?

He was in his recliner in the den. The venetian blinds were slatted open on the streetlight-lit night.

Who will give the nailers a job? And bandy-legged Solly?

One lost one's balance in this chair.

He floated over Far Rockaway, over all the ranch houses. And I flew with Louis in the small airplane and we banked right and we banked left, little sinkings until your feet find the floor. We followed the tracks of the Long Island Railroad, which ran parallel to the boardwalk, which ran parallel to the beach and the ocean, the waves coming in spaced so. Only now it is all milky dark down there, and I bank right and left searching. Happily the television glow is on, for otherwise I would not know where to land.

It was day. There was blood on his underpants. He called the doctor.

At nine, a large bouquet of blue and white flowers was delivered. What are they? he thought, standing in his bathrobe behind Dora.

What are their names? What are their qualities? They are beautiful. But Dora accepted the flowers into her arms frowning, as if at the expense, as if, who sends flowers on Yom Kippur, as if, who sends flowers to us now?

He held the card out to read it, it was addressed to Dora, it was signed by Artie. "What a nice thought," he began. But she threw the flowers to the floor.

"Don't do that," Ben said.

"I don't want his lousy flowers!"

"Princess, the world is collapsing about me."

She turned on him and said with a bitterness that had no limit: "Samson!"

Later the doctor bandaged him and put him to bed.

"The stitching's come loose," Ben said. "Ha! ha! ha!"

The doctor said if the bleeding did not stop in the next few hours they would cauterize the wound at the clinic.

Sol stopped in on his way to the synagogue. "It's not the same without you."

"Of course it isn't."

Louis came from Lawrence to keep him company. That was good, that was like the drive to the city every morning. He had little conversation, squat Louis. He needed an audience to be a clown. Ben could read in his serious manner that he had decided to stay with him all day long.

"A little gin rummy, Louis?"

Anna and Fred came from Woodmere with Larry and Max, who were spending the day with them.

He had not been to see Leah since before his operation.

"How is she?

"So, doctor, what do you say to this? Is it a good bandage?"

Louis watched Larry critically. Someone had to approve Larry's competence, he would be stern.

It occurred to Ben that there was a gathering now about him. He could wink at Max for Max had been to Paris. Louis was like a strong right arm. Now came Jonathan from the city with his darling wife.

"One shouldn't drive on Yom Kippur," he said, smiling.

"I fast," Jonathan said, smiling, indicating his limits. Ben nodded, approving.

Sam came with Margo and his boy. He had been on his way to his sister's split-level house in Amityville and thought to stop in here for a while. Now he would not leave, and he called his sister and she said she would come too.

So in the house there was the sound of children playing. Anna, Larry, Max, and Sol's daughter were playing bridge in the den. It was a little like a Sunday.

The bleeding got no worse, but he felt the beginning of a fever.

"Do you want to rest, Uncle Ben?"

"Yes," he said, putting down his cards.

He knew he was sick then because there were whispering sounds about him. He would close his eyes a little. He felt the not-unpleasant heat at his forehead, he felt heat and languor in his calves.

When he woke, the doctor was there and they were going to the clinic. No matter, he was surrounded. They would go in three cars, all the nephews about him. They would protect him with their bodies. Dear boys!

"No, princess," he said to Dora, "you'll wait here. It'll only be an hour or two."

"Come, give me a kiss," he said to his daughter Elaine, who stood waiting for his call.

"Larry, you stay at my side." He patted the first-year medical student's hand. "You are my doctor."

He was given a private room at the clinic, his dressing was changed. Another doctor appeared. It was already four o'clock in the afternoon.

Fred brought Sam from Rockaway. He shuffled in, his hands trembling. Then Fred brought Sol from synagogue. Ben counted them. He said, "We're almost a *minyan*."

They came to take him to surgery.

He said, "I want the boy with me."

His doctor said, "Well, he is a medical student."

They waited in a bunch in the empty corridor outside surgery.

Though they were all fasting, some smoked. They wore dark suits, some wore city hats. They were two brothers and five nephews.

Where is Jack?
Where is my son?
What are they doing to me?
Cauterize!
Aie! It hurts! It hurts!
He thought he smelled flesh burning there. He began to writhe. But then he saw Larry's face. It is the doctor's boy, it is Eshka's boy.

He was floating again. He was in his recliner floating over the ranch houses and the railroad tracks. He was on a big bed in a small hotel room and a big fan was turning slowly overhead.
He thought, Where am I?
I am short of breath.
There is a word on the tip of my tongue.
Din! Din! Din!
I can't breathe.
I'm sinking.
Aie, who will tell her?

Why did it take so long?
They saw Larry 100 feet away. His mouth was agape, and there was a sudden craziness in all their spirits. They were rushing to the boy. His still acne-marked face fell apart.
"He's dead, he's dead."
They began to moan.
The tall doctor appeared behind Larry, his face confirming.

They cried out their anguish, his brothers Sam and Sol, and his nephews Jonathan, Louis, Sam, and Max. They beat their breasts.

Louis exclaimed, "They killed him! They killed him! The bastards killed him!" He meant the creditors, he meant the world. His hands were fists.

And Jonathan's lips were drawn tight as if for vengeance, and even gentle Sam's lips were drawn tight. Sol stood with his hands open at the height of his shoulders, not knowing which way to turn.

Larry said, "His heart stopped beating, and my God, you should've seen how fast he was in there, the precision of the cut, and the hand massaging, oh, that was remarkable, I could hardly think this is my uncle, and . . . Oh my God, he never checked him before! Oh my God, he never checked him before they put him on the table!"

He turned to the doctor and he said, "What kind of doctor are you?"

The doctor turned white. "Louis," he stammered to his friend.

"Get out!" Louis shouted in the corridor, closing his eyes not to see.

Now someone had to go back to Far Rockaway to tell them. Sol and Sam would sit with the body of their brother.

"How will we tell his son?"

They were Jonathan, Louis, and Sam in an Oldsmobile with Larry and Max.

"I am his son," Sam said and began to weep.

"We are his sons," Jonathan said.

"Who will tell David?"

"You will tell them," Jonathan said to Larry. "I'll go in with you and you'll tell."

"I'll need smelling salts."

There were ten cars parked close to the ranch house. Joe was there with his wife, and his son and his family had come, and his daughter and her family. Starobinetz cousins had come from Long Beach. It was twilight, and Jonathan and Larry got out of the car and entered the house.

And then there was the first scream, and that was Dora's, and as she continued to scream her sister began to scream. And Fanny was screaming, and Mima, and Ben's daughter Elaine was screaming, "Papa! Papa!" And in the car they heard the screaming of the women, the rising and falling wailing, and then people were coming out of the house and they were walking like crazy people, their hands at their heads and wailing as they breathed.

4

Jack stood on his property near his unlit house in the cold night beneath the sky filled with numberless stars and thought, We own nothing, we are only caretakers. He spoke up into the night and there was anger and bitterness in his voice: "We own nothing. We are only caretakers."

He wore his earmuffed cap and his long overcoat. He was looking at the stars from a crouch. There was a burning always in the center of him, and he could not hold himself straight.

He said, "We do not own the land though we work it! We do not own the trees we plant! We do not own our houses! We are caretakers of the land and of the fruit-giving trees, and of our houses. We own nothing."

He was pacing, his head bent, the fever at his forehead, his eyeglasses halfway down his hooked-almost-to-the-mouth nose, the burning at his center, his hands rising sometimes to the level of his shoulders as if to burst a way through. He was wearing his high shoes, and the land was not yet hard. He paced heavily as if he were walking in mud.

We are only caretakers. We are only caretakers of the land and of the fruit-bearing trees, we are only caretakers of our houses, even when we have built them and built them of stone.

I should have liked to have planted a thousand trees, I should have liked to have had sons, fine healthy tall straight sons, I should have liked to have lived long on the land, to have grown old on my land, in my house, with my sons and their sons, with my stores of honey and apples sweet as wine.

He laughed aloud.

All we own is words and money.

Wearing his earmuffed cap, his long heavy overcoat, his high shoes, he passed the elevator lobby information window of the office and pushed through the swinging doors into the showroom. He was so big, he occupied so much space from his moving crouch, was so clearly going somewhere known that the switchboard secretary, standing from her post at the information window, not recognizing him—who had had his hair cut every week at a lunch hour, his morning shave always close, his shoes always shined, who had been straight and measured if not slow—began but did not finish, "You'll have to go by the service . . ."

He did not turn. In him was such burning and intent that the world around him had become distant, like deafness. He saw a model standing, a customer seated, and had already crossed the showroom when Sam, wearing a duster, carrying a fur coat over his arm, entered from the vault and, seeing the model standing as if to protect the customer, the bent back of the man, the images in the facing wall-high-wide mirrors, said, "Who's that? Who's that?"

Jonathan was seated behind the desk in the private office, and Jack smiled malignantly as if, I knew you would be here. Jonathan stood pale. Jack heard, "Uncle Jack! Uncle Jack!" from far, from years before, for Jonathan's lips had not moved.

"There!" he said, taking from his inside pockets and slapping them to the desk envelopes stuffed with bills (that they would later count into piles, $70,000). "For Ben's boy!" he said that they know it was not for them, it was that Ben's boy not have scandal on his head, that he have something to start with.

Sam was standing in the doorway behind Jack, and he had begun to weep and now he dropped to his knees and came to him on his knees and took his hand to kiss. Jack wanted to tear his hand away, but this was Sam, who had been like a son, and he let his hand hang limply, and he was then leaving, and they were following, the model still standing, the wide-eyed customer caught in a whisper, the coat Sam had had over his arm dropped on the carpeted floor. He walked less fast, the weight gone, this showroom that we planned and saved for, that he would come to me with drawings of, that we *did*, oh, to have all a floor of this building! These mirrors, these tables, the armchairs that Ben would bring me from the factory to look at and approve. He was even then drawn to enter the factory, *his* place, as he had ten thousand times, and he even veered, to see the faces of the workers, to nod perhaps, cousins, neighbors, landsmen. Yes— ha!—to visit as had once a worker come back wearing a suit in which his shrunken body swam!

Jonathan, following his uncle, almost at his side, his own cool rooted graceful manner useless now, awkward, no manner at all from which to reach this man, longed with all his heart to stop his uncle, to take hold of him and against all fight hold on, but did not as if no matter how right one is one is somehow forbidden to so touch such a man, uncle. He was become so pale he would later have to lean his head against a wall to recover, the image even now imprinted in his mind of the beginning yellow-tinted face, the nose hawking down, and the smile when he saw him.

Sam was weeping, he was at Jack's elbow as Jack went through the swinging doors. He said, "You can't go, Uncle Jack. We'll go to lunch together! Come, we'll go to the New Campus together! *Where* are you going? No, you'll come home with me!"

But the elevator was there, and Jack went in, and Bob, the uniformed Negro elevator operator, saw that this was Jack and saw the nephews and hesitated and looked from Jack to the nephews and back, and Jack pointed his sewn-together fingers at the operator's lever and Bob shut the doors, and halfway down he turned to Jack and said hesitantly, "It's good to see you, Mister Jack."

The door to Leah's private room was shut, there was a small window in the door. Jack carried his heavy overcoat over his arm, he held his cap in his hands; he wore a double-breasted suit, the collar of his shirt was buttoned to, but he wore no tie. He had come earlier and had sat an hour at her side. She had been operated on a second time a week before, she was thin and pale, her lips were cracked, her hair was dry. He had closed his eyes and thought, She carried her purse high, as a schoolgirl carries her books. Her eyes had opened, and she had seen Jack and frowned and asked, "Where's Edith? What's wrong she doesn't take care of you?"

Now, where he had been seated was his nephew Max, who was, Jack realized, studying his aunt. Jack stood crouched in the corridor at the door and saw his nephew take a small notebook from his jacket pocket and write something there.

What are you writing? What are you stealing from the dying? What is he stealing from us when our eyes are closed?

He saw him wipe with a handkerchief the guilty sweat from his hands.

Out! he wanted to cry. Out! For he was like them all, money and grasping. But he knew then that the boy had done this at the side of his mother, yes, at the side of his father, and he sensed then that the boy lived with them still, that he spoke to them in the night. And he is doing the same with Leah. As if as long as he carries them with him they will not be buried. And does he already have a piece of me?

Why not bury them? Why not bury us and be done with it?

Dressed as he was, carrying an overnight bag, he entered one of the fifty such hotels in this neon neighborhood of bars and street-corner telephone booths and peephole movies, of high-heeled whores leaning out of dark doorways, their eyes blued. He climbed a narrow staircase and stood at the reception desk, where a small man with the head and beak of a bird looked up at him and passed him a numbered key as if he had always had his room here. Then he searched for the numbered door in dark narrow fetid twisting corridors, the overflowing smells of people, of what we eat and what we leak and what we defecate.

In each room is a man or a woman alone. They lock themselves in and listen.

We long for more.

How can we be clean?

Now, in the neon light he had great pain that cleared his eyes of tears and memories. He saw through walls. He saw a naked man kneeling over a naked woman. They were sixty years old, her hair was gray and dry, her breasts were flaccid. They were reaching, reaching, reaching, she was twisting, turning, moaning. He saw a man seated by a fire escape window listening to a small radio he held at his ear. He saw a man counting his pennies, nickels, dimes, and quarters into stacks, and the stacks of them were growing, growing, growing! He saw a woman coughing, bent over herself. In another room, Mary was dying. And in another room, Leah was dying.

The neon invading his room changed pastel again and again. And waiting still in another room was Eshka. His brothers were waiting in another room while Edith, almost sightless, gasping, was twisting on the floor of another.

It is waiting for us here, it is waiting for us there, it is everywhere. It is in every sister's body, it is in the love of brothers, it is in every kiss. And we feed it by copulation! And it grows in us like judgment. *We long for more.* We copulate—ha!—for more! I have sensed the underground sources of life!

The pain had become gigantic, his body could hardly contain it, the room was too narrow, he was butting into the walls. He dressed quickly, missing buttons, mislacing his high shoes, and he went out into the neon night. Only now with the great pain in him that cleared his eyes.

We shall be buried.

We bury this one, and it is a part of us that dies, and the next, and it is a part of us, and then we have hardly finished throwing the earth on this one that it is our turn and we are buried suffocating.

I have longed for more!

The pain was welling in him, and the sidewalk was become too narrow for him, and he was walking bent in the street between the parked cars, diagonally, and faster, like a trot, low, and the pain welling and the people disappearing from his sight, and only the cold, and the welling pain becoming a cry, coming then from the burning center of him to his lungs, filling them to bursting like the answer to all longing, and trotting still, criss-crossing the street, his cap on, his overcoat, heading toward the great neon avenue he, who would a moment later fall in the street, who would a week later die quite alone in a city hospital ward, was howling into the frozen cold with all the force of his pain and life, "Ow-ooo! Ow-ooo!"

CHAPTER *Twelve*

Four years had passed.

Wearing a Brooks Brothers topcoat and a dark city hat with a discreet feather in the band, carrying an attaché case, Anna's husband Fred arrived from Woodmere at the Long Island Railroad station in Pennsylvania Station. But then, instead of going directly to the IRT downtown local platform, as he did every morning since he had, three years before, closed up his father's fur business, he briskly made his way up out of the station into the clear spring day. He glimpsed as he passed out of the shade of the great pillared station the clock at the corner of Seventh Avenue and Thirtieth Street, the Saturday morning smaller knot of men beneath it, and he could indeed even here recognize passing furriers by their clothes and manner.

"Taxi!"

He had when he had accepted his cousins' offer to go into the shipping business—the offer made for Anna's sake, for he had long known none of "the boys," not Jonathan, Louis, Sam, or David, really liked him—thought his life was over, that he was a failure. And worse, had thought it his own fault. When he had been discharged from the army, he had gone into his father's then-prosperous business rather than start as a forty-dollar-a-week law clerk. Sometimes he almost blamed himself that he had paid off his father's debts dollar for dollar.

They, who had succeeded, whose success was to be celebrated, yes, even *launched* today, would not so have paid off. They would have settled a dime or a quarter to a dollar and then, with what was left, gone into a new business, a new venture. How had he fallen into their world! Years before, in the Oldsmobile driving to the city, Ben and Louis and even little Sol would never listen all the way through a sentence of his. One day he had said aloud, like stating a fact, a conclusion, "If I had a million dollars you'd listen to me." No one had even laughed, Sol had nodded sagely, but had he really heard? Well, now if he would ever have a million dollars it would be because they had a hundred million.

Still, when Ben had died he had felt grief as he had when they had learned of the death of Jack. And he had only discovered the extent of his loss when he realized there no longer was any place at all that he and Anna really wanted to go and take their children Sundays.

At Grand Central Station, he made his way briskly across the great hall toward a numbered platform entrance marked "SPE-CIAL," and shortly was installed just inside the gate at a table in an office armchair. He removed his hat; his baldness was to his wife's cousins—like his being a nonpracticing lawyer, like his being rigorously honest, like his having been Phi Beta Kappa (he wearing his gold key to work every day)—his very quality, all that he was to them, and the only way he had to defy them was to be that.

His attaché case open before him, he set to studying again the ten-page list of names and data he had prepared.

Soon the first of the office boys arrived. He heard a dull noise behind him and, yes, the train was being backed in. Two more of the office boys arrived.

"Did you bring your armbands, boys?"

He left the smartest of the boys at his place at the gate and went with the others toward the train. He marched ahead of them and pointed out each car: "Owners' car! Businessmen's car! Family car! Buffet! Friends and miscellaneous!"

A boy came running. "The caterers are here! The caterers are here!"

"Well, they know what to do," Fred said, for a chief had to be calm and, though he knew he would eventually be made responsible for the well-functioning of the catering, that one of "the boys" would say to him, "What the hell's the matter with the smoked sturgeon?" as if he had fished it, smoked it, and served it, he was still only in charge of getting the guests to their places on the train.

But even then his heart fell to see David limping in with his two sons, the beautiful nine-year-old-boy Michael and the six-year-old giant Gregory, David sitting now on the edge of Fred's table in such a way that one would think one leg even shorter than it was and that the next limp he made would be even wilder than the last, and he was so nonchalantly and scornfully going through Fred's papers that Fred thought he could as easily as not toss them off onto the tracks. And Fred was heading back, leading his armbanded office boys, thinking, Everything will go to pot! All my plans! All my preparations!

David said, "Fred, I count on you!

"This idiot," he said, pointing to the beautiful boy, who did not flinch at the word, "says that the capital of British Honduras is Georgetown. I *know* that the capital is Paramaribo. Who's right?" He was leaning forward bulldoggishly.

But Fred was grown strong. "Belize . . ." David flinched. ". . . on the Belize River."

"Belize!" David mimicked. "Belize on the Belize River!" he mimicked and then went off the way he had come with his sons, Fred hearing he could not tell who saying, "Fred for facts! Fred for facts!"

Now the guests began to arrive. Dora arrived with her daughter Elaine and her sister Rose. Mima came alone by the Long Island Railroad from Rockaway by the sea. Sam had died quietly one night, snuffed out so gently that Mima had not been awakened. Sol and Fanny arrived. Jonathan's big colored maid came, she wore a fifty-dollar artificial-flowered Sunday hat. From Queens, Staten Island, New Jersey, came company ship captains with their wives and children. They recognized ship agents they had met in New Orleans or Rotterdam and who were friends of the Cohens, in-laws. Here was the union man, Philadelphia Blackie; he was a giant. Here was stiff-necked Joe and his small wife Lily. His hair was silver, he was sixty-five and trim, he wore thick Jack Benny eyeglasses. Even in-laws said, "There's Uncle Joe!"

Fred left his post to lead him through well-wishers to the owners' car, where he would be a privileged guest: leather upholstered armchairs, polished wood surfaces, deep carpeting, and bouquets and bouquets of roses. Fred showed him the private sleeping room that had been set aside for him in which he could, as was his habit, take an afternoon nap.

Here was Joe's tall boxer-shouldered son Marty. His hyperactive wife, like half the women here, wore mink. Of Marty's nine-year-old boy it was already said, He will break no hearts!

Here was Anna! She was going to celebrate today. You could see it in her eyes, in her manner. She looked like she owned it all. She owned the growing crowds of Nissnievitch, Starobinetz, and Feldbaum cousins, of in-laws and ship captains. How could Fred even think of cooling her ardor? If she had the quiet pride and fears of her mother Leah, today she would be Eshka, today she would not allow herself to be offended that her cousins-like-brothers did not esteem Fred, for today was somehow her triumph too, through Eshka, how to explain it, and Leah! Already there were tears in her eyes.

Fred would keep an eye on their boys. Anna had rights that he did not and that they would not. Jonathan, David, Sam, and Louis had divided 2 percent of their C-ways shares among the children of Leah and Eshka. Still his boys were not Cohens and would not be sent to schools in New England and Switzerland.

"Where's the bourbon?" Anna gaily demanded.

Fred explained, "They're not permitted to serve on the platform."

"You watch!" she said and introduced herself to Philadelphia Blackie. The giant laughed at her chutzpa and went off with her to the buffet car, and it was not a waterfront but she came back with a cherry- and orange-studded Southern Comfort.

Here was Zola Levi, the not-quite-five-foot-tall flowing-white-haired painter teacher of Sheila and friend of Jonathan. His regard was hawklike, his work was hung in museums all over America.

Squat Louis was the first of "the boys" to arrive. "Is everything all right?" he whispered gruffly, in lieu of greeting, to Fred at the gate.

He drank much. He had the temper and muscle of a fighter and builder, and Jonathan would send him out halfway around the world to fight something through, and it would be done.

Louis brought his Uncle Sol to meet Zola Levi.

"This is," Louis said, "our artist!"

Sol, like the artist, understood that he did not mean just that they bought his work, but that they understood it, and that it was Jewish, and that it somehow represented even the feelings of Louis.

"I've seen your paintings!" Sol said. "I've seen the sewing machine operators! And that's the way it was for us! I've seen the consumptive girls! And that's the way it was! Only you, you've brought your heart to bear!"

"You honor me," Zola Levi said.

"No, no!" Sol said. "You honor us! And we're indebted to you."

Louis was so surprised and moved by his uncle that he winked at the artist.

Here again was David, this time escorting Emma. She was a widow. Who did not know her story? The father who committed suicide, the daughter who committed suicide, the grandson who was forbidden to see her. She wore a pearl necklace and earrings so old-fashioned they were exquisite.

David's limp at her side was an attentive tiptoe.

Proud Sara, sister of "the boys," arrived. Her husband, who had always been loud, had grown fat and insecure. Their three children trailed behind, the youngest, Marybell, resembled no one in the family, she was plain and fearful, if you addressed her she might reply by an "uhhh" that seemed to have no end.

It was fifteen minutes to departure time, and bank directors, company chairmen, congressmen, city officials, judges were arriving. Jonathan's partner Dan Weber was happily there with his heiress wife to greet the most important of them.

But now crossing the Grand Central Station hall were Sam, Margo, their boy, and dogs.

"Is that Jonathan Cohen?" someone asked.

The way Sam held himself, swaying back from the waist as if to look at the populace, was royal. And the clothes he wore, almost English, almost pastel, were cut to his measure and ideals. He held the leashes of Margo's three sausagelike dogs.

The eight-year-old boy was dressed as a cowboy and had toy guns that shot caps and that he was shooting even now, Sam half-amused, Margo, wearing flowing dark mink and multistone-studded almost masquerade eyeglasses, and rings and bracelets, sometimes saying, "Stop that noise!" and sometimes, "Shoot him for me! That one! Ha! ha! ha!" They brought a good-natured hilarity with them to the station platform, the dogs that risked being trampled, the boy shooting his guns as at a rodeo.

Now came Jonathan and his party. The clear blue-eyed man had no need of flamboyance, there was a core and grace to him, and in his perfect calm one could see that he had had the dream and was bringing it to life.

He had seen ships. He had seen fast ships crossing the seas. He had seen ships that docked next to rail and trucking centers, he had decided, We shall carry containers, containers that can be dropped whole onto truck wheels or onto flat rail cars, containers that can be sent across continents as across oceans. He had begun by buying old ships that no one wanted and renovating them. Now he was building new. He had agents in ten American ports, in European ports, in Asia. Subsidiary companies were developing methods for faster unloading, tens of companies were renovating to receive subcontracts to service the Mediterranean, the North Sea, for South America and Africa. In America, on every highway, one saw fast C-ways trucks.

Today, in Baltimore, would be launched the prototype of five new C-ways ships. Each ship would carry 900 twenty-ton containers. The prototype was twice as big as a Liberty ship and yet was more than twice as fast. Unloading would be accomplished in hours instead of days and weeks.

The rate for shipping a twenty-ton container from New York to Rotterdam would be $1,500. In a month's time of two round-trip voyages, each ship would earn $3 million. No dirty or sticky hands would touch cargo. You would load and lock your container at your plant, it would go by rail or truck to a port, it would cross the sea fast, it would be unloaded and put on another truck or train to be delivered where you wanted it to be. The speed of container shipment was revolutionizing the entire shipping industry.

The company had a tanker division. Supertankers. The company had ships under three flags.

A senator from the state of New York and his young wife were with Jonathan as his guests, as was the widower senator from the state of Rhode Island, who was escorting Jonathan's handsome mother-in-law. Sheila, on Jonathan's arm, was very pretty and there was something about her that made it seem she would always look younger than her years.

Now, the special train speeding south through America, Fred took it on himself to follow waiters serving caviar canapés and champagne with fresh champagne. He discussed with the caterer captain the lunch plan, and later, when the caterer fell behind schedule— for the guests were called to go car by car to the buffet car to get their lunch, and many stopped midway, and guests from other cars joined the stream, and though there should have been room enough, every car a clubcar, there were bottlenecks—he sent his armbanded office boys to help out, to indicate the way, to announce and repeat which guests were being called to the buffet car, to bring back lunch plates for the older guests, to be, as he commanded, ever available. He himself went through the family, businessmen's, and friends' cars with a growing ease, and who was not pleased to be greeted by name by an official, for Fred remembered all names and qualities: "Can I get you some more Médoc, Captain Carmichael?"

He thought it wrong that no one paid any attention to Dora and Elaine.

"Is there anything I can get you, Aunt Dora?"

"So how are you, Fred?" she asked. "And your boys?" She wanted to know, and was delighted to hear, and yet was leading up to what everyone really wanted to know and be reassured about: Was it real? Was it solid? Would the train arrive? Would the stocks continue to rise, rise, rise?

"Champagne gives me gas," Elaine said, pouting as if to belch.

"So?" Dora asked, raising an eyebrow. "What does an insider say?"

Fred spread his arms and shrugged as if to say all at the same time, Look around you, Who am I, only an office manager, to know? How can anyone know what the future holds?

But she answered, "I've seen big shows before!"

Emma asked Anna why Max had gone to Europe. Anna was embarrassed.

Max's first novel was soon to be published. She had read it in manuscript and told Jonathan and Jonathan had told Max: "You won't hurt your family! How dare you even think of publishing things that'll hurt your Uncle Ben's widow!"

In telling Jonathan, had she, Anna wondered, acted toward Max like a sister?

"What I don't understand," Fred now said to Emma, "is the memorial stone." It was apt to speak to Emma of that since Eshka, like the doctor, had been buried gratis on Emma's plot. Though Emma immediately seemed more troubled than anything else. She had buried gentle Mary there too.

"Anna put up the stone. He never paid his share for it," Fred said, blaming the doctor's son for his lack of rigor.

Anna said angrily to Fred, "I never asked."

"Well, he never thought of it."

"If he were in Israel," Emma said, "then I'd understand. That's where we can be most useful. But in Europe, what is he but what our fathers and grandfathers were before, an exile?"

Anna was astonished at Emma.

And during the day she was drawn to Emma as Emma was drawn to her. Much later in the day, flying back to New York, Emma came to her and gave her her pearl earrings from her ears and promised to leave her her necklace in her will. But Anna was high by then, and had cried more than once, and what a day it had been, and she could not care less about necklace and earrings, but she said, "Oh, honey, why don't you give me the necklace now and leave me the earrings later?"

They had passed Philadelphia and the train was slowing.

"What's this? What's this?" Fanny said, thinking they were arriving and not understanding why there was no water close by, no ship.

"Where are we?" Mima said, she too thinking they were arriving and so taking now and dropping into her purse to put later among all her other souvenirs, bric-a-brac, pinecones, an ashtray marked "Baltimore and Ohio."

"It's Lazarus!" someone said, pointing to a uniformed navy officer holding his infant child in his arms, his wife at his side, on the station platform.

It was squat Louis, more at home here surrounded by his family than in the owners' car, who said, raising his glass, his eyes twinkling, "This is Katzville! We're at Katzville, Pennsylvania!" The joke spread through the car.

The young medical officer and his wife and child boarded, and everyone kissed and hugged them.

"So how's the doctor?"

They told him the joke and asked him, "Is this Katzville?" He did not know if they were laughing at him, at Katzes, and so he laughed that he was as good as anyone and explained that he had told Jonathan he would not be able to get off duty earlier and Jonathan had said, "So we'll stop and pick you up!"

"What's this place?" someone said as they passed, hardly slowing, another station.

"This," Louis said, making a gift of it to a clan of cousins close by, "is Starobinetzville!" And then was Nissnievitchville. "Feldbaum, America!"

But by now Louis was maudlin. He said, "We came from nothing!"

"Schmuck!" David exclaimed, as if in necessary and perfect counterpoint to all sentimentality.

Louis said, "Ben! Jack! Joe! Even you, Uncle Sol!"

Sol was thinking of his brothers and was nodding.

Mima called out, "And my Sam!"

David stared at her and then nodded up and down and acknowledged, "And Sa—sa—sam too!"

Louis said, "He'd take me for haircuts." They all knew of whom he was speaking.

"When we came to America, he took us to buy suits!"

Larry said, "He'd take Max and me for lunch to the New Campus restaurant and then give us each a dollar for a haircut."

Anna said, "The pinochle players. Where are they all? The fortune-tellers."

There were tears in many eyes.

"Schmuck!" David said softly to Anna.

Children went from car to car following Mark, the son of Sam and Margo. They lost him, he would reappear, making his way easily through the big people, and they would brighten to see him. He had a radiant smile, a galloping energy, he overflowed with ideas.

Who did not notice his kindness to Marybell, Sara's five-year-old autistic child? That an eight-year-old boy should be so understanding and treat her even as a sister. He perched her high on a barstool in a corner by the front of the family car, where she waited almost breathless with excitement.

Now he reentered, shooting his guns at the head of his band, calling out, "This is a hold-up!" Gregory, David's giant son, pointed his fat fingers as guns.

Fred glared at his own sons so that they would not join this wildness, and Marybell was looking on, her mouth hanging open with pleasure, perched over them all. Fred saw then that as the children pushed through the car playing their game of hold-up, the adults playing along, passing imaginary and real bills and silver, Ed, Marty's son, was going through overcoat pockets at the coatrack near the front of the car. Fred closed his eyes and shook his head, something about the ugly boy had seemed to him dwarflike, dreamlike, the excitement, pleasure and triumph in the boy's face, and then he grew stern as if to go and collar the thief, but how to do that to his friend Marty, to Uncle Joe. No. He would have to make the boy, and only him, know that he knew, he would have to put a guard over all the overcoats, he would have to tell the office boys to keep an eye on all purses everywhere in the train. Even then Mark was standing before him, his six-shooters at his belly, and his mother Margo had come in and was laughing, laughing, and said, "You can shoot him, honey. Go ahead. Ha! ha! ha!"

There was still more than an hour before arrival. In the owners' car Uncle Joe had gone for a nap in the sleeping room, and though the monotonous sound of the train covered most other sounds, voices now were muted. The senator from New York and his wife had gone for a stroll through the train. At a window table Philadelphia Blackie was playing gin rummy with Sam, who, holding the leashes of his sausage dogs, was trying to lose enough for the other to let him go.

Jonathan had had the time to call Larry in from the family car to ask him about himself. The boy was troubled, should he continue in the navy? Larry had said he would surely be a captain, perhaps a rear admiral. That's something, Jonathan thought. Am I to say it's nothing much?

Those sitting about listened carefully. They were his wife and mother-in-law, his sister Sara, they were friends who knew the value of his silences as of his opinion.

"Is it what you want?" Jonathan asked.

The young medical officer, his acne still not gone, reddened as if attacked. The others were nodding their heads at him encouragingly.

"I could be a surgeon," the boy said. He raised his fine hands as if to prove it.

Jonathan understood that the boy wanted to be complimented on his not becoming a surgeon, and he sensed then that there really was something else he wanted to do. He smiled widely at the boy and asked, "What are you now, a lieutenant?"

"Lieutenant junior grade," the boy corrected.

"And in twenty-five years you'll be a captain or rear admiral? When I go to Washington, captains serve me my coffee. 'Black or with cream, sir?' "

"Oh, Jonathan!" Sheila exclaimed.

But he maintained his wide smile on the boy, and he knew the boy would understand: Rank and pension are nothing.

He was served a drink. He made sure the women were served before he drank. His wife drank Coca-Cola.

He asked his sister Sara, "Where are your children, darling?" Her children were so far from her mind she thought that a reproach. He had only wanted to see them a moment.

His decorator opened a portfolio to show him projects for their new central offices.

Zola Levi spoke of a Russian-Jewish painter who captured the everyday life of the *shtetl*. "The colors! The barnyard animals! The fantasms!" Jonathan said he would visit his studio.

He sipped his drink and nodded at the decorator's drawings on the floor before him.

He thought Sam's dogs could use a walk, and he stood, and Sam gratefully passed him the leashes. Everywhere in the car people were glancing at him, What is he doing now? I am taking my brother's dogs to pee for no one else has thought of that. And he was smiling when he stepped out into the brisk day on the car platform, holding the leashes hard.

But now, the fleeting tracks telescoping, he was glad to be alone. He thought again, What are you building? What are you proving? You are forty years old, you will have no posterity. These thoughts were so familiar to him they came to him colorless. No matter, he thought, it would come clear. He would go on building bigger and bigger, he would be mightier and mightier, and all would come clear. He was who he was for a reason.

The dogs had peed, mere cupfuls like toy dogs. He smiled and bent to caress the ridiculous dogs.

Louis said, "You should have seen Uncle Sol!"

And many in the owners' car were already smiling, for squat Louis stood just like Uncle Sol, his little belly forward, his arms hanging low, his sad clown's lips.

"What did Uncle Sol do now?" Jonathan asked.

"I introduced him to Zola here and he said, 'I have seen your work! I have seen the sewing machine operators! I have seen the *con-sump-tive* girls! And that is the way it was! You have seen them with your heart!' 'You honor me,' Zola said. 'No, sir, you honor us!' "

"Did Uncle Sol say that?"

Zola Levi nodded his flowing-white-haired head. "Your uncle is a man of real grace."

Louis was nodding. "Where did he learn that from? Was it success that brought it out?"

They were smiling still, but Louis's manner had changed, he had become so ponderous and substantial no one knew if he were still joking: "I want to do something for humanity. I want," he repeated, "to do something for humanity!"

The smiles faded. He would crush opposition, he would crush details. And too, he had caught a chord of the moment, there was some great and almost desperate longing in him that was in others.

Sam had put down his cards. He was radiant and said, "Yes! Let us too do something for humanity!"

Wives were interested as they had not been before. Each had a favorite charity.

Louis said, "Zola, you have done something for humanity. You have touched people's hearts. Now it's time for us to help humanity."

He looked at Jonathan for the approval and support he took even for granted and perhaps Jonathan's warm, calm waiting smile was that.

David said, "Humanity? Why not!"

Zola Levi said, "It's part of our heritage to fight for social justice. We have always been in the forefront of that fight."

"Disease," Sam said. "Let us fight disease!"

"Multiple sclerosis!" Margo said, for she was North Shore committeewoman for the Multiple Sclerosis Foundation.

"Too local!" David shouted scornfully.

"Cancer," Larry suggested.

Before the pall of that word could drop over them all, Sam said, "The heart!"

"The heart!" Louis said. "We'll cure the heart!"

Then, after the noise of general approval of that idea, they felt so good they began to clown it up.

"How much?"

"How much for humanity?"

"How much for the heart?"

Uncle Joe just then came out of the sleeping room.

"How much, Uncle Joe, will you give for humanity?"

"A man can't even get his sleep!" the stiff-necked uncle said, but when it was noisily explained to him, he was not against, he would give too.

Zola Levi said he would contribute a painting. Dan Weber said he also would contribute. Still Jonathan said nothing, but smiled at them all.

In any event, he was, like everyone there, filled with good feeling, and it was like a confirmation of all our ways and decisions and of our expanding horizons that shortly, after the train pulled to at the shipyard, after the short parade to the ship's enormous hulk, and after everyone found his place and Sheila stood ready at Jonathan's side to launch the ship with champagne, the vice-president of the United States of America, whose motorcycle-and-black-limousine arrival had made everyone solemn, made a short speech about our role in America's future.

The
Ambassador

PRINCIPAL CHARACTERS

THE KATZES:

Esther Katz-Nissnievitch, sister of the doctor, has lived in Israel since 1930. Her husband is *Abba*, her son *Abisai*.

Dan Katz lives in Paris with his wife *Tanya*.

Sonia Katz lives in Russia and has a son.

Anna, daughter of *Harry* and *Leah* Katz, married to *Fred*, who is now employed by C-ways; they have two sons.

Eli, Anna's brother.

Larry (Lazarus), older son of the doctor and Eshka, married and a father. He is a professor of psychiatry.

Max, son of the doctor and Eshka, married to *Madeleine*, father of *Saul-Daniel*.

THE COHENS:

Joe Cohen, stiff-necked, most successful of the Cohen brothers.

Sol Cohen, smallest of the Cohen brothers, married to Fanny.

Dora, widow of Ben Cohen.

THE "BOYS":

David, who limps, whose girlfriends are *Sadie* and *Mary*. He has two sons, *Michael* and the giant Gregory.

Sam, who is gentle and generous, married to *Margo*, has one son, Mark.

Jonathan, who has risen, married to *Sheila*, childless.

Louis, married to gentle *Rachel*, has a yacht.

Sara, sister to the "boys," is the mother of Marybell and another girl and one boy.

Marty, son of Joe Cohen, married to *Julie*, father of Ed.

Elaine, daughter of Ben Cohen.

Marvin, son of Ben. He is married and has taken over his father's business.

Gregory, giant son of David.

Mark, son of Sam and Margo.

Ed, son of Marty and Julie, grandson of Joe.

Marybell, daughter of Sara.

OTHER:

Emma, widow of *Bill*, her father and daughter committed suicide, rich cousin of both the Katzes and Cohens.

Selma, niece of Emma.

Herman Friedland, self-important chief of the Friedland clan, link to the Cohens.

Dan Weber, partner to Jonathan Cohen.

Stanley, retarded nephew of Dora.

CHAPTER *Thirteen*

1

I N 1933, Esther Katz, against her parents' will, married a cousin twenty years older than she and went with him to Palestine, where he was already a political figure. Three times the British imprisoned him, their son was born while he was in prison. Poland was overrun by the Germans. Her parents, her sisters, their husbands and children died or were killed in Warsaw. The one survivor, her niece Ruth, came to Israel and died not long after. In America, her brothers Harry, Irving, and then the doctor died. Her husband died suddenly in 1955. Early this year, 1973, word came to her from Dan in Paris that their sister Sonia had died in Russia, Dan having received the news months after the fact in a hand-carried letter from Sonia's son as if not only would he never write to Israel, but was afraid of having further contact even with Dan, who had visited Sonia in Russia. So that now in all the world there was only Dan childless in Paris, and in Russia the son of Sonia, and in America the sons of her brothers. Barely two months before, at Yom Kippur, Abisai, her only son, who had already fought in one war, had been called up for duty and had been killed.

She mellowed the pain in her by thinking of all her dead.

She sat at her kitchen table looking through photograph albums. She took down from high shelves shoeboxes filled with unmounted photographs. She found rubber-banded letters spanning almost the time of her life, the many languages and nations of her family, the marriages reported, the children born, an uncle barely dead, a child given his name. She read again in a letter numbered and stamped by censors the last mention of her sister Judith, who had always left letter-writing to someone else. She found herself staring at a photograph of a young and handsome cross-belted Soviet soldier straight even as her Abisai had been. Who was he? Whose son was he? Who embraced him a last time? What had become of him, blood of her blood?

She wanted to let go, but there was in her, as there is in certain widows, as much man as woman, her husband's own pride and rigor. And there was then a bitter time when she thought she should change her name even as, at their marriage, her husband had changed his, he taking, as if seeing the horror ahead, the names of their already blood-allied families, Katz-Nissnievitch, discarding his given name and putting on himself the Hebrew name, *Abba*— Father of Katz-Nissnievitch. She was almost twenty years widowed and her son was dead and there were no grandchildren and what was left of her family was scattered and rootless. She would call herself Widow to the Family Katz-Nissnievitch.

Emma was seventy-five years old, and she was condemned. She lived now in a West End Avenue residence hotel, her small apartment crammed with porcelain and silver, gilt-framed mirrors and paintings, and antique furniture. From her bed in her scented and velvet darkened bedroom, the color television on, the sound cut for conversation, she—lipsticked and wearing silk—would have a silver serving tray or an ivory inlaid cigarette box brought out and shown to the visitor. "This is for you," she would say, only a promise, for the item would then be put back in its place.

She had black nurses in eight-hour shifts around the clock. Her mother's German-born niece Selma did her shopping and hung close, one eye on her knitting and the other on Emma's visitors. Many came. They flattered her, they told her of their chagrins: a son did not visit; a lawyer was slow to hand on dividends, perhaps he was embezzling. They were cousins, friends, widows; last wills and testaments had not been as carefully prepared as they should have been, there were disputes that had to be settled, there were greater debts than had been thought. Stocks were falling. What was happening to the world? Emma gave clear and precise advice to each: "Invest in property, stay away from mutuals." She kept iron control over her own investments and lawyers, she would not be cheated now.

So when she received Esther's letter, coming only two months after the news of the death of Esther's son—the strange pain in her then, for she had hardly known the quiet handsome boy—she wanted to think, Only another with a tale of woe, but she knew better. She felt a touch of satisfaction too for visiting in Israel she had offered Esther help and had been refused.

She showed Esther's letter to Esther's own niece, Anna. Anna read the brief letter and said, "What do you want me to say?"

"Well, should I help her?"

Anna too had a share in Emma's will, and if Emma enjoyed posing the question, she also enjoyed Anna's quick response, "Honey, that's your business."

But that evening at dinner in the city with her bald husband Fred and her tall boxer-shouldered nearsighted cousin Marty Cohen and his small nervous wife Julie, Anna said, "We need this like a hole in the head." For Emma had commissioned her to buy Esther a round-trip air ticket from Israel and to make reservations for her in the same residence hotel.

Anna had never met her Aunt Esther. She thought her proud, she sensed in her the Katz pride that had insulted her mother and, even more intolerably, her Aunt Eshka. She knew she disapproved, even as had her husband, of all Jews who had not *returned*. Nor was it the right time. It was a lousy time. The very city was going bankrupt, they were selling gasoline only every second day, things were up in the air and could fall apart. And what was happening in the world was happening to each of them, crises everywhere. Fred was become too tense; Marty, after fifteen years, had returned to his analyst. Anna's older son could not get into medical school; her younger boy did not know what he wanted to do, he had long hair and a filmy beard and read Vonnegut and Brautigan and spoke about a return to nature. Marty's boy Ed no one spoke much about, what limbo was he living in? Anna played bridge three times a

week, she was sharp sharp sharp. It gave her pleasure to be sharper
than the others. But she sensed that, even in her, something terrible
was happening and joked about that: "I've got the hundred-year
runs."

Marty, only a cousin to Esther, had met her once in Israel. Perhaps he was thinking of her apartment, and how it could get cold in
Jerusalem, and how it was miserable to sit looking at a photograph
of one's boy, for his eyes were teary. He explained, "She must get
depressed."

She was leaving Israel for the first time in forty years. They were
to take off from Lod at dawn, their luggage was opened and examined piece by piece, they were X-rayed and in curtained-off spaces
were frisked.

A blue-eyed policeman asked her, "Where are you going, mother?"

"I'm not your mother," she replied, because she did not like his
familiarity and hated it that anyone could even think a Jew might
quit Israel. And her prayer—in the rush of fear in the terrible
mounting jet noise just before flight, she who had never flown—was,
Let me live to return. Even then the 707 began its run and then they
were aloft and it was all so fast, and they were thrusting roaring up
and fear was leaving her as when a child is lifted high but then
realizes he is firmly held. She wanted to laugh that she had until
now disapproved, even if unconsciously, of flying, as honest people
disapprove of what they cannot afford.

She thought the plane was suspended above the earth's movement. She thought, How beautiful is the sea! She thought, seeing
the patient curve of the earth's horizon, How grand is the world,
how vast is the sky! It occurred to her then with a rush of sadness
that it was forty years since she had seen autumn leaves and autumn
colors and that she would be too late to see them now.

She thought, I am returning to the world of the Gentiles, the
nations, I am returning to the world of exile. How can I excuse the
excitement in me? She thought, I have seen too much.

Abisai had, after the Six Day War, driven her into the occupied
territories to visit, even as Abba had taken her thirty-five years before, the mausoleum of Abraham and Isaac and Sarah and Rebecca
at the cool mosque at Hebron. Later, returning, he stopped the car

at what had recently been a battlefield, a field of stones and hardy wild plants, for the sun and wind there are harsh, and while she waited in the car, he walked alone, straight, thoughtful, in the field.

She had sensed even then that that time was a reprieve. It is too hard, too hard, she thought and for a moment was restless in her seat. Some weeks before she had taken the bus to Beersheba and had stood at the edge of the heat-hazed smooth-duned desert. She had felt it infinite, she had felt faint. What or who had called her to the desert? She had been at the edge of the desert before.

Now she slept. She dreamed of a wedding. Whose wedding was it? Who was she bringing back to life in her dream?

She carried, leaving the airplane at Kennedy, Abba's soft black leather briefcase filled with newspaper and magazine articles, with speeches and manuscripts he had written. She knew so much of his even by heart, as one knows poems, she thought she was even filled with his voice and that he would even speak through her.

But there was no one to meet her.

She was seventy-three years old, she wore a twenty-year-old cloth coat. She wore eyeglasses, her nose was hooked low to her wide mouth, the flesh about her lips was infirm as it is with old people, her legs had long ago gone thick.

She looked expectantly in all directions. Though a look as of deep fatigue fleetingly crossed her face when she accepted that no one had come for her, she was then off, head held high, her manner even more purposeful for her ducklike walk, as if she would never get used to the weight of her legs. But in the Carey bus, at the highway rise before the Midtown Tunnel, where she saw against the background of city skyscrapers what she had seen a thousand times in photographs and films and what had been a very symbol of hope, the glass-faced UN building now evening sober, evening gloomy, she thought with irony, Well, maybe they too have other business!

It was Anna who answered the doorbell of Emma's apartment. Esther had been sent photographs of Anna, this was a fifty-year-old woman who went to the hairdresser often. Still, she immediately knew this was her niece.

"Is it you?" Anna asked softly, the way people speak in sickrooms.

"Who's there?" a voice called from a further room.

Esther had glimpsed on a table in the entry a tall brass samovar and, now following Anna down a dim corridor, remembered straight-backed Leah as she had been in Berezin.

Emma was lying propped up against pillows in the center of her bed. Esther had last seen her heavy and handsome; she was shrunken, her hair was gray and dry and combed out so that her head seemed to rest in a web. Her mouth was small, cupidlike, she wore lipstick, lines of age had been carefully painted over with powders and creams; still there was a sickly puffiness to her face that was particular. And Esther sensed before she knew that there was nothing under the covers where one of Emma's legs should have been. Even then she glimpsed, seated in a dark corner of the room—a black white-uniformed nurse standing in another corner next to a color television, on but silent—a heavy round- and red-faced white-haired man holding a walking stick, who did not acknowledge her except to scrunch together his eyelashes as if to scrutinize her better, she knowing first who his father was, and feeling his father's darkness first and then his own. She was approaching Emma, and Emma's expression had hardened, and Emma said as if to stifle any pity, "No, I don't want your kisses!" Emma's eyes looked out proudly and defiantly now, as they had all her life.

"I won't change my will," Emma warned. "I've disinherited my grandson, but everyone else is in it, every cousin and second cousin."

Anna said, as if to soften the blow, "I'll help as I can. It is a lot of money."

"The money is not for me," Esther said.

"Isn't it?" Emma said, as if she knew better. "Anyhow, I have other debts."

Anna said, "What we'll have to have is more information about Abba."

Esther looked again at Anna. What did she want to know about him? His years in the desert, his years in prison, his last years when his countrymen stopped listening to him? What did she want, an affidavit! What was so false about her eyes?

She was suggesting that others might help raise the money, Esther sensed she meant even the man behind her; she thought, Even as I must know more about you. But she would not have been able to phrase what was troubling her—that *she* had been away, that *she* here was returning, that her wax-smiling niece and the white-haired red-faced man and Emma, somehow now like a hostess in her bed, knew a hundred things that she did not know and that what they knew was even *hers*. She was angry at herself, silly old woman lost in time change, and asked Emma, "Then why did you send me air tickets?"

But before Emma could answer, Esther turned and said angrily to the red-faced man, "Why don't you say hello to me?"

He was drunk. Still, he looked like an imp. He said, "Every time I say hello to a cousin, it costs me a fortune."

He had begun laughing even before he finished his joke, a nasal wheeze that somehow reminded her of a child's laugh. And Anna too was smiling at the joke, but also at her as if to say, "You asked for it." Nor could Emma, in spite of herself, restrain her laughter. She wedged herself into the pillows and the bed, her leg bent and her foot digging in. But suddenly she was in pain, her face and body contracted as if she, all her body, were concentrating to confront the pain. The very room grew larger and stiller for the force and darkness she was meeting. The red-faced man had stood and approached in a limp and lurch as if to bring Emma help. Then Emma was relaxing, moaning, and her lipstick was smudged and there was a sweet fecal odor and she began to smile and the smile for the lipstick smudge was all over her face and she said as if in answer to every question, "Do you understand now?"

I understand nothing, Esther thought.

The black white-uniformed nurse approached Emma with a pan and towels.

In the entry, Esther asked Anna, "Why didn't you write me?"

"Come," the limping drunk said, "I'll take you to dinner! Come!" he said, even beginning to propel them toward the door.

She said, "I don't know you!" And she opened the apartment door to go back to her own room and almost walked into tall nearsighted Marty. He had a bouquet of crumpled flowers in hand.

"I went to meet you," he said. His hangdog boxer's face was all contrition, his big eyes. "I looked everywhere for you," he said.

"But you weren't there," Esther said.

"That's right, I was late."

"So why did you look?" she said, shaking her head.

She would, she thought in her room, leave the hotel in the morning.

She held in her hands a leather-framed photograph she had brought with her of Abba, Abisai, and herself. Abisai, a boy in short pants, was leaning from one side to seated Abba, and she was leaning from the other side. Abba and Abisai wore open-collared short-sleeved shirts, she wore a plain summer dress. She was forty years old and could have been younger, her regard, directed at Abba, was of love and respect, the way her hands were folded one on the other was somehow attentive to him. She saw in Abisai's regard loyalty, a calm like resolution. He was only a boy, curly-haired, slender. How could a boy be resolute? Why should it so trouble her? Abba's forehead was so high the rest of his face seemed cramped, you could not for his thick eyeglasses really see his eyes, you saw there light like vision. She and Abisai were pressing to Abba, he was seeing ahead. But even then she saw her husband as he had been in the last year of his life. Often, at the sunset hour, she would come upon him slouched deep in his low armchair, motionless, unseeing, a cigarette burning out in an ashtray.

In the morning, Emma, attended by her cousin Selma, came to Esther's room in a wheelchair.

Emma said, "Darling, I'm going for treatment, do you want to come?" She wore a brown turbanlike hat and a black Persian lamb coat too big on her. Her leg was stick-like, her foot was pressed to the footrest.

They drove in a rented limousine across town to Mount Sinai Hospital. Selma wheeled Emma through corridors, other city-dressed patients and hospital patients converging to a large waiting room. At first Esther thought it was the too-bare and bright fluorescent light, and then she realized it was, in fact, the treatment, there was a puffiness to the skin of all the sick, there were patients whose eyebrows had been burned off, there were patients with reddish blotches on their skins, there were dark rings about their eyes. Their clothes were too big for them. They stared through their fellows as if fearfully and longingly at the barrage of lead-walled, red-warning-lighted, buzzing, and radiating machines.

Esther sat near Emma, her regard missing nothing.

Later, in Emma's bedroom, Emma told her that her husband Bill

had been unfaithful. Late business dinners, trips, lies. Hundreds of
lies! Her father had played about with showgirls—that was different! But he had put his stamp of approval on Bill even though he
knew Bill's real worth—tall good-looking merchandise—and so let
her do that to herself, to her life. And took his own life—the market
tumbling, his stocks worthless, notes coming due, but she married to
trash—kneeling to a pillow inside a kitchen stove, casually, com-
fortably, scornfully. So that when Emma realized her daughter was
a tramp, did that with everyone, she thought, It is in her blood. But
when she hung herself Emma recognized in her own pain and anger
that such fierceness was even in her.

Esther came to sit with Emma before lunch or in the early afternoon when Emma was most at ease. She would relieve Selma, and
though Selma was convinced it was Esther's intention to get what
she could out of Emma, she did not believe Esther worse than herself and so did not think that what Esther could do in several hours
she could not undo during the rest of the day.

Emma said, "What good is there in the world if Eshka could die
as she did? She weighed ninety pounds, her body was all pain, she
crawled up four flights of stairs in the nursing home in Brooklyn to
throw herself from the roof."

"I didn't know," Esther said.

"And then Leah alone in Lenox Hill Hospital. Her brothers hardly
visited as if to forget her. She accepting! Yes! Yes! Uncomplaining.
Though once she did cry for her Sonny who, give him that credit,
came once to see his mother. He too is in my will!

"I visited often with Mary. The burning there was in her breast.
And then spread to under her arm, and her hair growing dry, and
then to the other breast, and then to under the other arm, and then
to *here*. She couldn't bear to be with people, she hid from them.
She'd been very gentle, like a bird! But her hiding was now a burning, she was filled with hate and disgust.

"Do you," she asked suddenly, "believe in God?"

Esther had no answer.

"How can there be a God!" Emma exclaimed. But then she said,
"I've never loved. I didn't love Bill! I didn't love my daughter! I *did*
love Eshka!"

Esther put her hand on Emma's hand as if she were a sister. "Wasn't Abba married once before he married you?"

"She wants to suffer," Anna said. She was driving Esther cross-town in evening rush-hour traffic to meet the Cohens.

"I see," Esther said.

"She wants to suffer more than all the others," Anna said, as if she did not think Esther could see.

2

The C-ways vessel SS *Westways* was docked at the Bremerhaven container-port.

The ship was from bottom to top as tall as a twelve-story build-ing, from bow to stern as long as five city blocks. The ship's building was located aft and the ship would have had, free of cargo, a certain grace. But containers were piled five levels up all her length and width, and she looked, even docked, awkward, overloaded, and in a hurry. She carried 1,500 twenty-ton containers, each of which could be dropped on wheels to be hauled as a truck or onto a flatcar to become part of a train. Nor was she ever free of cargo, for she worked a circle—New York, Savannah, Le Havre, Bremerhaven— linking those cities, discharging and loading, in a twenty-eight-day round trip. She was seconded by three sister ships, so that every week, almost by the clock, one ship was where another had been. The operation was repeated at the other end of what the company called "The American Landbridge" linking West Coast cities to Hawaii, Japan, Korea, the whole C-ways system stretching across two-thirds of the globe.

The Bremerhaven container-port operated around the clock. Within half an hour of a vessel's docking, three black cranes taller even than the ship rode on twin sets of rails alongside the ship, lowered their black arms out over the ship, and began discharging now to load after.

The aluminum container to be discharged was clamped, raised, hauled in the length of the crane arm, and then dropped down to sit quite small between the crane's four giant legs. Immediately, even as the crane clamps rode out the arm for the next container, a monster machine flashing red lights and emitting a loud whirring warning noise, riding on four legs, approached and straddled the parked container, clamped it to its underbelly and, operated from a cockpit four flights up—such a machine could straddle two decks of containers—moved the container to its computerized place in the container-park.

Thousands of containers were parked waiting land transportation or secondary sea shipment—they would be loaded on smaller vessels going to Scandinavia, on barges entering the Continent.

It was the middle of the night, and the passenger, Max Katz, could not sleep. He was, after some years abroad, returning with his wife and five-year-old son to America. His wife, sleeping lightly at his side in the owner's cabin, was French. They were going to teach the 1974 winter quarter at a city university in Detroit. He taught writing, she, though a sculptor, taught French. Whenever their funds ran out, they returned to America to teach. They were now several thousand dollars in debt and did not have the cash even to take Icelandic, and so they sailed on this C-ways ship. Though Max saw his cousins, the Cohens, the principal owners of C-ways, only when he passed through New York to go midwest to teach, or on his return to France where he lived, he had only to ask the favor and it was granted.

His very house was as if a gift from them, the ten acres behind Sénanque on the plateau of the Vaucluse, the stone-upon-stone farmhouse ruin, the partial renovation of the house, paid for from the sale of C-ways stock his cousins had put in his name.

His very clothes came from them, a topcoat Ben's son Marvin had given him seventeen years before when he had come back from Europe after the publication of his first novel (he then still wearing the tailored Italian suits of his only paperback sale), the belted leather "genius" jacket and double-breasted blue blazer his cousin Sam had given him some years ago after the suicide of his son.

"What do you do when you need clothes?" Sam had asked, feeling him out so as not to insult him or be hurt himself before offering him his son's clothes. Though Margo, when he had gone to their Great Neck home that they were even then moving out of—the boy had committed suicide in the garage—had, going through the boy's closets and chests of drawers article by article, tens of suits, sports

jackets, held back this item or another as if she thought he, refusing
for belated pride this that or the other, was taking advantage of her
and she could get better consideration elsewhere.

"He was a genius," she said, her wet eyes flashing. "All his generation knew it. You should hear the way they speak of him. His film
would have made him famous!"

The cabin was full of tenebrous light. The wind had picked up,
and it whistled through wires and rattled the aluminum sidings of
containers like paper. He stood up abruptly. At the porthole he saw
that the crane arms were raised, the work had ceased.

All night and all the following day the wind would not let up, in
such a wind the loading could not be continued, the containers were
stacked too tight, there was not enough margin to risk lifting them
out. Already, since he had boarded the ship in Le Havre, there had
been delays. He hated the delays, but what did it matter, where was
he going, what was his hurry?

It was too cold to go out. He sat in the armchair before the walled-
in well-like dressing table mirror. He plugged his ears with wax so
as not to hear his son quietly playing or the clicking of his wife's
knitting needles. He watched them in the mirror as if he were
watching from the other side of the mirror. He walked alone on the
dock in the freezing wailing wind. He made an effort to play a game
with his son and wife, but midway stood up and moved off, the
others continuing their game, hardly disappointed, for he had been
nervous or absent while playing. He sat leaning into the well of the
mirror, day falling.

He thought, I told the others then, two months ago, I was going
to Paris for business, thinking, Let them figure that one out! And
gave them to understand they could be on their way too, Thomas,
the Detroit student I never trusted, and Madeleine's cousin Nicole.
The first time she came to this halfway house she was seventeen and
weighed ninety pounds, her mother was being psychoanalyzed, she
was smoking two packages of cigarettes a day and drinking cup
after cup of black coffee and scared when her hands began to tremble. "I'm paralyzed," she said. "Don't you see?" she said begging,
"I'm paralyzed." "Stand up!" I ordered. And when she would not, I
picked her up by her little-boy shoulders and said, "Walk!" And she
did, looking at me wide-eyed as if I had made a miracle. Only now

she was smoking less and she, her father, and mother were all involved in the same group therapy, and she was at the right school to get the right diploma, though still seeing a boy who was, she gave us to understand, involved with some guerrilla group, though there, with us, in the *mas* near Murs, she fell right in with Thomas, whose wife and infant child were back home in Detroit, he on his world tour and adventure.

In the morning, I had gone with my boy to the synagogue at Avignon. It was packed, hot, everyone was sharing the Yom Kippur fast. I saw the passing of snuff and remembered the same passing, hand-to-hand, in the East Bronx. But the men here were all out of the ghettos and suburbs of Tunisia, Morocco, and Algeria, and though there was something here of the Bronx, I had been gone a long time. And though I could remember the sounds of Hebrew letters, I had never learned the meaning of the words and prayers. And my wife Madeleine is French and Christian and my boy Saul is only named after a Jew.

When we heard the news, the first reports of the Syrian and Egyptian surprise attacks, Thomas said, "It was bound to happen."

He is the smartest of them, 100 years old, lithe as a cat. They are born with monkey wrenches in their hands, to tear down. They let their hair grow long and they swagger.

We went for a drive the following day. We drove up winding autumn roads to Sault and Banon. We met an old woman at the edge of the forest selling goat cheeses at twice what they cost in the grocery. There was no good news on the radio.

Thomas said, "If they don't win this one, they'll win the next."

In the night train going to Paris, the second-class compartment filled, the lights off, the shades drawn, but light still from the corridor, the other passengers dozing, they necked, twisting and turning, rubbing. All of this already lived through, every nuance and direction, and I sitting there thinking that I am thinking about leaving my boy, my wife, my home, but really thinking about Nicole, about making it with Nicole.

For I so necked once in an IND subway, in a rush hour emptying out into Queens, rubbed and pressed with a tall thin Jane whose needs were even as great and twisted as mine. My very first date was a so-pretty and sad Connecticut girl who, sitting cross-legged on a wall, told me her fairy tale: "I'm going blind." She had a boy's name, she had tiny breasts. But she was Connecticut, and to get to that wall she sat on we had passed through a living room with rugs and piano and glass sliding doors, and through a garden, and were as if still inside but were out under the stars. And I was from the East Bronx, and from Yiddish, and when I delivered fur coats for Ben Cohen, I would sometimes be sent to America, to Westchester, Scarsdale, and Stamford. In Kansas City where I did my army time, a Phyllis whom I fucked even the first date under the steering wheel of my car asked, "If I get pregnant will you marry me?" And there was no question. Because she was a Jew? Because it had been too easy? As in England, after Kansas City, a Yugoslav girl studying nursing once massaged my neck and so cured my headache, and later wouldn't let me come inside of her, or only a little, and after asked, "What if I get pregnant? Will you marry me?" When Madeleine came from Kansas City on her way to France and stayed with me, the Yugoslav girl pinned a poison flower to my cottage door. It was then that I entertained an Italian Commedia del Arte theater troupe. There was a blazing fire and good bread, sausage and wine. There were thirty of us in that small room in which I slept, ate, and worked, and it was now dark and flame-shadowed, and we sang and laughed, and then fantastically one of us was flying through the air, thrown back and forth, arms spread, and there was a moment of childlike astonishment, and I was sitting crowded on my bed next to the dark beautiful leading lady who had at that evening's performance been presented with an armful of flowers, and she gave me a flower and a kiss, a flower and a kiss.

"Sonny," I said to another *rejeton* come to our halfway house, we climbing into the Alpilles, the boy so close behind me I was uncomfortable, "do you know what happens when you walk in your father's footsteps?" This was a sensitive boy, who looked up to me, my dear cousin Anna's boy, but also Fred's. "He farts in your face," I said. The truth of the matter is, of course, that what a father wants of his son is that the son do what he did not have the courage to do, and the complement to that is that the son demands of himself to be even as brave as the father.

So the neckers went off into the Paris morning, and I went out to

Orly, where submachine-gun-armed blue-uniformed police were stationed all about the El Al counters.

I was wearing my genius jacket. Did I mention that when I first put it on I found a condom in a pocket? Under my genius jacket, I wore my fifteen-year-old blue woolen navy shirt that Madeleine had recently made into a short shirt-jacket for me, a sleeve pocket in which I kept my pocketknife and a ballpoint pen. I am thirty-nine years old, monk-bald, I wear heavy country shoes.

I purchased a one-way ticket.

There were a hundred of us waiting, now the line was moving forward. One by one we were taken to a far office. Why did I assume that the question would be, why do you want to go? Because that was in my mind? Because that was even what I wanted to prove?

In England, I read fifty books about the concentration camps. After some months, I would sit reading through the night, a kitchen knife at hand, and when I would hear a noise in the shrubbery outside I would quickly move with my knife into shadows. Vera, the Yugoslav girl, must have come in the night when Madeleine was there, to pin the poison flower to my door.

Because I married a Christian? Because her father was a lantern-jawed one-eyed Christian soldier? Because I do not live among Jews? Because I have not been a Jew? Because I have sinned by omission and by commission?

What I was asked was, "What is your profession?"

My brother Larry, in Europe for a conference of psychiatrists, visited us in St. Rémy. I had just finished writing a play that was drawn mainly from my readings in England, from my very mood in that cottage, and I read it to him. I read well and I believed in what I had written, and Larry was moved and during the visit he said I was a teacher.

That was in the Mas de Maria at the foot of the Alpilles. It was a 200-year-old stone farmhouse that we would rent for two years and then to America to teach for a while, and then back. That was where I first cut wood, split oak wood down a seam with an ax and iron wedges, split olive tree stumps with an ax, the wood breaking off in hunks, the olive wood odor rising rich, flooding up with each stroke, like wild mint or thyme or lavender when you walk through a field.

Madeleine had her sculpture studio downstairs next to the small room with the big fireplace where we spent our evenings. Our bedroom above was unheated, and in my study above that I had set up a cast-iron coal- and wood-burning stove that glowed at its vents.

The walls and floor of that room were irregular. My heavy table was at a narrow window from which I had a view of a field of olive trees, and then 100 yards away a rising slope covered by pine, and beyond that the Alpilles, the small mountains with the contours of a giant mountain range. The wind blew from the Alps down the Rhône River valley, across the plains, and rolled up these mountains like waves licking up, and the sky in a mistral, sunlight and star-light, turned and whirled, the twisted forms of the olive trees, the lines of tall wind-breaking cypress trees bending, bowing, whistling.

Larry said he gave my books to the young cousins, the hard cases, who were sent to him. Even the second book that he did not like, the masks. "That's what we're doing," I explained, "putting on masks."

"Yes, yes, but the first," he said, "the family book, that's origins, that's connections. These are kids who don't know what to connect to, who don't know who and what they are."

The Teacher, the *Melamud*, would, for his height and his tall black hat that he did not remove, bow into a room. He came to us from the Tremont Street neighborhood already turning black, the elevated Seventh Avenue subway there, its noise and shadows in-vading the apartments of old Jews my father treated. My mother took me once into that neighborhood to visit with a gypsy fortune-teller, and I sat waiting for her in one empty room while down a long corridor she sat in another with the fortune-teller. The *Mela-mud* came up Hunts Point Avenue looking like a diplomat, he wore a black jacket and vest and black-and-gray-striped trousers, but when you looked closely his clothes were not clean and were snuff-stained, his fingers were tobacco-stained. He taught us to read Hebrew, though not to understand it. What could he think of us?— we did not even speak Yiddish. Sometimes we had lessons in the dining room at the big table where a hundred family photographs lay in no order on a lace cloth beneath a glass top, sometimes in our bedroom at a folding bridge table that served as our work table, the afternoon view from our corner window of Hunts Point Avenue and Lafayette Street, the trolley that roared by. His long finger smoothly underlined the words, and he nodded his head to the singsong rhythm he wanted. He would slap our hands to punish us, or grip our wrists so hard it hurt. Sometimes he would grow absentminded and the finger would stop though we would continue, sometimes he would push his hat back on his head, partially revealing the skullcap he wore under his hat, and close his eyes and nod.

One year Madeleine had a miscarriage and the next an operation for a fibroma and the next she was pregnant again. Because of the fibroma operation the birth was to be a Caesarean, with our blood types there was the risk of an accident. She carried too low, too big, the last months she was confined to bed.

It was the approach of winter, and we lived in a small, flimsy, storm-windowed house among a thousand flimsy storm-windowed houses dropped like boxes in the otherwise unbroken American cornfield, the roads always going straight, the angles always right. They are houses I have seen put on wheels, sailing the highways.

We had no friends, we doubted everything. My last novel had been bought for peanuts by a publisher who had been like a mentor and who now said his partners refused to allow him to publish it. I could not find another publisher. I was knocking on doors, only I was in America and New York was 1000 miles away. It was the year of the student riots, of the assassination of Martin Luther King. Madeleine began the year spotting, and when had she last sold a sculpture? Rejected second sister, she doubted everything about herself, believed herself able only to give stillbirth or monsterbirth, or useless sculpture birth. Thin, yogurt-eating, unappetited woman with yet, months after she had done any serious sculpture, the hands of someone who has worked with her hands all her life, and the often distant regard of someone who sees forms behind forms. She had always been her own person, she left her parents' home when she was eighteen and, come to America, worked as five-dollar-a-week *au pair* in Connecticut and Kansas City suburban homes where husbands would come sneaking up back stairways to plead at her bedroom door and wives would insist she call them by their first names and would use her as their maid. Stubborn, silent. If there is an appetite in her, it is for poetry, for a deep, pure, and formal seeing.

I am speaking about her, but I am speaking about me. For if she came to me in England, I went after her to Provence. Going for the fibroma operation, she muttered about walls—"I must pass the wall" —and after, there were monumental sculptures of the wall, of reaching to climb the wall, of forms within walls, she dwelling on the passing of the wall as if she had not realized that the wall was then passed. But she had decided for life, for the pregnancy. Decided or intuited, or simply felt, or became. For can one make such a decision? And it is not given to just anyone, and it does not happen at just any time.

One day she complained of pain. The Caesarean was scheduled for a week later. We went to the hospital, and though they were sure it was only psychological, they found her a bed.

At home I was awakened at midnight by the phone, I was told not to worry, but that she had begun labor and that they would operate, and would I please come to the hospital?

When I arrived she had been prepared for surgery and sedated. She told me she had gone to the bathroom and there the water had burst out of her. They wheeled her on a stretcher to an elevator, she held my hand, her gaze was on me, but then, as the doors closed, was lost upwards.

The waiting room was next to some narrow labor rooms, and in one there was a woman in labor sitting in a barbershop-type chair, her husband at her side. I remembered Madeleine's miscarriage. She had been hemorrhaging, and I had brought her to the hospital at Arles where, when I left her to buy newspapers and magazines, she was taken from her bed and made to straddle a chair, her legs strapped bent and apart. She was left that way, the door open, nurses and interns passing by indifferently, as if to be shamed for the miscarriage, as if they thought every miscarriage was suspicious, the very will of the mother. She maybe thinking then, in that posture, that it maybe had been her will, maybe thinking, Why did I not stop sculpture for the time of the pregnancy? Early the morning of the miscarriage she had screamed from the cold dank bathroom downstairs in the Mas de Maria, "Max! Max!" "What is it?" "It's going! It's going!" So that when she was looking at me ten minutes before, telling me of the water bursting out of her, she was maybe thinking of that.

"What happened to the baby?" Margo, our simple-minded neighbor, asked later. She was seventy-five years old, hunchbacked, a very witch in appearance, a mole on her lantern jaw. (Whenever neighbors had a litter of cats to dispose of, they would ask for Margo, and she would carry them in her full apron to the canal and open her apron like opening her hands into the canal.) I returned to the hospital with newspapers and magazines, but Madeleine's bed was empty and it rushed on me that I had gone to my mother's semiprivate room at Mount Sinai once and her bed had been empty and stripped, her things gone, and I am always witnessing my mother's death. And every time I open a door or wait for news, I am waiting for that.

I am pacing the waiting room—next door the woman is controlling her breathing, she is only at the beginning of a long labor—and Madeleine is upstairs, and I am waiting again for such news. All my life I have been waiting again and again for such news.

I force myself to think of the Mas de Maria, of the sky on a day of mistral. I hear Claire Galron's voice like a birdsong. Even for you I think of her, Madeleine. I would come back in the cold night from the hospital to the empty Mas de Maria and I would find the stove stoked and on the stove a pan of something good simmering. Claire would have come up with it, or she would have sent her bent sister Margo with it. "Where is Galron?" we asked her of her husband when we returned once from America to the Mas de Maria. She said, looking up at the clear sky, "He's gone to the Great Garden."

If it is a boy, his name is Saul.

Didn't Madeleine tell me that in her dream he came to her and said, "I want to introduce myself, *maman*. My name is Saul-Daniel," she finding in her father's father's name a link joining her family to mine. For even as I have not been a Jew, what is she? For all of yours are dead, or indifferent, your parents are dead, and there never was a reconciliation, though it did happen that your father, looking at you, saw his mother. You are here, Madeleine, in the center of America without even your work, and so little of me, and only what you carry in you.

Next door she is breathing loudly, surely his hand clasped in hers.

Is this for me? I begin to stand.

"Mister Katz?" The nurse is smiling. "It's a seven-pound boy. She's fine too," she says nodding. "We're finishing up, and we'll be taking them down in a moment."

I am standing by the glass-enclosed nursery, and a stout nurse enters it from behind carrying a black-haired baby, my son! But what is the nurse telling me, she is counting the fingers of both his hands, she forms the sound on her lips so that I will understand— ten—and now she uncovers his feet and begins to count his toes, and counts carefully so that there will be no mistake, and she looks up at me and again enunciates—ten. She's telling me, and this is, I begin to realize, very important, he is all right.

They are wheeling Madeleine in, her eyes are closed, her breathing is light moaning. I say her name, I say, "Madeleine, Saul-Daniel is here!" She is in pain and only semiconscious, she opens her eyes, her smile is radiant.

I go home and I make a couple of long-distance calls and wake people up, and then I am quite alone in the kitchen and I begin to dance as all my life I have wanted to dance, foot-stamping, hand-clapping. Then I am leaning on the kitchen counter, my head is in my hands, I am, I think, trying to catch my breath, but no, I am sobbing. My boy will bear my father's name, and it will go on.

In the morning, so Madeleine told me, even before they brought the child to her to nurse, the flowers began to arrive. There were a dozen red roses each from Jonathan, David, Sam, and Louis Cohen. There were flowers and telegrams from uncles Joe and Sol Cohen, from Joe's son Marty Cohen, from Ben's widow Dora, from Emma, from cousins Madeleine had never even met, from Anna and from Larry, with whom I had spoken during the night, from Dan and Tanya in Paris. The long window ledge of Madeleine's room over-flowed with flowers, and there were flowers on all the tables and shelves about her, and baskets of fruit, and telegrams. For that time, for Madeleine's radiance, for her being foreign, for the celebration about her, the nurses thought they were caring for a princess, that a prince had been born. Madeleine was in pain still, but she laughed.

It was a time of success. The play was optioned, the novel was sold.

One day Larry called and told me that Sam's boy, Mark, had

committed suicide. He was twenty-one years old; he signed his suicide note to his father, "Traditionally yours."

In Connecticut, on our way back to France, we stopped with my
brother and his family. The very day we arrived, Marty Cohen, his
wife Julie and son Ed drove up from Great Neck, Long Island.

The boy was twenty-one years old. His face was acne-covered, his
nose without the acne would have been big and bumpy, his lips
were as if swollen, and his large eyes were closely spaced. On his
father the very same features were somehow not unattractive, an
alertness still in his tall lean boxer's body as in his expression, his
eyes.

The boy had visited us once in Milwaukee, where we taught a
season, and he had been all loose and at ease, he had kept us laughing describing and acting out "The Three Stooges" television program. He had been arrested that year at the University of Illinois on
drug charges, and six months later at a school in Florida. Both times
his father had been able to have him gotten out of jail. But now Ed
had been arrested even in Great Neck for selling hashish, and Marty
knew he was using heroin, and he did not know what to do. He had
been advised that he could keep him out of jail now only by institutionalizing him.

We were drinking coffee and eating coffeecake. The boy had gone
to sit alone in Larry's study. Larry said to Marty and Julie that he
could see to it that Ed be institutionalized, but they would have to
agree to all institution policies, they would have to come up twice a
week for treatment with their son.

"Whaaat!" the mother said.

She was an intelligent woman, she was herself doing part-time
counseling, and she knew generally what she wanted. She had had a
mastectomy several years before, the threat of illness was on her
still, she was tired and high-strung. She immediately explained herself, "But it's two hours each way."

The boxer-shouldered man said they would come.

My son was crawling at his feet, and the boxer's hangdog look
became the clown's face as he stared into little Saul's eyes, widening
his own until they were astonishing.

He did not, he said later, know what to do with himself. His father had just sold his fur business to a conglomerate, and his own share of the stocks given in exchange would make him a millionaire. He wanted to go back to school, he would fulfil his dream of being a schoolteacher.

"He's escaping!" my brother's oldest boy called out.

Ed had opened a study window and climbed out. Immediately the boxer and I were running through the streets after Ed.

Once, years before, visiting Marty, we had gone to the local school playground to play stickball, the father pitched, the son batted, I fielded. A gray day in Great Neck, pitching, or hitting the ball, or lunging to catch a drive, settling in under a fly.

We ran across backyards into the parking lot of a supermarket, and I glimpsed Ed crossing the main avenue. Marty let go then, and he was fifty years old but he left me far behind, the nearsighted man, eyeglassless then, flying across the avenue, already overtaking his son, the son turning breathless, hands raised and open at his chest as if to say, "Stay away, don't touch!"

We were circling each other on a sidewalk, between bushes and parked cars, in front of a small white bungalow.

I said, "You're throwing everything away. Don't you see? You're throwing away everything good."

He looked at me, his father's large eyes, only hurt beyond consolation.

"What do you want, what is it you've always wanted? You can have it still, you can come back to it still. I don't know what you want, but the things I want, the things I love, I'll never give up."

He said, "I don't want to be locked up."

"What can I say? Larry says it's not like that, and that it's in order to be able to come back stronger. Larry's all right, that's his business, it's his life, he knows what he's about, and he doesn't give up on you."

"Is that why he let you run after me?"

"Can you see him running through the street?" Larry was very big and had given up cigarettes and smoked cigars, and he wore thick eyeglasses and had a psychiatrist beard. Ed smiled.

Marty's eyes were wet. I felt I had won. We walked back together, quietly, slowly.

We all drank diet cola.

Larry began to make calls, Ed went back to the study.

The next time it was evening and no one saw him escape, and we did not know which way to go. Marty, Larry, and I each drove to a different bus station downtown and waited, but we did not find him.

Some days later I was in the city on Second Avenue on the Lower East Side. I saw Ed walking alone and I caught up to him. He was surprised and not unpleased.

We went to a candy store for milkshakes. I said, "At least speak to Larry."

"No."

"What are you going to do?"

He stood and said he had to go.

"Give me a number where we can reach you."

"No."

He walked off. I followed him. He came back on me. He said with anger, but satisfaction, as if he had figured me out, "What are you bucking for now?"

He swung off, and this time there was a real I-couldn't-care-less bounce to his walk. I watched him walk down tenement- Puerto-Rican-crowded Fourth or Fifth Street.

In the middle of the night, a day or so later, Marty called Larry. He was at a city hospital, Ed had had an overdose, he would be all right; could he take him up to the institution that afternoon?

We met them at the institution, and while the formalities were being accomplished I played hearts with Ed in the social room. He was pasty white. At tables about us were tens of boys and girls, some drinking Coke, one playing a guitar, something like a college dormitory social room.

The 35,000-ton ship was highly automatized. The wheel, though always controlled by the deck officer and sailor on watch, was most often on automatic. The engineer on duty was not required to be in the enginerooms, he could be called by computer-controlled alarm signals in his cabin or in the officers' mess or lounge. There was a complicated shipwide system of alarms and signals, which shortly after the ship left Bremerhaven for New York, began to malfunction. At night, alarm signals like fire signals would start ringing through-

out the ship and the passengers in the owner's cabin would be
awakened by an alarm bell ringing on a wall just outside their door.
But with the ceasing of the alarm would be a stopping of all the
ship's motors, a sudden silence in which you could hear the sounds
of the sea. And the enormous ship, top-heavy with containers, pow-
erless during the time of repairs, would begin to roll heavily in the
always heavy seas.

In their cabin, unattached chairs would topple, books and toys
would slide wildly. They would have to hold onto the sides of their
beds. The five-year-old boy had been sick since they had put to sea.
The husband and wife went down for meals in turn so that one
would always be with the boy. The chief mate one day, when the
other officers were gone and Max was finishing his coffee, told him
that some months before there had been an accident on a sister ship.
Periodically a deck officer and sailors inspected the lashings of containers. The chief mate of the sister ship had made his tour, found
everything in order, but shortly after he and the sailors who had
accompanied him had become violently ill. The captain had gone to
repeat the inspection; he too had discovered nothing out of the
ordinary, and then he too had become violently ill. The ship's officers and crew numbered twenty-six. The captain and the chief mate
were unable to command, four sailors were ill. The manifest, which
the remaining officers examined and reexamined, did not list any
poisonous cargo. The ship was in daily radio contact with its home
office in New York.

"What's happening to us?" Other sailors were complaining of
headaches, a sailor who had not been among the containers had a
vomiting fit.

The ship was one day's sailing from Europe; it was ordered to cut
speed. A helicopter was sent to the ship and dropped aboard a new
captain, a doctor, and two men who, in gas masks and special cover-
all suits, went among the containers and corrected the situation. For
a day there was a regular helicopter traffic as cargo was removed,
and then the ill, replacements arriving.

There was no doubt in the chief mate's mind that the cargo had
been sent by a US government agency. He wanted Max to understand, but would not out of politeness or regard be explicit, that
someone in the corporation was at fault for having accepted the

poison gas as secret and unmanifested cargo. The chief mate of the sister ship was still hospitalized and would perhaps never fully recover. Every man who had been aboard the ship at the time of the leak had had aftereffects. It could have happened that through the accident of the leak, a slight shift in the wind, and the ship's ventilating system, every man aboard would have died, and the ship, on automatic, would have gone on sailing toward the Continent.

He thought, sitting in front of the mirror well in the owner's cabin, What am I afraid of? And he was suddenly smiling, thinking that until now he had thought he was on the verge of breakdown, but that he was really only on the verge of seeing something he did not want to see. Nor would the ceaseless sea let him go, he could not here end his thoughts on an irony. Outside it was all gray mist, drizzle, and the ship fog-horning through.

He thought, I have gone with a hundred whores. I have gone with the blackest whores and never seen their faces, and what I have done is too low. I have gone with girls I used as whores. And even then I longed to be loved as a child is loved and caressed. I have longed for my wife to be with me as a whore, and I have hated her for my own longings.

In Paris, a whore, understanding me, sat on me, straddled me, attached me, and then sitting up on me began to slap me, left cheek and then right, and pinch me, and she yelled at me, "Don't move, don't you dare touch me or I'll really hurt you!" I am thinking of that, and in the mirror I see Madeleine knitting, I see my son pale and still in his bed.

I am incapable of love. Whom have I ever loved? The dead. Did you love your mother? When she was dead. Did you love your father? When he was dead. Will you love your wife only when she is dead?

You have loved only in your work. And so you have lived among shadows, among what might have been, or what should have been. But now, having written about Madeleine choosing life, you realize that that is almost nothing. It is almost nothing to choose life, but how you live is something.

"Have you ever hit someone with your fist? I mean like this?" Big Mike, who had been my student, said to me one night drunk in

Cobb's Corner in Detroit, banging his fist into his palm. "Has anyone ever been afraid of you? You use too many commas to make enemies! Ha! ha! ha!"

He had written, "The sky was a flaming raging red-hued yellow-streaked battleship and I am jumping into its saddle and . . ."

"My aching back!" I had said.

He had stood up from the seminar table and had said, "In five years I'll be the biggest writer in America! I'll crush you!"—in a class, with sophomores too. And in five years he had published 375 poems, and garnished this fellowship and another, all the while gobbling up degrees and becoming a famous local disc jockey. He was prosperous now, he weighed 250 pounds, he was telling me about America, the money world, Clark Gable, F. Scott Fitzgerald, the great Smith estate, the cars, the women! He was tearing down twenty grand, and everyone knew who he was! When he interviewed the hypocrites who came through town to sell this bag of tricks or another, he ate them up! "I'd eat you up too only you're not even big enough for me to invite on my show. And besides, you've got nothing to sell!

"We're all hucksters and you gotta get in that arena and pitch your voice out to the bleachers! No, we're *gladiators*, and before you're even allowed to try to sell, you gotta kill off the others, the weak and delicate ones, the cripples, the starry-eyed ones who don't know how to take what they want!"

The place was rocking with jukebox poetry, kids were arriving and leaving, every one of them parading his costume—RAF, SS, leather genius jackets. Big Mike was wearing shades and what he called a boss hat.

"Go back to Faye," I said.

"We're dying!" he exclaimed, spreading his arms, "and all you can tell us is, 'Go back to your wife!' Tell us about heaven, about hell! Are you a poet or what?"

I chose Provence, ten acres behind Sénanque.

The first time we went to the twelfth-century abbey, the tall lean Père Grégoire, one of the handful of monks still living there, pointed up from the cloister to the long roof of the church, flat, tabletlike stones fitted to a gentle angle, line upon line, the stones weathered together, gray- and black-mottled, and said, "The intellect is vertical, the heart is horizontal." His gesture followed the gentle angle of the roof, swept it, and encompassed as well, as if that too had been part of the original conception, the flat mountain against whose flank the church roof seemed even to be an ordering of.

As for the modest-gardened cloister with its double line of columns, each column smaller than a man, its wide alleys for meditation, and the well where the monks would wash early in the morning, with its sweet irregularities, lines that slope to meet, its every gentle rising arch falling gently to a horizontal, its being enclosed against and yet attached to the church as to the mountain, as to the sky, it is of eternal intimacy.

The Cistercian order has rented the abbey to a multinational corporation for ninety-nine years; Père Grégoire is now a hermit, only he too lives in our time and he hermits in a ruin he has arranged into a sleeping cell, a tiny kitchen, and a room as a chapel. He raises raspberries and sells them dear.

We live high on the gently rising plateau of the Vaucluse. Our son began to go to school at the school at Murs. We live in a farmhouse ruin partially redone, the roof of old rounded tile interwoven over and under, an earth orange that melts like autumn rust into the all-year, season-nuanced green foliage. The house is of stone upon stone, the inner walls stuccoed and then whitewashed for light, for there are no windows facing north and even the windows south are small, for when the mistral blows it finds ways even through the three-foot-thick stone and mortar walls.

There is a main room, and above that two bedrooms. There is a kitchen and bath and a room for me. Madeleine works in a drafty outhouse. There are small farm buildings in ruin all about the property.

All the constructions, like the house, are of stone. The stones were removed from the fields that have been worked, on and off, a thousand years. They are the same stones with which men built high walls and low, and terraced their fields. It is an austere country of weathered stone walls, small hardy trees, and the clearest of blue skies. The fruit trees that prosper here are olive, almond, cherry, and quince; the most hardy of all is olive, though all of them died in the frost of 1956 and the olive trees of now are new shoots the trunks of which you can still encircle with your hands.

There are stone-terraced fields of olive trees barely five yards wide, and one stone-terraced field leads by a ladderlike stone staircase to another. The olive tree shoots here have not been trimmed, the land has been let go, you walk in dense shrubbery, live oak is everywhere, low, the silvergreen of olive trees reaching up through the tiny-pronged evergreen live oak leaves. You stumble over a stone-laid drainage system, foot deep and wide canals to feed rainwater from terraces to underground cisterns. Men here tended their stony land rigorously.

On our property there are low stone buildings that we have been told were *porcheries*. There are no pigs nowadays in this region, wells have gone dry, underground streams and springs have been lost. Now you only rarely see sheep, and the people who keep goats for cheese are often people who have left the city.

We have chickens and pigeons. When we bought we had no thought of that, just as we had no thought of a vegetable garden. In St. Rémy, where we rented a house, we had no garden and no chickens. But leaving the city you are sooner or later returning to the land.

Marty told me I had spoken to his boy as all his life he had wanted to, and I thought I was embarrassed for him but it was really for me. When Marty looked wide-eyed at my boy was he seeing even my father, Yes, doctor, here I am again. When he ran after his boy, when he stood wordless facing the wary boy, what did he think, what did he feel? How dare I play teacher? What am I bucking for? For whose approval?

When, wearing my genius jacket, I left my wife and son in the house behind Sénanque, why did I too take a condom with me? Later, when I returned home—the Israelis did not need writers—I condensed the experience in my journal: Russian roulette in Paris. Is that all it was, and not even that?

When I told Madeleine I would go to Israel, she became pale with anger. I said, "It's for my son." I said, "How could I ever face him, or myself, if I don't go now?" She said, "Then *we* should go."

Outside the kitchen door, at the rear of the house, she coming from hanging out the laundry.

Our house is closed now, we left our animals with a neighbor. My study is shuttered and dark, the fireplace in the main room is blocked at the flue. I went from window to window and brought the shutters to and hooked them in place. We left at night and did not look back.

All we have of that place are the keys, and we are arriving in America.

What is that house to me?

I cannot sleep. There is dim corridor light in the cabin. I despise myself that I am traveling in the owner's cabin. I feel I am imprisoned in this cabin. I am imprisoned by my wife and my son. They are sleeping lightly. Where am I taking them? Where am I going? What do you really want? You asked the boy, now ask yourself. What do you really want? What is it you are hiding from yourself? What longing is in you that you are afraid even to uncover?

3

The ambassador and his wife arrived at Le Bourget, were met by a young man and a chauffeured limousine from the embassy and driven off immediately on a belt around the city for Orly, where a reservation for the ambassador's wife had been made on a transatlantic flight to New York. It was winter, and though it was barely four o'clock, the heavy often bumper-to-bumper automobile traffic had low lights on and the city, rising in new skyscrapers everywhere here, was for the ambassador a welcome sight. Where he had come from everything was heavy monumental statue and stone, here it was movement. Though, looking at him, one might have wondered if he were not of that other world. He was fifty-five years old, he kept trim, but his face had thickened. He wore a dark hat and a soft heavy dark coat, he wore plain black shoes. And there was something about his gently ironic and surprised blue-eyed gaze that made one think he lived on an altogether different plane from others. Though now, with his small and handsome wife at his side, she wearing a dark mink belted coat and toque, unlipsticked as if she had begun mourning even when, ten hours earlier, she had received the cablegram and begun to dress for this trip, particularly thoughtful as she rarely was with him, lost in the solemnity of parting, the rushed voyage, her purpose, he felt deeply attached.

He knew something of what she was feeling. Her teacher was dead, she would now have to be worthy of him. Whatever she had been until now, she had been as if sheltered by him. Now it was her turn to be central and exposed. She was fifty years old, there was that about her still that he sometimes loved her and thought of her as a child.

What would she say about the artist? Would she use the folklore? —the man so small he had to stand on a chair to paint his big canvases. His subject matter had been limited, he had been ignored by a generation. Yet those who had stuck with him had been reminded by his work of hard times and more generous impulses. He wondered if he had ever made a perfect painting. Did he make even one painting that went beyond possession and could not be owned?

It occurred to him that he had never had a teacher.

She would see her mother too, in an upstairs wing of their apartment. He wished for an instant he were arriving there too, for their quiet and handsome things, the cleanliness, order, the hundred paintings, the grand still spaces, the building lobby still like a great palace, the door captain standing from his place to greet you, his words soft and lost in the space and marble. Bibi, they called her; she was eighty, and the recent rush of age on her had been terrible, for she had always been young, like an older sister to her daughter. She would see no one now, she was wheeled in a chair from one room to another.

They were all dead or dying, all that generation, and he, who had been an orphan very young and who had never not been a man, thought that one could not be a man before one's father's death, or the sudden aging that announced a father's death, and suddenly one was a man only to realize it was your turn. Joe was almost ninety years old, Sol was eighty-five. Joe's mind was slipping; when he called Joe to honor him for a birthday or just to say hello, Joe spoke the tough New York Yiddish he had not used since the 1930s. His own half-brother Louis was sixty-five, David was almost that, Sam was sixty.

"He did good work," he said to his wife, who looked at him grate-fully.

Their kiss, at the departure gate, a stewardess waiting to accom-pany her aboard, was brief, she moved hesitantly away and half-turned to him when she reached the accordion passageway that would take her even into the plane, but he nodded and smiled at her and she was gone.

Now he felt quite alone, free of his wife, of all the boundaries of his offices, and he thought he could better consider his own mission. He would bathe, dine lightly, drink enough to sleep. He would want the morning for study and last-minute checking. In the afternoon, he was flying back into that other world, but to its very center, where he would renew the interrupted negotiations.

"Your Excellency."

He turned and thought, We are even like gods.

"The Plaza Athenée," he said.

There was but the barest change of expression on the young man's face, but the ambassador could read that the young man now al-lowed himself to think he was of the losing party.

The president had said to him, "And if you can, bargain out a few Jews."

When Jonathan was contraried, opposed, his smile was even more self-satisfied.

"Monsieur Cohen," the *concierge* said warmly as he, removing his dark hat, stepped out of the revolving doors into the Plaza Athenée, "how are you?"

For he had come here as a furrier, and his uncles had stopped here. For an instant he had the feeling that any second now Sam Koch, the dirty-old-man furrier friend of Joe, would loudly turn into the lobby, but he was dead. And he remembered being here with his Uncle Ben, and it seemed to him it was 100 years since he had loved anyone with all his heart.

For, he thought in his bath, they could not speak to him without putting the touch on him. His sister Sara insisted on the love and consideration he and his brothers had always reserved for her, but she had been divorced, she had had a nervous breakdown, she was on drug therapy, often up or down. She had had three children, two had flown the coop to California, she was left looking sterile and barren with Marybell, the autistic third child.

Louis thought he had been betrayed when he had accepted the presidential appointment and left Dan Weber chairman of the board. David had always envied and despised him, and mocked him. Only with Sam had he been able to feel at ease, but gentle Sam had taken to mediating, to representing brother, sister, uncle, or cousin to him, and, in spite of all their experience, no one but Dan Weber understood that what one could give was only money and had nothing to do with happiness, that money was another language altogether.

When Dan's wife had shot off a rifle in her mouth, he had gone with the tall proud quiet man to Greek islands, to classical museums. Dan had given millions in his wife's name to brain research as if what she had done had been the result of an organic disorder and he would fight the disorder. But the ambassador had not long before glanced at a report of the foundation Dan sponsored and read that one of its lines of research was the freezing and subsequent reanimation of sheep brains. One does not, however, laugh at a partner's dream.

Dressing, it occurred to him that he did not want to dine alone and wanted even to speak Yiddish, and he called his cousin Dan Katz, who said he would come and pick him up.

Dan Katz had never asked. They had more than once offered. He was semiretired now, but he had had a metal business and some years before had had serious difficulties. Jonathan had learned of that and had had his bank call its Paris director, who had then called Dan for an appointment at his home where he had told him he had a blank check, he could have as much credit as he wanted, literally.

Dan would never forget that as he would never forget David's finding him and his wife in Paris after the Liberation, arriving at their apartment with duffel bags full of rations and chocolate, and sugar, coffee, cigarettes, and silk stockings.

He was seventy years old and short and heavy, yet he had very fine hands, and his feet were small and he wore soft fine Italian moccasins. He had the broad Katz smile, and perhaps because he had been the youngest of five brothers and four sisters and had been small and not as studious as the others and had loved and looked up to his brothers and lost them so early, there was no trace of irony in his smile. When he would greet or bid good-bye to a nephew or friend, his eyes might grow wet as if he thought every such meeting was a chance and every departure was momentous. Still, he would afterwards eat with appetite or watch the latest American "The Untouchables" episode on French television.

It was dark, they drove across Paris. It was a comfortable car. There had been a silence after their meeting. Now Dan said, as if to renew that first warmth by sharing what had been so deep for him, that he had seen his sister Sonia in Moscow before she died, he had had a week with her, they had sat drinking tea at a kitchen table.

He pulled to on a narrow street of the old Jewish quarter behind the Hôtel de Ville. "I buy a special salami here. There's no salami like this salami. I'll buy an extra one for you."

"That's all right," Jonathan said, smiling, shaking his head.

Dan bought like a prince: salamis, corned beef, smoked salmon, golden-skinned smoked whitefish, pickles. He bought a bottle of Polish vodka. The two men in their expensive hats and coats in the sawdust-floored delicatessen, the old Russian-Jewish proprietor in a full soiled apron, speaking Yiddish, some neighborhood Jews who had emigrated from North Africa ten years before looking on. The narrow brims of their hats were angled sharply, they probably used this place as others used cafés, meeting here, talking deals.

"What can I buy?" Jonathan asked.

"Do you want to insult me?"

Dan's father-in-law, to whose small apartment halfway again across Paris they drove—by the Seine, "Parees by night!" Dan said (Jonathan looking behind at the facade of Notre Dame, the fast traffic, the city lights, though now, two months after the Yom Kippur War, a dimming even here)—was ninety-nine years old. Dan said he was almost intact. He greeted Jonathan as Your Excellency and said that in English, a language he hardly spoke, so unctuously one might have thought he had been dealing with ambassadors all his life and not voluntarily confined to this apartment thirty years. He was of average height, but for his bearing seemed tall. He was slender, his lips were thin and drawn. His smooth enormous forehead glowed, but somehow almost as if from within, as if the skin pulling taut to bone had begun to reveal the real inner glow. He had lost everything once in Russia and once in Germany, in France he had lived five years in hiding. "Rutabaga!" he would say of that time.

"Your Excellency," he asked when he had dropped back into his tall armchair, "how goes the world?"

"As it always has," Jonathan said.

The old man permitted himself a smile of complicity and closed his eyes.

"He predicted it," Tanya said.

She too was become heavy, round, and she too had fine wrists and her ankles were so fine you were afraid they would fold under her weight. The living room of the small apartment was crowded with heavy wooden tables and chairs, there were big-shaded lamps, the big television in a corner, and Tanya and Dan bringing platters from the kitchen, their little chihuahua yapping, Tanya cooing to the dog in passing, Dan wagging his finger at it. By now the table was spread, Russian sprats in sunflower-seed oil, creamed and smoked herring, one of the salamis sliced halfway, smelling thickly of garlic, the corned beef, the smoked whitefish and salmon, the smell of pickles, sturgeon just a bit stiff-stale as if it had been sliced the day before, and cold chicken in quarters, and Dan had popped open a bottle of champagne, and they raised their glasses and said, "*L'chayim!*"

"Where will it lead to?" Tanya asked. "The whole world wants only and always to destroy the Jews! A hundred million Arabs. We are always David against Goliath! And in Russia, they will not let us out!"

"My nephew," Dan explained, "the son of my sister Sonia. He and his family are in Moscow. . . . Eat," he invited.

"Is that your work?" Jonathan asked Tanya, indicating colorful paintings of Russian peasant women on the walls.

"A hundred years ago," Tanya said. "I've changed. You'd never believe what I'm doing now." She wanted him to guess. She had a girl's charm and real intelligence, she had a woman's quick intuition.

"Erotic!" she said, blushing. "At my age."

Dan smiled as if he had reason to be proud.

"I came to Paris," Jonathan said, "to put Sheila on a plane to New York, her teacher just died."

He wondered why he was telling them that. She was still in the air, her mink coat and toque probably on an empty seat at her side, probably still composing the speech she would make: A man who did good work. A small man standing—ha! ha! ha!—on a chair in order to even reach his ambitious paintings, a ridiculous man who never knew how much he wanted money and esteem, who never could even begin to understand what things were all about. They were all prima donnas, artists, each thinking he was the most beautiful, he was the only one worth listening to, one loved them like dogs, mascots. When he thought of truly great artists, he knew they were like sleepwalkers, they lived their lives elsewhere, though once, after a visit to the Sistine Chapel, he entered a great domed building and tilted his head back to look up, expecting and almost fearing he would see an insect-like figure crawling in the dome creating clouds and angels.

He turned abruptly to Dan and asked, "Does he really want to be let out?"

Dan understood immediately. He was again as if poised over a blank check. And he was suspicious, afraid and angry. Why doesn't he say clearly what he is offering, how he will effect it, what are his terms and conditions? And Tanya had paled, for she could even read her husband and she had learned many lessons and one of the most difficult was that one could not decide for others. Even then she sensed risen into the room the years of fleeing and hiding, of not being able to look anyone in the eye, for not only were you without a country, you were no one, your name borrowed, your papers false, the years of being hunted and ashamed, ashamed even of not being dead, though that had come later, was the very bottom of it, that one had lived only to survive, to keep husband alive, and father and mother alive.

"Why do you ask?" she demanded.

But the moment was already past. He could and would have done it. He thought, They think I can only hurt their nephew, and there was a distance between them, and he smiled warmly and did not answer Tanya and said that the salami was wonderful, that he was lucky Sheila was not there for she did not like garlic.

"Have I told you," Tanya asked, "how much I like Sheila's work?" This he knew was *politesse*, but he smiled warmly at the praise.

They were little people and afraid. You offer them a way, but they want it at no risk. Yet he sensed something else when Dan, tears rising to his eyes, asked, "Did you know Esther's boy?"

"Do you know," Tanya interrupted, "he came once to Europe, a boy, ten years ago. He hitchhiked! He didn't very much want to see us, we were only Jews, the other generation. Nevertheless, he came, and though he was a very quiet boy, we were very close. He spoke about his father. When he left us, there was one last stop in Europe on his itinerary, he was going to the aquarium at Monaco."

Jonathan thought strangely and sadly of his simpleton niece.

Dan was nodding at the story, the memory. He said, and Jonathan knew it was this he had wanted to say before, "*He* was a hero."

The old man stood in the silence that followed and raised his arm as if to still conversation. He had a fine little mustache, his tie was knotted big. He smiled as if he were about to say something well worth listening to, as if he could win the attention of all the world by his superciliousness. The chihuahua looked up at the raised arm, alert.

"We are," he said, "the chosen people. But," he said, now barely able to contain his mirth, "not democratically."

He was laughing as at the very best *bon mot*, and he somehow lost his balance and began to fall, the chihuahua retreating straight back, yapping violently. He fell, remarkably, as if superciliously, absolutely erect, slowly, and in a wide arc. Jonathan caught him under his arm, twisting him around, his own arm encircling him, the weight then in his arms astonishing, tremendous.

The weight in his arms, Jonathan now knew, had seemed like stone. He was seated up against pillows centered in his large bed, the large room, the high molded ceiling, lit only by a bed-lamp. There was on a wheeled tray at the bedside a half-empty fifth of Scotch whisky, an ice bucket, and a platter of sandwiches, there

were several sharpened pencils in a glass on a night-table. He had
asked the floor *concierge* to see to all that, he had pleased the *concierge* almost as much by the sense many people had with him of his
importance as with the one-time folded tip he passed him. Nor
would he ever finish the bottle, would leave it capped and neat, a
quarter or a half full. He wondered briefly if the second gold digital
watch had been packed with his shaving things, for he always traveled there with several gold watches and often returned with
Russian-made ones, the importance of the people one dealt with
there seen even in the gold fillings in their teeth. He removed his
heavy-framed reading glasses and pushed aside his dossiers. The
facts and figures were already imprinted in his mind, margins alone
now were unknown even if felt, the margins of push and price, of
luck, your mind always alert.

He had thought that the ancient man in his arms had been hardly
startled, as if it made no difference to him where he was, the eyes all-
seeing, the brain all-knowing. He began to smile, that man too, and
not entirely without reason, thought he was immortal.

The issue, he thought, is even the memorial speech, or—ha! ha!
ha!—the farewell.

His head was pleasantly warm, Sheila was in New York now, only
there it was six hours earlier, time for her to have been driven to
their building—he had had C-ways cabled. He thought of the mu-
latto chauffeur Luis, who would have told her perhaps about his last
trip home to Puerto Rico, big on New York–earned dollars, no doubt
doing big things for his numerous family. He recalled having, some
years before, visited Tony, in the chauffeured Lincoln, in Yorktown,
a walk-up, a gift-check for Tony and flowers for his daughter, a case
of vodka to arrive after. Tony dying then, the limping clean-up
"boy" from Berezin like them, only not family, not Jew, had discovered them in America by accident, had been given a job in Ben's fur
business as clean-up and delivery boy, and had never learned English and had unlearned Russian, so that his every second word was
sonofabitch and the rest was gibberish, but landsman still, and
more, the gibberish like secrets, his life stretching beyond Jonathan's past into the dark, Jonathan sitting in the daughter's living
room, smiling, listening, searching, What is he trying to say?

There would be time, he thought, for Sheila to sit with her mother and ask about her health. She could not wear contacts anymore and would not wear eyeglasses and so was button-eyed, and had kept herself slender as her daughter and was now all sticks and fragile bones, and would speak like them all about the stock market and the muggers, and gas pains. Sheila would listen and smile when called to and would think of the other, of her speech, and drink a Coke, as she did throughout the day and never even belched, not even a ladylike one. She would bathe, she was even cleaner than him—their maid, always on hand, would have laid things out for her—and then would dress and go out to the funeral home, Luis leading her even from the car to the dead room. Would his brothers be there? They had bought the little man's work, their first painter, but then had gone their own ways, discovered their own artists. David's *masterpiece* was a wall-large hide-and-seek that looked at from one angle was not what it was from the other, human figures that changed shape in a fleshlike forest of pinks and violets. Sam had discovered Renoir. "Who loves Renoir as much as me?"

He thought, I have built. He thought, And at each stage I would think this is as high as I will go, and that is too bad for it is even the next landing that would give it all meaning.

"I want," he said, having almost immediately, almost like thought, reached his brother Sam in New York, "that we honor Uncle Joe. I want a big party, Sam."

Sam nodded. His pleasure at receiving this call flew back across the ocean to Jonathan. "But how," he asked, "can we have a party for Joe without one for Sol?"

"Of course," Jonathan said. "Sol too will be honored."

"I'll speak to Anna," Sam said.

"Of course," Jonathan said, smiling wryly, not for Anna but her husband Fred, that he was the seating arranger, the arbiter almost, How can you invite this one and not the other? He himself would have to make the speech.

"It's important," Jonathan said, but he really meant, Fast, fast, fast.

He told his brother that Sheila was in the city, did you read that Zola is dead?

Sam nodded transatlantic again. "I'm going to the funeral," he said, deciding.

Neither said anything for a moment.

"What time is it?" Sam asked, always delighted that the world really did turn round. But then he asked impulsively, "Jonathan, when are you coming back? Without you . . ."

"Good-night, Sam."

4

We gathered this Tuesday evening to meet for the first time our cousin Esther Katz-Nissnievitch, whom Anna had said she would drive over, and to welcome our cousin Max and his family, who had just arrived from Europe on one of our ships. We met, as we did most Tuesdays, at Sam's "Versailles" thirty-eight stories over Central Park, tall Fifth Avenue and Central Park West buildings like a frame to the park, the nighttime haze of light beyond that was Harlem and far beyond that was the Bronx. A cloud could have passed through the living-room window.

Jonathan had been the head of the family. Louis, who had once been Jonathan's most loyal ally, now said of him, "He thinks he's taller than his asshole." It was not an idle comment, Louis had begun to think that things went wrong when one thought one was taller than one's asshole. And things were going wrong.

C-ways stock that had been at eighty was now at seven and was eroding every day. Container competition had become cutthroat, rates were down, the Justice Department had just won a rebate case against the company and the company had been fined $1 million.

Louis thought C-ways had expanded too much, they were involved in too many different operations, had too many subsidiary corporations, they required the use of batteries of giant computers and teams of lawyers, accountants, and technicians, whose findings only other computers, lawyers, accountants, and technicians could verify. Louis was paid $125,000 a year to, he would say, *worry*!

He was squat and neckless, his face made one think of knuckles.

White-haired red-faced David, with whom he shared an executive suite and whose broad desk was flush to his, would answer Louis's principle with his own: "Amateurism!"

At home, things were going no better. Louis's thirty-year-old son, an air force pilot, remained a bachelor, when he was home on leave he would see no one of the family, he yelled at his mother when the laundry came back not clean enough. He rarely even said hello to his father. "If it's a hotel, you can pay rent!" the father would cry out after his son when they would have passed each other without a word on a staircase or in a corridor of the house. The son would not answer, the father would put more stock in the son's name for tax purposes.

His daughter, bright, nervous, was here with us this evening. She lived where? Who knew? In disorder. Her brother was a patriot, she might have been a world revolution, Palestinian liberation, women's rights activist, except that now she was on a meditation thing, traveled with drums, and at the oddest times would go off to a bathroom, a rooftop, and sit cross-legged and beat out a mental pattern like a message across space to herself. "Why don't you shave under your arms!" Louis would scream at her. She had been a pretty girl, dark; she had learned to sneer.

David's older son lived with a woman ten years older than him confined to a wheelchair; the younger boy had been using drugs since he was a child.

David was here with one of his several girlfriends.

Sara came with her daughter Marybell.

Marybell stood with her Aunt Sheila because she was closest to Jonathan, and Jonathan had taken her out of "school" for holidays and trips, and a weekend at the beach. Sometimes she would confront a cousin her own age whom she saw only, as now, at family events, but every year, several times, his changes, the way he grew up. "Hi!" with enthusiasm that then waned, as if they had taught her at her "school" to break into our world with enthusiasm, but had not figured out how she could then stay in the world. She was so plain she made you think of servants' quarters or the country.

Anna's younger boy had called Max and Madeleine to see them alone first. He was six months out of college, he had a dewy mustache, his father was eating away at him to get a job, to cut his hair. His mother had always encouraged him to read and love literature, but he could tell that she, even more than his father, now needed a winner. Something bad was happening even now to his father, his mother was becoming hard, brittle. "Is this the kind of book I should read, Max?" You should read in order to do what? Max was about to ask, but he knew the answer and did not want that kind of conversation and so said, "Sure." He knew what he should say: You want to write, write! You want to join the Peace Corps, do it! You want to go to law school, go! But he wondered whether it was worth saying—the kid wanting only that, to be told by him—like wasting a blessing, or the blessing was too compromised, all of him compromised though he putting the blame on the kid, thinking what might even have been true, This is a loser. He had had the boy on his back for two weeks once—at his back, wasn't it?—and he could not do for the boy what the boy had to do for himself. Louis's daughter too had come through Provence, but she had come hitching, adventuring, and, yes, had come looking for direction, "'a viable alternative," the Max-Madeleine art-producing team. Surely she had respected their work, Madeleine's sharp-edged sculpture, the sculpture called *Miss Carriage*, the mountain legs raised and spread, the way we bleed. But Max, alone with her one day in the *Deux Chevaux camionnette*, talked about his longing for money, success, and hadn't she been able to see and even smell that that longing led right into another, she there for direction, he almost reaching out to touch her and take from her?

I have been even a monument, he thought, though he did not realize how much until later that same night when he, Madeleine, and their son went with Anna and her son to spend the night at their home in Woodmere. Fred was there, the bald normally fastidious man pale and quiet in a terrycloth bathrobe, his stiffness and silence even like a cry of distress though no one was yet listening. The older son who could not get into medical school came from his room and spoke of a career as a tennis pro, and his attitude was, Fuck you, Max, I'll make it my way. And the second son said to Max, "Come on outside, we've got something to show you." And the two boys playfully jumped him in that handkerchief lawn between fenced-in handkerchief lawns, the ever-present roar of giant airplanes coming into nearby Kennedy, Max understanding it really was not a joke, they getting back at him as you do at someone you believe in or want to believe in who plays you false, and maybe for that he struggled with them and they had even to pin him.

Anyhow, Max was then at "Versailles," and there was tall decent Marty, and Max asked him about his boy. "How's Ed?"

"Don't you know the story?" our host, the mild Sam, answered for the boxer.

He was sixty years old, plump, curly-haired, permanent-waved. His smile was warm and open as a child's, though there was in his clear blue-eyed regard something sad, permanent, and quiet. He had had 1 million shares of C-ways stock and had sold more than half when the stock was still well above fifty.

Sam told the story: "When Lily died, she left five thousand dollars to each of her grandchildren. And when they finally located Ed, he sent the check to Marty saying, 'You can use this better than me.'" Sam was beaming and Marty was nodding, It's true.

Sam's wife Margo brought out a toy dog that walked, barked, and she assured everyone, even peed. Margo had become huge, her face was blurred, she wore jeweled eyeglasses, she moved feverishly, panting for breath, a cigarette hanging from her richly lipsticked lips.

Anna finally arrived with Esther.

But Margo was then showing the dog off, walking it across the long enormous living room even to the giant window—the reflections in it, the pastel-tinted night sky—the dog nodding its head, its short tail wagging, and then she promenaded the dog back through the guests to little Saul-Daniel and said, "It's for you! You can have it!"

The dog frightened the boy.

"What's the matter? Can't he speak English? Here, take it!" she said, pressing the leash into the boy's small hand, and then turning abruptly from him—panting, breathing smoke, a moist film over her eyes—to Esther, her new guest, she said, "Darling, who are you exactly?"

There were different levels in that long enormous room, and there were people center and in nooks, and there was Anna, who was Esther's niece, and Max, who was her nephew, and Anna's son, and Max's son Saul-Daniel, and there were Louis, Sam, and Sara, who were her cousins, and David, who was the last person to have seen her mother and who had found and perhaps saved her niece Ruth, and there were other cousins and other children, and our flatterers, some of whom were cousins and Berezin landsmen, and we were, from every part of the room, looking at her, her thick legs, the plainness of her shoes and dress, the old-woman lines on her face, the flesh drawn about her mouth, and we sensed other people in her and others in ourselves, and yet we did not reach out to her. Perhaps it was Margo's question and immediate impatience then with Sam's explanation, perhaps it was that we permitted Margo, hostess here, to speak first. Sam said, "Esther is a Katz by her father and a Starobinetz and Nissnievitch by her mother. She is thus three times and doubly my cousin, her father cousin to both my father and mother, and her mother cousin two ways to both my father and mother."

"I understand nothing!" Margo exclaimed, "except that it all sounds corrupt, ha! ha! ha!"

Esther too had been thinking, Who are they to me? Their faces were painted and powdered, she had never seen lips as blue as Sam's, his wavy hair had been curled as a woman's. Who are they? she thought. What has happened to them? They all talked and laughed at once. And just then she saw the little boy being led to her, and he seemed to her, for the way the dim rich light caught his fair face, his perfect features, his high forehead, the deep eyes, beautiful. She moved heavily to him, bending, and said in French to him even before she could be sure who he was, "I am Esther Katz-Nissnievitch, who are you?"

"*Je m'appelle Saul-Daniel Katz.*"

"We must be related," she said, smiling, nodding, and embraced the child.

Madeleine told Esther about her son's visit to them in Provence. She said, thinking of meals in the small, low, small-beamed, big-fireplaced dining room in the Mas de Maria, "He didn't speak much, Abisai."

"He was not a talker."

"He went off climbing into the Alpilles. He found fossils, he came back with a bag full of stones. We lived in St. Rémy then, we took him to Sénanque. There were still a handful of monks there, Cistercians, the graves of dead monks in a line by an outer wall, small mounds almost as if for children, small plain white crosses. The abbey is truly nestled in a valley, surrounded by mountains. The monks cultivated lavender, and there's still a very long field of low lavender bushes there.

"It was very hot, we had to wait a little outside for a monk to let us in, and we stood in the shade of a big oak tree, but then we entered and that was very special. It wasn't just the sudden cool, it was the space, it was the way space is held, enclosed, is *stilled.* Abisai wasn't particularly tall, but he was particularly straight, and he was stilled, and I see him in the church now—the way the great arches curve into columns and fall then into horizontals—and he turns and discovers the oculus high in the church wall behind him. He's standing in the body of the church, and there is that beam of light entering the church, and we had been outside in the light, but now inside we see it. Every passageway there, every staircase, is large enough for a man and another, so that when you see one person passing into another place you sense even by his absence another at his side.

"We walked in the cloister. The cloister is central, like the open heart of the abbey. Here are wide arched arcades where the monks would walk in prayer and meditation. Beyond the arcade, veiled by slender columns, is the simple garden, and in a corner of it, a well. From the center of the cloister you can see the flat-stone-slab roofs of the abbey against the stone of the mountain, and against the sky are the stone-capped chimneys and the bell tower highest but still as if within reach.

"When Abisai left, we drove him to Aix-en-Provence, the National Seven, the big road south."

Just then Sam dramatically switched on a panel of lights, and the gigantic window suddenly became a mirrored wall and treasures in this room we had only glimpsed before now sparkled twice. They were gold, silver, crystal, and jade, they were ivory and silk. They were heavy gilt-framed *paysages*, and lit and apart like icons were two Renoir portraits of rosy-faced children.

"The colors!" someone exclaimed of the Renoirs.

"*La joie de vivre!*" Sara brought out.

"The colors of genius!" Sam said.

Then down, down, down we went in a team of elevators that had gathered at our landing that none of us would have to wait. The women wore their furs over their shoulders, for we were not going out, but to our restaurant in our building. There were television camera-eyes in the elevators, in the lobby corridors lined with display windows for furs, jewels, paintings, were black-suited guards. Like passengers on a ship, we never had to leave this building, and we knew all our stewards and waiters by name. This evening we passed through the tables of our neighbors, waving or smiling hello, into a private dining room.

"There's folly in every genius," Sam said, "and when a genius is destroyed, for even when they destroy themselves, it is that they were destroyed! It too is like a sacrifice."

Marty, who understood something of what Sam was feeling, nodded deeply. Sam too was nodding. What he had to say was very important, he wanted to reach this wisdom across to his younger cousins and maybe, yes, even to Esther, that she know even what he lived by. But he had drunk a little and the words would not form, and he sighed deeply and smiled warmly and looked at us so tenderly that we nodded to his every thought.

"My son," he said to Esther, "was making a film when he was struck down." Margo was panting-waiting, as if for Sam to make everything clear.

"We do not forget him," a flatterer said, feelingly. And we nodded feelingly.

And the presence of the beautiful boy rose at the table. So to him was it we ate caviar, smoked salmon, and smoked sturgeon. We ate, our eyes tearing, scampi and cherrystone clams. But we were troubled still by the presence of the old woman.

"We're Zionists," Louis said to Esther.

"It's a land of milk and honey," Marty intoned, tone-deaf. "Truly," he intoned as if to convince everyone there.

"Yes, we're all Zionists!" David said of his fortyish girlfriend, "This is Sadie, my Jewish girlfriend, ha! ha! ha!"

Sadie was embarrassed before Esther and said, "It's been so long."

"*What's been so long?*" David exploded.

"It's the psychiatrists who don't understand," Sam explained softly to Esther. "They don't let people be, they confuse them."

Rachel, the timid wife of Louis, said to Esther, "We're not real Zionists . . ."

"What are you talking about!" Louis exclaimed.

"You've given millions," Anna said that none of them would have to say so.

"Tens of millions!" another said.

"Still," Rachel insisted, whisky sours she drank to keep her husband company loosening her tongue, giving her courage, "we're not real Zionists. But how could we not love Israel?"

Louis was staring at his daughter and he said, "What do they know of us? Do you even know where I was born? Do you know after who you were named? She wore a wig! Ha! ha! ha! Do you know the cities I lived in before I came to *La-wrence*?"

"I know only what you've told me!"

"Do you know the darkness we come from?"

"I know darkness enough," she said bitterly.

Marty was at table like a swimmer all alone and far out.

Esther addressed Rachel softly, "When I first arrived in Israel, I knew I'd been there before. We long even for Zion."

"Oh," David said, "what do we not long for!"

And Sam, who wanted only to tell Esther more about his son, said, "I don't know if we can help you."

And so it was out.

But Esther perhaps had begun to sense what was in Sam's heart and in ours, and what she had come for that had been so important was part of something else now. She felt no chagrin for what Sam had said, though that was even—she could see in the faces about her, the embarrassed looks and the firm, Marty, facing up to his responsibilities, looking her squarely in the eye, all the hurt in his eyes—a general policy. No, something else was gathering about her, about them, and was it good? And was it bad? Flying was in it, and returning to Israel, a blood-red sunset tinting the desert, and the cloister where her son had walked was in it, the garden veiled by columns, the flat-stone roof against the flat mountains. My son is waiting for a ride still on the side of the National 7. This beautiful fair boy is part of it too—his mother said he was born with black hair—even as she, gentle Christian with the hands of someone who works, is in it. Still, she was here and they were staring at her, and she said to unhappy Sam, "Perhaps you should wait until I ask."

David turned to Max and said, "Schmuck, do you know what *mama loshen* is?"

Everyone was suddenly smiling and laughing, and squat bifocaled

Louis was like a scholar swaying and nodding appreciation over Esther's interpretation of a difficult text, and then all of the men were scholars at a dinner, and Louis said, "Schmuck, *mama loshen* is mama soup!" And he was lapping it up, and even his daughter was laughing.

But shortly Esther said she was feeling tired, and Anna said she would take her back, and Max said he would, and David insisted he would, but she said she wanted air and to be alone, and we let her go, she would not even let us get her a taxi, in her cloth coat, and her purse like the kind our mothers carried.

"Seventy-five thousand dollars!" Sam had said with astonishment when Anna had dryly told him of Esther's embassy. "That's enough to commission a statue!"

"What?" Louis demanded. "Does she want us to pay for a statue to her husband?"

"No," Anna corrected, "she wants you to pay for the publication of all his writings."

"So how many books did he write?" Louis demanded.

Marty said, "Supporting her might be interpreted as *our* taking a position on the Israeli Right."

But though some of them nodded, they all sensed that it was not that. In any event, there was their heart foundation, their own Zionist causes, and Ben Cohen's fur business was operating heavily in the red, and Sam, who had been Ben's partner, would not let Ben's son sink. What did it matter that Ben's son spent $50,000 a year and only earned $20,000? It went for his house, for his children. In a deep and confused way, Sam believed in nothing but beauty, children, and sorrow.

All this evening, Sheila had been preoccupied and when she said she was leaving, Sam said he would accompany her. He did not like the idea of her taking a taxi alone at night. The street of her building by the East River was deserted at this hour, and though the taxi would go from door to door, doorman to doorman, the nighttime city was, for Sam, filled with furtive shadows.

Sheila let him accompany her to the door and then told him that she had Luis, the C-ways limousine chauffeur.

"Ah?"

She said, "They're attacking Jonathan."

His eyes and mouth formed astonished O's. Did she mean Louis and David?

"In Washington," she said.

He was almost relieved, perhaps Jonathan would be forced to return. He said, "I heard your speech. It was beautiful! Beautiful!" He saw her impatience, she was fighting not to cry. "What is it?"

"It's nothing! Nothing!"

"Let's go!" David said, but did not move.

It was 2:00 A.M. Now and then the white-haired red-cherubic-faced man would do an isometric exercise, he would grip his hands and pull at his tenor's barrel chest, or he would lean forward and breathing hard pull behind his back as if at bindings. Sometimes his blue eyes would lid over and he would seem to be sleeping.

"Let's go, darling," Rachel said to Louis. She alone had stopped drinking, she never knew when Louis might need her to take the wheel. For he was too drunk to drive, but would. "Darling?" she called.

The squat man's eyes were closed behind his bifocals. He made a sound that was neither yes or no, and Rachel was yet reassured.

Sadie was tipsy. "Honey, come on, honey," she said, pulling uselessly at David.

Sam, his back to them, was swaying, dwarfed at the gigantic window full of reflections.

"Stay a while," he said.

None of us knew how to sleep.

Marty said to David, "Sooner or later, you're going to have to. You can't go on like this, not even you."

"The *balagola*," Sam said, smiling sadly, looking still into the park.

"Why does he dye his hair?" Margo demanded.

"Who dyes his hair?" Sam asked, interested.

"The Frenchman!"

"How do you know?"

"I asked him."

"He answered what you want to hear."

"Hair so black it must be dyed.

"Maybe she dyes his hair! What does he want of us? Why does he come to us now? Why does he bring his boy to us?"

"Honey, let's go!" Sadie said.

"*Where* do you want to go?" he exploded, for he had been thinking of that too, troubled by that idiot question as if it could be a clue to something. Where would they go? To a nightclub where tired gypsy violinists would still be fiddling?

Marty said to him, "You have to think of institutionalizing. You can't carry it all on your back."

"What can you know, schmuck," David demanded, "of what Quasimodo can carry on his back!" But then he turned his anger and scorn down from his tall nearsighted cousin, for his cousin was speaking to him out of his own need. For I am the very hunchback of Notre Dame, for I am the very *balagola*! I throw sacks of grain onto my wagon, I am seated high, the reins in my hands. Aie! His sight dimmed, and he who had never been other than operatic operatically brought his hand to cover his eyes.

"What is it?" Sadie asked, terrified.

"A ghost! Ha! ha! ha!"

"It's true," Sam said, coming back toward them, nodding as if ghosts were on his mind too, "what can they know of us?

"I never told Mark about us. What could I tell him? That we were furriers? How can you explain who and what we were to kids?"

Marty said, "Nevertheless we're at fault."

Sam said impatiently, "I tell you that in a hansom cab in the park the boy put a blanket over my legs. It was a cold winter night, and I said, 'Motke Bulba,' and he took me, his daddy, for a ride under the winter stars and the bare trees against the sky, and I told him about Motke Bulba, the *balagola* of Berezin, and I said, 'You are the *balagola* now.'"

"Was that before or after he engaged Orson Welles?" Julie asked to encourage Sam.

Sam said, "Orson Welles told him he was a genius, it's true. But the disease had already gotten to him."

After a moment, Marty said, "Ed writes that he's singing." And we saw the hurt-eyed acne-faced boy bent over a guitar. "He composes his own songs."

Sam nodded his warm approval.

"The thing is," Marty said, "we've worshiped the golden calf."

"Oh!" Sam exclaimed, thinking of his charities.

Sadie looked up with interest. "Is it the circus you're talking about?"

Margo asked, "Where's my dog?" She dropped to her knees on the floor to look under chairs and sofas. "Where are you, darling? Where are you?" Rachel went to her knees to help her look.

Sam had gone to stand again at a side of the giant window.

David had seen the Queen of Spades, he had seen Eshka turning up cards at the dining-room table.

"Call the doctor!" Louis said to him. And David was stunned as if Louis, half-brother only, but deep brother, sharing in all the darkness, had read his mind. "Call Larry! Arrange it!" Louis insisted.

"It's the middle of the night," Rachel reminded them.

"What's the middle of the night?" Louis demanded, gesturing toward the giant window and night as if it were day.

"I called Larry too," Sam said.

And Marty was nodding.

"I call him, I call him," David said. "I call him sometimes in the middle of the night."

"They're no good, those doctors, no good," Sam said.

"What's a doctor for," Louis explained to Rachel, "if you can't call him in the middle of the night?"

"What does he say?" Marty asked.

"Schmuck!" David exclaimed. "He's a psychiatrist! He *listens*! Ha! ha! ha!"

"I'd weep into the phone," Sam said nodding.

"Honey, let's go," Sadie said to David.

"Darling, come on," Rachel said to Louis.

"Darling, we're keeping everybody up!"

"Nobody's keeping me up!" David said.

"You see," Louis said to Rachel, winking at David.

"Darling," she called, but now without any force.

Louis too was claimed by ghosts. Sometimes, driving home in the

Rockaway Boulevard mist, he was even almost with them. Sometimes, near dawn, at home in bed, he might fall off and then begin to toss and turn, toss and turn. "Where'll we go?" Louis asked David.

David was pulling hand against hand at his chest. "To Brooklyn," he said.

"Ah, to Brooklyn," Sam said, tender, tender.

But David was thinking of the orthodox in broad-brimmed black hats and black kaftans, he was smiling thinking of little boys with earlocks.

Marty was pale, for he had never forgotten dying Eshka sitting up in her bed and addressing the nephews. Maybe they're better off dead, he thought of their sons, and then he wanted to hurt himself because what he really meant was, Maybe we are better off when they are dead.

"We are orphans," he said, not quite knowing what he meant.

"We're orphaned by our fathers and orphaned by our mothers," David said, "and then we're orphaned by our children, ha! ha! ha!"

"I dream of visiting Eshka in Brooklyn," Julie said.

And David knew again that one was always going backwards.

"Backwards to Brooklyn," he said to Sadie when they were alone an hour later.

"You want my *tushie*, honey? Here's my *tushie*."

Maybe that too—ha! ha! ha!—was what he meant.

CHAPTER *Fourteen*

Backwards to Brooklyn

1

"THE SHARKS! The sharks!" Louis yelled, pointing.

"Kill the bastards!" David cried.

It was dawn Sunday, and they had gone out on the rear deck, drinks in hand, to watch the sunrise over the sea. They had been sailing and drinking since Friday evening, eating Beluga caviar, and bagels, and smoked salmon and sturgeon, and sour pickles, tongue and corned beef, and once Rachel had insisted they eat a regular meal, and the white-jacketed Puerto Rican steward had prepared steaks and string beans and served them at table, but it had been an intrusion and they had already been drinking too long and steadily to be able to sit even the time of a meal in one place.

David had told Louis, and Louis had said, "How can that be?" They had screamed at each other.

Finally, late Saturday night, they had called Sam at "Versailles," the call catching him still at dinner, *his* ship restaurant, the message thus beaconed ship to shore, channeled thirty-eight stories down, and he listening in on a receiver plugged in for the call to an outlet at his table. Sam had said he would meet them at the yacht club, Louis had said they would be there at 4:00 A.M., but it was already dawn and they had forgotten Sam, for later Louis had said, "The doctor! If we're going to straighten things out, there's that!" So they had called Larry in the middle of the night, and Larry had listened as he had tens of times and said, "Uh-huh . . . uh-huh," for he had learned that people, that family, called him in the night not to hear him tell them the truth but to find it in themselves, and that they had to force it out of themselves. And so he listened to the facts and held the line open, and there were long silences, and Louis could not look at David bent over the phone, and then David had hung up.

And Rachel had gone to bed her eyes red, for every time someone talked of children she thought of hers, and why couldn't the girl marry and give Louis grandchildren? and why couldn't the boy come home? she never knowing until now Louis's dream for him, what he wanted so ardently he kept it secret not only from her but from himself, he not even now telling her, she overhearing, David having then to explain it to him, "Schmuck, is that what you want?"

And they had started and stopped conversations, and they had picked up night shows, the reception as they cruised back toward the city becoming better. And then David had said, "Look, the sky's breaking." And they had, in their shirtsleeves still, gone out into the chilly morning and breathed deeply, and then Louis had cried out, "The sharks! The sharks!"

Louis lurched for the door, and David knew what he was after and, swinging his walking stick like a blind man to locate the doorway and precede him inside, he lurched in after him. The squat almost no-neck man, already through the large richly carpeted still smoke-filled salon, was up three stairs at a landing where rifles were kept in a glass-faced case, finding a key on his keyring, calling out to the bridge deck above, "Full stop, please, captain! Full stop, please!" Only it was not the captain at the wheel but his drunken hobo of a mate, and almost immediately, the rifle case open, Louis handing David an army carbine, the 100-foot vessel seemed to be caught and stopped in forward movement, and then thrown back, all motors suddenly off, the vessel's movement suddenly chaotic, David falling heavily against a wall, the walking stick dropped, he now using the stock of the carbine like the point of a stick. Louis had no time to curse, he was gathering up clips of ammunition, passing some to David, stuffing his own pockets. Rachel appeared from the sleeping cabins below in her flower-brocaded robe, her eyes heavy, red, and worried.

"Sharks!" Louis explained in passing.

"Yes, darling."

They went out onto the deck, but David could not locate the rifle at his shoulder without losing his balance, and he called out, "Steward! Steward!" even as Louis called out to the bridge, so that they would not be firing into the sun, "Get around them, schmuck! Around them!" And the motors started up with a lurch. But this time when Louis called out, "Full stop, Goddamn it! Full stop!" the vessel glided to a stop, Louis not forgetting to call out before squeezing off the first time, "Thank you, captain."

Now, day breaking behind them, the half-brothers stood in their shirtsleeves on the rolling expanse of rear deck, the captain and mate looking down from the bridge above, Rachel shivering in the salon doorway, the Puerto Rican steward, his white jacket on, kneeling by David, holding the barrel-chested man around the waist, both of them taking the recoil, Bang! Varoom!

The sharks, their metallic fins cleanly cutting the sea, had followed the vessel as if it were a prey and now, with the sudden blood, were moving erratically, churning up the surface of the sea. The captain kept the vessel moving to keep the hunters in position, and the hunters were killing their enemies. They fired clip after clip into the churning and blood-frothed sea.

The sun was risen.

The captain cut the motors, the sea was still, the vessel began to turn idly. The two men lowered their rifles, David shrugged off the Puerto Rican's help, they looked at the bloodied sea. Then they saw like an apparition the distant eyeless towers of the World Trade Center beyond the Brooklyn shore.

Sam was waiting for them in a limousine, the motor running, the chauffeur sleeping, when Louis, on the bridge, the captain at the wheel, brought the yacht abreast the quay. There was no one to haul in their lines so the mate jumped ashore and Louis fed him lines, and shortly the big boat was tied to. Sam was by then standing in the cold, and though he had been angry that he had been kept waiting more than an hour, he nodded admiringly at Louis like a

connoisseur of docking maneuvers. He wore a sable-collared coat
and a Borsalino tilted over an eye.

David, watching him from a salon window, wondered what he
himself looked like to others and recalled that that Friday morning,
in the midst of the beginning of all this, he had, in his apartment
building elevator, happened to glance at the operator and had seen
a look of hate on his face. He could not remember what he had done
to him, what he had—ha! ha! ha!—been to him. No matter. Though
later that day, he had been bowed to. On Houston Street on the
Lower East Side, where he had gone to buy delicatessen for the
weekend, struck immediately by the smell of fresh-for-the-Sabbath
bagels, eggrolls, and challeh. The round old bearded owner himself,
in a *yarmulka*, a full apron on over an old sweater—his sons too
wore *yarmulkas*—served him. "Ah," David said, catching sight in a
corner of a line of coin boxes he had not noticed before, "so that's
where you hide your *pushkas!*"

"It's the old way," the old owner explained apologetically and
shed years as if before the ancient. "Their mother," he said proudly,
blaming his boys, "insists I keep them."

But David was studying the picture of *yarmulkaed* earlocked boys
studying Torah on one of the *pushkas* and was then drawing out his
checkbook and scrawling in a sum. He folded the check into the
pushka, and when he went back to the taxi waiting double-parked,
the owner and one of his boys brought out his purchases and the
owner bowed to him.

He sat opposite his curly-haired blue-eyed brother, Sam's lips
blue. Louis stood off in a corner as if he were not here or did not
want to be here and so would stay. What Louis had revealed, why he
could not now help, the project he had that would require all his
funds, David—a morning sobriety and clarity come over him though
he had not rested, though he had not stopped drinking—could not
reveal to Sam.

David told Sam he had bought 25,000 shares of a stock then at
twenty using C-ways shares then at nine as collateral. The stock had
risen, but he had neglected to sell. Then when the stock began to
fall, he had gambled it would not fall far, and then it had begun to
plummet even as C-ways had reached rock bottom. His collateral
had shrunken 85 percent in value, and his stock, purchased when it

was worth $500,000, was worth $50,000. He owed over $400,000. And the factor's interest on that was $10,000 a month.

"Oh," Sam said, nodding tiredly, "it can be done, we'll find a way."

He looked at Louis, who would not say anything or even nod, and now Sam paled. But even as he would not question David—How could you hold on so long? What have you done with all your capital?—he would not question Louis—Why do you say nothing? What are you hiding from me?

"I'll speak to my broker."

"I need fifteen thousand dollars now."

"A Sunday morning?"

"Tomorrow morning then," David said, finishing the conversation. He needed the cash now, Louis would not help, that was that. Should he tell him the rest, how every morning he had to go through the boy's closets, drawers, and pockets looking for pills, how he had set down the law: If I find that poison once more, I'll throw you out, do you hear? And how he had found Friday morning, not the poison, but the boy himself poisoned, and had taken from him his keys and the few crumpled bills he had and said, "That's that, if you go out to get your poison now, you don't come back in. Do you understand? You can go out for your poison, but you won't get back in!"

How tell that to this brother—"Traditionally yours," his boy had written—how tell that to this orphan who wanted more than anything only that things be as they had been, who had come here in the middle of the night even as years before one would go, well after the factories had shut down for the day, giving the bosses time to catch up on matching and cutting, to the private office at Ben's, all the Cohens arriving from every direction in the fur market, to reach family decisions, the safe there behind the desk.

He did not know how to show affection to this brother. "A game of gin rummy?" he asked.

But Sam shook his head, rising. He would not be bitter. "Margo's waiting up for me at home," he said, putting on his sable-collared coat.

Home, David's English girlfriend, black-haired red-lipped Mary in a black sweater and black short skirt, and a mustached flatterer her own age in a modish-cut suit were waiting for him in the black leather armchairs in his wood-panelled den, the bar open, the color TV on, the flatterer rising for the introduction: "This is Reggie, dear." He was, Mary said, English too, an opera producer.

"What do I know about opera?" David protested, for he had never even told his sons he had sung.

"You like opera, don't you, Mr. Cohen?"

Oh, you schmuck, I am opera!

"I've produced operas in London and Amsterdam."

"Go on! Go on!" David encouraged, the light under his number blinking, he picking up the telephone receiver.

He sat, his dark glasses on still, tieless, wearing a discreetly pin-striped double-breasted dark suit; Mary had brought him a drink in a hand-filling cocktail glass and sat down on the arm of his chair, her hair was in his white hair, she put her arm on his shoulder, her side, her breast, pressed against his arm. She blew into his ear, "Isn't he a darling, dear? We went to school together." He looked at the slender lithe girl and thought of all the things she could do in the dark. Where had she come from? What suburbia? How do they learn? He knew that her almost every word was lie, but it made no difference, for her truth was money and in her mind money could be transubstantiated and love of it was even love of flesh.

On the phone, Sam said the money would be brought to his office in the morning by a messenger.

"What movie did you see?" Because Sunday afternoons Sam and Margo went to a midtown movie.

David asked the flatterer, "Where will you produce?"

"In the Academy of Music."

"In Brooklyn?"

"No, he's not here," he, having again answered the phone, said to Larry without any drama. For he had assumed the boy was gone when he had tried to call him earlier in the day and had known for sure when he had entered the apartment, barely nodding hello to his guests, limping first to the kitchen and then to the boy's room, al-most reassured at the gigantic disorder, the stereo equipment not fully off, that the boy had only gone out and would have to call to be let back in. Let him cool off!

But then, the receiver still at his ear, he holding on as the psychiatrist held on, the TV on, the flatterer continuing to list his accomplishments—he had filmed an opera, he had almost had the Callas in his pocket—almost hearing what he almost heard in the back of his own mind every time he spoke with, held on with the doctor, it occurred to him that the boy might have taken something to sell. Immediately, furiously as if outsmarted, he was lurching through the big living room looking for theft, lighting the room like a stage. What, anyhow, would anyone steal here? Lamps? The stores are full of such lamps. Antiques? The factories are mass-producing them! Who wants this stuff! Who needs it! "Hide and seek!" he said, gesturing with his stick at the big painting in so wild a way that the flatterer wondered if he meant that that was what they were now doing.

"Without support," the flatterer said, "without benefactors, without impresarios, there'd be no art."

David stopped where he stood. How much did the boy think he could get out of him?

"For every benefactor, there are *five* impresarios, and for every impresario, there are *fifty* artists. We pick and choose, and bring the best out into the open, into a framework. I tell you, I have discovered such talent!"

This boy was deep, deep.

David began to do isometric exercises at his barrel chest, encouraging the boy to follow his example by nodding quickly like a Chinaman, do! do!

"Sopranos like birds!" the flatterer continued, nodding.

"Who?" David demanded, again at the phone. The secretary to the Mezrivitcher *what*? Ah, the Mezrivitcher *rebbe*!" A smile like a laugh spread over his face. Earlocks, *yarmulkas*, gefilte fish.

"You got my check? Ah, I see." He could not remember if he had written a check for one or five hundred dollars. Would they invite him to dinner for one hundred?

Mary was at his ear. "Dear, why don't you write him a check?"

"Did you at least check to see if my check was good?" he asked, smiling at his court as if to share the joke with them. But he dearly did not want to let go of this line. "Wait! Wait!" he called out. "I am a soul in torment! What should I do?"

The answer did not come immediately.

"I do already."

Again there was a pause.

"Then I should make—ha! ha! ha!—*two* prayers a day?"

The flatterer said, "They're always alone, a single voice. You can't imagine how narrow the singer's view is."

And he knew who the flatterer was, and this is what we have taught them, and this is all we have taught them, this boy organizing talent, pocketing it, trading it. Go home, he wanted to say, start all over again, from scratch, this will get you only pain. But, of course, it made no difference, what Mary had whispered into his ear about him was lie; he was perhaps even her brother. This was an age of vipers.

"How much do you need?" he asked cunningly.

"Who is it, dear?" Mary asked.

For it was Max on the phone and David's mood had suddenly deepened. His name came from far, and it was not just the gefilte fish but the place and time, the very making of the fish, and Leah too serving, the grapefruit halves, and then the fish, and all of them gathered at the same table and someone saying, "A miracle!" and each then with his way of praising the fish, the fish, *the fish*! His name came even from that far as if he still lived in that time or was coming from that time, his father, and David remembered going to the East Bronx to visit with his father Sunday mornings, with his boy, sitting with the doctor, talking politics. For there had always been that too, the world and how the world turned, and the doctor had understood much even if he had, after all he had seen, all he had lived, believed still in the future. He had told the doctor about Berlin, about ruin and spies, the marching off of thousands to camps, and the avid stupidity like cruelty of our side. He had sung those stories to him with his ha! ha! ha!, but the doctor had understood that singing so he was hurting twice, for them and for himself that he was what he was. For the little doctor had listened and nodded, and then at the end, when he would abruptly rise to leave, he, who virtually each time he shook hands found occasion to wash his hands, put his hand on his shoulder and even held him so a moment. But now, suddenly, David was suspicious, wondering, What does the psychiatrist tell his brother? What does he tell about me and my pain? What does he tell him that he won't tell me!

"What do you want?" he asked impatiently.

"I want to spend a couple of weeks in the city, I want to make and renew contacts. Can you put me up?"

"Ah," David said, "contacts. You want to make *contacts*! Of course I can put you up!"

But then, looking at the flatterer, the TV, Mary's hand inside his jacket, caressing, he wondered, Why me? Who am I to him? and thought, No matter, he will come to me as a spy—ha! ha! ha! His hick clothes, his hayseed clothes! Even his father's spy? Her hand was in his fly, and the flatterer was speaking fees, and it was as if they were accomplices in each other's deceits. Only he was almost three times their age, and the lessons they had learned so easily, he had learned by wounds. Only he had put whole cities into his pocket, Istanbul, Naples, Galveston! And he could destroy them for in him there was also a rage. He could rise and throw them out. Ah, he understood Louis, he understood Louis's dream—"Schmuck! Is that what you want? Is that all you want? To be partner with your son!"—father and son against the world. There were tears at his eyes and he sighed—Mary's grip tightened, her fingers like necklaces about his thing, but then the pad of a finger upward caressing—for he was thinking of his older, beautiful boy's choices, of his life now, living with a wheelchair case! His boys had been sent to live with their mother in California, and when they would come home from school they would never know if she would be there or in Africa taking pictures or in Paris writing poetry or in an institution for alcoholics. And by the time he had stepped in, there had been drugs and the nine-year-old giant had already tasted drugs, and he had sent that one as if for punishment to a military school, and the other had been expelled from the *best* private school in America, not for sniffing glue, but for refusing to tell with whom he had sniffed! And all those years I lived only half awake, and now the dreams are all—ha! ha! ha!—coming true. He would come like an ancient potentate in her hand, and the flatterer would pretend nothing had happened. He raised an eyebrow at Mary to indicate they should go to the bedroom.

"Dear," she whispered, "I'm on the rag." He shrugged away from the impurity, and she fell to the carpeted floor and still, breathing in

sighs, was as if calling him to touch her, Money! money! money! He
hated, he felt dirtied, by the impurity.

Again the light under his number was blinking.

"What do you mean, I'd better come down there?" he said furiously to the doorman. "What do you mean, *better*?"

But then he paled and was lurching out of the den and through
the living room and out of the apartment and down down down, his
stick in his hand, but no overcoat on, no hat, and the doorman
triumphantly leading him out under the canopy and halfway across
the Sunday-empty street, in the evening twilight, he saw his boy
seated like a giant on the roof of a Volkswagen as if on a throne, his
legs crossed onto the hood. He was staring off into space as into
another world. His light hair was electric, it hung like wire to his
shoulders, it radiated about his head. His face was even his own, the
same fine features, the blue eyes. There was a ring of onlookers like
admirers about him. He recognized the batiste shirt the boy's
mother had sent from Bangkok, and then he saw that he was hanging out. And even as the blood rose to his eyes dimming his sight,
and even as he thought, Who would he have to pay off now? Door-
men even! he knew that this, what his boy was doing, what his boy
had become, was his real debt, was what he somehow, some way,
would have to pay off for, was paying off for now, only where would
he get the means? And even then he was lurching to his boy, his
stick raised as if to beat him, but the giant did not move, saw beyond, beyond, and the white-haired, dark-glassed, barrel-chested
sixty-five-year-old man dropped his stick and threw his arms about
the unmoved giant and began to sway against him as if he were
rocking an infant in his arms.

2

Once again I could not sleep.

There is no night at our apartment at the Belair Hotel in the
center of Detroit, it is milky night there, and all through the night
come the wild wailing sounds of police sirens and fire engines, sometimes a police helicopter hovers almost at our seventh-floor win-

dows. They are big rectangular windows dirty with the traces of wind-blown rain the color even of sulphur. All our windows give east on rows and rows of low ghetto houses, and our horizon is broken only by factory buildings and warehouses. In the distance I can see the nighttime ghostlike procession of car headlights on the Ford Expressway where it rises between monumental car cemetery piles, the procession is endless.

The hotel itself has seen better days. Its spaces are large, its furnishings are run-down. One or the other of the two elevators is generally out of order. The hotel serves the giant university, accommodating transients like us and also handicapped students who cannot be accommodated by student housing. There are a certain number of blind students in the Belair, and a great number of students in wheelchairs. We come back from year to year, and we know them to say hello to, and one is English and his head seems gigantic, for his limbs are atrophied, and one tall straight boy was some years ago on canes and now uses an aluminum platform that he swings into place before him and then leans on, dragging his legs after. There was a fire on our floor in a vacant apartment being repainted the other night, and when the firemen located the fire and opened the apartment door black smoke gushed out into the wide carpeted corridors, billowed out toward us waiting for the elevators, and the firemen, giants in their wonderful hats, their caped waterproof coats, their floppy boots, lined up the wheelchair students by the staircase door, ready, in the event of worse, to lift them—who waited so quietly—into their arms and carry them down.

"Madeleine," I had said, gently waking her, for this time in Detroit she would be very tired after teaching language classes and correcting papers and preparing for us, and was, I began after weeks to realize, like someone deserted, "you better get up, we have to go downstairs." "What is it?" she cried, staring at me. One day, Saul-Daniel and I were in a bus coming home from his school and were passed by three patrol cars zooming into a bookstore a little beyond the hotel. Policemen dashed out of their cars, revolvers in hand, and took up television poses flat against walls, pistols pointed up.

"Daddy," Saul-Daniel said to me one evening.

"Yes?"

"I think about when I'll die."

Kathy, who had been Madeleine's student and had stayed with us in Murs, baked us fresh bread every week. She did not want to go to graduate school just yet, she worked in the kitchen of a cheap restaurant. Mel came once a week to eat with us, to play chess with me, or just to sit. He is black, six foot two, and his voice is never more than a whisper, and what I know of him is what I glean from what he writes, only he puts it down slow and has to work at this job or the other in order to keep going. His play is being produced at the university. I went the other night to a rehearsal, and when it was over all the actors and all the technical help and Mel gathered in a circle to talk it over, and then they stood and held hands and swayed in place an instant, and then Mel said, "God bless," and they all said, "God bless."

He came to us in our house near Murs and stayed some months. He has migraines. He comes from the South, he was raised by a stepmother and then by an uncle on poor farms. What worlds lie in him? We went once into the low Alps, and it was summer, and we were on a *crête* that here rose in rich green and distantly was covered still by snow. The air was mountain-cool, mountain-thin, and we had to stop a while, but he went on, and he is a runner, and when he walks alone he lopes, and he loped off toward the snow.

I see students all afternoon long. In a ghetto journal, I read that a product containing a colorant that all the major networks have announced will shortly be taken off the market because it is more or less poisonous is put on sale in a ghetto supermarket and is instantly sold out. I want my students to write about what is important to them, and if for some that comes out as the-girl-of-my-dreams or the job-of-my-dreams, for others it is the marriage breaking up, the children sick, it is the day's rhythm, getting up, the job, school, the car breaks down, or is a Sunday family visit.

Thomas, who visited us at Murs only some months before, is now separated from his wife and does not see his one-year-old daughter. He is twenty-one and tough and cunning, but wants to be a writer. He tells me he is not cynical enough; in the no-man's-land in which he lives, who will know if he dies? He too comes regularly to play chess, he comes one evening and his eyeglasses are broken and his clothes are torn. "I'm sorry I'm late," he says. "I was attacked on my way over by a crazy."

Big Mike, who was my student, announces himself by sending a disciple to me. The boy is talented, and he does have the force, his story about cocaine and craps and being hit in the head by a brick and the world becoming flying bricks, and now he is running through the streets a flying brick, watch out! He says to me when I suggest he submit a story to a university contest, and he is only a boy, "Yeah! yeah! I want to beat them all out!"

Big Mike himself shortly makes his yearly visit to us at the Belair. Two hundred and fifty pounds, a half-gone fifth of bourbon in a briefcase, a play about America he wants to read to me. But first, as always, he must tell me how much money he is tearing down, and then how much ass he is getting, and then of his successes as a poet, of his growing fame. We live at the Belair in a kitchen, living room, and bedroom, and Madeleine is correcting papers in the kitchen, and Saul-Daniel is watching television in the living room, and I am listening to Big Mike in the bedroom, who is really saying only, Listen to me, motherfuckers, listen to me! I am the biggest! And I begin to hate the sound of that as if it came even from inside of me. I say, "Enough, Mike! Good-night, Mike!" And the big man, it seems to me for an instant, is almost grateful, but now he is standing by the door, and he, who has a weak heart, who has been in and out of A.A. and drying-out farms, who has a boy Saul-Daniel's age whom he loves and whom he can see only every second Sunday, won't let go, won't give up, is pushing at me and demanding, "Who do you think you are, you son of a bitch, Norman Mailer? ha! ha! ha!" Madeleine is holding Saul-Daniel to her, and I begin to propel the pig out of my apartment. And maybe he even knows I am really pushing something of myself away for he doesn't resist.

I pace the night through. I think of money, of rank. I am speaking of night upon night, though some nights I pace the narrow Cass Corridor—flop houses, a six-story mission house, bars and whisky-selling drugstores protected by wire mesh, a drunk weaving the sidewalk, a neon-lit storefront Chinese restaurant that has still not moved out, sharks cruising the street in their silent cars, a great twenty-story hotel gone bankrupt and vacant though you know things are crawling and scurrying about inside. A whore leans forward on frozen legs out of a doorway, an alley, and beckons you urgently.

This night too I cannot sleep, and suddenly I hear a terrible sound from the bedroom, and it is my son gasping, wheezing, for breath.

The bedroom is a dormitory, one, two, three single beds. His mother in her nightdress is at his side holding him in her arms, his head by her face. He is wheezing still, he is looking panic-stricken at her and is trying to say something. Finally, he says, "I couldn't speak!" and he begins to sob.

It is 1:00 A.M., he is running a high fever. There is no question of calling a doctor, no doctor will come out in the night. We bundle him up in blankets. He is five years old, an in-between age, he is become so big, he is yet so little. He is too heavy to carry long in your arms, though you can see that he wants that even as you want it. You sit at his side and hold him in your arms. He begins to cough, and his cough is so big it fills all the room. "It hurts! It hurts! Mommy, Daddy, it hurts!" We know, we know.

I carry his mattress into the kitchen and lay it on the floor, his mother arranges his bedding and props him up with all our pillows. She lights the gas and puts water on. When the water boils, we put the gas low, steam begins to fill the room. "Go to sleep," we say, "go to sleep." But the fear is still in his eyes; I could not speak, which is really, I could not call Mommy.

"You have to sleep," I say, for I am thinking also of us, that Madeleine has an 8:30 class and that I am suddenly very tired. "Do you want a toy? Do you want me to read to you?"

He says he wants *his* car—an old white Saab whose hood, trunk, and two doors open, the paint has peeled in places. He rolls it up and down the hills of his covers, he looks at us, and then the car in one hand, his other hand in his mother's, he is sleeping.

We turn off the light, the gas flames light the room blue. I tell Madeleine to go to bed, I'll wake her later. I sit at his side, in the strange blue light, holding his little hand.

Now he is breathing regularly if noisily, and a great desire comes over me to sleep. As if after all these long nights, I shall be able to rest, as if all my worries and fears have been resolved or put aside or taken out of my hands. I have always loved to give in to sleep, to lay myself down, to tuck myself in, and to let myself drift off, to fall, drifting, deeper and deeper into sleep. The lassitude is in all my limbs, my eyes cannot stay open, my hands are weak. The boy is all right, let go, let go. There are such dreams waiting for you. I stand, he stirs, his eyes open, he sees me in the blue gas-flame light, his look is uneasy as if he hardly knows who I am or as if, at this moment, in this light, he does not know what to expect of me. Yet his eyes close. I pace softly, one, two, three, and back to him, and each time I must look closely at him, for this night I know he could suffocate in his sleep. He could wake gasping for air and think he is trying to call his mother when what he is really doing is gasping for air and life.

Never in my life have I so wanted to sleep. Dreams come to me even as I pace. I can almost taste them. It is so long since I have had such beautiful dreams, like fruit, like flowers, like everything you have always longed for. I see a procession and a woman in white, surely a wedding procession, who is she? Madeleine is standing silent to a side. I want to go past her into my dream, but I know I must address her. She is so distant, she is ghostlike. Is she dead? I have no language with which to reach her. I cannot speak French, the words don't come, and English I know is no good, no good. What is it I want to say? Looking at her I am full of sorrow. Is all I want to say the key that will let me follow after my receding dream? I feel then rising from deep within me another language, I am looking at my son, whose breathing is again labored, the wheeze at the end of every breath, the blue gaslight flickering on him.

We were three for the circus. We had seen its arrival at Murs in the morning, some run-down trucks and trailers covered with painted-on circus signs, a woman in a glittering costume standing on a horse, roaring lions. The circus people had immediately begun to set up their tent between the bare plane trees of the village square.

"Can I go? Can I go?"

"Yes, we'll go."

It was late autumn and the days were shorter, and in the evening there was a mistral and it was chilly. We drove back to the village, and the square was lit up but there were no crowds.

Inside the tent, benches had been fixed in three concentric circles, and one sat high, low, or in between, one's feet on the bench below. We were perhaps seventy, many children, and their excitement was great. But no one was more excited than Saul-Daniel; it was his first circus. He studied the ropes, the bars, he was thrilled by the phonograph circus music.

It was a family circus, and the father, a tall lean mustached man, was impresario, acrobat, and clown. The mother was the ticket-taker, and though she was a bit dumpy, she did acrobatic feats too. The seventeen-year-old daughter was the equestrian artist. There was a boy no older than Saul-Daniel, who with a sister two years older did somersaults and jumps and was hung from a low trapeze and did leaps, the father standing by, alert and then relieved. The boy would, regardless of applause, look for his father's silent approval. But the star was a young man who played drums and a bugle no bigger than an outstretched hand, he was acrobat, juggler, clown, and unicyclist. In all the clown dialogues with the father he had the last, if idiotic, word, in all things he did he was always just on the point of disaster. Riding a unicycle, weaving between bottles, he would be about to fall when crazily he would go backwards or his whole body would go forward and the unicycle would remain in place, his body hanging over the precipice.

Our boy's laugh each time the young man retrieved himself from some irretrievable situation was full of astonishment and delight, was so natural, golden, honeyed, so much like a song that spectators turned to look at him, and the young man himself searched him out with his gaze as one looks at an unexpected gift. The boy's laugh was even contagious, and many of us were soon laughing as certainly we had not laughed in many years. And we, the parents, were very happy. And I remembered other circuses, men who somehow threw themselves or leaped through the air fifty feet, one after the other, one leap more unbelievable than the last. I remembered cossack horses being raced into a small ring and cossacks virtually flying about the horses, leaping on and off, the horses racing, racing, the cossacks leaping to hang from one side to the other like butterfly wings, hanging then from the stirrups, their heads inches from the ground. Bears! Bears! Bears! Bears running so funnily on their hind legs. We up in seventh heaven in Madison Square Garden, sugar candy, my mother.

"We'll have more chickens," I said to Saul-Daniel, his cheek against mine in the blue gas-flame-lit kitchen.

"A hundred chickens!" he said.

"A hundred chickens? What'll we do with a hundred chickens?"

"The eggs!" he said, rubbing his hands together in imitation of me.

"We'd have to open a store to sell them. One hundred egg-laying chickens makes eight dozen eggs a day! Besides, who'll take care of them? You were supposed to take care of last year's chicks. You never did."

"I was too little!"

"I'll too little you!"

"Mommy," he said, having had a brilliant idea, "will take care of them!"

"Mommy already takes care of the chickens we have, and the pigeons, and Mommy already takes care of the house and takes care of us and bakes us cakes into the bargain. Who's going to take care of Mommy?" We thought that over.

"Did you ever see a swarm of bees?" I asked Saul-Daniel. "When there are too many bees in a hive, the colony divides and the new colony goes off all together in a swarm, and the buzzing noise is almost cheerful, they take with them several days' food, honey, and they alight onto a branch somewhere and just hang there like a living swarming beard, or moss, and the beekeeper has known for some time that something was about to happen and he's been keeping an eye open, and now he knows where the swarm is, and he brings a new hive to the bees, and he gently cuts the branch down with pruning shears and lays the swarm right at the door of the hive, and the bees are now really joyous and they beat their wings in place and enter right into the hive as into a Palace Hotel."

I said, "Maybe we'll have bees this year."

He looked doubtful.

"Bees for honey," I offered.

Still he was doubtful, he had been bitten once.

I was thinking of planting a field of lavender. "We'd call our honey, Katz Lavender-and-Thyme Honey. What do you think?"

"I want a dog."

"I know, I know."

"But that's what *I* want."

"Well, we'll think about that too."

I awake in the middle of the night, in the Belair in the empty heart of Detroit, in the living room on the couch, for again I had a headache and I needed room to pace, and again I think of my work, again that it is nothing, and again of my rank, again that I am nothing, and that I am committed to nothing, and that I believe in nothing, and I think of my wife, sleeping now in the bedroom with my boy, that in fact I do not live with them, I do not live with my wife, I do not speak with her, I use her, that using her in the ways I do I am even suffocating the life in her. And I know that what I need to pull me out has a name and it is money, and it is liberty, and it is will, it is will to do, to explode, to rise, to let go, to make love, even to hurt, and that everything else is constraint. I know that, compared to my real needs, house is nothing, garden, chickens, and bees are nothing, that I'll be a no worse father by being a more successful man, and that if marriage is to slowly kill the other off, then marriage is wrong. That if what I really need is money, money, money, then I should now take hold.

I know without looking (the every-night milky sky too bright for my headache-hurting eyes) that on the Ford Expressway cars are still advancing in endless procession, and I shall hear, hardly hearing, distant pulsing wailing police sirens, and suddenly I hear in the distance a dog howling. I am standing quite still and I hear a dog howling in the distance and I look at the milky sky, and it is a snowstorm and the thick swirling snow is being driven against our windows, and out in the snow, in the distance, there is a dog howling, and I hear then a voice across all the empty city and night, *Shma Yisrael Adonoi Elohaynu, Adonoi Echod!* And then I see, eyes open, the snow settling down, a snow-blanketed village of steep-roofed houses, and only here and there a light, the quiet of sleep, and then I see sitting ponderous on the ledge of an attic window an old woman hunched over herself.

I know I have had a vision, and for a long while my heart beats rapidly and strong, but I am a writer and have had other visions. And in the morning I begin to try to call David, thinking of leathered den, of money, of dark secrets, that when I send Madeleine and Saul-David back to Provence so that I can renew contacts in New York, I should stay with him.

3

Anna wanted to get closer to Esther.

"Woodmere," she said, adding reason to reason for Esther to visit, "is as American as American apple pie." They were seated across a small table from each other at the spacious Metropolitan Museum of Art cafeteria, the large clear fountain-fed pool at their side. "All of us who moved out there were from the Bronx and Brooklyn, many of us had been to college, and we wanted our children to go to better colleges yet. My oldest boy, you know, could be a tennis pro."

She laughed at herself because Esther could not understand that just as she would not be able to understand that she had a season ticket for all the football Giant home games.

"I want to show you the school my boys went to."

But the more she spoke, the more she realized the inadequacy of what she was saying. I couldn't care less, she said to herself, but she did care, and she could already feel cramps beginning. And the funny thing was today it had something to do with Rembrandt!

For the thick-legged seventy-year-old woman had stayed long among the Rembrandt portraits and Anna too had looked, and it was not like looking at a person. For when we look at a person it is to admire or criticize, we think of who he is, of what he does, and we find clues in his clothing and manner, but when we look at these Rembrandt portraits we think of what the subject has lived and suffered, of what he has seen and felt. And there is between the subject and the viewer an immediate intimacy that could be very heavy to bear for it makes us think of those who have been dearest to us, whose pains we have known, and it might make us think of ourselves.

Even so, Anna, speaking of Woodmere, trying to suggest what the move to the Island had meant, what living and raising children here meant, was thinking of what her mother had looked like the year before her death, and it occurred to her that she herself looked like that now. She was almost at the age at which her mother had died. Her bowels were knotted. Esther was watching her, her hand over her cup as if nursing the heat of the tea. Her broad mouth, the flesh drawn about it, the still-stubborn chin, the nose hooked for age to her mouth, the thoughtful gray eyes behind her plain eyeglasses. And suddenly Anna knew that her cramps were that she was afraid for her own life.

She closed her eyes tightly. She knew that her cramps were what she would never allow herself to say even to herself: that Fred was a failure, that he had failed her, that she was afraid that her boys too would be failures, that her cramps were her fear of answering the phone and discovering that she was a widow, that she felt her own death close upon her, even in her. She had to have a cigarette, her smile was tough and brittle, and she looked at her aunt and it occurred to her that this old woman looking still at her had been her father's sister, that her father had watched her grow up and had surely played with her, and teased her, and lifted her in his arms, and that she had seen her father a soldier, a husband, for her father had married in Berezin—the love in her mother's eyes, she looking up at *her* Harry—and that looking at Esther now she was even seeing in her something of her father and something of her mother (and I would have her see in me too a little of Eshka), and that was very comforting, and there was a deep reaching out to her aunt in her.

"Come to Woodmere," she said.

And it was like a sign that arriving home they were met by Fred with such good news that she was even in the street both laughing and crying, their oldest boy, who had not been able to get into medical school and who had begun work for a master's in biology, had finally been accepted at a medical school. He will be a doctor! And she was embracing Esther in the street. Could Esther understand what she was feeling? Thirty years before, when he was eighteen, her brother had graduated Phi Beta Kappa from college and had been rejected by every medical school he applied to, and Larry, son of the doctor, had been rejected and rejected, and Eshka had died before he was accepted, not knowing that he would be a doctor. And Anna wanted to share this triumph.

They entered the house. Mrs. Lewis had been there, and it was neat and clean, and there was the wall of mirror above the long deep sofa and facing that the wall of books, and the big vase lamp in the big front picture window, and the brightness of the house, the airiness, the American textures, the wall-to-wall carpeting except, a step down, in the fully-windowed flagstonelike-floored den, that room airier yet, a window communicating directly to the kitchen so that in the summer they could take their meals here as in a patio, passing the dishes directly from the kitchen to the table. There was a wall of books here too, above the built-in bar, the built-in television and stereo, for Fred had discovered in himself a love of opera, Gigli, Bjorling. And she realized now that he was standing straight for the first time in a month, and she felt for him a surge of the same affection she had felt when she had first known him—Phi Beta Kappa law student—when she had been drawn to him, bright, college-successful, upright, dutiful. He had put champagne on ice, and he popped it open now and served it in champagne glasses, and they drank to their boy. And Anna said, "To my father and mother! To the doctor! He put me to bed when I began spotting." She was smiling and crying, and she had to remove her contact lenses, and Esther thought, That is even it, that is the falseness in her regard, and without them she is tender.

Fred said resolutely, "We'll have to see him through four more years."

Anna allowed him to take her in his arms.

He said to Esther, but also to Anna, "We didn't send them to private schools, but we gave them a good home."

"It *is* a nice home," Esther said nodding, looking to Anna too.

"We've had to soundproof it, Kennedy's within a few miles and the big seven-forty-sevens sometimes come in directly overhead, and we've had to burglarproof for the city *throws its shadows* even on us, but it's our home, that we paid off over twenty years! And our boys grew up here."

Anna reached her boy long distance.

"I did it!" he said.

"Oh, honey, you did!"

"There were a thousand applicants, there were only one hundred acceptances!"

Fred said to Esther, "He's named, you know, after your brother."

Esther was surprised. "Which brother?"

"His Hebrew name," Fred explained.

Anna caught the flash of irony on her aunt's face, and she blushed remembering that she had told her mother, "It wouldn't be fair to him to name him Harry."

Fred was addressing her. "Why don't you call *them*, honey?" He told Esther, "They'd send me to their childrens' schools in Switzerland and Vermont. When a son was expelled, they'd send me to find another school, to offer the school a gift for their library, stadium, scholarships for the *underprivileged*! When a son was arrested on drug charges in Colorado or Wisconsin, in Canada or Mexico, they'd give me air tickets and cash envelopes to bail them out. Come on, Anna, call them!"

"Do you really want me to call Sam? Do you want me to boast to Sam?"

He was just as suddenly pale for he too liked Sam.

And this too was her cramps, her blood loyalty, and her loyalty to her husband, and yet another loyalty, like a conscience, that she had always sensed and now, leaving the den, even glimpsed in the again deeply brooding face of Esther. For somewhere deep in her she was concerned with what was right and what was wrong, and what good was an honesty that was only lack of imagination and lack of courage? And seated in the bathroom the question came to her, What is the link? And though she did not really know what she meant by that, the words had a magic of their own, and she unknotted, and she smiled then at all the ironies—What is the link?

But in the night she could not sleep, the sound and vibrations of the airplanes, and Fred had taken a pill and was snoring lightly, and she did not tonight want to take a pill, hated that sleep that left one restless and resolved nothing, and tossed and turned and finally left the bed and in the living room felt Esther awake in the den and went there and Esther was sitting up on the bed-sofa, the lights off, the blinds open; she wore her eyeglasses, the shape of her cottonnightgowned body the shape her mother's body would have been. Esther excused herself as if Anna might think it impolite that she could not sleep in her house.

Anna said, "It's true, we should have named him Harry."

"Don't you know," Esther said, easing her, "that Saul didn't really want to be a doctor, but all the places for Jews in engineering school were filled, and only then did he become a doctor."

Oh yes! Anna remembered. "Oh honey," she said, "I want to take you to the cemetery."

Again the flash of irony, the return in her own eyes, the jokes not said, the understanding immediate, that I want to show you where they are buried, I want to take you to them. And the other's unspoken answer, I want to go even though I would not have thought so, I want to go to the cemetery.

They sat in the den in their nightgowns in the milky light of the Island night sky, the million all-night lights, the airplanes coming in, the house soundproofed, but it hardly helped, and there was a deep silence between them, a link between them, and Anna thought, *She is even the link!* Still, how to speak to her? I should want another language to reach her.

Esther said, "You know, I left my parents and ran off to marry Abba, I left Poland for Palestine. There are things I've tried hard not to think of. His first wife surely died in Warsaw even as I would have died had I remained. I've dreamed not only of my parents, sisters, and their children reaching out to me, but his first wife.

"They were pioneers together. They'd left Russia in the same group and had arrived in emptiness, and went to work with only what they had learned from books, and their . . ." she searched an instant for the word, ". . . ardor. She went off into the desert, and for two days they couldn't find her, and when they did she was burned and *not well*, and they had no way of treating her, and it happened a second time, and she lost a child, and there was nothing they could do, and he went back to Europe with her and he left her in the care of her family.

"Once I went with Abba to Eilat. There, at the opening of the Red Sea, with all of Desert Arabia before me, I knew I had been there too before. It was very hot and the light had been very bright, and it was very unpleasant, an emptiness and promise of emptiness beyond all emptiness. In my dreams, I'm often at the edge of the desert."

She paused. She turned to Anna, smiling gently as one does at someone younger and dear to whom one is trying to give an idea of all a lifetime. "I hadn't been a Zionist.

"He wore thick eyeglasses, he was thin (he would grow hunched). There was such absence of personal ambition in him you knew it had been burned out of him, there was such intensity in his regard you knew the vital purpose of his life and work. In Europe I heard him speak to a large audience of Masada. He spoke of the desert plateau over the Dead Sea, the painted palace of Herod, the hanging gardens, of the Zealots using it as their fortress. He told how the legions of Romans came first from the side of the sea up the Snake-path and were repulsed and made camp at the base of the mountain and besieged the Zealots. Of how the Romans then came from behind, from within the desert mountains, and were within striking distance, and how the Zealots chose to fight even after there was no hope, and then chose to die by their own hand rather than surrender and die slaves. Somewhere in his speech, he changed pronouns and whenever he then spoke of the Zealots, it was *we*, we chose to fight, and we chose to die rather than die slaves. Abba knew this long before anyone ever dreamed of Warsaw.

"I heard him speak of his leader, Trumpledor. Listen: The house he fell at, our Trumpledor, was but a clapboard building among clapboard barns in a land still wilderness. He told the Arab aggressors come under a flag of truce that they could enter the clapboard house to assure themselves no mercenaries were with us, and so they entered and on the second floor of that clapboard house, which our men and the two women with them had built, they pointed guns at us to disarm us. Trumpledor called out, 'Betrayed! Fire!' And we killed the Arab aggressors, and Trumpledor fell and dying he said, 'It is good to die for one's country!' In Palestine in nineteen twenty-one.

"We named our boy Abisai to be a soldier of David. I knew without knowing he would die young. When they came to tell me, I already knew. A mother knows, and a mother who is a mother as late as I was knows. And his father's name was Father. Only," she said, some deep hesitation in her now, "Abisai knew too. After the

Six Day War of sixty-seven, I felt that his life had been reprieved, but now when I look at photographs of him even when Abba was alive, when he was only a boy, I see that he knew even then. And never said a word. After that war, he began the work that I shall finish of editing his father's writings, and he told me a dream he had had.

"He was at Qumram in the desert north of the Dead Sea, north of Masada, not far from Jericho, and he was drawn to the cave-pocked hills where the scrolls had been found. And then he was climbing in the heat, and he was approaching a cave, looking for he did not know what, and he went from cave to cave and he found debris, broken jars where scrolls no doubt had been kept. Now he reached a cave and it had been very hot, the sun is white hot there so you cannot distinguish it in the sky, and he stepped into the cave, and it was cool and his father was there writing, bent over his writing, even as in his study.

"We sacrifice our sons to our dreams. And even if our dreams are *right* and *just*, we are full of doubts and darkness, and we have a need that goes beyond being right. We think we have been right (perhaps we have only been proud), but then at the end we stand alone at the edge of the desert.

"I am looking still for my son."

Anna did not understand all that Esther said, but there was a longing in her too. They were sitting in their nightgowns in the den in the milky Island light, and Fred was sleeping, and there were tears at her eyes. She was thinking of her own sons, she was praying that her boy become a doctor as the doctor had been a doctor, by being, by seeing the way we live, by feeling our need for a doctor.

No matter that Anna had been many times to the Beth Israel cemetery in Queens, she never could find her way. First she would get lost in the maze of cemeteries surrounding Beth Israel and then would be unable to locate the main entry and so might park and enter by a service gate. Then for a rare cluster of trees or an ornate mausoleum she might think she had found her way and would go off on a shortcut and so would get hopelessly lost among the crowded burial stones.

It was almost spring, and it was a bright and sunny morning, still it was cold. Esther could see Anna was lost and so did not even try to keep up with her. Once Anna turned to say something and not seeing her became very excited as if now she had to find her too. But then she saw her, her thick legs, her ducklike walk, trailing her purse, coming slowly forward among the low stones.

Several times they were approached by orthodox Jews, old men whose very city hats had something different about them. They offered to accompany them to the graveside and make prayers for the dead. For few mourners remembered the prayers or understood them, and there were complicated injunctions about when to make which prayer. When Anna had gone to the cemetery with her mother and Eshka, they had each put a pebble on the stone of the grave they visited, and the custom had become so natural to her she continued to do that. Now she hired an orthodox for prayer, hoping he would be able to help them find the plot where two of Esther's brothers, the doctor and Irving, were buried. The orthodox was tall and unshaven, his heavy coat had seen much use; he was condescending, and though he said he knew his way about the cemetery and led them off confidently single-file, Anna after him, Esther last, they soon realized he too was lost. He had led them up a gentle hill so grass-soft and round you almost thought it was alive and breathing. Beyond the cemetery and the quiet two-family-house flat Queens skyline, they could see the tops of city buildings, the UN building, the soaring towers of the Empire State Building and the Chrysler. They stood for a moment, as if locating themselves in reference to the city, and then each went off, in a different direction, bending to the stones, looking.

Anna felt, this is the place, and she walked quickly forward expecting to see the low stones that had been put up for the doctor and Eshka, and she saw instead her father and mother's graves, for she had found the Cohen plot.

"Look!" she called.

It was almost as if she expected her aunt to say, "Yes, it is my brother Harry."

The orthodox said an *El Mole Rachamim*—God Full of Mercy.

Now there were the Cohens among whom her parents were buried to visit.

She turned, thinking to find Ben's grave, but no, it was Uncle Sam's.

"Sam," she said, smiling through her tears, introducing him to Esther. "Because of the way he played pinochle, the doctor said of him, 'His hands stutter.' He chose always to live by the sea."

Here then was Ben's grave, and Ben, wearing the fur worker's white duster, rose from it like turning from the matcher's table, and he was smiling so broadly, and he greeted her, Dearie. But then he said, Why has no one found a husband for my daughter?

Anna turned, and Esther was standing behind her, low over her thick legs, her forehead heavy like stone and her so-deep frown.

Anna led them through the maze of low stones, turning sharply this way and that, for the paths were at right angles to each other and stopped here to continue there, and seeing the Nissnievitch plot stopped at a distance, the tall, tall-hatted orthodox almost walking into her, and they waited for Esther to laboriously make her way past them.

Esther stood before the twin graves of her brothers. She almost silently made the mourner's prayer for them, the brothers she had only known young. She felt Harry's daughter standing behind her. Here, to the right of Irving's grave, was Mary's. She had never met her, she had died alone. Here, to the left of the doctor, was dark Eshka.

Behind her the tall orthodox was again intoning the *El Mole Rachamim*, his rocking movement like the swaying of a reed in the wind.

Esther stood low, her hands hanging as if reaching toward the earth.

"To what do I owe the pleasure?" Sol Cohen said, gesturing his niece and cousin into his seventh-floor Brighton Beach apartment. He was almost eighty-five years old, he was short, broad, and almost neckless. He was deaf in one ear, and to hear better he often turned or tilted his head. His mouth was wide, and when he was sad he seemed very sad, and when he was pleased he seemed very pleased. His question was (though he greeted most visitors with it, though Anna had not only phoned before coming but arranged to meet Max and Madeleine here) more than formal, more than his way of giving pleasure. During the more than ten years he had been retired, he rarely left Brighton Beach, and for the last five years his wife Fanny had been sick. She had had strokes and been paralyzed, she had had a breast cancer. She was recovering. And he had always, in his first apartment in the East Bronx, and then off the Grand Concourse, and then in Far Rockaway, and in his small place of business, and now in Brighton Beach, truly felt honored by visits of members of his family. Why should they come out of their way to see me?

Anna he embraced, but Esther he bowed to, for he remembered her from Berezin and she was the doctor's sister and she was from Israel and her son had died a soldier of Israel. He said to her, "I was remembering you to my wife, and telling her how beautiful a girl you were."

"Ach!" Esther said, feeling for an instant that she could still blush, "you're thinking of my sister."

"No! No! Of you!"

"Of Sonia," Esther insisted. "Sonia was beautiful."

"Maybe that is the case. Still, you were all beautiful girls."

Fanny was seated in an armchair, heavy still but nothing to what she had been. She was fifteen years younger than Sol, she wore a housedress, she looked tired. And the fair-haired beautiful little boy was seated on the big flower-brocaded deep-cushioned sofa. The television was on.

"*Comment vas-tu?*" Esther asked.

"You've grown!" Anna said.

He was timid.

"I kidnapped him!" Sol said. "They went to visit Dora. I said I'd take you all over when you came."

He whispered to Anna, "They sent him to a ghetto school. Can it be safe?"

"Who can say?" Anna said, having learned that a good tactic with Sol was to answer a question with a question. Sol nodded as if the answer were sage.

Sol whispered, smiling as if with astonishment, "He speaks English with a *schwartze* accent! What do you think of that?"

"That's America," Anna said.

"Ah," Sol said, nodding as if Anna had answered several questions.

Fanny said to Esther of Sol, "The things he did for me no one else would do. He was my nurse, always. I cannot tell you the things he did for me."

"Sh!" Sol said.

"I could be sick a hundred years and no one would come to visit me."

"Sh!" Sol said. And he explained to Anna as if she had asked a question, "It's a long way to Brighton Beach, and maybe—ha! ha! ha!—it reminds the young people of the Bronx."

Esther was looking at a Zola Levi dark oil painting of a thin perhaps consumptive girl sitting at a factory sewing machine. Sol said, "I'm not a rich man, but I bought that original painting. Because the painting shows the way it was. I met him, you know. Zola Levi, *olavasholom!*"

In the bedroom that, for what Fanny had said, for the neatly arranged rows of medicines, the utensils of sickness, made Anna think of the things Sol had done for Fanny, through months of days and nights, the image of him going from bedroom to bathroom, from kitchen to bedroom, nursing, she thinking also, inevitably, of her son, would he do that? *Would I?* Sol told her, using her as others did as intermediary, that it was not right that his nephews make a party for Joe and him and not honor at the same occasion Ben's widow, Dora.

"Do they have to spend so much money?" he asked.

"They do," she replied.

They walked on the boardwalk with the little boy, Anna having stayed behind with Fanny, toward Dora's apartment building, for Dora too had sold her house in Far Rockaway to move to Brighton Beach by the sea.

They were in no hurry, it was a visit of pure form, and it was pleasant and relaxing to be with this small squat man and this little boy named after her brother in the ocean wind, on this clear cold almost spring day, the saltiness invigorating.

The boardwalk was wide as an avenue, and even the expanse of wooden boards, horizontal here, diagonal there, weathered by the sea air, was pleasant to look at. There were few promenaders, and they were older people dressed warmly for walking. And one walks better on a boardwalk, easier no matter that she was seventy years old and thick-legged and he eighty-five, and the boy five and a half. Esther held one of the boy's small hands in hers, Sol held the other.

Tall new apartment buildings almost lined one side of the boardwalk, on the sea side the beach was broad, the sand was white. There was something untouched about the beach as there is at the end of winter, the winds and rains having given it a crust so that every footstep is clearly marked. The sea was 100 yards away, and the tide was coming in, the pulling in and out of the waves, waves bursting on beach jetties, the wind driving the spray, the sharp fresh air of the sea washing their faces, in their lungs, the never-ceasing sound of the sea. In the distance, entering or leaving New York harbor, were oceangoing ships small on the great expanse of sea, the sense of the depth of sea beyond.

With an embarrassed smile, Sol asked Esther, "Tell me, how can you speak Hebrew all day long? How can you speak about business, about food, in the holy language?"

She said in Yiddish, to put him at ease, "Sol, we are home and so we speak our language." But it occurred to her that she too had more than once wished and searched in herself for a secret language.

Sol nodded as if they were in agreement on the question and said, "I have lost the meaning of many of the prayers, but the sound of them! The sound of prayers!" He was smiling like a boy who has been too enthusiastic, and he turned his head to the sea.

"The moon," Esther said, pointing over the sea to a daylight ghost of the moon.

"I assure you," Sol said after a moment, "you were very beautiful."

She was grateful and said nothing.

Sol said, "It's a long time." She nodded and sensing then that he also meant by that that it was a long life, and not easy, she looked at him. He was wearing a dark city hat, a little green feather in the ribbon, the expression of his face, his wide mouth, was poised delicately, philosophically, between sadness and fulfilment.

Just then she felt the boy's hand in hers go tense and saw in the distance, on the hard flat part of the beach by the sea, Max and Madeleine. They were alone on the beach. Madeleine wore a short coat, she seemed tall in pants, Max wore a dark jacket over a sweater, his black hair, her light hair, were windblown. The boy let go of Esther's hand and Sol's and was running across the boardwalk to a stairway to the beach. "Let him go," Esther said as Sol reached after the boy.

She and the small old man approached the boardwalk railing. The boy had flown down the stairs and was now running across the empty beach in a long diagonal toward his parents, who still had not seen him. There was a welling up in Esther's heart as if she would now kneel into the sand to receive her boy into her arms, and just then there was an uneasiness in her for she saw in the way Max and Madeleine walked that they were apart. The boy had stopped, Sol thought he recognized the figures by the sea and said their names wonderingly as if they had stepped out of the sea, Esther sensed even what the boy felt, that he too knew they were apart, knew they were *still* apart, the pain that the boy had lived until now!, that she, holding his hand, had not been aware of!, that he, all this time, had been hoping, hoping. Did he have images of them together? The three of them, each really aware of the others?—father, mother, son! Paralyzed now that he would have to go past one to reach the other, would have to run past his father to reach his mother. And so she was moving, to the stairway, the impatience she felt with the parents doing this to the boy—with the gentle Christian sculptor mother now all closed in on herself but who had spoken to her of her son at Sénanque, with the son of her brother—bursting open a so much deeper impatience that was even general, that was as if with all the world, with everything and everyone but the boy, as if with the boy all could start anew, but only with him, as if all had its focus on the boy. She was moving heavily, urgent, running almost in the sand, her feet bursting the beach-crust just at the side of the broken-crust footsteps of the boy. The parents had finally looked up, pride, guilt, and hurt written on their faces, they seeing the boy standing, the old woman coming in a ducklike run across the sand, swooping to their boy as if to stop time.

She had felt while running a presence behind and now, as she stood with the boy, the parents approaching, she heard Sol call—he too surely sensing something, perhaps he too trying to put off the moment—addressing his nephew and niece, "Are you coming from our Brighton Beach pride, from our aquarium?"

Esther turned, realizing in a flash what the peculiarly curved buildings just off the boardwalk were, and saw Sol, in his city hat, his shoes buried in the sand, a little breathless, smiling.

"No," Max answered, "we were just walking."

But Madeleine had heard the echo and she looked at Esther, and Max now saw Madeleine's expression and he too understood, remembering the upright boy left at the side of the National 7—of course, he was going to Monaco to the aquarium. And already Esther was walking through the sand, at a new diagonal toward another stairway almost at the aquarium. The boy looked to his parents and they looked at each other as if to give approval together, and then he ran after Esther and caught up with her and walked at her side.

Sol, trudging after with the couple, said, "I come often. The dolphins I like. I like to look at all the fish, the big fish, the little fish, even the *trafe* fish! Ha! ha! ha!" But when they were at the boardwalk, he rushed ahead to pay for their tickets.

Inside the main building there were few people and it was dark, the glass-faced exhibits lit from within, and they, facing an exhibit, the coral, the undersea green, shells, were as if walking on the sea bottom. They followed Esther on the sea bottom, they stood at a distance behind her—all but the boy, who stood with her—looking past her at the giant slow leather-back turtles who lived 100 years, they looked at the brightly colored rarities, the rainbow colors, the starfish, the flying fish. Esther had taken the boy's hand and now in front of the big funny bottle-snouted dolphins spoke to him. For as she knew that this was as it had been, she knew that this was as it was, and this boy was here with her. She told the boy how smart dolphins were (who knew for he had watched "Flipper the Dolphin"), that they could speak to one another even through water, that they had a language still secret from us, how they were the sailor's sign of good weather; and speaking to him she began to know what the longing in her was, a coming together, Abisai and this boy, this morning in the cemetery, and Sol Cohen, and those two behind her, and all who were in her, a longing for it all to come together even if only for an instant, and they were then watching the swift sharks, and the room where she would again be this evening, the lipsticked minuscule dying woman, and they were looking at the dark blind creatures of the deep, and she did not understand the sense of her longing, and the boy's hand was in hers.

All the rest of the afternoon she was gentle, even after she learned that Madeleine and Saul-Daniel were flying that very evening back to France, that Max was staying on in David Cohen's apartment, a calm come over her that was like distance and yet that made Max, Madeleine, and Saul-David even more dear to her.

"Good-bye," she said to the boy and to the mother, looking deeply at each of them.

Graceful beyond grace had been the young ice skaters this Saturday afternoon at Rockefeller Center. They skated in time to gay music full of small steps and leaps. Among the skaters were stars who did remarkable jumps and pirouettes. There were couples who skated hand in hand—and look! He is lifting her up off the ice and now she is flying effortlessly. Even so did we skate in Russia, in Berezin, when I was a girl, with my sisters Sonia and Nuissa, with my brothers Lazarus and Dan, and with my prince Irving, who was of all the young men the most gallant, the most daring.

She had been standing with Sam Cohen above the rink. He wore a Borsalino hat and a fur-lined coat. They had met in his thirty-eighth-floor "Versailles"—with the grand view of the park like the park at Versailles, all the roads in the park like garden lanes, and the Renoir garden portraits of children too beautiful and happy—and they had gone down down down to his building restaurant for lunch and afterwards Margo had gone back up for a nap and Sam had suggested a walk and they had walked out on Central Park South where she had walked that first night at "Versailles," though then on the small-cobblestoned park side, at the very edge of the city and park shadows, the darkness she had felt at table even in her, where she had, glimpsing a horse-drawn carriage alone on a road inside the park, suddenly longed for her son and husband, she who until then had accepted their deaths as: how they lived, so they died; as if their dying for Israel was no longer enough, as if she would no longer even allow herself to think she was reconciled. Sam had walked her down proud Fifth Avenue to here. For he too had been an ice skater, and, he had told her, he had, when he had still been a furrier, some

Saturdays when he had not gone to business, taken his son here from the Island for an afternoon of skating.

"We were good skaters."

"Should we?" she had asked.

"We'd be the best," he had said.

He had led her downstairs to the rinkside café. He had called no one to serve him, but his clothes were so rich and generous, his manner so gentle, people made way for him and waiters hurried to serve him. He brimmed over, delicately, with appreciation. He himself helped Esther off with her cloth coat. He ordered tea and *pâtisserie* for her. She thought, And maybe it is true I was beautiful, and maybe it is true young men did, when I was a girl, crowd about me. Sam ordered Scotch whisky, he held his drink well, it gave him a glow as if he were on the verge of some great joy.

His lips were blue for bad circulation, he had removed his Borsalino, there was something artificial about his hair—The way he combed it to hang a little, evenly, over his forehead? That there was not one gray hair? He wore his coat still, the dark sable collar framing his face soft.

There they had been separated from the skaters only by a glass. Looking up, Esther had seen the spectators and the beginning of the enormous rise of the center's skyscrapers. Still, wonderfully, there had been sunlight in a corner of the rink on the ice.

They had watched a young girl standing awkwardly on skates at a rink entry, her white-stockinged thighs and calves had seemed thick, but Sam had nodded to Esther as if to say, You will see, you will see. She had begun to skate and had been instantly transformed, all youth, swiftness, and beauty. Sam had looked as if his heart were filled to bursting, proud as if the very magician.

Esther had earlier wondered why he had called; it had occurred to her then: Even as a cousin might call a cousin. For I have been away, and he has known mine even as I knew his, and our memories of them are living links between us. And she had thought, What can I do for him? (Thinking now, that evening, seated in the sitting room of Emma's apartment, waiting since half an hour to be received, Emma's cousin Selma sitting dour at her side, I thought then for the first time of what I can do for one of them, I was suddenly awkward for I had come to America without any gift for any of them, as if I had never even thought of them, as if I have nothing for them and came only for myself.) She had said to Sam when the music had stopped and the skaters paused, "Thank you."

"Ach! For what?" he had said almost irritably, for he had still done nothing for her.

"I haven't watched ice skaters in so long I'm afraid to tell you."

"Ah," he had said smiling, "you've no ice in Israel?"

"We've two million skaters, but no ice." He had laughed. She had said, "Even in Jerusalem we haven't a real winter."

She had looked into his gentle eyes and offered him a confidence. "It's forests I miss, and it's autumn."

He had been touched and troubled.

"I remember our forests, I think of the autumn colors, the rust colors."

He had seemed pained.

He had said, "Would you like a trip to the country?" He had beamed and offered, "Would you like a trip to Miami?"

"Thank you," she had replied, shaking her head, smiling.

He had nodded. Of course, autumn and Miami were not the same thing.

Now, thinking of that, of him, of him back in "Versailles," of his park stretched out before him, she wondered why had he stopped at Miami? Why had he not insisted? Did every refusal of his magic put a new crack in it? Had he again begun thinking of his son?

He had looked deeply into her eyes and had said, "Jonathan's coming home soon. Things will be different then. Without him, you see," he had said, his eyes glistening, "we're rudderless."

Selma said, "Do you know I have a daughter?" They were alone in the room, seated on the same side, facing dark antique tables on which were laid out silver trays, a silver tea service, silver candlesticks, there was a locked antique cupboard filled with things and things, the high molded wall.

"My husband had left me, my child was twelve years old when she had her first *breakdown*." She spat the word scornfully. "I asked Emma for help. She sent my child to the best doctors, Park Avenue doctors who knew what to do! Seven times Emma paid for shock treatment. I could visit my child only with Emma, and it was as if, when I visited, I was the stranger, I was the cousin. They took her away from me, to treat her, to make her better, to torture her as if by punishment to teach her how we live! I never got her back, she's thirty years old now, and I don't even know where she lives."

The pain was the stranger in the desert, the pain was what she had not yet allowed herself to think of, the stranger in a room in a city where the walls were always pressing in. The pain was the dying person, cast off, forgotten. The pain was this woman at her side laying her claim on Emma before her, waiting to be paid back for her child and hating the creditor even as the debtor. And Esther wondered then, What am I waiting for here? Sam is waiting for his brother the ambassador and she is waiting for what is due her, but what am I waiting for? For Sam had given her to understand that with the return of Jonathan they would reconsider, they might finance the editing and publishing of Abba's work, but that had then seemed to her a mere detail. *What then am I laying claim to?* She was softened suddenly, feeling Abba's presence close, not the prophet, not the fiery orator, but Abba as he had been in the last year of his life, tired, unable almost to concentrate, the cigarette forgotten, burning to ash, as if what he too had been waiting for, *was* waiting for, was not the publication of his work, but something else. The nurse said Emma would receive them. They entered the dark perfumed bedroom, the color TV on as if Emma had been watching all this time and not suffering and dying, and Abba was with Esther, and Selma's daughter was there too, and Abba's first wife, and they were there waiting as if for the minuscule smiling cupid-lipsticked woman at the center of her bed as at the center of her web to show them the way accomplishing it, and Esther knew then by her repulsion that what she was waiting for was even and also in her, deep in her, was as if all around her and yet was at the very source of her.

Other visitors came and there was conversation, and shortly the room was full, as if of spectators, and they talked softly and they waited.

4

My topcoat is frayed at the cuffs and one of the buttons is not one of the originals. I wear no hat, I carry—heavy with manuscripts—

my many-pocketed, zippered army flight bag, my 1956 (paperback sale) Olivetti 22. I am alone in the city.

This day I came with my wife and son from my brother and his family in Connecticut to Brooklyn to greet, on our way to Kennedy, my Uncle Sol. Sol sent us to visit Dora, whose real pleasure at our visit embarrassed me, for in my mind she was always dragging Ben down. He called her princess, but she was his maid, she never believed in his good luck. When he expanded his fur business, she warned him; when he made a friend, she warned him; when he bought a house, she said it was *his* house, *his* dream. Still, here in Brighton Beach twenty years after, she and her unmarried daughter, who is my age, live here with him, tenaciously. There is an oil portrait of him hanging in their crowded living room, there are photographs of him, I am sure there are gold relics of him, his wristwatch, cufflinks, tiepins. He looks here like the president of a synagogue board of directors, like a man of social prominence. This is not the Ben I remember; I think of the "countess" calling me the day after his death, asking only, Is it true? Yet, if I think about it, this too was Ben.

I walked with Madeleine across the white beach. Her silence is like a wall. She has more than once told me about her grandmother Petitjean who, widowed, her son, an army officer, away, locked herself into her house and died there quite alone, neighbors discovering her after. When Madeleine was a child she would go with her family to her grandmother's house for summer holidays. She remembers seeing her grandmother during a thunderstorm going with a candle and crucifix from room to room in her house closing shutters, muttering prayers. She has told me that when she was a girl and ran away from home, quietly, stubbornly, and lived in a tiny maid's room, the beginning of years of living in maid's rooms, she began to think she too would die like that, alone and *within*. She is so quiet and deep a person. Her pleasures are miles and miles inside her, and one has to have patience and persistence, and one has to himself be quiet, to reach her.

When I told her I would go to Israel, she said, Then we three should go. In Detroit, when I told her I would stay on in New York, she said nothing at all, as if I were already gone or as if she were already gone or as if a part of her were already locked within. When she led the boy into the Icelandic embarking area, he turned to look at me once more, through a glass partition, unbelieving still.

David wears dark glasses. His face is red with drink, his barrel-chested body has become large. He shows me my room, he hovers near, what does he want? Seeing that I am tired, he abruptly says good-night.

I pull back the covers of my bed, and I see a note that reads: "What are you trying to get out of my dad?" The boy's room is next to mine. It is soundproofed, but I can tell the stereo is on loud for the music beats in the walls.

I try to sleep, but I am thinking of my new book, I am thinking of Sundays in the East Bronx, the arrival of the uncles, I hear my student Thomas telling me, "In the place I live, who'll ever know if I die?" I fall asleep. I awake hearing a scream: "MONSTER!" The music is beating still. I feel feverish, it was a scream of fury and anguish and came as if from my very dreams.

In the morning, my agent tells me she has heard from an editor who is enthusiastic about *The General, His Daughters*. The editor will fight for it. That is encouraging, we must push harder, I must broaden the front. I call college friends, first-book friends. They invite me to lunch, dinner, a quick drink before a dinner appointment. One knows the wife of the publisher's brother, another will put in a good word at another publishing house. I go uptown and downtown, I walk five blocks up and five blocks down not to arrive too early.

It is a time when everyone is speaking of Watergate. We are out to get the president. We have been out to get him for so long, for even twenty years, that I hardly listen until, at lunch one day, my ex-editor, a sort of dean of American publishers, explains to me patiently why we shall now succeed. What the president has done is, yes, intolerable, but what America needs now after Vietnam, at the beginning of the economic crisis, is a real cleansing and purifying. His publishing house, in any event, is committed to getting him. He is a man in his sixties, he too went to Columbia, and he has published good people. He has had a heart attack, and he moves as if he is still partially paralyzed. He tells me again how good a book *The General, His Daughters* is, how if it had been by anyone but me he would publish it, but I have lost money for the firm, his partner has lost faith in me. I tell him of the editor who said she would fight for the book. He is sincerely pleased. He says, "Max, good luck with the bitch-goddess Success!" He says it with such meaning, as if that has been the secret evading me, that I think it is perhaps with her that I have an appointment.

My agent tells me I am being considered for a $25,000 playwriting fellowship; she tells me to mobilize support.

At David's apartment one afternoon between appointments, I catch hold of the boy. The first day, I left the boy's note on the bed, and at night when I returned it was gone. He is a foot taller than his father, 100 pounds heavier, he lurches from his room through the apartment propelled even like his father, but there is no substance to him, he moves like a giant flying shadow.

I say, "Let's talk."

We sit in his father's den, the maids are playing cards or watching television somewhere in the apartment. He offers me Scotch whisky, he opens a giant bag of potato chips and spreads the chips toward me across a dark leather embossed table, he eats them negligently a handful at a time. Still, there is something delicate about him, a giant's delicacy, bottom buttons of his shirt are open on his belly, but they are simply too far for him to be aware of it. He is barefoot, his light hair is shoulder-long, stiff as if electrified.

I tell him what I'm doing in the city, my career is at ebb. He asks me what kind of things I write, he likes science fiction. He asks, "Do you read Kurt Vonnegut?"

"I've always wanted to."

He lurches to his room and almost in the speed of thought he is back with a handful of well-worn paperbacks.

I tell him Sunday mornings his father used to take him to the Bronx to visit my father. My father, I tell him, was a doctor.

"Then Larry's your brother?" he asks, looking at me, suspicious. He says, "The damage to my brain is irreparable."

I have drinks with a college acquaintance who is now a Pulitzer Prize poet, a visiting professor at five great universities, New York's, if not America's, authority on French literature, on Emily Dickinson, on all his competitors. I mention that my ex-editor wished me good luck with the bitch-goddess Success. He is pate-bald, proud as if beautiful, even at college there was something of a high priest in his manner. Now he throws up his arms and says, "Darling, I am even she!"

One day I take the Sixth Avenue subway. I sit down and see that opposite me is a man wearing a single earring. Well, that's interesting. As I then look around the car I see, in another place, another man wearing an earring. The third man I can't be sure about. I stand, I cautiously as if casually edge my way around. Yes, he too is wearing an earring.

One day I go down to the fur market. I'm walking on Thirtieth Street past skin dealers' street-level shops. There is the entrance to Ben's building. Here is the liquor store. On the street I see Stanley, Ben's retarded nephew. He still wears an earmuffed cap, he walks in a hurry.

I attend a meeting of writers, editors, and agents at a reading room at the Forty-Second Street public library. A couple of hundred of us are crowded into the room, it's standing-room-only. This evening's question is: How are we going to get the power from the commercial interests?

A young man interrupts the speaker: "Cooperatives!" he calls out. "No more of this ego trip, 'I'm more important than you!' Everyone has something to say, so publish! publish! publish!"

"I have something to say," someone else in the audience says angrily. "You're all full of shit! We have to destroy the system!"

"I have something to say," someone says. "Fuck! Fuck! Fuck!"

"Boo! Boo!"

The chairperson tries to call for order. A motion is made to adjourn for sandwiches.

I come home late. Outside the building diagonally across the street is something strange that strikes my eye. What is it? Yes, it's David's boy, it's Gregory, he's sitting enormous on the roof of a Volkswagen. I approach him, no one is there, maybe he just got there himself, maybe I can save the situation. I say, "Hi, Gregory."

"I am Thor," he says.

I see that his fly is open, he is hanging out.

"Greg?"

He is looking mournfully out at the street. A taxi passes. The buildings are all new, twenty-five, thirty stories high, there are canopies at all the entrances.

I have the doorman call David, David is not in. A police patrol car pulls to.

"Where is my father?" he asks. "Where is Odin?"

"Take it easy," I say to the spaced-out mournful boy.

"What do you want?" he says to me before shrugging himself down into the hands of the policemen.

I have, of course, been here too before.

I watched the acne-faced guitar-playing cousin strut down a tenement sidestreet off First Avenue toward Avenue A. And a day or two later I sat with him, he overdosed pasty-faced, in the social room of a hospital into which his father was committing him, other kids there, one playing a guitar, we playing hearts.

"One-to-one," I once said to Big Mike, speaking to him about husband and wife, father and son, obligations, he on the brink of leaving his wife and son. I said, "Mike, the only way we can help one another is one-to-one." So when he was drunk and I pushed him out of our apartment at the Belair, and he let me, he muttered, "I am one, and you are one, and is this one-to-one?"

Maybe, I am thinking, sitting now in a black leather upholstered armchair next to David in his, each of us with a water glass of Scotch whisky gold in hand, his English girl Mary in his bedroom, he sometimes phoning into the night, the lawyer, a judge—"I WANT HIM HOME, I WANT HIM OUT"—calling his half-brother Louis—"WHAT AM I TO DO?"—getting up, his pajamas open, buttons missing, barefoot by now for he would lose one slipper and kick the other violently off, lurching into the kitchen for ice, Maybe, I am thinking, thinking of him, it is all nothing. "Schmuck," he has said to me, "do you need a suit?" "Schmuck," he has said to me, "what can you know? Schmuck, let me fix you a steak!" Maybe, I am thinking, it is all only that and that is nothing, that what is happening to his son is nothing.

I think of the boy and I wonder, What does he want?

I think of the English girl—waiting? napping? rubbing her thighs together?—in the bedroom. I think of Madeleine and Saul-Daniel arriving in Europe, waiting for trains, making their way from Luxembourg, in the night, sitting up through the night, Madeleine not letting herself fall asleep, and why have I not allowed myself to think of that until now?—of their arriving in the morning at Murs, and the house is shuttered, the stone-upon-stone house is shuttered, and the doors are locked, and I am standing alone with my many-pocketed suitcase before the shuttered and locked house.

And I know now that this is all about me. I am at the center. And if it is all nothing, I am at the center of that nothing. I begin to understand that everything I have gone looking for is not *it* and that what I want, or what I think I want, is not *it*. What do I even mean by *it*? The word surrogate comes to me, and it seems to clear up something, a little. The whore's caress, I conclude, is a surrogate. The bitch-goddess is a surrogate! And I am longing still for my mother's love! Oh you go far, Max Katz! You are a hero, Max Katz! You have been longing for Ben's gifts of dollars-like-love, his hope-like-love! You have been, hero, longing for your father's esteem!

"Ha! ha! ha!" David is looking at me and laughing nastily. He says, "You know what you are? You're a spy!"

"That's right, I'm a spy!" I say angrily. And it's true, I have always been, and there's no way out. No matter. What I want to know is what surrogates is your boy calling for? What mother-for-mother, what father-for-father is he calling for?

"Why don't you tell me the truth?" David says over the phone to my brother.

"You," he says to me, "are the doctor. You're just like your father was."

"I've always thought I was like you."

"Like me? Who is like me?" he demands. He is gesturing and dancing before me. Mary comes from the bedroom, she is wearing a sheer black night-thing, she is all slow, plump, and as if wrinkled from sleep. "You're little like your father was, you're a failure like your father was."

"No," I say, "I'm a Goddamn spy!"

"That's right, you're a Goddamn spy in my country!"

"You have a house in the country," Mary says. What is she thinking of?

"WHAT AM I TO DO?" he screams into the receiver as if to break his brother Sam's heart.

Mary is on my lap. The corruption is in me. I see the points of her breasts through the sheer dark material, I feel the underside of her body against me, I see her thighs on my thighs, her hair there, living, the secret longed-for place. My hands want to touch even as I want to be touched—Touch me! touch me! My hands are swollen with longing to touch—Well, why don't you? Take! David is even smiling. Take! Take! The corruption is in me. Not in him. It is in me! The issue is me! David brusquely says, "Leave him alone." I am only a little man. Her hand caresses my cheek. She says, "I've always wanted to live in the country."

I think of Esther standing on the beach with my son, I think of David's boy hanging out, I think of Ben in Paris. I am thinking of my book, of all the people hanging over it like gargoyles.

David answers the phone. The boy will be released in the morning.

"NOW!" David shouts. "I WANT HIM RELEASED NOW!" But already he is thinking of the next time. "He'll kill me yet," he says.

They are fucking in his bedroom.

The corruption, I know, is in me.

I am the runaway.

I sat with my boy once when his mother was in Paris, her train not due back in Avignon for several hours, and we were looking at a book together, and there where we live near Murs it is very quiet, you hear every sound, but we are fifty kilometers from Avignon, and he said, "Sh!" I asked, "What is it?" "I hear Mommy's train." I said, "No, you don't," but I smiled. And a moment later, he said, "Sh! I hear Mommy's train." And we listened.

And growing in me now is a cry: BURN IT OUT OF ME! The words themselves are like a brand: BURN IT OUT OF ME!

I stand in David's den, the TV on, the nighttime city, the pearl-illumined city bridges, the giant lurching sixty-five-year-old father in his bedroom with the twenty-year-old dark-haired girl, and I call silently into the night, BURN IT OUT OF ME!

My hands are dripping sweat, my clothes are old, wrinkled, shapeless. I am a little man, too small, too small. I am too weak, too afraid; is my heart strong enough? It will burst!

BURN IT OUT OF ME!

Mel had said good-night and good-bye to Madeleine and Saul-Daniel and he had sensed something, and now we were waiting for the never-coming Belair down-elevator, and I saw tears at his eyes. I was embarrassed that he was crying at good-bye, nor would he look away or wipe away his tears, which began to flow, as if to force me to look and see. I understand now that the tall quiet runner was not crying for good-bye, but for me, that he forced me to look into his unblinking tear-filled and flowing eyes that I read in his eyes his prayer for me.

I pray, BURN IT OUT OF ME!

In the morning, David calls me from downtown and says, "You and I are going to Brooklyn tonight."

5

David had called Brooklyn back once.

"WHAT AM I TO DO?"

He had insisted he be connected with the *rebbe*. The *rebbe* had listened. He had begun to speak of Gregory, but as if in a parable, there was a good son and a bad son. Was the other boy caring for a cripple the good son? He spoke of Baal and Astarte though he knew that his boy thought he was Thor and that he himself in his boy's cosmogony was Thor's father Odin. He worships Baal, he goated out. And squat Louis at his desk across from and flush to his ran the tickertape through his fingers more quickly.

He told the *rebbe* the sharks were feeding off him, his very brothers were doing him in. He told him about his son being uncovered, and the *rebbe*, who until then had said nothing but an occasional and encouraging yes, said, "He saw you uncovered?"

"In the street!" David shouted. "Before everyone, before strangers, he was uncovered." But he had heard in the *rebbe*'s voice that the other sin, the biblical one, was on his mind. He saw *you* uncovered. What kind of sin is that?

"*Rebbe*, I curse the day I was born, I curse the night I was conceived! *Rebbe*, if I fear a thing, that thing happens. I cannot rest, I cannot sleep."

He was breathless half the day. There were times he thought his heart was cracking across all his chest.

"I am at the bottom of a well. I cannot breathe."

He was holding onto the receiver, and he heard then the truth in the voice of the doctor: "Too late! Too late!" the doctor said. "Too late! Too late!" And even then the *rebbe* said, "Mister Cohen? Mister Cohen, it is not too late."

"How did you know?" David demanded. "*Rebbe*, you are a *tzadik*!"

Though shortly after, he began to wonder, What secret knowledge does the miracle worker have that he should say it is not too late? Do you know the boy's brains are *scrambled*!

My debts are like mountains! *Rebbe*, I wait for dividend checks in the mail, but there are thieves—ha! ha! ha!—even in the postal system!

Louis said, "What do you mean, too late?"

"Leave me alone."

"What leave you alone! Leave you alone to eat your heart out?"

David laughed. He called his secretary in. "Take a letter! To the president, vice-president, chairman, and vice-chairman of the board.

"Gentlemen:

"I'll go on relief before I take a cut in salary!

"Bring it to me to sign!" For they had dared suggest he take a cut in salary.

What could Louis say? Could he say, "Institutionalize"? Louis knew there is no cure. He knew we are all such rotten and inept nurses.

He said, "David, let's get out. We'll buy an island somewhere."

David was laughing to choke. The squat man did not mind, at least a joke.

"Who'll we take?" Louis demanded.

"Brother Sam and his ghost!"

"Sara and Marybell!"

"Marty and his boy!"

"Can we leave Anna behind?" Louis asked.

"No, we'll have to take Anna. But that means we'll have to take Fred!"

"Who else will organize the seating arrangements at the crazy house!"

Too late! he thought. Too late for Gregory, whom I sent to military school. Even as it is too late for the other, who nurses a wheelchair case. Too late for Sam's boy, *"Traditionally yours!"* Even as it is too late now for Sam, his flawed heart. Too late for Sara, whom we loved and honored as if she were our virgin mother, too late for her when she gave birth to an unwanted child for whom it was then too late, for Marybell who decided even at birth to want nothing, to, rocking back and forth, ask for nothing.

Too late for all our children!

He said prayers in the morning and prayers at dusk, and he said prayers in the pit of night when the longing in him was greatest. He called God for help, he praised God, and though there were moments during the prayer, during the rocking expression of his longing, when he felt all weight gone from him, he returned from prayer to see that nothing was changed, the night was as deep as it had been, he was even who he had been, the boy was still who he was, and there was a light on under the boy's number—"HANG UP, MONSTER!"—and no matter what he did the poison would filter through, and the longing in him might go elsewhere, sink in him to there, want to be scratched, or caressed, and there was Mary for that, and Sadie, and a third and fourth. And he thought then that all he really longed for was to believe as if to remember, to be able to believe as if to remember, to stop everything and believe as if belief would restore him to life, as if before his birth he had believed.

Maybe, he thought, this is what the *rebbe* meant, that just when it is really and finally too late, then you are closest, then you are ready! He made the prayer for wine when he drank Scotch. He would praise God until God would take notice, he would praise God when he fucked, ha! ha! ha! He would praise God when he came from behind, ha! ha! ha! He would praise God in the scented temple, the color TV on, of Emma's bedroom. He would praise God for what was happening to Emma, that her other leg had been amputated, that she was undergoing painful radiation treatment! He would sit with the congregation in that darkened temple and sing God's praise, and maybe God would listen. A surgeon called him—he had recently undertaken to pay her bills—and said that a third amputation would be necessary. "What do you want to cut off now?" He arrived at West End Avenue with an armful of flowers, of every color, holy tall-stemmed flowers to be put around the large bed as if it were a bridal bed, and when the nurse had arranged the flowers, he ordered everyone out. "OUT! OUT!"

Emma was shriveled, and her hair was falling and hung out like wire from her head; she wore pearls, but her lipstick would smear after no time at all. She was smiling.

He was suddenly timid as he could be before a woman's suffering. Here it was her life that was being cut away. He blurted out what the surgeon had told him. "Yes!" she said so readily he thought she already knew. "Yes!" And he read in her pride his own. For she too had had a father, and he had done that to her, and she had had a child, and she had done that to her. And somewhere there was a grown young man who was her grandchild and who would not even now come once to greet her! But she was then complaining petulantly, "Why doesn't Joe come to visit? After all the business I sent him! I brought him, you know, tens of clients, good clients!"

He wondered if she had heard him earlier, if the "Yes, yes" he had heard had been an answer. Joe was almost ninety years old, he lived in retirement in Miami. Then he saw her smile and he understood, she was asking even for what The Great Cohen, for it was as that that he had advertised his fur business, had not given his sisters Eshka and Leah—had been off on business trip or holiday when they died—and David loved that justice, and David understood: She is asking for her due. She is paying back her debts, and so she is asking too for her due, and maybe even for what was due Eshka and Leah.

"I'll tell him," he promised.

"Tens of clients! The business I brought him!"

The other guests filed back in. Sam who was, David realized, wearing a wig; Esther bent, her legs become like stone pillars, her frown like stone; the cousins; the friends of Emma, some of whom came even without hope of gain to honor the rich—they would later, when he told them of how Emma had said, "Yes, yes," be full of new admiration—though one whispered to David, "Mister Cohen, is now the time to buy C-ways stock?" As if too their closing down their shipyards, their dry-docking ten giant tankers, the stock's being at rock bottom was a device with which to realize new and unheard-of profits.

"Darling," Emma said to Anna, "I'm so happy for you! He'll be so good a doctor, it's even in his blood! Tell me, is he a good dancer? Does he sail? . . . Tennis? I never knew," she lied, smiling, and even then she was dialing with bonelike fragile fingers. "This is a fine girl," she said, and fine was of course money, money, money, though one had to wonder what other debts were involved in Emma's matchmaking.

"There," she said, having had Selma bring her a five-dollar bill from her purse and giving it to Anna, who, nonplussed, accepted, "for their first date."

Even Anna. As we live, so we die, so we watch ours die.

He sat in deep and almost laughing admiration, for he too was being dunned now, was paying back his due. But even then he heard from somewhere in the congregation a childlike crying. In the color-TV-shadowed obscurity, Rachel, Louis's gentle wife, was crying.

He thought, As I live, so shall I die, by—ha! ha! ha!—debts! But who am I paying back now?

I was afraid to hold my boy in my arms that I'd drop him and make him like me!

I cannot speak, I cannot think, the pain is so large in me!

"WHAT AM I TO DO?"

But he could not this morning, no matter how he intimidated, get through to the *rebbe*. He left a message: "Tell him I must see him privately tonight even if only for five minutes." They called back and said this evening's dinner was a festive occasion, the *rebbe's* time was precious. He said, "Tell him that Mister Cohen says, 'Soon it will be too late!'" And so then they called back and said he would have exactly five minutes with the *rebbe* before the dinner, and he felt suddenly so good he began to hum a hi-diddle-diddle Yiddish tune.

6

We are driving in the Lincoln down the East River Drive. It is six o'clock and the traffic is heavy, and Luis, the small dark Puerto Rican chauffeur, does not, for the length of the Lincoln or for its dignity, or for David's, weave from lane to lane. Luis does not wear a uniform, tonight he is even a volunteer; it is clear by his manner he is devoted to David as one is to a prince. I wonder what act of generosity earned David this—A roomful of flowers for a sick mother? Delicate heart surgery for a baby girl? It occurs to me that it is not that David wants to be treated as a prince, but that he wants to treat others as a prince would. We have, in fact, a case of Johnny Walker Black at our feet.

He told me about the *rebbe*, the miracles people credited him with. "It's a worldwide movement of true believers. Business people come to him for business advice, sick people ask for medical advice. And the miracles do happen, ha! ha! ha!"

He is darkly dressed in a fine double-breasted suit, a pale blue shirt, a dark rich silk tie. He wears his dark glasses though it is already night. His thinning hair is snow white, his face is red. He is humming almost inaudibly to himself. Is he drunk? Are his eyes closed? When he came home this afternoon, Gregory was in his room sleeping or feigning sleep, and the father stood once after entering and once before going out in his doorway looking pensively but calmly at him.

I want to leave the city. I have seen everyone who will see me. I have a sense that everything is about to fall through. Why should anyone give me a fellowship? Why should a publisher risk losing money on my work? What have I to offer? It is as if I can have no confidence in all my relationships—How dare I ask for anything? To whom do I bring profit or pleasure? Should I teach? What can I teach? It is not enough! But how can I go home now? Nothing is changed, I am as I was only I know me better. I would go back to my wife only to long again to be unfaithful, to go on using her and go on killing her. Am I using my boy? How have I been using my boy? I have nothing to bring them, so stay away!

We are driving in heavy traffic on the East River Drive. I think of my father. We would come down the drive, in his two-door Chevy, to visit his brother, or we would accompany him even to here, to the towering New York University Medical Center, where we would wait in or near the Chevy for him ·as he would, often with his brother, attend a lecture, sometimes he returning with his brother, the tall professor and the small doctor, my father always proud as if strong in this brother's presence. What shadow is in the back of my mind? We are passing the UN headquarters, I look at its face up, up, up. Larry and I played two-handed pinochle, "a thousand," almost all day last Sunday. Larry senses where I am, he says little. I felt, playing pinochle, playing fast as we learned to play fast with my father, very close to Larry, to my father, to the Bronx. I called him "Lazy" as my mother sometimes did, I called him Lazarus as my father always did, I called him Eleazar, for that was the name of the great-grandfather my father's brother was named after. He told me he had given a lecture on community mental health care at the Bronx hospital. It is now all black and Puerto Rican in the heart of the Bronx, the hospital is run-down. After his lecture, an eighty-year-old Jewish doctor, his black medical bag in hand, approached him and asked, "Are you Doctor Katz's son?" Larry has already been asked this question here and there, and his answer is, "I am the son of Doctor Saul Katz of Hunts Point Avenue." The old doctor, still practicing medicine in the heart of the Bronx, nodded and nodded, his eyes wet.

Now we are approaching the great webbed bridges of lower Manhattan, the Williamsburg, Manhattan, and Brooklyn bridges, these old bridges that even as a boy I sensed led backward, and that are for me, I realize, we turning now into the city to gain access to the last, the Brooklyn Bridge, bridges into the past. As we rise within the webbing over the river, I recognize the melody David has been humming and I understand he is happy as is a traveler coming home. The lights of the city are behind us. I am so sure I am entering the ghetto, I smell gefilte fish, *tzimmis*, brisket! I push-button open the window; we are descending into Brooklyn, the air is warmer, stiller, there is something mournful in the air, and I remember seeing first green at Larry's house in Connecticut. Yes, it is spring.

We are passing through a black ghetto. I have been here too before. When we were still looking for a location for the liquor store, my mother and I came by subway to measure off the 1500 feet required by law between liquor stores. *She*, of course, has always been waiting for me in Brooklyn in the back of my mind.

I see in my mind great bushes of the sharp yellow *genêt* that in this season yearns up from our stone-terraced land near Murs.

7

The Lincoln was moving very slowly between rows of cars parked bumper-to-bumper, spaces only at the fire hydrants, down the one-way narrow streetlamp-lit ghetto street, searching for the address. But David, seeing people on the sidewalks converging toward a narrow brownstone, already felt part of the flow. Here was a young husband and wife; he was bearded, he wore a narrow-brimmed hat, she was wigged. Here was a large family, the bearded father hurrying not to lose his place at the celebration, walking belly forward, the mother sharply glancing the hatted earlocked boys, the timid girl, into his shadow. A yellow taxi ahead of them had pulled to at the brownstone, blocking them. A Manhattan judge? A rabbi from the suburbs? David told Luis to park farther on; he spoke to him generally in Spanish, Yiddish came to his tongue now, but Luis understood. He wanted to sit a moment, he sensed the interiors of these crowded squat apartment buildings, the two- and three-story brownstones. He sensed in backrooms heavy mothers hurrying, in the midst of their complicated dressing, here and there, hurrying a child on, helping one, taking a cake from the oven, putting perfume behind their ears; he sensed grandmothers lighting candles. He sensed somewhere a dark beautiful big-eyed girl soon to be a bride.

He forgot that these were Jews who worked in the city, who wore Bond or S. J. Klein suits. He thought they were Jews from his childhood, from his village, from even before his century. In his mind they were preparing for the Holy Sabbath, and he remembered vaguely that the Sabbath too is called a bride, as if, it occurred to him, every celebration is a wedding. He felt his heart hurting for joy for he had seen these very streets filled with the dying and the doomed, but here the earlocked boys were alive and radiant in their parents' shadow.

He told Max to carry the whisky, for though it was a little thing he did not now want to appear with a *goy*, a member of the nations. So Max picked the case of Johnny Walker Black up almost to his chest and followed after his snow-white-haired, dark-eyeglassed lurching cousin to the brownstone to which Jews were converging, the crowd at the stoop progressing up slowly for they were family groups and would enter together, and many were carrying bulky packages—one smelled cake as well as perfume—and at the door were burly squat bearded men who had that coplike look, and they wanted to know who everyone was and those whom they did not know they checked out by name with an upstairs office. David and

Max were shunted off to a side in the entranceway by the wall mailboxes, and they waited there, one of the guards kept glancing suspiciously at the case of whisky at Max's feet, though many of the guests came with bottles and packages of bottles. The guests, once past the guards, separated, men from women, the boys going with their fathers into what David could see was a many-tabled banquet room, the women and girls going up a wide staircase. A harried-looking man brought the word down that David and Max could enter, and they were given seat numbers, but David said, "The *rebbe*! I have an appointment to see the *rebbe* now!" The very word stilled people and caused them to turn and stare. But the harried-looking man said reluctantly, "So come with me, Mister Cohen." David began to follow him, but one of the burly guards grabbed him by the arm and said, "Are you a Jew? Why aren't you wearing a hat?" Neither David or Max had thought of that. Still, David angrily shook off the guard's hand. The harried man said firmly, "No, Mister Cohen, you can't go up without a hat!" A boy was sent to find paper *yarmulkas*, and David's was broad and stood up from his head like a desert tent, and he, feeling it then with the tips of his fingers, was humbled again as if by memories. He followed up the stairs after the harried man, his stick hooked to his arm, he pulling on the handrail, past the women in dark and flowered dresses, girdled, corseted, wigged, their ornate hats. He glimpsed, past a group of them at a doorway on the first landing, a banquet room, and he guessed, still looking in that direction as he followed the harried man up another staircase, darker, more narrow, that it was a terrace to the lower banquet room. A flock of hatted earlocked boys, fleeting like a dream, hurried down past him, laughter on their lips. And now he was breathless, pulling up, and there was whom he immediately knew was the *rebbe*, the teacher, waiting in a lit doorway for him, and he said, "Father! Father! What am I to do?" But even as his heart so spoke, his dark-glassed gaze was taking in the man, his mind was remembering things he had heard about him, his pride was telling him, I am the man who put Istanbul and Galveston, Texas, into my pocket, I bought all of Qatar and was like the very emir for a week! And knowing one did not shake hands with the *rebbe*, he nevertheless put out his, and the *rebbe* let his be taken, not quite limp, he, darkly dressed, perhaps fifty years old, blue-eyed, pale, a muscleless pallor as if he had lived all his life in such rooms in such ghettos.

Where have I met you before? You look like Fred, you look like a bookkeeper, you look like you couldn't fight your way out of a paper bag! Did I call you father? And even that he realized had been for pride, for he had heard that the pain of the *rebbe* was that he had no children.

"Father," he repeated, this time half-seeing his own—squat battler, conniver, fur-coated god, twister, destroyer!—"What am I to do?"

The pale troubled *rebbe* turned his back to David as if to avoid the theatrics of his dark-glassed expression or as if to be alone with the question: What am I to do?

The *rebbe* asked, "Do you believe in God?"

"Oh I long to!" David answered quickly.

The *rebbe* nodded.

"Do you pray?"

"I pray!"

"Do you pray often?"

"Often! Often!"

The *rebbe* was nodding as if praying. "So now you must study the Law. Everything begins in longing, but only the Law is revealed."

Downstairs in the terraced banquet room, David leaned right up to Max and urgently whispered into his ear but loud enough for their neighbors to hear, "So what are the commandments? Don't you remember the Ten Commandments?" Max was embarrassed.

But the heavy-hatted bearded men about them looked away, and only a silk *yarmulkaed* golden-earlocked boy watched them.

"There is one God," Max whispered.

"It's more than that!" David insisted.

"We mustn't worship other gods."

"Astartes! Baals! Golden calves! The sabbath is another commandment."

"Honor your father and your mother. Thou shalt not kill, steal, or lie."

"That's only six or seven, what are the others?"

Above, women had brought their chairs even to the railing about the terrace, with their ornate hats they seemed like squatting birds.

David smiled, thinking that the golden-earlocked boy could recite
for him in an instant all of the Ten Commandments, no use, no use,
flimsy like the strands of his hair. He had said to the *rebbe*, "My son
is not even a Jew!" not sure in his own mind if he was telling him he
was outside the Law or if he was asking him if he, the *rebbe*, could
perform a miracle for a non-Jew. Oh, he had troubled the troubled
pale man, but the *rebbe* had said, "He is your son." "*Rebbe*," David
had said, "he sits on top of a Volkswagen exposing himself!" "Still,
he is your son." "Yes, he is my son," he had said, answering what he
had begun to understand the *rebbe* meant, that, no matter what, the
connection was there, there was no exception: Pray, Long, and
Study the Law! But he had also begun to sense something more,
something enormous, the boy was *waiting* on the Volkswagen. They
ate, oh bad! bad! The gefilte fish came from bottles! The olives came
from California in cans and were giant tasteless things. For drink,
there was celery tonic! The chicken was steeped in fat. Still, the guests
were happy, people ate with appetite, a song almost on their glistening
lips. When the meal was finished, a bottle of whisky appeared by the
rebbe, and bottles then began to appear at all the tables, and David
took a bottle from the case at his feet and gave it right, and gave
another left, and again and again. The *rebbe*'s assistant had like a
cupbearer poured a glass for the *rebbe* and tasted it first himself,
and then the *rebbe* raised his glass and toasted, "*L'chayim!*"—
Life! And after, he honored certain guests, calling out their names.
"Shmuel Bernstein!" And Shmuel Bernstein would rise and raise his
glass and toast, "*L'chayim!*" And everyone would drink. And David
thought looking at the Jews about him, Even like us, as we then were,
with a tall solid Jack, and there are five Bens here, and of our Sol there
are a hundred. And even my father, though none that he saw had the
glint in his father's eye, and then the *rebbe* called him by name and he
almost laughed thinking he too, his father too, had a place here. Hypocrites! he thought, raising his glass. "*L'chayim!*" he called out, happy.
And the people about him, seeing this newcomer in the desert tent
paper *yarmulka* being so honored, wondered who he was. Perhaps
rumors were already spreading, a great shipper, a prince from the city,
returning to his people and his faith. Life! he called out happily. Life
for me and life for my son and life for my tribe.

The *rebbe*, who in his office had worn a *yarmulka*, now wore a heavy black hat over it, its brim wider perhaps than that of any hat here, his pale face shaded, indistinct. He stood and the guests grew silent and in a quiet lilting Yiddish, he began to speak.

This, he said, was a day of celebration for his movement, still, he would speak of the Law, for the Law he said is what is *revealed*. The first three commandments are concerned directly with our honoring God, but the fourth, which is the beginning of the social commandments, Honor your father and mother, is also an honoring of God. This is clear even in the phrasing of the commandment, Honor your father and mother so that your days on earth, given to you by God, be prolonged. So that each commandment, even the commandment against adultery, is a commandment to honor God. By His Law we honor Him. As if through His Law our relations with one another are all sacred.

But David was listening with a smile of irony, for honor your father was his father and his son, and adultery was all his whores. And Max could not understand so much Yiddish. Indeed, as the *rebbe* continued, developing his thought, others in the assembly who had perhaps eaten or drunk too much, closed their eyes and began to nod.

Max thought the *rebbe* was saying nothing, was elaborating on a pinhead, and yet he felt a flame close by. The Law. Of course, the Law! Of course, BURN IT OUT OF ME was even that! But it would not burn until he took hold of it. It was there as if hovering over his head, and he had to rise up, reach up, take hold! That was a decision! For above his head was nothing, but the Law was there. He felt he was glowing, and he began to understand. You will not worship golden calves! You will not worship Astartes! You will honor your father and mother so that your son will honor you and his mother. You will honor your son so that he will honor his son! He saw his fair-haired clear-eyed son Saul-Daniel! You will be faithful to your wife so that your neighbor will be faithful to his and your wife to you, and his wife to him.

Even then there was a commotion at the entrance to the banquet room, and two of the squat burly bearded guards entered, pulling by the arms David's Puerto Rican chauffeur Luis.

"A spy!" someone cried. "A spy!"

Men who had been minutes before joyous almost to singing were rising angry from their places.

"KILL HIM!" someone cried. For they had been mugged and robbed, their daughters had been raped, their synagogues had been desecrated.

"BLIND HIM!" someone cried.

The wigged ornate-hatted women above were shrieking piercingly.

The world was dark dark dark. David was at home. Here in so dark a place we maim our children. We bring them into the world and maim them. The *rebbe* was still standing, so small within all the passion of his people. Someone spat at the spy.

"*Señor* Cohen!" Luis called out, still not seeing him.

David was standing, tilted like a storm. Max stood now loyal and guilty at his side. "Let him go!" David commanded.

"APOSTATE!" a Jew shouted.

"APOSTATE!" David almost sang back, triumphant. For he wanted to be driven from this place. "That I married a Gentile? That my son's not a Jew?" he accused the *rebbe*, who had no answer.

"APOSTATE!" a woman above cried down like throwing a stone.

"APOSTATE! APOSTATE!" bearded Jews threw at him.

"HYPOCRITES!" David shouted. Thinking, knowing, I am even descendant of Aaron, and my son is Cohen, descendant of Aaron, and by our birth and blood we are even priests of Israel! And he led as if through a gauntlet Max and the Puerto Rican out.

Now the silent Lincoln drove on deserted streets, through rubbled streets, the shops gone, the A & P windows boarded over. They saw the low flat rooftops of Brooklyn, they passed an elevated subway station, the metal staircase, the flimsy sheltered platform barebulbed lit above.

David was dark-glassed in a corner. There was nothing he did not see. He saw through walls. His heart this night was big enough for him to feel the suffering of all the world. The beast in the jungle was in pain too, the prowling lurking jackals and hyenas here were as if searching the sky, only—ha! ha! ha!—they did not know which way to look.

"INTO THE CRAZY HOUSE WITH YOU!" David called at his son seated barefoot and belly-free in the black leathered den before the color TV.

The giant boy rose in a lurch and already halfway across the living room said, "This is the crazy house!"

"INTO THE CRAZY HOUSE WITH HIM!" David called into the receiver to his half-brother, real brother, Louis. David was sprawled barefoot in his pajamas in his chair. "INTO THE CRAZY HOUSE WITH HIM!" he repeated, but by now the sound had a meaning of its own, the cry had a tenderness to it, and he knew only that his child had to be severed, his heart had to be broken. His eyes were closed, he saw himself in a long corridor trying to catch up with the giant. "INTO THE CRAZY HOUSE WITH YOU!" he called after him, and Louis, in his den, did not respond, for he knew that David was most of the time connected here and there, up and down, and one had to hold on. David was alone in the corridor, and he saw coming toward him his older boy pushing a wheelchair. "Hello, boy," he said softly, but the boy put his finger to his lips to still him, he was busy. He stood in a doorway and Sam's boy Mark was in a hospital bed wheedling his weeping father, "Dad, Dad, it's a hundred-dollar book by *Bernard Berenson* and Marboro's selling it for only forty-nine ninety-nine." Marybell opened the doors of the crazy house; like a visitor, he followed the idiot-faced girl, and there was the girl's mother, his sister, grown old and skeletal, coming toward them with her princess hysterical laughter.

"We've opened the gates," David said into the receiver.

"There's no stopping them now," Louis said.

"INTO THE CRAZY HOUSE WITH YOU!" David said, pointing, reaching, as if playing a game of tag. And now he went through his apartment opening doors, only he saw and addressed couples making love, sleeping children, nursemaids and their infant charges sleeping at their side. "INTO THE CRAZY HOUSE WITH YOU!"

"David! David!" I implored.

"Schmuck! It's the wilderness!" he confirmed. "We live in the wilderness!"

He had the phone in his hand, it was the doorman again.

The Volkswagen was across the street. The boy was bellowing,

"WHERE ARE YOU, FATHER?" And now, as the boy saw him approaching, he cried, "KILL ME, FATHER!"

David's heart began to break. He stood bursting like a statue on tiptoe.

The boy had come down from the Volkswagen, and he took his father by the shoulders and violently began to shake him. "KILL ME, FATHER!"

For David had already, as he had himself.

David saw the turning flashing red light of a police car and saw then the police running, revolvers drawn, and then even felt them beating at the monster, and David, already paralyzed, gasping, the rage in his bloodied eyes, supported now by police without whom he would have fallen, stared at them and all the world with hate, strangers to me.

8

Emma's will kept her alive.

The brass samovar in the entry of her West End Avenue residence hotel apartment glowed darkly in the dim light. The faces we saw there were in this sorrow twice familiar, our own faces in this light reminded us of the old Jewish faces of our parents. No matter that none of us lived any longer in the Bronx, that the East Bronx where we had lived was now for us only the quickly glimpsed Hunts Point exit on the Bruckner Expressway to Connecticut, that Hunts Point Avenue was a darker part of the city wilderness, we thought of Sundays in the East Bronx, of visiting Grandmother Cohen in her small apartment behind the doctor's office, of Eshka and Leah sitting, on warm spring days, with neighbors on folding chairs, knitting, talking, at the street corner near the red fire-alarm post.

Emma, who had never really been one of us, who had come visiting us like a *grande dame*, or who had brought us clients, who had not spent her summers with us in Rockaway, but who had loved Eshka, reminded us too of that time, of those dead. And in her proud dying—I shall die as I have lived—we were confirmed in what we had learned: This is the way things are!

She had said to Esther, "Don't you know what we do? We erect statues to ourselves! We take our dead husband's suits from the closet and offer them to his nephews, we take his hundred-dollar shoes from the closet and lay them before a nephew thinking, Keep them alive, keep him alive, but the nephew says, 'Don't you have something to go with my plaid suit?' We make heroes out of men who died heartsick! And we convince ourselves, by erecting statues to them, not only that we loved them but that we had *something*!"

Her hair was gone. Her eyes seemed, perhaps because her face had become so drawn, very large. Sometimes her eyelids dropped half and remained so, as if she had found a resting place between sleep and waking. For when she was awake she was filled with pain, and we knew what the little doctor had suffered in his bed and how he turned yellow and how he spit into a spitting cup, and we knew what Eshka suffered in Brooklyn and how for her suffering she *crawled* up four flights of stairs, and we knew how Leah was abandoned and how Leah cried for her son, and Mary, burning inside, locked herself away, and Jack, full of pain like disgust, called Anna before coming to visit that he would meet no one else, not even a brother. And she had all that in her, she had in different places in her body the glowing burning medals of pain, and in her mind her father was in a tuxedo and had decided not to come home, and her husband was doing something cheap but would always be tall and proud, and her daughter was hanging by the neck from a crystal chandelier. She was sitting in a taxi waiting for only a glimpse of her grandson, she was knocking at a door and a black servant was telling her to go away. What do you mean? How dare you? She was the best of us, the proudest; she would not bow her head.

It was not often now that we were allowed into the bedroom to visit with her. The light was dim, the color TV glowed, the odors about her were, no matter what products were used, sickly sweet. There was always a nurse on duty. Esther and Selma sat with her or were on hand, for her dressings had to be changed several times a day. They would uncover her and lift her to place a rubber sheet beneath her. Then one would hold her hard by the shoulders, staring into her big-eyed skeletal face, while the nurse removed the dressings, and the other would take the soiled dressings and then hand the nurse new ones. The flesh of her leg stumps and of her arm stump would be washed clean and would be baby-red, and even an instant after small wounds like cracks would begin to suppurate.

Sometimes Anna, unasked for, came into the room. What am

I waiting for? Anna thought. To see even how we shall die?

Emma had not asked for David since his stroke. But she asked again, "Why doesn't Joe come? The things I did for him!"

Anna did not know what to do.

David was still not out of the hospital, but a hundred creditors no one had ever heard of had begun law actions against him, his women had called Sam and Louis and spoken of promises.

Fred told Anna the banks were pressing C-ways, there were strangers in the wide corridors of C-ways, they went to private meetings with the chairman of the board, who was not one of us.

A Senate committee was now loudly investigating Jonathan's appointment as US ambassador. They had discovered traces of substantial presidential campaign contributions that might make it seem Jonathan had bought his appointment. Why didn't he defend himself? Where was he? He had not yet been back even to visit his brother.

What could Anna do?

She listened for messages.

Sol called her that the brothers should stop sending him money, he could make do with what he had. He said this was no time for a party. She called gentle Sam and told him. She told Sam someone would have to pay the nurses.

She told Marty what Emma said about his father. Would the tall, hangdog-faced boxer tell his father, remind the old man in Florida, The things I did for you? In any event, Marty came often. Darling! Anna thought. For he was like her, he had never broken the circle, loyal to it.

She called Larry in Connecticut to get out of him something she might use to encourage others. "He's doing all right," Larry would force himself to say of the still steadily sedated Gregory. And Anna would phone that back to Sam, who if he was bitter at anyone was bitter at psychiatrists and yet would repeat that to David, who did not respond.

Fred wanted to know if at the party for the old timers, for Joe and Sol, the Feldbaums should be seated with the Friedlands. Who would he put Ben's daughter Elaine with, for she was a deadweight and Dora would have to be with Joe and Sol at the table of honor.

She said, "Not now, Fred."

"Yes, now! They gave me this to do, and I'll do it!"

"Put her with us," she said.

She called her second son often. "How are you, dear? How are you, Sonny?" Holding on then as if without another word she would pour on him love and consolation. For what kind of brothers will they be if one is a winner and the other is a loser?

In Woodmere, she played bridge.

"You're a murderer!" an opponent said to her.

"That's the only way to play!" she said angrily.

What am I waiting for here?

9

It had seemed to Esther she had entered a world of luxury and waste where suffering was terrible because life was meaningless, and then she had suspected that such suffering was in her too. It had seemed to her that her cousins here had almost no link with her, that by the way they lived they had become strangers, and now she felt they were even in her blood, that what they had lived in America was in her. She thought of Emma as her own dark sister, she thought of her niece Anna even as she should have thought of her niece Ruth, daughter saved out of Warsaw. It seemed to her that there came a point at which many lives could intersect and at which time we all have but one voice. When they spoke of their children, she thought of Abisai. Was it for her guilt? That they had named Abisai to be a soldier of Israel, that she had taken the place of the wife who had gone off crazy into the desert, that he had put that wife into the hands of others so that he could go on with his life? We live in blindness, she thought, we wake up one day and realize that we have not prepared ourselves right, that all the while we have been doing this we have been omitting to do that. There are twenty-year mistakes and lifetime omissions, there is no certainty. We meet and have one voice in uncertainty.

The old woman sat late at night at her seventh-floor window looking out at streetlight-lit and deserted West End Avenue like an empty stage. Her thick legs were pressed to the wall, her forehead sometimes touched the cold window, her nose hooked almost to her wide mouth. She heard the wilderness wailings from east of Broadway, the screaming city sirens, she thought of Selma's daughter in a city room somewhere. She thought of Sam's suicide son who had driven a hansom cab in Central Park and whom Sam had called, his eyes wet, the *balagola*. She thought of the park and of death and was then afraid she would be buried here. What difference would it make?

She thought that in America one, or one's children, could have everything, and yet, and look!—she knew that those grabbing onto this or that were yearning still for something else, and those who were refusing this or that and thought they were even refusing all were yearning too. All of them. In the middle of the night when they awake sleepless, they are never yearning for money, though a minute after they may think they are.

She thought, Perhaps Israel is nothing. Perhaps Israel, not only that it is encircled and endangered and may be destroyed, but in its very *idea*, is nothing, is like everything else. Or is part of something else! And then it occurred to her, Israel would survive even Israel. As if the accomplishment of Israel were not Israel, but something beyond.

She knew that her fear of dying here was a longing to be there, and the longing came from so deep in her she knew it was right and did not have to know how or why, and then she again saw herself entering the desert.

Sam said to her, "I have put you in my will so that if anything happens to me before . . ." He was embarrassed at his generosity. He whispered proudly to her, "Jonathan is saving the Russian Jews."

She did not understand.

It was a secret, but Sam thought Esther should know.

"He is buying them out of Russia."

"Who has put them on sale?"

He did not understand.

She said, "They risk their livelihoods, they risk imprisonment, they are buying themselves out."

"You don't understand," he explained gently. "Without American grain, without our wealth, what could they do?"

She would not argue, she would not say, Without Israel?

Even Sam had a role.

She wanted to say good-bye to him as to a son. Soon I shall die, I want to die at home. But still she could not decide to leave. What am I waiting for still?

She sat in the night by her window and thought of flying, of flying over the sea, she thought of flying at night, among the stars above the earth glow. Already she had seen her return to Israel, arriving at sunset, the sun-tinted desert below, a density and presence in the air that was not only the return home but the return home into time, into an unbroken sequence of time that took her back thousands of years. For she had passed in her mind from this century of our homecoming into the centuries just out of darkness, and there were yearnings in her now even as there had been in us then.

After the Six Day War, she had gone with her son to the Wall of the Temple, where they had been separated, he with a thousand other men, mostly like him, in uniform, but wearing skullcaps and prayer shawls, and she at the smaller partitioned-off women's section. She had begun a prayer of thanksgiving in the rote way we, who do not know if we believe, have, and had, perhaps because of the swaying prayer movement, kept repeating prayers and had begun to think of Abba, how much she wished Abba could be there, and so, regardless of the words she said, the prayer was, I bring you here. Then, rocking still, a prayer for her favorite brother Irving: I bring you here; and then Saul, Dan in Paris, Lazarus, who died alone in Russia, Sonia, who then had still been alive in Russia. She had prayed for all her sisters, and their children, whom she had not known, and for her parents. It had been the prayer of: I bring you all here. And she realized now it had been, I bring you all back together again here.

She sat at the side of her dark sister.

Emma asked her why the radiation treatment had been discontinued. Esther lied, "It is only temporary." A smile played over Emma's cupid lips. Emma was fed intravenously; the pain was, regardless of the drugs administered, constant. Still, she would not complain, she would not cry out, still, in that instant when she wanted to draw in her breath and close her eyes for the pain that made her think her legs and arm were still there, she would catch herself and would smile.

There were five women in the darkened deathroom; there was the nurse, whom we did not know or try to know for it was one day one person and the next another, and there was Selma, Anna and Emma and Esther. But with Selma was her daughter, and in Anna was her mother and sons and husband, and she would save them all, and in Emma was her father and her suicide daughter and the other suicides, and, of course, was Eshka, though Emma kept that even from herself as if somehow that way paying Eshka back, and was gentle Mary like a bird, and in her, in Esther, old woman, was them all, and even the Cohen brother whose name she had forgotten who had chosen to live by the sea.

And so they were together and some others were occasionally allowed in, bringing with them their parents and children. And, of course, Esther realized, they were all yearning. They had been yearning in "Versailles," and they had been yearning in Woodmere, and the dead had been yearning in the cemetery. And Emma, now at their center, was yearning all the more that she refused anything she could not buy. She smiled with pain, but it was like a cry, it was like, Do this to me for I will pay! It was, My father did that to me, and my daughter did that to me, and her son, my grandson, will not even visit me, and why should it stop now?

It was, Pay me back for what I have done! Cut off my other arm! Blind me! Give me more pain!

And who could say—for her suffering was as great as her pride— that she did not magnify the wrongs she had done. For all she could know of what she had done was only the punishment of herself.

As I have lived so shall I die.

What could Esther answer? For the waiting frowning old woman knew that Emma was calling out and that she had to answer. And there was a point at which if there were no answer one became as if stone. And she thought, all of them, and Selma, and Anna, and each one that they carried in them, even the yearning dead, they needed an answer, or the beginning of an answer. It is not death that closes us off, but death in life. They were all here to visit and watch Emma, to wait with her—the sound of the color TV so low it was only a murmur—but she knew now they were even waiting for her to answer. Only, her voice was the voice of Abba, for forty years her voice had been the voice of Abba, and the father had nothing to tell them now, and what did an old woman have to say to all these people she had brought and was keeping together? What did an old widow, mother whose son had died, have to say? Then she saw in her mind the timid gentle wife of Louis crying as she had in this room, and she too began to cry.

She was unaccustomed to crying, who had not cried at the death of her husband or her son, the sound of it was like that of hiccoughing. Her body began to let go in the prayerlike rocking movement though she was seated, and her sternly frowning face had fallen apart. The others looked at her without understanding. Anna saw she was crying and she was not one to let another weep by herself, and so there were tears at her eyes, she wondering first why Esther was crying but then crying on her own. Esther was weeping finally for her husband and her son, that they were gone, that she was alone, that Abba had died uncertain and Abisai so young, unfulfilled, she was weeping for her brothers and sisters. Still it was not enough, though Anna, sobbing now, Kleenex from her purse in hand, was even, for her contact lenses, gasping with pain. Emma said fiercely, "What is this, my wake!"

Esther did not understand the joke, and the words came from her uncalled for. "Forgive me. Forgive me," she said, and was weeping still, to the woman whose place with Abba she had taken, to Abba, to Abisai, to each of her brothers, to her sisters, to their children, to her father and mother, whom she had left. "Forgive me," she said, "forgive me." And in the enormous calm now coming over her she knew but did not say, We buy back nothing, we pay back nothing, forgive me. Looking at Emma she did not say, For others will die this way, even the children, even their children. We are never the last to die, or the only one, and we do not die alone. "Forgive me," she said to Emma, and it was so deep a request that Emma turned away.

Anna would have dropped to the floor and crawled for forgiveness, but she thought she was not important enough.

Esther went on praying, "Forgive me," knowing it was already so if only for now, and she remembered then the boy running across the beach to his mother Madeleine and saw now the thick eyeglassed mother kneeling to the sand to receive him in her arms.

That evening, Emma's pain became very great and her will broke and she began to moan and cry.

CHAPTER *Fifteen*

1

IT OCCURRED TO HIM as he walked from the taxi to the
entrance of his apartment building at the East River, leaving the
tumult behind him, Kennedy airport, the evening Belt and city
traffic, even before entering the large marble hall, two guards,
across all the length of the hall, on duty at a long table, a glow of
evening light behind them, the sound now of his leather-soled special shoes, for his arches had always been weak, that this place, this
quiet and echoing, made him think of dreams and tombs. One of the
guards rose to bow slightly; Jonathan acknowledged with a nod.
The guard was tall, the dark uniform so discreet one could not really
tell it was a uniform. Sometimes, here at the elevator, he would
meet another owner of this building and they would nod, each respecting the other's silence and dignity as his own.

Sheila kissed him on the cheek. She had anticipated his mood, he
did not want to talk, she had come in a smock from her studio and
was ready to return. Still, he had to greet his mother-in-law, she was
upstairs in her wing of the duplex apartment. He came upon her
sitting absolutely still in her wheelchair, her eyes open. She was a
little deaf, she seemed like stone, he took the narrow waiting elevator back down.

Sheila said, hesitating still, "Honey, do you want a drink?"

He knew that his small doll-like wife had these days answered a hundred calls for him, that she was waiting only for him to call her, but he could not. He wanted that she return to her studio, not that she be hurt, but that she go on with her work. He did not want any touch, even hers.

He walked through corridors of his apartment like galleries of a museum. His paintings, but not one he wanted to look at. Even at the beginning, Sheila had insisted they buy paintings only by living artists. That had been interesting, meeting artists, supporting their work, but it had come to seem to him that all those paintings, which, like their artists, had at first seemed so vibrantly demandingly alive, were flat or incomplete. They were too loud, too insistent; those that had seemed pertinent were dated. He wanted then to own great art, but he did not permit himself to buy any. He thought briefly it was for loyalty to the artists he had supported, it was for the good principle of helping living artists, but he knew that it was because he would never be able to hang his wife's work with great art. As a private joke, he began then to divide paintings into two classes, those he could afford to buy and those he could not. And the more he wanted to own great art, the more unpurchasable and untouchable some paintings became.

He knew many museums of the world. He was sometimes in his dreams alone in museum corridors walking in stillness from gilt-framed oil painting to gilt-framed oil painting.

He thought, sitting now in his library-balconied den, the lights off, of Sheila wearing a smock, working, retouching, at her easel in her studio—the two-story church-high river and bridge view there. He thought of her models, the tall worn girls she chose for some sadness in her, she chose dancers, even in silence she listened to their unhappiness, and you could see some of it in her work. They sat awkwardly on the floor by the view, they had had deceptions, they were alone in the city. She would work the day through, but she would never be more than a few minutes late for dinner, and she would be so handsome, fresh, and young, one would think she had spent all her day preparing to meet him.

He had a bottle, a glass, and a bucket of ice, he was in a comfortable leather upholstered armchair, the window light was the city glow over the river.

He had sent ships around the world, he had been an associate of the leaders of his nation; now all over the world his offices were laying off employees, some branches were being closed, they were selling off ships and equipment that they had even innovated. He had gone too fast and been caught short. This day he had resigned his ambassadorship.

Sometimes he allowed himself to think this was only a period of consolidation and that he had seen worse times before. Then when he had risked everything, the first Liberty ship for two, the two against four, everyone's holdings, his uncles' very houses and businesses against the first giant tanker. But he knew that everything was different now. He knew that his withdrawing from touch was that he felt vulnerable. What could still happen? Would they try to strip him of his very dignity? Would they accuse him of being a cheat and profiteer? He knew what they were worth. The best of them were merely ambitious, the others were idealists until they became impatient, they lived by principle until they became jealous, they were intellectuals until they became angry. And it pleased them now to join together to tear down their betters. For we had *imagination* and we *rose* and some of us *built*.

Everything but one thing that could happen had happened. For David was paralyzed, and Jonathan had never been able to help his brother. And their children were null and void. After them there would be nothing.

He saw in his mind a somber painting. He remembered, it was a Rembrandt. At a distance a man was seated before what seemed to be a table or desk, most areas of the painting were obscure, light came down steeply from high windows—the shadows of the windows' intricate leading fell magnified on the wall. The man's head was framed by the light, but his features were unclear; he was not young, he could be meditating, studying. Surely what was on the stand before him was an oversize book. The man wore a beretlike hat peaked forward and pointing at the book, but the light that entered the room did not seem to illumine the book inclined as if to receive or reflect it, and only reverberated against the wholly dark right area of the painting, and seemed really to rise again, even as a steep passageway upwards. There were lines suggesting a rising spiral in the darkness.

Only as he saw himself looking at the painting so full of calm mystery that he felt mystery in himself did he remember how small it was.

He woke in his armchair in early morning light, he was quite stiff. Sheila had laid a blanket over him. Surely she had, upstairs, helped Bibi to bed.

He remembered, thinking of Sheila helping her mother out of the wheelchair, We weigh like stone. Standing stiffly, he thought with a wry smile that his legs were already like stone. He walked through the corridors of his apartment. In the giant living room with the sweep-around view of Brooklyn, the river, and lower Manhattan, the red sun barely risen, the morning light soft, he saw his idled Brooklyn shipyards. He could distinguish the office building, the chimney stack above the power plant, shipbuilding webbings, giant cranes. He smiled wryly at the great C they had raised hundreds of feet above the yards. Here, south, taller than his own building, imprinted on his view of Manhattan, the bridges, was the UN building, its glass face receiving the morning light and glowing. He turned, and his eye was struck by a small painting he had not noticed before. It was by Sheila, it was new, he approached it.

A woman was center kneeling to a baby on a sofa. The colors were the pastels of apartment interiors. The baby was sleeping on its stomach, its head turned to the mother. The mother's hair was combed simply to a bun. Her chin was pressed to the back of her hand placed on the edge of the sofa, her other hand was laid lightly on the child's back. The painting was awkward, perspective was shortened, there was pathos in the daydreaming mother, but clearest of all there was such disappointed longing in the artist that the mother, even touching the sleeping child, could not believe the child real. He knew Sheila had painted this now while he was being attacked. He thought, To show me she shares my pain she searched into her heart and made me this gift. He thought for the pathos that even reached out of the awkward painting and made him too its subject that he was being mocked. It seemed to him then that all was mockery, and he felt that he could shatter to pieces. But he would not and he smiled then at the painting to enjoy the joke.

2

We gathered, 100 of us to honor the last of us. Never again would we so gather. Friedlands, Feldbaums, Nissnievitches, and Starobinetzes joined with us, in-laws whom we had never met but who had heard of us, children so stunningly like their parents we had not seen in twenty years that we stopped where we stood and stared. Cousins took their old fathers or mothers out of nursing homes to attend. Eighty-year-old self-important Herman Friedland had insisted that all of his clan come, for if the Cohens were falling it was that they had been high and they could do them favors yet, and Herman and his had shared with them and he was proud of that. He had been brother-in-law to Jack Cohen, and even as Jack and the Cohens had struggled to rise, he and his brother had struggled to buy a bar and grill, and struggled to make a living. They too had sent their children to college; was not his daughter married to a doctor? None of his clan could refuse his call, there was not one he had not done a favor for. In hard times he had found jobs for one or the other, in good times he had not forgotten those less well off and had visited with gifts, with projects, with hope. He had taken his nephews to the fights, to Dodger ballgames at Ebbets Field.

Now he moved from cousin to cousin like an elder statesman and perhaps that is what the clan chief always wanted to be, mediator, link. He was not by a decade the eldest at this party, there were old people like ghosts of themselves who wandered about looking deeply into every face. Sweet Lily Friedland, held securely by her daughter, smiled at everyone who came up to greet her and asked, "Who are you, dear? Who are you, darling?"

Herman said to Larry, "Do you remember, professor, the photographs under the glass on the dining-room table in the East Bronx?"

The tall heavy psychiatrist with his neat black and silver psychiatrist beard said, "Do I remember!"

"Do you remember, professor, when in thirty-nine we would meet in the East Bronx around the big table and your father would tell us, between games of pinochle, what we had to do for our cousins in Europe?"

"I remember," Larry said, wondering what Herman was getting at.

"Do you remember my sister Edith going with your mother to Texas and Chicago?"

"Herman," Larry said, nodding then as if to assure him—Herman, we are related, Herman, I'll never deny that we are related, no matter how successful you think I become, I'll always be willing to listen to you and yours—"I remember."

Tuxedoed musicians were arriving, their cased instruments under their arms. Fred stood at the ballroom entrance and made sure that every guest took his seating ticket. "How's business?" some guests whispered. He frowned at the question, this is not the place, this is celebration.

His boys arrived. What matter if one still had long hair? Go boy, he almost said to the older, circulate, enjoy yourself, be big.

Marty's boy Ed arrived wearing a pea jacket, tight jeans, high-heeled boots, he carried a satchel and a guitar in a case. His face was all giant staring eyes, big nose, thick lips, and flaming exploding acne. Fred greeted him warmly, though no one had expected him and no place had been reserved for him—who did not know Ed's story?—and besides, Ed was grandson of The Great Cohen whose party this really was.

Our hosts arrived.

We could trace in the newspapers how C-ways was being eaten up by its creditors. Only the container division North Atlantic line was operating, everything else was shut down, or being sold, or draining funds while unable to find a buyer. The container division itself was operating at a loss, government agencies were investigating other government agency contracts with the corporation, new officers of the corporation, giant shareholders, wanted the corporation to sell the container division, to become a paper holding corporation. All of us would have sold our stock then had it not been for Security Exchange Commission restrictions on the sale of family holdings. Jonathan was alone at the helm. He was drinking heavily, though he too, like his brothers, could never be drunk.

Sam, at his side, wore a curly dark reddish wig. His lips were blue, but there was a fine touch of color to his cheeks. They had come walking from "Versailles" across Central Park South together, the brothers in their $500 topcoats, their wives in mink, Margo wearing a dark lustrous horizontally fitted mink that hung on her like mink quilting and looked like it could blanket ten or twenty and that yet, for her big head even more than her body, for her contact-lensed staring eyes, her huge breathlessness, was a just fit; Sheila bright and bubbly in her casually belted mink, looking from any distance at all like a girl barely eighteen years old.

Sam greeted many of us with an embrace. He turned to Fred and said, "Fred, I don't care how you've arranged it, but today we're honoring furriers, and I don't want to sit with anyone who isn't or wasn't a furrier!"

Who had not once been a furrier? Nevertheless, Fred was not one to be caught off balance. "You mean you want a Traders' pastrami sandwich!" And then he brought out of his pocket a dollar bill and began reading it the way they used to when they were all in the fur market and would play serial number dollar bill poker to see who would pay for everyone's lunch. Sam laughed warmly as if Fred had made him a gift.

Louis arrived with David. Louis had left C-ways and bought three tramp steamers, which he ran himself from a small office downtown. But the squat bifocaled cigar-smoking man had acquired some of the habits of a titan, and he too was losing money hand over fist.

David's hair was snow white, his skin gray. We looked at him and sensed where he had been, and nodded our heads slowly to tell him we understood. He stared at us fixedly.

Tender Rachel was with Louis, taller than him and yet within his shadow, softening the space of him. David's Jewish girlfriend Sadie wore eyeshadow but no lipstick, she devotedly wheeled David about.

Sol Cohen arrived in a C-ways chauffeured Lincoln from Brighton Beach with his fat wife Fanny and his sister-in-law Dora and Dora's fat unmarried forty-year-old daughter Elaine. Sol too was to be honored today, and Dora, because she was Ben's widow, had a place at the table of honor. Many people came to greet them, but Fanny was tired and they went to their seats at their dais-raised table and received well-wishers there, and Sol, pleasantly deaf and grown quite farsighted, occasionally fished, squinting, at arm's length beyond the heavy ornate silver settings, between triads of sparkling crystal, an olive or a stalk of celery from the small salad plates. Elaine was to sit with Anna and Fred, she stood alone, her little button eyes stared this way and that, and she would not smile until someone smiled at her.

They came up to Jonathan aggressively, humbly, democratically. They addressed him as Your Honor, Your Excellency, Mr. Ambassador, and if he could answer their questions, praise, or expression of support politely enough, he smiled at each and them all as if he were enjoying them from on high. His sister was at his side, never was a brother more considerate of a sister, her every wish and whim, and yet when she addressed him he now smiled at her too so. Across from him was his sister's autistic daughter Marybell, whom he had taken on trips, whom he had taken to Fifth Avenue stores to buy clothes for, on whom they continued to spend $40,000 a year that she be weekend presentable.

"Why doesn't your Aunt Dora wear a girdle?" Margo accused Anna.

"To show us," Anna said, knowing Margo's impatience.

"To show us what?"

"That she's not happy."

"What the hell do I care if she's not happy! What the hell does she mean showing us she's not happy!"

Tall boxer Marty and his hyperactive wife Julie arrived with Marty's father, The Great Cohen. Joe Cohen was eighty-eight years old, stiff-necked as always. But the ramrod-straight man was become thin, his shirt collar was too large on him. Immediately people rose and went toward him. He had come from Russia sixty-five years before, he had succeeded.

"You've got a thousand-dollar tan!" someone said.

His nephews came up to him. "What's happening?" he said, for he had been all winter in Florida. "What's happening to business? What will I be able to leave my children now?"

For even his name, The Great Cohen, was mortgaged, it belonged at his death to his son-in-law. And if his son had again given up his idea of being a teacher and had gone back into the fur business, he had done so without fanfare, without energy or will.

"What's happening?" he repeated, afraid to look around for he might see David—What did you do to yourself now?

His nephews had no answer for him. Jonathan smiled, Louis looked at him through his bifocals frowning.

Fred whispered to Marty that his son was here. Marty looked about nervously, he wanted to go looking through the clusters of cousins for his son, he would have to prepare his wife, he would have to tell Joe. "Come," he said, leading his father toward the table of honor. "Dad," he said, "Ed's here."

"I don't want to see him!" the almost ninety-year-old man said.

The music began. Joe sat silently at the side of his small brother and looked unseeing out at us.

Tall Marty, not finding his boy, thought with some relief, Maybe he's gone. He thought, What does he want? And he despised himself. Where is he? He saw the boy sitting with Julie, the mother in evening clothes, bright and belonging, always masked hard in this world, knowing all the faults and all the arguments—No one will put anything over on me—and the boy in a Western shirt, boots, his flaming blushing acne; he had been in and out of schools, and now in and out of institutions and jails, and jobs, and on the road, and now no longer was a boy, was the oldest among his friends, scarred, a veteran.

"Hey, Ed!" the father said, wanting to embrace the big boy, but not knowing how the boy would respond.

Julie only glanced at him and went on talking, she had the ball, she knew what she was doing. "Honey, if you write songs, you've got to sing them. Maybe somebody here has contacts, maybe somebody here can help. You don't know how big your family is! I bet we'll have a nightclub date for you by the end of the evening."

"I just came to say good-bye," the acne-faced boy, who did not want to seem diffident, said.

Julie had tears of anger in her eyes. "Honey, you're always just coming to say good-bye! Stay a little!"

"Stay!" Marty appealed.

"Do you want to see my songs?"

"Oh," she said, "I want to see them and I want to hear them!"

Fifty uniformed waiters began to serve us.

Jonathan thought of his speech.

Larry sat with his wife and children, with Anna, Fred, and their boys, with Elaine, with an older couple he vaguely remembered from summers at Rockaway—the husband, an in-law, reminiscing about Eshka telling fortunes, she his link to the Cohens? to the great and powerful? to me, the professor? who knew? to his own past when he would visit his in-laws in Sam Cohen's rooming house at Rockaway? Dark vibrant woman, he said, she knew things, telling then about the little doctor playing nickel, dime, and quarter pinochle on the porch, a proud man, how fast he played cards, how he snapped his card down, asking Larry's oldest boy, "Will you too, sonny, be a doctor?" Larry wanted to leave. This man too shared his past. Sharing, they deformed. Tomorrow was Sunday, but he had to prepare the annual fight for his hospital's budget, had to cut money here, get more money for there, had to know what services were most important. Teaching! Research! Community Care! But what kind of teaching, which research, what kind of care could they afford that would be most useful? No, it was that he wanted to have a quiet Sunday with his children. He too was a man, he too was getting on. He wanted to spend the day close to his children, walk the boardwalk with his children. I remember my father wearing, one summer Sunday, a straw boater hat and a short-sleeved open-collar shirt, he, Max, and me walking on the boardwalk. Of course, Elaine, that Ben always wanted me to marry her, that Ben always thought he could buy her a husband, buy her a poor nephew doctor! that she sits there all loose and spineless like his very living disappointment. "How are you, Elaine?"

"Oh . . ." she began, suspicious.

"Elaine," he said, "I never forget Ben."

Her eyes sparkled. She said, her very city accent becoming noble, "It sometimes happens when I meet somebody new that he or she asks about my family, and I tell him or her I am the daughter of Ben Cohen, the furrier, and the new person changes in a second from a stranger into an old friend."

Between courses the hosts circulated in the chandeliered and parquet-floored ballroom from table to table, even Louis and David, the paralyzed man staring now at one, now at the other, occasionally gesturing Louis down to him and Louis putting his ear almost to David's lips.

"What does he say?" red-wigged Sam asked.

"What should he say?" Louis demanded.

Sam bent to Fred. "You mean you arranged such a dinner and there's no chicken!"

Anna said, addressing herself too to Sam because she thought he should hear, he might understand, to Larry because she sensed he would be leaving before the end of the dinner and she wanted him to take this away with him, "I went to say good-bye to Esther at the airport. I was there before her, I waited for her at the El Al desk. I saw her coming." She was speaking too to her sons, to the winner and the loser.

But Fred was anxious that she announce the punch line. "First tell about Dan's call."

"That was after," she said, irritated; Fred only understood facts. "After she left, Dan tried to call her from Paris and then called me. He wanted to tell her that he'd received word that our cousin and his family are coming out of Russia."

"Is that so?" Sam said, marveling, turning even then to look for his brother, the ambassador, his eyes filling.

"So that, in effect," Fred explained, "she was going home to meet the Russians."

Anna felt she was losing it all, going to meet the Russians was only part of it, only the beginning of it, she had been going elsewhere, but she did not know where, did not even know how to make clear the little that she did know, the enormity that she sensed, already in her the rising need to tell a joke—the *thousand*-year runs! She could see that her older boy's attention was elsewhere, that even the loser's interest was fading as if he knew she had nothing to tell him—sonny! sonny!—that even Larry was thinking of other things, what could cousins whom we have never met mean to him?—photographs under the glass of the dining-room table—that Marty, now standing behind Fred, had come over with his own problem or story, that the distant cousins seated at this table would interrupt her in a minute with *their* Israel story. "She walks low, bent forward, like a duck, and watching her you have the feeling

she's leading in her shadow all a flock of children ducks. People give
her way, even in a crowd. She was carrying her old suitcase, her
husband's briefcase, she was wearing her cloth coat—she wouldn't
let me buy her a coat. And you know how one is coming out of
mourning, that seriousness, that awakening awareness, and there
was something else I don't know how to describe." Maybe, she
thinking, because I don't understand, Maybe because it seems so
crazy. "She was pale, only days before we'd wept for Emma, and
yet, I tell you . . . she's seventy years old, and her nose comes down
to her mouth, and she wears eyeglasses, and, she still not seeing me,
there was a radiance about her that made me think of a *bride*."

Elaine began to cry.

"She went off like a bride!" Anna said, still not understanding.

Sam was beaming at the image.

Fred took advantage of Sam's mood to stand and whisper to him
what Marty had asked of him.

"Of course!" Sam said, as if offended that anyone should think it
could be otherwise. "Of course, the boy shall sing! He'll sing for us!"
And for the warmth and spontaneity with which Sam said it, magic
happened. For in the back of our minds we were afraid Ed would
sing as he looked, that he would embarrass us. But Sam's heart laid a
magic veil even over the boy, and the news went from round table
to round table, from Starobinetzes to Friedlands to Feldbaums to
Nissnievitches to furrier friends, table-tangenting cousins whispering, Marty's boy Ed is going to sing, it's Joe's grandson, The Great
Cohen's grandson is going to sing.

Shrimp cocktail had been served, giant and iced, and a tomato
soup whipped almost to cream. We were waiting for the meat, most
of us were drinking Scotch whisky, but some had asked for wine and
famous Bordeaux was served them.

Fred caught the maître d'hôtel, the maître d'hôtel frowned but
held back the uniformed waiters, the mother was whispering fierce
encouragement to her boy.

Joe asked half-deaf Sol, "What are they saying?"

"What?" Sol asked.

Then Joe, he too grown farsighted and blurry-eyed, saw his
grandson stepping out alone from all the tables and looking like
what he had always feared his boy would look like, the fantastic

acne like the sign of weaknesses, and, Boy, why don't you wear a suit? He was tall like his father, he wore a Western shirt, jeans! He had his guitar. Boy, he thought, you've got to make a living, boy, don't you understand yet? You've got to make money. The boy saluted him with a gesture of his guitar, and there was in his thick-lipped big-eyed smile a warmth, a confidence in his affection, that made Joe think of Eshka.

Now the boy stood, one foot planted on a chair, tuning his guitar. A silence descended on us. He sang, "I only stopped in to say good-bye." Marty's eyes were as big as his son's. Tears sprang to many eyes. We thought of all our children. Sam's boy was within reach, the park! the park! The paralytic was staring. Many of us stood to applaud.

Herman Friedland crossed the ballroom floor and said to The Great Cohen, "What a future this boy has!"

The boy was surrounded by admirers. Someone asked, "Have you made a record yet?" as if such talent had to have been recognized.

"Isn't he a genius!" his mother said, pushing, pushing, allowing herself to be desperate again for her boy.

There was among us a throaty-voiced distant cousin whom we discovered had once sung in nightclubs. She spoke energetically with the boy and then with his mother.

The boy sang two more songs, then the waiters had to begin serving the red meat three inches thick. Such steaks were the steaks of dreams. What else could we have given the boy? We made appointments for him, we would give him a push; were the conjunction better we would do more. We gave what we could! Only Joe acted as if he did not understand that for once there was hope for the boy. He said to Sol in Yiddish, "Why didn't they do more for him?" Sol thought he was speaking of Marty, and he nodded, for he too had thought the brothers should take Marty into the shipping business, and his own son, and Dora too was nodding—ho ho ho—for her griefs were innumerable. Why didn't they do more more more? Who? For her it was everyone. Why didn't they visit, why didn't they remember? The stiff fragile old man could not bear to listen or to *look* at her griefs. He stood and went circulating table to table. He said of his nephews, addressing the old timers, "Why didn't they do more?" And all the old timers understood, for no one had done enough. What did it matter that this dinner cost $10,000, a drop in the bucket, money down the drain? Why hadn't they done more more more? We all had sons-in-law who could have used better jobs, who were selling cars, stock, or real estate, and why hadn't they bought from them! We were eating our three-inch steaks and didn't they melt like sugar in our mouths, and we were drinking our whisky and wine, and Joe, farsighted, blurry-eyed, stiff-necked man in a shirt whose collar was too big for him, in a Florida sharkskin suit with pearl-snapped flapped pockets, with his Florida tan on his old-man reptilian skin, was asking, "Why didn't they do more?" But as he met echoes wherever he spoke, as his own grief grew as if by echo, he thought he saw shadows among the crowds of a hundred bankrupts, of his own brothers and sisters, his slow brother Sam whom he had pushed out of his business, Ben and Jack whom he had not wanted to take in as partners, and Eshka and Leah! Oh, I did what I could! And for an instant the old man was as if facing down shadows, turning between tables: I DID MORE THAN I SHOULD! His son Marty, torn between him and his own son, came to him to lead him to a table of some old furrier cronies with whom he could speak of good years and bad, of those passed on, of famous gin rummy games, and Joe said quickly, earnestly to his son, as if it had been him who had sung, "Enough of this poetry business! You're not a child to believe in nursery rhymes! Everything we do, we do behind money." Even then the old man's hand was gripping the boxer's arm tightly, for he had seen at the Friedland table a dark beauty.

Some band members had begun to circulate table to table, fiddlers, a saxophonist, surely sons of the old country for they played so sweetly Yiddish and Russian as well as Broadway favorites, and as we ate, and as we drank, we almost swayed with the music.

She was a dark Friedland, twenty-five years old, whom we had not seen since she had been a girl. Her dark hair glistened, her eyes were large and laughing, she wore long earrings. Perhaps her evening gown was a little loud, but there was about her that ripeness beyond innocence that is pleasure. Her bursting bust, as the flash of her smile, was pleasure. She was the kind of woman on whose dark sunburned shoulders you wanted to lay and smooth the finest furs.

Joe approached the Friedland girl, who was honored by his attention, and he said, "Darling, will you dance with me?"

The mustached husband was a member of a branch of the family that had, coming from Russia, veered south to Argentina. He was not as tall as he was solid, you could tell he had the build of a lifeguard. He rose to Joe and old-fashionedly introduced himself and even escorted his wife with Joe to the dance floor.

So before the steak was finished, the dancing began. The Friedland girl was light on her feet, she swayed happily, smiling at her partner. And if stiff Joe took smaller steps and seemed to have to concentrate more, he was still good. And when he bowed out to the girl's husband, some of us now standing about began to applaud, he was eighty-eight years young! As for the Argentinian, he was a sensation. He would this evening dance the *kazatchka* like a cossack and the tango like a gigolo.

We who had taken lessons danced about the Friedland girl and the Argentinian. He had been born to dance. We wondered, Who exactly is he? What does he do for a living?

Fifty uniformed waiters were clearing the tables, there was only the dessert to come. Champagne was served, and we knew we were now entitled to a speech, and we were heated from dancing, and we sat down again, though now Cohens sat with Feldbaums and Friedlands with Nissnievitches. Larry had gone. A tall silver-haired candy salesman Starobinetz was looking for him, he had a nephew who was getting his doctorate in psychology.

Eighty-year-old self-important Herman Friedland, asked by Fred to introduce the speaker, stood between the table of honored guests and the round table of furrier cronies, and said, "Ladies and Gentlemen, Friends of the Family."

Even waiters caught at that moment at the tables or coming or going stood still, adding to the solemnity. We were a family and people who loved speeches, that greater will rising, that union listening.

"We are gathered together to honor Sol Cohen and Dora, and by Dora the memory of Ben, whom none of us will ever forget, and maybe some of us will think in passing of my dear sister Edith's husband, the greatest gentleman I ever knew, Jacob Cohen. And we are gathered, last but not least, to honor The Great Cohen. I'll not do him a dishonor by introducing his nephew, our speaker, as another Great Cohen. Ladies and Gentlemen, Friends of the Family: Our Ambassador, Jonathan Cohen."

There was much applause; we had, of course, all come *also* to see and be with him. He had gone further than any of us, he was the highest point of our ascension, he had made us rich, and he had qualities that went even beyond money. How could we not know that this man was above all a builder? For how many times could he have bought and sold, and made profit, and speculated on this or that, but always he had chosen to build, and now, when things were darkest, he was fighting on alone. How many ideas are there in a generation? He had had one: Containers! He was the kind of man who has ideas and who lives and fights to build! At the back of our applause there was that, even more than his wealth, even more than his rise or than our sympathy for him in his troubles now. For if he had been good to us, it was too long since he had been warm to us. And in each of us there had always been and would always be a longing to build.

He was good-looking, fair-haired, blue-eyed. His manner had always been that of a man pleased with himself. He was standing at the table of the hosts, his brothers, he looked out at us all and said, like someone accustomed to being listened to and who weighs his every word, "You know I have been to Russia."

Herman Friedland sprang up from his place and pointing a finger at Jonathan declared, "We know! And we know what you've done!"

Jonathan turned, his surprise merely an amused waiting smile. He could read the old man's warmth, still this was the Friedland who had once put lawyers on his back for the return of his family's investment.

He said, "I've done little."

"We know what you've done! You've been a holy man in Egypt!" Herman said, the allusion apparent to many of us. "You've done God's work!"

"Actually," Jonathan said, "I was only doing my chief's work," and we all knew who his chief was and, sharing in the enormous irony, we smiled and we settled down like Herman—content now that he had said his piece, that he had shown his fealty—his head tilted sideways in an attitude of profound attention.

Jonathan had seen here cousins he had not seen in many years. Our growing old had spoken to him of his own aging and reminded him that not even Sheila was untouched. David had been struck down; what was one to do, raise one's fists to the sky? Squat Louis no longer spoke about humanity. He had said, I want to do something for humanity, and we had set up foundations, our own Beacons of Hope, but we are humanity, and look what we have done to ourselves! He smiled at the hard-eyed cynical daughter of Louis, he smiled at Marybell, who tried so earnestly to listen to conversations. Where was Sam's Mark, what movie would he have made to change our lives? He had spent $200,000, and after his death they had not discovered a foot of film! Marty's boy was one of those miserable unwashed creatures always on the side of the road walking proudly or not. But even as he had been thinking that, his attention had been caught by the Argentinian and he had thought, understanding him instantly, young man on the make, new blood—ha! ha! ha!—for the family!

He had come out of Russia an infant, he had not known his father, all that he had of his mother was a blurred memory of her smiling at him, the radiant smile mothers can have. He had been raised in the Bronx by his uncles, he had gone to work for them in the fur market when he was thirteen. What kind of speech should he make for them? What kind of giants were they? Who would even bother to remember Uncle Sam who had been syphilitic? *What* was to be remembered about him? Should he speak of how tight-fisted Sol always was? With his workers, his partners, his wife and children? That as soon as he could afford to Joe moved to Yonkers to rise in the world, to live far from Jews? What should he say to honor the stiff-necked man?

All is mockery.

He looked at Sheila; she too had made a speech, looking at her he saw her skeletal mother in her wheelchair staring blankly ahead.

The truth is we have always followed one line, and that has been Keeping Ahead, Keeping Way Ahead, Winning. And it is all only movement, and after the movement there is nothing.

"I have been to Russia," he repeated, "I have been to Berezin, and our Berezin was burned to the ground and what was rebuilt there is nothing to us. Where you wrestled, Sol," he said, suddenly remembering that quality of Sol, "there is nothing. Where you, Joe," he said, suddenly remembering that of him, "galloped across fields by the river"—and were seen by Eshka, who told us of that, how she loved you, Joe—"there is a paved road and a factory. The forests that we owned and worked in no longer exist."

He was thinking, The past is null and void, and we live only in movement and that is the present. He could not say, We come out of nothing and we go to nothing and all that is is only now.

He said, "There are no Jews left in Berezin. In the war, Berezin was destroyed. There is not a trace of us there!"

Was it the way he said it? Something in his manner? Something in us? We were relieved. It was as if he were telling us our links with Berezin, with the past, were cut, and that we were new. It was as if a weight had been removed from us and we were suddenly more *here*. And now Jonathan said with new force, "We came from Russia and we worked hard and we made a living and we succeeded." He spoke then energetically and at length of the rise of the brothers. "And look," he concluded, his irony only half, for the publicity for The Great Cohen was national, "wherever we go nowadays, people ask, Are you The Great Cohen?"

He was even then, palm upward, indicating first all the honored guests, for they too shared in the title, and then, raising his hand a degree, indicating Joe. We had risen and were applauding. Joe was saying something, but we could not hear. He repeated louder, "I won't settle for less than a hundred!" Some of us did not understand, but all the furriers did. The words were repeated and explained and we laughed and applauded all the harder: He is not going to settle for less than a hundred years. "Nothing less!" he was saying now, stiff fragile man smiling broadly, triumphantly.

Again we were dancing.

Jonathan stood in a ring around the dancers with Sheila and his red-wigged brother Sam, and popeyed short-of-breath Margo, her long miles of silk and gauze black evening gown. He had come forward to tell the Argentinian, "Let's get together, call me for lunch." But once there he began, like his brother and Margo, to, watching the Argentinian, move rhythmically in place, smiling hard, Margo smiling hardest, breathing hardest, as if they were impatiently and insatiably hungry. Suddenly he felt someone touch him from behind. He whirled. It was Marybell, who, frightened, began to cry. She was so ugly and so unhappy and what had she come so far to tell him? And he was disarmed facing her with his miserable smile, and he almost knew what she had come for, and he said, contrite and so slightly ironic that she who felt every hesitation was confused, "Darling, will you dance with me?"

She was awkward and ill-coordinated, she tended to make two steps for one for fear of not getting there in time. But he held her steady, and then she let herself be led, was aware only of this beautiful uncle, who dancing with her—the musicians playing slower, the Argentinian dancing modestly, everyone giving Jonathan and his niece room—thought warmly, though not without irony, of Ben's countess, of his own sister, of all our princesses. He would sit with his Sheila this night on the sofa in the long wraparound-view room of his apartment, and he would take and hold her hand in his. Anna, seeing Jonathan with Marybell, felt tears rising and she rose and took her second boy's hand; this was their dance too. Nor was Fred insensitive to the moment, and he stood to ask fat pouting Elaine to dance, but even as he stood, he winked—*noblesse oblige*—to his older boy, You do it, fellow! Gracefully, the older boy asked Elaine to dance with him, and she for all her spineless weight danced well enough, her eyes sparkling.

David indicated squat bifocaled Louis down to him, and Louis put his ear at David's lips, and then stood up frowning.

Anna, dancing now with Fred, who had cut in on their son, gave in entirely to him and thought that a hundred times magic had been close to them all, had hovered over them, had even touched this one or that, but that now, as if with the music, the magic was fading and would forever be gone.

3

The road from Murs turns descending.

I carry my bulky bag, my Olivetti. The sky is blue, the sun is bright, the mistral is blowing cold. It blows the sky clear, it blows at my back. The road is lined with thick-trunked plane trees trimmed to fists. Sloping fields of cherry trees are in flower. I turn off the main road onto a dirt road. Here is the border of my stonewall-terraced property, here is the wild field where I will plant lavender. I see the roof of the house, it is tile over and under, the color faded almost to that of the country about. Madeleine is in the garden terrace below the house, her back is bent, she is wearing my worn mackinaw. She is hoeing the garden.

I can almost feel her hands on the hoe. Her hands are strong and marked, all day long she is using tools and her hands.

She turns to me from her work. She looks at me without surprise, she says nothing. Her face is thinner, there are age lines about her mouth. Twenty years we have groped.

The wind is blowing hard, the sound of the wind in the trees is like the sound of the sea. I hear the cock crow. I ask where is our boy, she replies he is at school. I am very tired, it is the wind, we are 1,000 feet up here, I have been traveling long, I am happy I will already be home when I meet him.

In the house I go to bed. I sleep lightly, I hear occasional noises downstairs, my dreams are mysterious, small groups of people I am sure I know are waiting as if for a solemn ceremony outside Sénanque.

When I wake, my boy is standing in the afternoon light looking at me, his smile is fragile, timid. I reach to him from my bed, and he is in my arms. Together we go out to look things over. The chicken coop is solid enough for now, there are six chickens and the cock, he is as big as a turkey, he wants me out and attacks me, chest forward, wings opening in a jump. I push him back with my foot, he continues, chest out, to lunge at me. I ask Saul-Daniel how was school; he tells me what he ate at the school *cantine*. The mistral is glowing, it blows in threes, three days, six, or nine, it sweeps the sky perfectly clear, it blows down from the Alps and sometimes, in the sun-warmth, you can taste snow on your lips. The pigeon coop she has always taken care of alone. This year we have only three couples, there are no young pigeons yet, we do not kill the young until they have learned to fly, I am pleased there are no young now. In the storehouse where we keep grain for the chickens and pigeons, and our tools, I look at the cultivator. It has six four-pronged wheels, they can work the earth to about six inches. I have lost parts, I have pottered things together. The almond trees have already flowered, the cherry trees are in flower, I can still trim the olive trees before they flower and work the land about them. I can still, before planting, work the garden terrace over lightly.

At dinner I do not ask her any questions, nor does she me. We sleep in the same bed, we say good-night. In the morning she is up, as always, well before me. I hear the cock crowing. I open the chickens, she has prepared the feed, and she comes to take care of the pigeons. The wind, which lets up at dawn as in the evening crepuscule, is blowing again. I get my cultivator working, she is going to take the boy to school. He comes out to say good-bye, he is very proud of his briefcase, which is strapped to his back. I work the garden terrace first, the earth after the winter is dark, damp. Every now and then I stop the machine to lift a stone out of the ground and put it by one of the terrace walls built even so 100 or 200 years ago, this land worked and lying fallow across tens of centuries. I work the field from outside in and when I am finishing, in the center, I turn all around, pleased. The turned-over land smells rich. The wind is blowing.

That day and the next, I work the land about the olive trees. I have never done enough here. I shall trim in function also of my machine, that no branches get in my way. I have 100 olive trees to work and trim, they are young, they give little fruit. You can encircle their trunks with your hands. They will age, little taller than a man, thickening, gnarling.

The boy is home from school and is watching me. He follows me. We cannot speak for the noise of the machine, but he watches me carefully. No doubt it is the machine that interests him, but he is watching me, how I use it. Last year he would not eat the pigeons, but said he would taste them one day.

I have not entered her studio, but today I am passing and I do. I smile and keep my distance. She is constructing a sculpture with two forms, they face each other. She works in reverse, carving in sandblocks. Her forms are hidden by her material, no matter, I can sense the two figures facing, the still space between them.

I buy a beehive and put it in a place sheltered from the wind at some distance from the house. I pick up a bee, holding it with my fingers by its middle, I study its parts. I begin solidifying a crumbling stone wall of the storehouse. I mix lime and sand, the mortar sears cracks in my fingertips. I write letters to the university. We must assure our jobs for next year, we shall again go in the winter when we can best afford to leave the house uncared for.

Every night I am very tired.

Still I do not go to my studio.

One of the hens is acting peculiarly, she does not want to leave the laying nest, if you touch her she pecks at you. Madeleine brings Saul-Daniel to look. "There will be chicks," she says. The boy likes the idea.

She makes a nest for the hen in her studio, where it will be warm and will not block the other hens from laying their eggs. We gather all the eggs of this day and the day before, eight, and we put them in the new nest, and we bring the hen and she hardly even looks around at the new surroundings and waddles right into the nest and delicately sets herself down on the eggs. The days pass, the hen learns techniques. When she returns to her eggs after leaving them for a moment, she sets herself in and then, like a person using his elbows, wings and wiggles the uncovered or half-covered eggs back into her warmth. She eats so little we worry for her, she sits in so concentrated a way on her eggs, she seems even desperately attached.

It is getting warmer, the wind has let up, but the sky remains clear. We have planted potatoes, string beans, salads; I have begun my work. Irises are in flower, *genêt* has flowered and remains in flower. Thyme flowers in medallions, whole fields glow with low medallions of thyme. Bees hum, it seems, about every flower. My eyes have gone farsighted, I must change my eyeglasses.

This morning the first egg hatched. It is a yellow chick. It chirps. It chipped its egg open, it moves in little runs, the mother folds it under her wing. Saul-Daniel is very happy. Are the others hatching? Saul-Daniel must go to school. In the afternoon we see that four have hatched. They chirp, they don't go far from the mother hen. The following morning we are all there for the feeding, in Madeleine's studio, with her two-form sculpture rising on her work table, there have always been links between the forms. There are seven chicks, two are black. It is gay about the mother hen, how they nudge their way in under her wings, against her body, how they look out tremulously at the world, how they take little runs.

The eighth egg does not hatch, we gently break the egg, the chick is stillborn.

In the evening after dinner, Madeleine is ironing in the kitchen, I am reading on the living-room sofa, Saul-Daniel is playing quietly at my side.

It is his bedtime. Madeleine puts him to bed, and I come up as always to kiss him good-night.

This night I say, "We'll make a prayer together." I ask him to repeat after me the *Shma Yisrael*. He does, and she, standing behind me, does too.

We are gathering here at Sénanque, twelfth-century abbey, quiet and holy place nestled in a valley on the Sénancole, the church building almost against a mountain flank. The roofs of the church are of flat stone laid at a slight angle, the stone has weathered and softened and, seen from a distance against the steep mountain flank, seems like a single cultivated field, for the mountain is otherwise all low shrubbery, live oak, flowering *genêt*. We are lucky to have clear weather; when it is gray here the mountain flanks are as gray as the church stone and inside it is cold and damp. The buildings are low, horizontal. They meet crossing, and the crossing is marked by a simple rising roundness that covers a chapel and the main space of the church exactly where the nave is crossed, and rise then briefly to a single sharp point at the bell tower, it alone rising vertically, as if to give voice. When the bell rings here, sounding in all the valley, it is an announcement, we look up and wonder what part of the ceremony we are entering now.

Our cars are parked, more are arriving. We are wearing our best clothes, dark double-breasted suits, tall city hats, the women all wear hats, some wear furs. Still, if we are gathered to celebrate, we are gathered solemnly.

I see Herman Friedland in the middle of his clan, he raises his hand and smiles at me in greeting. My Cohen uncles are all here, there is Sam, come from Rockaway, shuffling, there is little Sol, there is stiff-necked Joe. Ben, father, is smiling his million-dollar smile at me. Strong Jack nods his head at me in greeting and approval.

The bell rings, stillness rises, and everyone looks up and I know it is time to enter, and I indicate the way here at the edge of a long

Katz-Cohen

440

field of lavender on the point of flowering. The monks cultivated this field that stretches rising to the end of the valley. They buried themselves here, at the foot of the church, at the edge of the field of lavender. It occurs to me that I might speak of these things to my uncles and cousins, and I wonder then where Madeleine is.

The entry hall is crowded. Anna is there, and I am glad to see her; she too is glad—when she is like that she moves about in small steps like dancing—for her tall brother the biophysicist Eli has come back to us and is with us here today.

Larry, with his family, is, of course, here. I think of him every day. Still we hug each other.

He wants to know what is happening next, he is looking for an overview. I cannot tell him, though by now I have realized people think I am the master of ceremonies. I am then putting two and two together and have just determined this must be my boy's bar mitzvah—that would explain why Saul-Daniel is nowhere to be seen—when I notice my Uncle Dan. Surely he has come down from Paris for the occasion. He is standing alone, he has grown old and is round, his feet are very small. He thinks no one recognizes him, no one remembers him. We move toward each other, when we kiss like Frenchmen do, we truly kiss the other's cheek, and there are tears frankly in his eyes. I introduce Eli to him, they last met thirty years before, they beam at each other.

There are the "boys," Sundays-in-the-East-Bronx-young. They have come late as always, who can tell where they come from. They are full of life, David, Jonathan, Sam, and Louis.

I see Leah. She carries her purse against her breast as a schoolgirl carries her books. She is small and heavy, but her back is straight, she is proud and radiantly quiet, and I sense suddenly that her presence here announces another, and then the bell rings, the sound resonating, and as we leave the entry and enter the abbey there is Madeleine wearing a monk's habit, hooded, keys attached to the rope at her waist. She is, I have always known, the keeper of the keys.

She and I are walking alone in the cloister, and I know by the feeling rising in me that she is taking me toward where I have always wanted to go. She has opened the cloister door to the church, and this bare simple holy church is filled with mine, I am breathless,

I know that here are all my living and my dead. They have come across seas and deserts, they have come out of smoke and mist. I see Mother Cohen surrounded by her sons, I see my aunts Mima, Dora, Fanny. I see David's older boy standing behind a girl in a wheel-chair, I see both of Anna's boys. They are craning forward, side-ways, standing on tiptoe. Now I see by the simple altar my father, small slender fragile doctor. And then I turn to see my mother being led up the aisle of the nave to the altar by her favorite brother Joe, but he too is so young I think for a moment he is my dear cousin Marty. My mother is more beautiful than I have ever seen her, beautiful in white as with my eyes closed I long for her, her black hair is drawn back tight to her temples, her dark gypsy eyes glow. I long to reach out to her, to touch her one last time, I too am on tiptoe, I too am reaching. But she is already beyond me, she is standing at my father's side facing the altar, their backs to me, and still I am reaching, and they, and we are all reaching it seems to me, and above us the arched space is suddenly filled with painted images. I see there my father dressing to answer a call in the night, I see my mother on the rooftop staring out over all of Brooklyn, I see David carrying a duffel bag up staircases, I see Ben dancing at Maxim's, I see Jack turning the soil over with a spade. We are all here yearning, and the light in the church has become burnished gold, and the bell tolls, its sound echoing, stilling, and Madeleine is turning me away, for my mother and father have turned again to stone, and everyone here is turning heavy and featureless to stone, and I am now again in the slender-columned cloister left alone with the monk-robed keeper of the keys, who removes her hood, her light hair tumbling, and I awake and it is morning and Saul-Daniel in his room is calling insistently for his mother and she is, of course, al-ready up and maybe there is a light in my face as I look at her, for she turns to me and smiles radiantly at me.

We go toward God by his absence, we are like orphans who have forgotten everything of our father but our longing for him. We must find the way ourselves. We must make a living, we discover our deepest longings, we try to find our dimensions, we lose our way. We make his Law for longing of him. In his absence we are always even at the beginning. We live longing for his Grace, though some-times it seems we are even at the point of awe.

2-2178

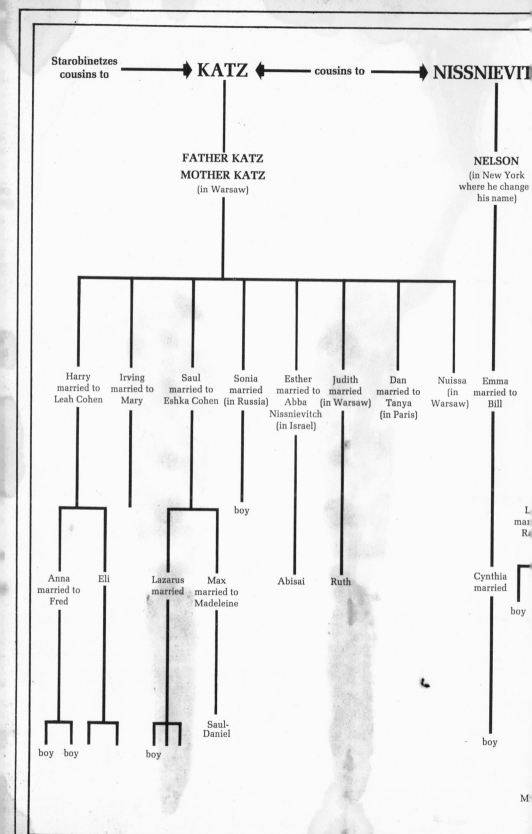

Starobinetzes
cousins to → **KATZ** ← cousins to → **NISSNIEVIT**

FATHER KATZ
MOTHER KATZ
(in Warsaw)

NELSON
(in New York
where he change
his name)

Harry
married to
Leah Cohen

Irving
married to
Mary

Saul
married to
Eshka Cohen

Sonia
married
(in Russia)

Esther
married to
Abba
Nissnievitch
(in Israel)

Judith
married
(in Warsaw)

Dan
married to
Tanya
(in Paris)

Nuissa
(in
Warsaw)

Emma
married to
Bill

boy

L
mar
Ra

Anna
married to
Fred

Eli

Lazarus
married

Max
married to
Madeleine

Abisai

Ruth

Cynthia
married

boy

boy boy

boy

Saul-
Daniel

boy

M